OUR ANIMAL HEARTS

OUR

Dania Tomlinson

ANIMAL

ANCHOR CANADA

HEARTS

Anchor Canada and colophon are registered trademarks of
Penguin Random House Canada Limited

Library and Archives Canada Cataloguing in Publication

Tomlinson, Dania, author
    Our animal hearts / Dania Tomlinson.

Issued in print and electronic formats.
ISBN 978-0-385-68985-4 (softcover). ISBN 978-0-385-68986-1 (EPUB)

    I. Title.

PS8639.O458O97 2018   C813'.6   C2017-905247-0
                                              C2017-905248-9

This book is a work of historical fiction. Apart from well-known actual people, events, and locales that figure in the narrative, all names, characters, places, and incidents are products of the author's imagination or are used fictitiously. Any resemblance to current events or locales, or to living persons, is entirely coincidental.

Cover and book design by Jennifer Griffiths
Cover image: Kidsada Manchinda/Getty Images
Interior images: (peach) The Annunciation to the Shepherds, Abraham de Bruyn; (sea monster) Design for a Plate with Thetis on a Shell in a Medallion Bordered by Sea Monsters, Adriaen Collaert; both Metropolitan Museum of Art; (peacock) H.M. van Dorp; (leopard) De Ruyter & Meijer; (wolf) Hermann van der Moolen, all Rijksmuseum.

Printed and bound in the USA

Published in Canada by Anchor Canada,
a division of Penguin Random House Canada Limited

www.penguinrandomhouse.ca

10 9 8 7 6 5 4 3 2 1

Penguin
Random House
ANCHOR CANADA

For anyone who calls the Okanagan home,
in recognition that this land is ancestral
and unceded territory of the Syilx/Okanagan people.

Discover thou what is
The strong creature from before the flood,
Without flesh, without bone,
Without vein, without blood,
Without head, without feet,
It will neither be older nor younger
Than at the beginning;
For fear of a denial,
There are no rude wants
With creatures.
Great God! how the sea whitens
When first it comes.

THE MABINOGION

WINTER 1941

This lake has no bottom. The monster glides through waterways beneath the mountains to get from lake to river to ocean and back again. Some say the lake monster used to be a man, an evil man, and this evil man committed the first murder. I don't know how he ended up in the lake. That was never part of the story. What I do know is that evil never dissolves, only transforms, changes shape, drifts from one body to another. Maybe a mob held the evil man underwater until bubbles no longer slipped from his lips. Maybe, overcome with shame, the evil man filled his pockets with stones or held a boulder to his chest and walked along the lake bottom until he lost his way to the surface and sank into the black infinity.

Other people claim the lake monster is a descendant of the biblical Leviathan, or the Kelpie, or the Loch Ness, or the Mizuchi dragon, and that the creature travelled to Winteridge underground, or was brought here from the green lakes of northern Wales or Japan or the Mediterranean Sea by an immigrant, its larval form hidden under a hat or sewn into a bodice or sucked at like a stone in the mouth of a child. And still there are some who claim that the lake monster was never a man or a descendant of some foreign monster, but has existed in this valley long before the settlers came with their books and relics and shrines, before the first people canoed from shore to shore to hunt the forests surrounding the lake, even before the lake itself, which arrived long ago in the form of ice or poured from a hole in the sky. They say the monster is the spirit of the lake, the very face of the deep.

Now, so many years later, scientists poked and prodded and vaguely concluded that the lake monster is not a monster at all but a fish, perhaps a sturgeon. But back then we cast our own shadows onto the lake and each claimed the monster we saw there as our own. We called our monster by name. We called our monster by many names.

These days I try to avoid the lake and all it brings.

Morning sun pours crystalline onto the fresh snow blanketing the small garden and fruit trees in my backyard. I have taken the blue fish from its hiding place in the attic cabinet and set its jar on the windowsill above the kitchen sink because the world is far too still, too white today. The fish spins and spins, as blue as flame. I am washing dishes, recalling an old poem my mother would recite whenever it snowed. She claimed it was much prettier in Welsh. It went something like—

> Mountain snow, swift is the wolf, she haunts the edge of wilderness.
> Mountain snow, the stag is swimming and fish are in the deep.
> Mountain snow, white everywhere, yet there is no hiding evil, no
>   matter where.

I still find the words chilling.

Right then, there is a knock at the back door—a single, ominous thud. The door whines as I open it. What I find makes me choke. I clutch my throat. An enormous buck lies at my doorstep, splayed on its side, hoofs twitching against the steps. The deer's branching antlers are enormous and force his head upwards, neck arched back to reveal a pulsing throat. Blood spills from three parallel slices down his belly and melts the snow beneath him. Steam huffs from his nostrils. His eyes are black as beetles. I scan the yard for paw prints before I go to the kitchen for a knife to bring the buck relief. I know the deer is both an offering and a warning.

She has found me once again.

1904 – 1911

In the beginning, there was nothing. Just the water.

THOMAS KING

1

Saint Francis came to us in a yellow biscuit tin. It was Christmas Eve. Frozen branches tapped against the windowpane like neglected ghosts. Wind wheezed through cracks in the walls and carried with it the yips of coyotes, making it sound as though the beasts were right in our kitchen instead of out in the orchard, tormenting the chickens and filling their dreams with teeth and bone. My father had made a fire and it steeped us in orange. Then again, some of my memories have this chemical effect: sepia. As a girl I would scrutinize old photographs and imagine myself into *that* kitchen or *that* field, or beneath *that* cold light. I would dream myself into the bodies and minds of those apparitions. Fantasy might replace memory, or meld with it, a double exposure. I remember things I could not have possibly seen in a photograph, like how my mother, Llewelyna, pricked her finger while sewing pearl buttons onto her wedding dress. She brought that bead of blood up close to her face and held her breath, as if it were some kind of miracle, as if, were she to breathe, it might disappear. I can also see the very place my brother, Jacob, died. The poppies nearly black in the dark, my little brother belly-up and gaping at those billions of stars as chlorine gas itched his face, his eyes, his lungs. And so, *sitting room steeped in sepia* could be a cinematic effect. The room might have been bright with refracted light from the snow outside, or it could have been grey despite the flames. But I remember it as sepia. Orange pekoe. Warm.

Llewelyna was seated on the yellow chesterfield, her red hair electric in the glow. She was bent towards the fire as if it whispered to her alone. The chesterfield's claw feet were poised and shining. Jacob was cross-legged on the floor beside me. He hopped his toy soldiers along the hardwood like chess pieces. The soldiers were a gift from my father, who had just returned from one of his many trips overseas.

My father spent most of his time in England and Wales, where he managed my grandfather's coal mines. Even when my father was home, he often had business of some kind in the city, a day's trip by boat from Winteridge, our small community huddled on the lakeshore in southern British Columbia. My clearest memories of my father are of him departing. The image of my father waving to Jacob and me from the lakeboat, his top hat arching above his head in steady sweeps, is so vivid in my mind that his short presence in my life can nearly be summed up in that one continuous moment of his perpetual leave-taking. I can distinguish his arrivals by the gifts he brought home for us.

Jacob's tin soldiers had tiny red coats and black trousers painted on them; some carried guns or swords or rode horseback. Hushed explosions and screams and murmured calls for help came from the battleground Jacob had built from kindling and newsprint. In my cupped palms I held six glass marbles; "handmade in Germany," my father had said when I slipped them one by one from their velvet satchel. Until then, the marbles Jacob and I played with were clay and painted like Easter eggs. These new marbles were of another breed, far too intricate and precious to play with. I held my favourite up to the firelight. It was blue as the lake in the summer with pin-thin white and black tendrils swooping through it in a kind of dance, as if continuously falling through time and space.

My father came in from the kitchen carrying the yellow biscuit tin and a crystal tumbler half-full of scotch, a rare treat for him. He was wearing his brown suit, the bow tie crooked at his neck. His moustache twirled up at the tips.

"Here, Lew," he said as he handed the yellow tin to my mother.

My father was the only one allowed to call her Lew. Jacob and I were forced to stumble through her entire name. She told us to pronounce the Welsh double "l" by pressing our tongues against our teeth as if about to say "l," but to say "shh" instead. "It is a voiceless sound," she said. "Made in the throat." I thought it sounded strangled. Even after our practised elocutions—"Shoe-wellen-nah"—she would complain that not even her own children could say her name right—would ever say it right. She wouldn't have us erase her with our *Mother this* and *Mama that* either. She said it made her invisible, almost as bad as being called Mrs. Sparks. Most people in our town could not pronounce Llewelyna's name. To her face they avoided it, but eventually, behind her back, they called her other things. Although she refused to return to Wales, she resented that Jacob and I were not Welsh but watered-down Canadian Brits.

Llewelyna's eyes narrowed at the yellow tin my father passed her. She set it on her lap. Tiny red flowers slinked up the sides of the tin. On the lid was a girl in a white pinafore and bonnet. She looked lost amongst the gaudy flowers. The paint was scratched along the top; one of the girl's feet was missing.

"But the drapes, and the gloves, and the . . ." Llewelyna motioned her arms in the air as if conjuring these items with her words.

"You don't give a damn about all that," my father said. He winked at me. "But could just be old biscuits, for all you know."

He sat in his wingback chair and pulled at his bow tie until it came loose. Jacob and I climbed up onto the chesterfield on either side of Llewelyna and waited for her to open the lid. Her hands hovered. We stared at her long fingers until we looked up to find her smiling at our anticipation.

"Maybe I'll wait till tomorrow," she teased.

"No," we squealed and jostled her shoulders. The tin bounced on her lap.

"Stop!" my father said, his hand stretched out towards us, his eyes steady on the tin. "You'll break it. Iris, Jacob, back on the floor."

Jacob and I slipped off the chesterfield. We sat with our hands in our laps and looked up at our father until he leaned back into his chair and smiled at us.

"That's better. Go on, Lew." He watched her face carefully, the tumbler of scotch balanced on his knee. He had one hand up beneath his chin, a finger pressed against his moustache. I loved the way he looked at her when she wasn't watching.

Llewelyna snapped open the latch and pulled out some scrunched-up newsprint and folds of cotton and put them on the cushion beside her. "What in God's green and blessed earth, Noah . . ." She smiled so broadly she revealed her crooked bottom teeth. Cross-legged on the floor, Jacob and I craned our necks to see what was in the tin.

"It's your peacock," my father said. "Should hatch in a week."

Llewelyna picked a large pink egg out of the tin and held it out for Jacob and me to see. The shell had a thin crack I ran my finger along.

"Don't touch it," my father said, "or the hens won't take to it." I removed my finger. He didn't seem concerned about Llewelyna's hands cradling it.

"How fantastic," she said, admiring the egg from all sides.

"With luck it'll be a cock. But there's no way of knowing," my father said.

"I can hear him in there," I whispered to Jacob.

"You're making that up," Jacob said.

"Listen."

Jacob's red eyelashes fluttered. "I don't hear a thing."

"You can't hear that?" I said, incredulous.

"Hear what?"

"He's singing 'Georgie Porgie, puddin' and pie' in there."

❧

Llewelyna once told me that, as immigrants, we would never truly belong to this land unless we died here. And so, at seven years old, I would lie in the freshly churned soil of Llewelyna's garden, sprawled amongst her beloved marigolds, with a halcyon smile on my face, and imagine I were dead. I watched blue carnations with the same crinkled edge as my dress sprout from my belly and my brains. This was back when the peach trees on my family's orchard were just scraggly things, tied to wooden stilts to keep straight. This was before the trees grew taller than the house and filled our yard with dense, darting shadows. Before the peaches grew to the size of a man's fist and, still unpicked, fell to the ground like grenades. This was before the peaches piled up at the feet of trees, before they grew out of their skins, were pecked at by birds, and carried away by ants. This was before the house filled with the swamp smell of rot and the footsteps of so many ghosts. This was before the fire.

Jacob and I were barred from Llewelyna's overgrown garden. The only one who roamed it freely was Saint Francis, her beloved peacock.

Francis could not fly. Once he was full-grown his train of jewelled feathers was too heavy to carry into the sky. Llewelyna pointed this out to me at a very young age so I would understand the cost of such extravagant beauty. I had watched her then, green eyes flashing, her hair a fantastic orange, her nose delicate and small. Features foreign to my own. My round ears poked through my thin dark hair, I had a crooked, aquiline nose like my father and eyes the colour of puzzle-bark. The only attribute Llewelyna and I shared was our bow-tie lips and crooked teeth. Jacob, on the other hand, was a miniature of my mother: red curly hair, green eyes, and pale, freckled skin.

It was difficult not to gape at Llewelyna. Her hair stood out, surely, but there was also something in the symmetry of her face, the slight angle of her eyebrows, the perfect dip of her nose, and the pull of her green eyes that made her magnetic. Men gawked shamelessly and women, confused by the attraction, struggled not to.

Saint Francis followed Llewelyna everywhere. He waited for her on the shore, tail fanned, while she swam in the lake, and followed her down the road whenever she went to visit Henry, her only true friend in Winteridge. When my father was away she let Francis in the house and he would sleep nestled at the bottom of her bed. I scavenged for his feathers and kept them in the bottom drawer of my wardrobe like relics from another world. Sometimes at night I pulled the feathers out to let them glisten in the candle-light. They reminded me of Llewelyna's stories about mermaids and monsters, dragons and saints.

It was said that the real Saint Francis preached to the birds, and the birds spoke back to him, and so Llewelyna spoke to her peacock as if he were a person, and the bird apparently spoke back. Llewelyna claimed that the peacock embodied the spirit of her favourite saint. He told her things. Often he could foresee the future and shared his visions with her.

Llewelyna said when Saint Francis, the man, had died, he was resurrected as birds. Not just one bird but all of them. I pictured the saint's body like an eggshell, cracked into the tiniest of pieces until he was only a pile of dust. And then slowly from the pile, a dove emerged, itching at her puffed breast with her beak. Blue-and-red parrots shuffled out next and flapped the dust from their wings. An array of colourful birds followed: hummingbirds, finches, budgies, robins. Then, finally, all the colours of the world used up, the crow limped out, his *caw-caw* muffled by dust. This vision was confused a few days later when Llewelyna and I were sitting at the cliffs watching sparrows play in the air currents and I overheard her say to herself: "Birds are only fish dreaming." Her eyes were bright and wide with the revelation.

Llewelyna gave her weekly confession to the peacock. "Who more pure and thus better connected to God than his blameless animals?" she would say. Her Catholicism blended with the stories she brought with her from North Wales, where beautiful women turned into horses or owls or disappeared into pools of water. Llewelyna claimed that long, long, long ago, a fisherman fell in love with a water nymph, and ours was the last of their bloodline.

Llewelyna found in Saint Francis a loyalty she thought humans, especially her children, were incapable of. She never considered the fact that his attachment to her was only natural since she refused to find Francis a peahen. The shrill of his desperate mating calls gave me headaches. When Francis's feathers grew too long, Llewelyna would trim some off and tie them into our hair. She told me peacocks were mythological beings. In North Wales the faeries used peacock feathers to cast spells on their human lovers.

My mother both terrified and fascinated me. As a small girl I often hid in the lilac bushes that enclosed her garden to spy on her. Sometimes she brought her easel outside with a pitcher of lemonade and sat all afternoon painting Francis rustling amongst the flowers. Other days she cut back the relentless poppies and deadheaded carnations, the pink flowers she said first blossomed from Mother Mary's tears the day Jesus carried the cross. One summer she called the garden her *room*. I helped her drag the yellow chesterfield outside. Francis would perch on the armrest and fan his tail while she sprawled in the shade like a house cat and smoked cigarettes and read. I flipped the cushions to hide the burn holes from my father.

On very rare occasions Llewelyna invited Jacob and me into her garden. She waved us in as if we had never been so emphatically excluded in the first place. While Jacob played with his tin soldiers in the soil, I posed on the chesterfield for one of her paintings with Saint Francis settled beside me like an ornamental cushion. His tail feathers tickled my cheek. Llewelyna gazed at me over her canvas, her eyes hard on my ear, my arm, my knee, my lips. It was a strange kind of attention. My body transformed into curves and shades. When she painted my face she looked at my eyes so seriously I had to turn away.

"Irie, look up," she said, her hand motioning as if to lift a veil up over her own face. "It's the eyes hold the magic, innit."

Her eyes were so severe, so focused, seeing the details, the skin, and yet somehow seeing nothing at all. I looked above her head and followed the bough of the maple tree up towards my bedroom window, where leaves and the maple-keys Jacob called frog-wings chimed against the glass.

"Irie, look here." Her finger pointed to her nose. "If I can't paint your eyes right den you're nothin' but a husk." Llewelyna's Welsh accent would come out unexpectedly and at the strangest of times. Often it would be when she was telling a bedtime story, or distracted by a book she was reading, but sometimes it was mid-sentence. My father, if he was there, would look up at her and grin, remembering her again as the woman he had met on the other side of the world.

One summer, while Jacob and my father were in the city at the northern end of the lake, I peered through the lilacs and watched Llewelyna knead the earth. Bees droned around my face and ants trickled across my bare feet. The leftover summer heat had softened the geraniums and dahlias; their heavy blossoms slumped on stiff necks. A sticky, sweet smell wafted up from the orchard and swirled with the balm percolating in her garden. Francis strutted along the garden path making soft clucking sounds, *gwlaw, gwlaw.* Llewelyna said when Francis made this sound it meant a storm was on its way. *Gwlaw* is Welsh for rain. As secondary proof, she would point to her marigolds. She claimed the blossoms closed ever so slightly when the weather changed. Sometimes Saint Francis approached Llewelyna and fanned his train of feathers about his tiny body in a show of trembling brilliance that made even the garden appear drab and grey.

I remember Llewelyna humming. She was always humming. I could never recognize the tune, but it made me think of the green forests, rivers, and lakes she told me about on the Isle of Anglesey. She was kneeling at the base of a rose bush, wearing a canary-yellow chemise that didn't quite cover her thighs and dipped low at her chest. The dry heat made her batty. Her knees pushed into the soil, staining the lace along the hem. A nest of red curls sat atop her head. Loose strands twisted and twirled down her back. With a flick of her wrist she pushed a ringlet over her shoulder. I mimicked that gesture with a tangle of my own brown hair. She refused to wear the special gloves my father had purchased her for gardening. Her fingernails were always lined with dirt, her hands chapped and callused. Llewelyna clawed at the stubborn weeds. Their roots snapped like tendons.

Suddenly she stood up, rigid in front of her rose bush. At first I thought she had seen me, and I leaned back into the lilacs to hide. I felt a raindrop on my cheek and wondered if she had felt one too, if this might explain her stillness as she waited to confirm the sensation as rain. Then Llewelyna's head lolled back and forth and her eyes slowly open and closed.

"Iris? Are you there?" she called. "Iris?" She reached out for balance as if blind, and found none. She fell backwards, right into the rose bush. I jumped out of the lilacs and into the garden. Francis squawked, flapped his wings in warning. I leapt past him and stood at her feet. Her arms were stiff. Hands in fists. She thrashed. I tried to pull her out of the rose bush, and thorns pierced my arms and legs. I called her name but she didn't respond even though her eyes were wide open. Her entire body convulsed. Speckles of blood and rain made patterns along her cheeks and bare arms and legs like constellations. I tried to hold her feet still but they jerked out of my grasp.

It seemed like hours before her body finally went still. I shook her awake. She sat up and blinked twice. Rose petals were stuck to her glistening skin.

"Iris?" she asked again.

That night I stood on a chair with a wet cloth and dabbed the scratches on her arms and neck. I watched her in the mirror as she observed herself, bloodshot eyes unblinking as if afraid to look away. "We must keep this a secret," she said, speaking to me but still watching her own eyes suspiciously. I nodded, excited to be a part of her strange world. "When your father comes home this weekend"—she licked her finger and rubbed a speck of blood off her cheek—"I'd like you to tell him we're having a grand time, just you and me." She smiled at me in the mirror then. I absorbed her warmth like a cactus clings to a single drop of water.

2

Our bay remained unsettled much longer than most spots on the lake. We called it Winteridge, but this was just one of the many names given to this strip of land on the steep hillside. A name first used by the European fur traders who settled the land as if it were empty. As if it belonged to them already. "Winteridge" was a name understood only when grey ice crept up the shore and slid beneath the doors of barns and homes, stealing breath from cattle and small children. During the hot, dry summers, the name was the only thing that provided relief from the heat, like peppermint beneath the tongue.

A few weeks after her fall in the garden, Llewelyna, Jacob, and I lay in the yard and gazed up into the branches of the maple tree. Frog-wings spiralled down on us and sunlight turned the broad leaves into paper lanterns, like the ones the Japanese pickers later hung around the pick shacks on the McCarthys' apple orchard. Even the birds were lazy in the heat, their usual chatter low and dull. Llewelyna had spread her duvet in the shade of the tree. Jacob lay with his head on her stomach and I lay beside her. Saint Francis fanned his tail and strutted back and forth in the grass, glaring at Jacob and me, envious of our proximity to Llewelyna.

The maple tree in our yard dwarfed our three-storey house and was our only offering of shade. The peach trees were no taller than my father, who, in the beginning, spent his days tending to the orchard in shirtsleeves, often with a book under his arm. I would watch his top hat bob between the rows. Having grown up on an estate just outside London, my father was not a natural orchardist. He learned everything he knew from books. My father never thought of our time in Winteridge as permanent. He saw Winteridge as a place he could escape away from as easily as he escaped *to* it. He wanted Jacob and me to experience the deep West, to grow up a little wild, but to return eventually to England. We were meant to bring our extravagances and our bigness back to a motherland we didn't know, attend private school, university, marry reputable Brits, and settle down. He never imagined he might lose Llewelyna and me to this land.

The branches of the maple tree twisted up into the sky. In winter the tree looked spindly and dead, but in spring it grew lush and full of birds, bugs, and other secret lives. The lacework of spiders glimmered or returned to shadow and disappeared as sunlight moved through branches. Cool droplets of sap we would have to lick or scratch off sprinkled our arms and bare legs.

Jacob pointed out a troop of ants spiralling down the trunk of the tree. Their tiny army trickled onto the duvet. We covered our mouths to keep from laughing and stayed completely still as the ants tickled up and down our limbs as if we were merely part of their landscape. The ants scurried over the inside of Llewelyna's wrist, manoeuvring over a puckered scar, and down the other side. Once the ants had disappeared into the grass, Llewelyna rolled onto her side, making Jacob readjust himself on his stomach so all of us were facing one another. She looked at us in turn, grinned, and closed her eyes. The silence was filled with only the babble of birds.

If I had known then that she was about to open her mouth and in her next breath invent a monster that would haunt us the rest of our lives, I would have asked her to stop. I would have asked if she had thought out the consequences of her words, which were never merely words but, as in Genesis, had the power to create. What would have happened if, when God spoke the earth into being, there was someone there to ask him, "Are you certain? Have you thought it all through?" But like God, Llewelyna was reckless with words.

"I remember it like this," she said. Llewelyna often began her stories this way. As a girl her Nain had told her many old Welsh tales, and these retellings were Llewelyna's attempts to recall exactly how they went. She called some of the stories branches of the Mabinogi, and back then I imagined the Mabinogi was a tree not unlike our maple, with four long, unfurling branches and broad leaves as large as my head.

"There once was a girl who was seduced by a fish."

"What kind of fish?" Jacob was a stickler for details.

"A carp," she said. "Now, close your eyes, you."

Llewelyna always had us all close our eyes when she told stories. I squinted to watch her eyelids tremble as she spoke. It was like peeking backstage during a play.

"Every day the beautiful girl walked through a dark wood to bathe in a clear pond. In the privacy of the grove, the girl would take off her gown and undergarments and swim completely naked. Her beauty attracted the attention of the water spirits."

"Like Kelpie, the water horse?"

"No, not this time."

"Hush, Jacob," I said and pinched him.

"Ow, Iris."

"Must I stop?"

"No, don't stop."

"I won't say a word."

"Where was I?"

"The naked girl."

"Right. The girl's beauty attracted the attention of the water spirits and the jealousy of the queen nymph. The spirits would spy on the girl from between the reeds and when she was gone they spoke of her beauty and perfection, ignoring the queen nymph. Soon the queen nymph had had enough. She commanded her friend the pwca—"

"Puka?"

I elbowed Jacob.

"I just want to know."

"A pwca is a shape-shifter," she said.

"Like Taliesin?"

"No. A pwca is a creature that takes many forms, one of them being human. And Taliesin is a man that takes an animal form."

"But how is that different?"

Llewelyna's eyes were open now, and I was afraid Jacob had broken the spell of the story and we would never find out what happened.

"Taliesin has the heart of a man. A pwca has the heart of an animal," I said, wanting to show Llewelyna my keen insight of this otherworld.

"Don't be a fool, Iris. A heart is a heart." She tapped Jacob's nose with the tip of her finger. "It's a good question, my sweet. The difference is a mystery, really. Can I continue with the story?"

Jacob nodded, and we all closed our eyes again.

"The queen nymph commanded the pwca to seduce the girl. The girl was charmed by the golden carp and watched it whirl through the water. It disappeared for a moment and then a man with yellow hair appeared at the other end of the pond. She fell under his spell. His skin shimmered like scales, and if the girl had looked a little closer, she would have found gills behind his ears, for a pwca can never shift entirely. There is always something leftover. Months later, the girl became round and pregnant and she no longer attracted the attention of the water spirits. But you see, the girl was already engaged to marry. Her beloved was to return to ask her family's permission to wed. The girl was ashamed and mortified by the pregnancy. She tried everything to rid herself of the child: special herbs and jagged devices. Every day when she went to the pond to bathe she cursed her unborn child and begged God to take it away. She slammed her fists against her swollen belly and wept. The queen nymph took pity on the girl and released a spell to rid the girl of the child before her beloved arrived.

"And so, one hot day while the girl swam in the pond, her swollen belly bobbing above the water, she began to have labour pains. It was too early. The child hadn't fully developed. She stood and a tar-like liquid oozed down her legs. The pond turned murky, then black. The girl watched her swollen belly shrink. Something long and snake-like twisted out from between her legs, but she couldn't make out its precise form through the dark water. The water spirits and the queen nymph hid in the reeds. The girl began to walk backwards towards the shore. The creature rose to the surface. It had the head of a horse and the body of a snake."

I pictured Leviathan from the picture Bible I read in Henry's library.

"An addanc," Jacob whispered forebodingly.

"It was a creature deformed by jealousy and betrayal, unloved and unwanted by even its own mother. The girl screamed and turned to run but the water slowed her down. She could hear the creature splash towards her. When the girl was almost at the shore she tripped and fell to her knees. The creature sank its teeth into her wrist. The girl pried at its teeth. It was useless. She picked up a stone and slammed it against the monster's skull. It let out a horrible groan and let go. When she was finally free of it she ran up the shore. Blood trailed down her legs and from her wrist. When she turned back to look at the black lake, the monster was staring up at her, gnashing its teeth and whispering her name."

Jacob sat up, eyes wide as a gutted fish. Llewelyna's stories often turned dark. They not only fed our imaginations and filled our nightmares, but the creatures in her stories emerged into our day-to-day world. It was often difficult for me to distinguish between what was real and what was imaginary, and if such categories still hold when the truth of either is equal. Llewelyna's monster became that sound in the night, the creature coiled beneath my bed. It became that eerie sense of being watched while we walked through the forest. It slithered between trees.

"And then what happened?" Jacob asked. Llewelyna opened her trembling eyes as if returning from another place. It was the same look she gave when I interrupted her reading.

"The girl avoided the haunted pond. Only her sister knew what had happened but the sister promised not to tell. The girl's true love never found out about her strange pregnancy. He took the girl far from her village to a new land. Sometimes at night the girl dreams of the monster's empty eyes. But when she wakes in the morning and sees her love beside her and her children playing in the grass"—at this point Llewelyna touched my brother on the cheek and then turned to me and pressed her thumb to my chin—"she forgets the creature."

"But . . ." Jacob began.

Llewelyna twisted her mass of tangled hair into a neat, miraculous little bun that resembled a snail shell.

"What about the village?" he asked. "What about all the people the monster must have killed by now?"

Llewelyna froze—her narrow arm poised above her head, index finger and thumb pinching the long bone pin my father had brought back from one of his trips. She forced a smile. "I don't know, Jacob." She slid the pin through her bun and shooed us off the duvet. I was angry with Jacob for asking questions and forcing her to leave our quiet spot in the shade. He didn't understand Llewelyna's unspoken rules, though I followed them desperately. First: never question her stories. Second: never ask for a story. Third: never interrupt.

"Go on now and get a treat from the Nickels' shop." She gave us each a coin. "Hurry now, before it turns." Llewelyna said these coins were faery money, and if we waited too long to spend them they would turn into fungus. She flicked the duvet, scattering a world of leaves and ants and releasing duck feathers that were still floating to the ground when she reached the house with Saint Francis trailing behind her.

Although years later Henry told me it was impossible, and that the age-old demon he called Naitaka—a name he whittled down from something much greater just so I could pronounce it—had haunted the lake long before my family had arrived in Winteridge, for a long time I still believed that with Llewelyna's words, the lake monster was born.

Unlike the surrounding area, which was dominated by evergreens, Winteridge was thick with white birch trees that appeared to hover above the bay like ghosts. It seemed the natives considered the birch a bad omen. They had lived and travelled along the shores and connecting rivers of the lake long before the Ebers had settled in the hills and the birch trees grew in the bay. I didn't know it then, but Henry later told me that Winteridge was built atop a burial ground. There had been a brutal plague: smallpox. Henry had another name back then, which he refused to tell me. He had watched many of his people die. Their spirits still misted the trees. It was not until Henry told me a story about these people in the trees that I began to see them out of the corners of my eyes—faces in the forest or shadows on the beach. Once, I saw a woman halfway up a tree tying a rope to a branch. The wooden beads in her hair chimed in the breeze. When I got closer to the tree she disappeared, but the rope still hung from the branch. Another time I heard the snap of a twig and glimpsed a man with long grey hair picking berries. In the next moment he was gone. Llewelyna called these spectres Lake People. She said they were experts at camouflage and knew the land better than anyone because they were part of it. Created from it. They could turn into birds, bears, fish, and even trees.

"But weren't we also made from the earth?" I asked her once, thinking of Genesis.

Llewelyna bent to clutch a handful of dark soil from her garden and let it fall in clumps. "*This* earth," she said. "They were made of this very earth."

At night when coyotes yipped in our orchard, Llewelyna told Jacob and me it was the Lake People, transformed into coyotes and angry at us whites for stealing their land. My father would frown and shake his head at her in warning. In the morning one of our chickens would be ripped to shreds or a cat disembowelled on our doorstep. Llewelyna would nod at the evidence and look at us as if saying, *See?*

There was one coyote in particular Llewelyna was especially fond of. It was a silver runt that was always on its own, and seemed excluded from the pack. Although it was clearly not a wolf, for some reason unknown to me, Llewelyna tenderly called this coyote her she-wolf and left her bits of dinner at the edge of the orchard without my father knowing.

Llewelyna often told us the story of when, while she was pregnant with Jacob, she had gone for a long walk in the woods and got lost. It had been a scorching day and she had not brought any water along. Soon she came across an earth house. From outside it appeared to be only a hole in the ground with a log sticking out. An old woman emerged from inside the ground. She smiled down at Llewelyna's melon-belly and, seeing her exhaustion, invited Llewelyna to follow her through the opening. Inside it was dark and cool, and the ground was carpeted with deerskin. When her eyes adjusted she saw blankets folded neatly on one side of the space and a few wooden tools. Earthen pots and bowls and a low table were at the other side. The woman brought Llewelyna a mug of water. They sat together in silence and watched the dust sparkle in the light from the hole in the roof. Once Llewelyna had revived, the old woman led her back to the outskirts of Winteridge.

This woman's kindness had touched Llewelyna deeply, fascinated her. Later, once she had recovered from giving birth, she had wanted to repay the woman for her goodness and went back to find the earth house. It had been abandoned. The roof had collapsed. There was a bullet hole in a tree nearby.

Henry was the only native in Winteridge. He ran a library from his cottage in the forest. There was a worn path from behind the cannery through the woods to his front step. When settlers had first arrived in Winteridge, Henry helped them navigate the lake and forest. He would accept only tobacco and books as payment for his guidance. Henry had more books than anyone else in Winteridge, and so everyone borrowed books from him. Henry didn't believe in money and would not accept it. Instead, borrowers brought things to barter—cured meat, an apple pie, a quilt. Henry survived better than most on the goods he received for lending out his books.

There were many rumours about Henry. Some said he was a halfling, and that his white father was responsible for the plague of smallpox that killed his people. Others said his tribe abandoned him for dealing too closely with white men. I heard once that Henry killed a man for his books. I thought this might be true, as many of his older books had the name Stewart Brewster written in the top right corner. One time Henry was late coming back from delivering some books to old Mr. McCarthy, who was sick with influenza, and I wandered in the woods surrounding his house and found a small graveyard hidden by the dangling branches of a willow. One of the gravestones had Brewster written on it.

I asked Henry why he was the only native. He shrugged. "There are others," he said, but I had never seen any in Winteridge. Sometimes they glided past Winteridge in their low dugout canoes. They would watch the bay suspiciously and stay as far away from the shore as possible. I wondered then if Henry meant the Lake People who crowded the surrounding forests.

"You mean the ghosts in the trees?"

"You see them, do you?"

I nodded. "Are they angry?"

Henry smiled, but his eyes filled with sadness. "Not at you, little girl." But I understood what his words meant: *Yes, even you are part of their suffering.*

❦

I spent much of my childhood in Henry's library while Miss Maggie taught Jacob and several other children from the town in the schoolhouse. Llewelyna said Henry could teach me more than that stiff old spinster. She claimed the schoolhouse was only built to meet legal demands, while the quality of education escaped government scrutiny. For a girl, such a rudimentary education would lead to nothing but entry into ladies' schools.

While Henry dusted his books he told me stories about Coyote, the trickster, and the animal people, the first ones to inhabit the earth, long before Adam and Eve. Henry taught me the sacredness of water, air, and fire, and the purifying power of smoke. He read to me from Milton, and Kant, and Spinoza, his favourite philosopher. When we tired of books, Henry and I would leave the library for the forest. Orange pine needles covered the ground. I followed him along a path invisible to the eye. Henry was tall, the tallest man in Winteridge, and he said he still hadn't stopped growing. He grew an inch or two every year. He had to duck under branches way over my head. We passed a bush with dark berries and Henry stopped, picked one off the bush, and popped it in his mouth.

"Saskatoons," he said, and offered me one. The berry was sweet and gritty. We picked some for our pockets. Further along Henry ran his hand through tall grass. He knelt down and spread the grass open to reveal green spears of asparagus that we also collected. Later he showed me prickly pear cactus that survive even in the dead of winter and once peeled can be cooked on a fire and eaten.

"You need to know how to take care of yourself," he said ominously.

"Is something bad going to happen?" I eyed one of the Lake People slipping under the bough of a nearby pine. She walked steadily towards us. Whenever I walked around with Henry, the Lake People loomed closer than usual. This woman's eyes were on Henry hard, as if she wanted to embrace or kill him. Even from the corner of my vision I could see she had terrible boils all over her face and neck.

"Henry . . ."

"It's okay. She won't hurt us."

I knew if I looked directly at the woman I would no longer be able to see her. This was the way of these ghosts. The woman stood before Henry, as if to prevent him from walking any further. From my downcast eyes I could only make out the woman's feet, bare and covered in the same welts as her face. Henry did something unusual then: he took a clump of grass and sprinkled it with some curls of fresh tobacco from the packet he carried in his pocket. He held the grass between him and the woman and lit it with a match. He closed his eyes and hummed as the grass smouldered. I watched the smoke rise up to the sky. When the fire went out and the smoke stopped, the woman turned and walked back into the bushes.

"Who was that?" I asked.

Henry put the burnt grass on the ground and covered it with dirt. "My half-sister."

"Is she dead?"

"In a sense, yes. In many others, no. Not at all. Not ever."

"She seems angry."

"She has reason to be."

I remembered what Llewelyna said about us taking the land of the Lake People and thought perhaps the spirit was angry at Henry because he was with me. I didn't admit this to Henry because I was afraid it might mean he would stop teaching me.

"What happened to her face?" I asked.

Henry brushed his hands off on his pants. "Smallpox."

Jacob and I had received vaccinations for smallpox earlier that year. When the nurse pulled out the thick syringe, I fainted.

"What did you do with the grass?"

"Begged forgiveness."

With that Henry leapt ahead of me up a steep embankment. We walked for a little while longer and then he stopped and pointed up. There was a small shelter hidden in one of the trees. Someone had hammered branches and strips of bark to the outside walls to camouflage it.

"This is a secret place. Only come here if you're in trouble. It's the perfect place to hide. Go on up," he said. "I'm too heavy now—I'll tear the tree down."

I carefully climbed using branches and worn steps nailed to the bough. I lifted myself through a square hole in the floor of the shelter. Inside the tree fort was a can full of buttons, some pencils, and a children's picture Bible. The walls were covered with words carved into the wood. The words were in a language I had never seen before, full of accents, backwards question marks, and upside-down *e*'s. Amongst these words there were also ink drawings of animals, fish, and trees. I peered through a set of eyeholes on the side of the shelter. Something flashed between trees: the silver-furred coyote, Llewelyna's she-wolf. When I looked out for Henry, he was speaking with someone. I scurried down the ladder.

Henry said, "Iris, come meet an old friend of mine."

The man extended his hand to me. He had skin as dark and smooth as leather. One of his ears was missing its lobe. I eyed him suspiciously and wondered if this was Coyote, who sometimes took the form of a man. "You can call me Frank," he said. But I knew that, like Henry, this was not his real name. When we shook hands he slipped something into my palm and winked. I rolled the square object over and over in my palm as he and Henry continued their conversation in their own language. Once he left, I opened my hand and found a caramel.

After walking for a few hours through the forested hills surrounding Winteridge, Henry turned to me and held his finger to his mouth. He picked up two clumps of pine needles and passed one clump to me. "They must be dry, orange ones," he whispered. He held the needles to his mouth and blew on them. I did the same.

"What are we doing?" I asked.

"Shh. You'll see." As we stood blowing on the pine needles, Henry looked into the trees around us, waiting. Then he stopped, ducked down towards me. "You see there?" I scanned the trees he pointed to and shook my head. "Look harder," he said. "You have to practise looking. Learn to see."

I focused my gaze on the trees until I could see the black eyes and nose of one, two, three does peeking at us from behind tree boughs, their ears extended, alert. Further off behind them, a buck nibbled at some grass, vines stuck in his antlers. Later Henry showed me how to call out groundhogs by cracking my knuckles.

3

Winteridge consisted of a strip of three small businesses along the water and the schoolhouse that Llewelyna liked to call *the barn*. The Pearl Hotel was a white Victorian two-storey building with purple curtains and a wraparound porch where visitors sucked on pipes and watched the hundred or so inhabitants of Winteridge pass by. Old Seamus Pearl was the widowed owner of the hotel. My father told me that he had moved from Ireland to the Okanagan during the gold rush, but never earned enough to buy his ticket home. He brewed beer in the cellar of the hotel and served it to the guests and the few Winteridge folk deemed respectable enough to share space with them. His young wife died in childbirth, leaving him with a daughter, Juliet. Motherless girls like Juliet fascinated me because they were often the main characters of Llewelyna's stories and the books I read. I would spy on Juliet serving the men on the porch their morning tea and scones, or rubbing the windows of the hotel with vinegar, or transporting spent barley, still steaming, in a wheelbarrow to the Ebers' ranch to sell it as pig feed.

Next to the Pearl Hotel was the Nickels' dry goods store and post office. The Nickels' shop had everything from lentils to wrenches to chicken feed. Jacob and I often went there with our allowance to purchase penny candies and squares of caramel and chocolate. Charlotte Nickel, a plump, rosy-cheeked woman, and her two daughters, Daphne and Teresa, worked the storefront, while Ronald and his father, Ernest, unloaded goods from the lakeboats. Ronald was a friend of my brother's, they took swimming and diving lessons together in Kelowna, the nearest city. Ronald was tall, slim, and dark-haired like his father. Ronald and Teresa were twins but they looked nothing alike. Ronald was olive-skinned with high cheekbones and Teresa was plump and mousy-haired. Although the Nickel family worshipped Ronald, the only son, he was a humble, gentle boy and seemed unaffected by his family's devotion, if not a little embarrassed. Teresa was always trying to tag along with Jacob and Ronald, and because I knew she was such a nuisance, I wanted to be nothing like her. I kept my distance from Jacob and Ronald and rarely tried to join them on their fishing outings to the river or swims in the lake.

Beside the Nickels' store was the grey, windowless cannery. During the winters, when the orchard work slowed down, labourers sought jobs canning fruit from Mr. Shawcross. Mr. Shawcross was one of the first bachelors to arrive in Winteridge. He had greenish skin and small, squinting eyes like a rodent. I once came across him gnawing at chicken bones on the shore of the lake. He offered me an oily drumstick and I ran away. He was the only person in town my father didn't take kindly to. "Not enough sunlight," my father said once. "So much darkness isn't good for a man's soul." Llewelyna grinned whenever my father spoke of souls.

"Ah, yes," she said, clearly pleased. "His poor Neshama." She ran a finger along my father's jaw. "Nice to see the Kabbalist within hasn't been snuffed entirely." When Llewelyna was a girl in Wales, her mother had cleaned house for a rabbi from Swansea, and on warm days Llewelyna and her sister were permitted to sit with him in the shade of his garden and listen to his stories. Despite Llewelyna's attempts to locate a spiritual core in my father that might connect him to his distant Jewish heritage, my father claimed he was an atheist. Although his father, my grandfather, had been raised Jewish, when he married my grandmother, a devout Catholic, he had to relinquish *all of that nonsense*, as my grandmother called it.

The schoolhouse was down the road from the other businesses in Winteridge. It was a one-room log cabin with a pot-belly stove that failed to warm the building in even the fall months. The country school had little more than a blackboard and some rickety old desks. The few books found in the schoolhouse were loaned by Henry's library. Just a handful of children regularly attended the school; most families couldn't afford to lose the workers. I was forced to attend the schoolhouse only when my grandmother was in town, which was very rare.

I had once asked Henry why he didn't teach the children instead of silly Miss Maggie, the McCarthys' eldest daughter. Henry burst into a laughter that brought tears.

"An Indian teaching a room of whites! Now there's an idea," he said.

Across the road from the schoolhouse and past a thick strip of forest, our bottomless lake unravelled, so enormous that many settlers imagined it was the ocean. From my bedroom window on the third floor of our house, I could see the wharf where rowboats bobbed, tied up to pillars, and where the lakeboat docked to load and unload its goods. When my family first arrived in Winteridge there was only the McCarthys' apple orchard, which neighboured our own land, and Ebers' sprawling ranch way up in the hills. Our peach orchard was a small piece of forest back then, and I was only an infant in Llewelyna's arms.

A treacherous dirt road descended from the hill that separated Winteridge from the rest of the valley. Every once in a while a motor-car would attempt the journey to Winteridge. We could hear the rumble of the engine long before it appeared. Often they never made it to town, the road being better suited to horses, but when the rare motorcar did, we would all come out cheering and watch it parade past. What roads there were, were often washed out by floods and mudslides, and so most in the valley depended on the lakeboat for transportation. Anywhere the lake could go, we could go too. That said, until I was eighteen I had been out of Winteridge only a couple of times. When I was eight my father took Jacob and me to Vernon, a dusty, hustling city at the north end of the lake, and bought us pretzels from a street vendor to eat while we waited for him outside the bank.

When my parents arrived in Winteridge, my father had asked Henry to help build our house, and Henry agreed only because he knew my father had access to literature otherwise impossible to find. Henry and my father shared a fascination with books. My father would bring boxes of books back with him from London to pay for Henry's labour. While I crawled about and played with toys my father brought home for me, Llewelyna, pregnant with Jacob, would lounge on pillows in the rooms Henry built up around us. As he worked, Henry and Llewelyna exchanged stories—not stories they read in books, but stories they knew by heart.

Llewelyna dreamed up the design of our tall, narrow house and changed her mind every other day. From the outside, our home resembled a haphazard dollhouse, painted sea-foam green, with gaping windows and a long, narrow front porch that faced the lake. Inside, our house was a labyrinth. It had three floors, two staircases, three balconies, narrow passages, and even a few small, pointless, unfinished rooms. Our house was different from the neat, white-walled ranchers in the community, or the low-lying log cabins the Japanese pickers later built on the orchards.

Llewelyna knew the maze of our house better than any of us. Whenever my father asked me to fetch her, I could never find her. I would call her name but the walls of the house absorbed my voice. Then she would appear in the most ordinary of places, in the kitchen making a pot of tea or on the front porch reading a book.

"Quit your hollering. I'm right here."

It was incredible how she could appear out of nothing. Reminded of one of Llewelyna's stories, I told Jacob I thought she might possess the warrior Caswallawn's Veil of Illusion, which allowed him to defeat armies without being seen. I found a gold scarf I thought could be the veil. As a joke, I walked around the house with the scarf over my head. No one seemed to notice my prank and I soon grew tired of the game.

Once while exploring the house, I discovered a half-built room on the top floor. It was the size of a closet and hidden behind a bookshelf. Inside I found a wooden box full of photographs of people I didn't recognize. There were a few of Llewelyna and her twin sister, Gwyn. I could tell them apart only when they were both in the picture together, and even then it was difficult to determine what exactly it was that distinguished them. The sisters looked porcelain and cold in the black-and-white photographs. Their red hair turned to grey shadows. In one photograph they sat together on a staircase, with what looked like a piglet wrapped in a blanket on Llewelyna's lap. In another, the sisters sat stiff and sombre-faced beside a cage full of canaries. They were no more than six years old. They wore plaid aprons over their patterned dresses and ridiculous top hats that left shadows on the wall behind them. Some of the birds in the cage were caught mid-flight by the flash, and were nothing but a blur of light.

Before Llewelyna's family moved to the Isle of Anglesey after her father died, they lived in what she called the Valleys. There, her father had been a miner, and her mother bred canaries for the coal mines. Llewelyna told me she and Gwyn snuck into the mine one night to look for Carwyn, a fourteen-year-old boy they were both sweet on. He had been lost to the mine the day before. Llewelyna had dreamt of Carwyn trapped in a cave of rocks. She thought the dream showed her the way to him, and so the girls crept down the earth's throat into the eternal night. In the narrow tunnels rats nipped at their ankles and the ghosts of dead miners brushed past their bare shoulders and breathed on their necks. Gwyn could hear a bird tittering, and so they followed that otherworldly sound as if it were a sign. The trembling canary was barely visible in the liquid dark. The girls released the bird from its cage. It slipped out of Llewelyna's hands and scrambled, unused to flight, deeper into the earth. Soon they could no longer hear its eerie song.

Also inside the wooden box, I found a portrait of Llewelyna as a young woman. Her cheek was smooth and clear; there was no trace of the crisscross scar that appeared there after she fell into the McCarthys' barbed-wire fence during one of her wanderings. But in that reflection of her young self, Llewelyna's eyes held a secret. She was not looking at the camera but just past the lens. On the back of the photograph was something written in Welsh. I sounded out the words. They tasted like citrus.

My father liked to tell guests the story of the Welsh barmaid who forked his heart when she spilled his ale onto his lap. I preferred Llewelyna's version. She told me she met my father in a dream and had borne him a child before they even met. I liked to think that child was me, though Llewelyna never specified.

Llewelyna had been completely out of place in the rush of Cardiff, where my father had been visiting that summer to check in on the family coal mine. When he told the story of their meeting, he would stretch a long arm over Llewelyna's shoulders and pull her a little closer as he described how her hair had shone like bronze when she bent to clean his spilled ale and how her eyes had sparkled like emeralds in the dim lamplight of the saloon, and how he had not understood her apology, her Welsh accent so strong. He had made her repeat her apology again and again just to keep her talking, to keep her near. My father spoke of Llewelyna as if she were all precious metals and gemstones, as though she were some kind of prize. She smiled when the story was over, but when he turned away from her, Llewelyna's face would darken, the smile not matching her eyes.

My grandmother had viewed my father's engagement to Llewelyna as a rebellion. She gave permission to the marriage only when she discovered Llewelyna was Catholic. It was much later that she understood Llewelyna's Catholicism was a breed very different from her own. Llewelyna spoke of demons and saints and shape-shifters like others spoke of rosaries and wafers and teaspoons.

Llewelyna refused to wear a hat to church despite my grandmother's insistence that she cover her head. "It is disrespectful," my grandmother would say, her hands clenched in white fists. She stared up at Llewelyna's pile of hair as if it were a capital offence.

"Best leave judgment to *Gad*, Missus Sparks," Llewelyna said, exaggerating her rural accent to further torment her mother-in-law.

I was nine years old in 1907, when my grandmother visited us for the first time. We attended the small church in the valley that summer. She brought with her some gifts, one of which was a black silk hat decorated with pearls, dried rosebuds, and a long white feather. Llewelyna set the hat in the middle of our kitchen table and thanked my grandmother for the fantastic centrepiece.

Although Jacob and I were much too old for it, my grandmother insisted on bathing us before church. She scrubbed the dirt from under our fingernails and combed our hair until it sat flat against our heads. Jacob's hair was as wild as Llewelyna's, so my grandmother would spend extra time glossing his curls down with wax and oil. Five minutes later the curls would spring back up. My own dark hair, unaccustomed to my grandmother's fastidious grooming, fell out and collected into tumbleweeds that blew around our drafty house. Llewelyna and I wore to church matching pieces of yellow lace over our eyes and pinned behind our ears.

At church Jacob and I passed a scrap of paper back and forth over my father's lap in a game of tic-tac-toe. Llewelyna spun one of Saint Francis's small blue chest feathers between her fingers until my grandmother snatched it away. We lined up to receive the host. Father John set the wafer too far back on my tongue and it made me cough a little. When Jacob fell asleep against my father's shoulder I gazed up at Jesus, his ruined body contorted against the cross, and imagined the wafer inside me, now transformed into Christ. The sight of his sinewy muscles, yellowing skin, and decomposing body always made me a little queasy. I stared at the spikes in his ankles and wrists, and the thorns the size of my fingers that dug deep into his scalp. I counted the many red cuts on his body. Each time I counted there were more. When I told Llewelyna about the spread of these gashes, my grandmother overheard and said it was because my sins inflicted Jesus with fresh wounds. Llewelyna smiled, satisfied with my grandmother's response.

4

Although the peach trees in our orchard had now been growing quite beautifully for a few years, none had yielded a single fruit, which concerned my father. "It says here that if we put a branch in water and it blooms, then we can expect blossoms next spring and harvest next summer," he said, balancing a book on his knee at the kitchen table while Llewelyna dished us each out a bowl of porridge. He sprang up from the table and rushed to the door.

"But your breakfast, Noah."

"I'll be a moment only."

Jacob and I watched our father climb one of the larger trees in his suit coat with a small saw between his teeth.

"Lunatic," Llewelyna said, stirring her tea at the table.

He came back with a leafy branch. My mother had already filled a pickle jar with water. My father set the branch in the middle of the table. We all watched the branch silently, our bowls of porridge steaming into our faces, scared to miss the moment a blossom might curl out. Llewelyna waved her hands in front of the green buds like a magician. It took weeks for the branch to blossom. It happened at night, when none of us could witness the metamorphosis. The flowers were dark pink in the centre with little antennae sprouting out. The petals were thin and smooth as moth wings.

Llewelyna said that in Wales, peaches were imported from China and were extremely expensive. She had only eaten one peach in her entire life, given to her by my father, and it was the most delicious thing she had ever tasted. My father always said that Llewelyna had married him for that peach. I hadn't tried a peach yet. No one else in the valley was growing peaches. Despite warnings from orchardists in Winteridge about the fastidious and delicate nature of stone fruit, my father persisted with his peach trees. The promise of a peach orchard had been his wedding gift to Llewelyna.

Every year more people settled in Winteridge. The dispossessed reserve land was affordable to purchase, and there was plenty of work for newcomers in the surrounding orchards and farms. The Bells built their house in the plot next to our orchard. They were our nearest neighbours. Their white house looked quaint next to our sprawling, sea-green labyrinth. They were new in town, *straight from the motherland* as my father said. The Bells did not have any children. Instead they owned a dove they called Angel and a greyhound named King Edward VII.

Angel's wooden cage was designed like a palace. It had a tower and a little door made out of twigs that opened like a drawbridge. It was painted white and sat monstrous atop the liquor cabinet in the dining room.

"Isn't it darling?" Mrs. Bell said. "Phillip had it made for me."

Llewelyna stood in front of the cage and said nothing. Angel was perched on a long wooden pole. The bird looked at her sideways. Llewelyna and the dove stared at one another as if in a contest.

"I'll put some tea on, then," Mrs. Bell said as she turned

towards the kitchen, her eyes briefly exposing her discomfort around my mother.

"What's the wire ring for?" Llewelyna asked suddenly, still not moving her eyes from the bird's eyes.

"Oh, let me show you." Mrs. Bell rushed back. She pulled a thin chain from a drawer in the cabinet and held it as she opened the drawbridge. Llewelyna stood stiffly beside her, eyes cold and slicing. The dove cooed as Mrs. Bell reached towards it. "Now, now, Angel. Be nice." Mrs. Bell clipped the chain to the wire band on the dove's foot. She held her index finger out in front of the bird. Angel stepped onto it hesitantly. Mrs. Bell brought the dove out of the cage and nuzzled her nose against its feathers.

"Isn't she darling?" said Mrs. Bell.

"Yes," Llewelyna said, "darling."

Angel flapped her wings and rose towards the ceiling until the chain went taut. The dove flapped absurdly, suspended above our heads. The candles on the chandelier sputtered from the beating of her wings. Each flap was closer and closer to the flame, and I imagined the phoenix.

"Well would you look at that," my father said from the sitting room.

"One of Gracie's little playthings," Mr. Bell said.

"Women and their birds," my father said. Llewelyna's eyes flared. Mrs. Bell gathered up Angel by pulling at the chain inch by inch. She tucked the dove back in her cage.

"Go on and sit with the gents," Mrs. Bell said to Llewelyna. "I'll be in shortly with the tea." Llewelyna joined the men in the sitting room.

I wandered into a room off the hall lined with bookshelves. There was a large redwood piano at the room's centre. I ran my finger over the cool ivory of the keys and thought of elephants.

"Do you play?" Mrs. Bell asked from the door. She wore a white lace apron over her flouncy yellow dress. Her question startled me and I accidentally pressed down on a low key.

"No," I said and crossed my arms at my chest.

"In England every respectable girl knows how to play piano," she said, not unkindly, only stating a fact. She tucked the tulle of her dress beneath her and sat down on the bench. As her fingers danced along the keys her ruffled sleeves fluttered. Mrs. Bell angled her chin this way and that as if its position affected the tone. She was a skilled pianist and I could tell she enjoyed it. At one of the softer, rain-like portions of the song, Mr. Bell could be heard hollering from the sitting room:

"Lovey, there's a funny smell coming from the kitchen."

"Oh, dear. How I miss my cook." Mrs. Bell's slack face tightened. "Why don't you go play outside with Jacob, Iris?"

In the backyard the Bells' big black greyhound dashed back and forth. He whipped up dust and pebbles behind him. The dog ran towards me and jumped up to lick my face, knocking me backwards.

"Isn't he grand?" Jacob laughed from the other side of the yard near the garden shed.

I pushed the dog off and wiped my face with my sleeve. I walked carefully along the perimeter of the yard to avoid the dog. It had gone back to racing along an invisible path of figure eights. Jacob had his hands up against the window of the shed.

"What are you doing snooping about?" I said.

"Take a look for yourself."

I cupped my hands against the glass and peered through. Inside was a cabinet with long rifles on hooks. A pair of antlers was nailed to the wall.

"I've never seen so many guns," Jacob said. He went to the

side of the shed and tried the door. He pulled a piece of wire out from somewhere and jammed it in the lock.

"You can't just go breaking in," I said. "Jacob, stop that." He ignored me.

"Where are you, children?" Mrs. Bell called from the house. Jacob rolled his eyes. I peeked out from behind the shed. "Ah, there you are," she said. She rang a bell, smiling. "Dinner is ready."

On the way to the dining room I passed a china cabinet full of figurines. On the top shelf there was a collection of miniature glass cottages that looked just like the Bells' house. They had tiny windows, chimneys, and doorknobs. A jade deer and bouquet of porcelain flowers appeared monstrous next to the little community. On another shelf was a collection of real butterflies. The glistening powder of their wings dusted the wood board they were pinned to. I could see a faint fingerprint on the wing of an enormous monarch. The bottom shelf displayed a collection of tiny sugar spoons. Mrs. Bell caught me looking at them and went ahead and told me the story that belonged to each and every spoon.

"These ornaments are all straight from England. Collectables. They are all I have of home now." She smiled sadly. "You can come over whenever you like and look at them," she whispered. "Or if you need anything at all . . ." Her eyes drifted above my head to the sitting room where the other adults were. I nodded. "Good. That's settled, then. Go let the others know dinner's ready."

Mr. Bell's cheery voice boomed down the hallway. "These Japs are coming in hordes. All I'm saying is I don't think it right to supply them with jobs instead of our own."

Llewelyna and my father were seated on a burgundy loveseat in the sitting room. Mr. Bell sat in one of the two matching wing-back chairs facing them. My father's arm was around Llewelyna's shoulder, his knuckles white.

"Our own?" Llewelyna said.

"You know what I mean." Mr. Bell looked to my father for solidarity, but my father was looking out the window.

"No, I don't believe I do," she said.

"Dinner is ready," I said.

Mr. Bell looked up at me and smiled, no doubt relieved by my interruption.

We sat at a large table in the dining room. My back was to Angel's cage and I could hear the bird coo every now and then. Mrs. Bell came out of the kitchen in her lace apron. She set a steaming dish in the centre of the table.

"You folks are in for a treat," Mr. Bell said, rubbing his hands together. "Gracie here's made her famous shepherd's pie."

"I haven't eaten lamb in years," my father said.

"I've only made it a couple of times." Mrs. Bell reddened. "Phillip, darling, serve it up while it's hot," she said and returned to the kitchen. Mr. Bell cut out servings of the shepherd's pie and handed a portion to each of us.

"This self-service has been rather difficult to get accustomed to," he said.

"Did you employ many maids in London?" my father asked.

Llewelyna tipped back her wine and clinked the glass down on the table a little too hard.

"A slew. And didn't your family?" Mr. Bell asked my father. Mrs. Bell came back in from the kitchen and placed the sprouts on the table.

"Yes, my father's estate—"

"My sister is a housemaid," Llewelyna interrupted, her chin lifted too high.

"Oh, is that right?" Mrs. Bell said.

"Lew," my father warned. "Life is different in England." He

turned to the Bells. "Llewelyna is from the north of Wales, a rural—"

"Seems the English," Llewelyna said, "can't even choose their own clothes or pain their weak wrists and pour their own damned tea."

Mr. Bell smiled. "Well, you've got that right. You wouldn't believe how long it took me to put these on the first time I tried." He raised his sleeves to show his gold cufflinks.

Mrs. Bell wriggled in her seat. "So I hear you are off to London for school soon, Jacob."

"In a few years. Not until I'm thirteen," said Jacob. "I'm only ten."

"I think you will enjoy London. Have you been before?" Mr. Bell asked.

"Excuse me a moment." Llewelyna pushed back her chair and slipped out the dining room. The front door slammed.

"Oh, dear. Is Le-wall . . ." Mrs. Bell began.

"Llewelyna," I said.

"Is she ill?"

"Just needs some fresh air, I'm sure." My father took a sip of his wine. "She isn't fond of Jacob going to London. It's a difficult topic for her."

"Only natural for a mother to feel that way," Mrs. Bell said. "But surely she understands the boy needs a proper education."

"Do you attend the preparatory school in Vernon, son?" Mr. Bell asked.

"No, sir," said Jacob.

"Why ever not?"

"The country school is satisfactory for now," my father said, a little defensively, I thought.

"Satisfactory for country folk, but a young man looking to attend a British college, that's another thing entirely."

"The boat ride to Vernon is hours in each direction and Jacob is too young to be away for such an extended period of time."

"Have you thought of a tutor?" Mrs. Bell asked. "Or perhaps employing a governess for Iris too?"

"Henry tutors Iris."

"You mean the Indian?" Mrs. Bell asked, aghast.

Mr. Bell laughed. "You are a rather eccentric family, aren't you."

My father smiled politely. "Henry is our friend. He is very knowledgeable. He owns more books than anyone else in Winteridge."

"He can read?" Mrs. Bell said.

"A literate Indian, imagine that."

"He's read more than I have." My father took a bite of his shepherd's pie and swallowed. "A very learned man."

"And Iris, aren't you lovely," Mrs. Bell said, eager to change the conversation. "You're a slight thing, though. How old are you?"

"Eleven," I said.

"There is a ladies' school in Toronto my cousin strongly recommends," Mrs. Bell said to my father. "And if you would like to learn the piano, Iris, I would be happy to teach you."

My father looked at me expecting an enthusiasm I did not have. "Well, what an excellent idea."

"It is important for a young lady to have some talents," Mr. Bell said, a lump of potato in his cheek.

Llewelyna returned smelling of tobacco smoke.

"Mrs. Bell has offered to teach Iris piano," my father told her. "Isn't that splendid?" Llewelyna smiled at me mawkishly and served herself sprouts.

When Mrs. Bell went to collect dessert, I caught Llewelyna staring at the dove's cage behind me. The dove cooed to her. Then Mrs. Bell passed china plates of trifle around the table and broke the spell.

5

I didn't have many friends in Winteridge. I lived comfortably in my own head or in the stories Llewelyna and Henry told me. Jacob and I were the only children not sent to work, and this in itself distinguished our class, made us into an oddity. Not only children but adults too looked at us as though we snatched the bread from under their noses and then spat it out.

During the planting and harvest seasons, the country school was empty except for Jacob and Ronald Nickel. After their lessons, Jacob and Ronald played in the woods until dinner, and so, for the most part, I was left to entertain myself. Once, as I walked through the forest to Henry's tree fort in the woods, to do some reading Henry had assigned, I had the feeling I was being watched, followed. At first I thought it was a cougar and the hair rose on the back of my neck. A cougar had carried away the McCarthys' youngest a few years before, while the family was gathering firewood. Sometimes I thought I saw that redheaded toddler amongst the trees and fantasized about her growing up alongside those giant cats like Mowgli and his wolves. Then I thought it might be the child's ghost watching me. Or the silver-furred coyote. I had seen her the day before running through the peach trees towards our chicken coop.

I took my next step careful and slow. I moved my eyes around without moving my head and practised looking, like Henry taught me. I saw, between two pine trees, the flash of a girl's face. She had dark eyes and black hair, a Lake Person, a spirit. She darted behind the next tree. I followed slowly, then jumped into a run. When I got behind the tree I expected the girl to be gone, or transformed into a bird or a deer. Instead I found her panting with her back against the tree and her hair slick on her forehead. She looked down as if it might make her invisible. Her cotton dress was stained with grass and dirt.

"Are you spying on me?" I asked. She looked up. I recognized her now. Her father was one of the first Japanese pickers to arrive in Winteridge. He worked on the McCarthys' orchard. "What's your name?" She didn't respond. I pointed at her. "Your name?"

Just then my hair was given a hard tug from behind. I turned around and found another girl, a little smaller than the first one, but with the same dark hair and light skin. She wore a pink ruffled dress, untouched by dirt. Two tight braids hung past her shoulders. The two girls spoke to one another in Japanese. The smaller one pulled the first girl's arm, trying to get her to follow her out of the forest. The taller one shook her off and the little one fell, her pink dress soiled with dirt at last. The smaller one said something low and cutting to the first one and left with tears in her eyes.

We watched her go.

"Azami," the taller one said. She gave a bow.

"I'm Iris." I mimicked the bow. "Who was that?"

"Sister."

"What are you doing out here?"

She brought a cloth sack out from behind her back and opened it so I could see what was inside: a pine cone, a green bead, the porcelain handle of a teacup, a teaspoon, and some string.

"What's all this for?"

Azami demonstrated by tying the teacup handle and teaspoon to the stick so they clinked together: a wind chime. We scoured the forest floor for other items to tie onto her chime. She gave me some of her string so I could make my own. When our chimes were complete, I took her to the tree fort and we hung the chimes from the roof.

At first Azami and I communicated in half sentences. I opened the large book I had borrowed from Henry called *South America* and pointed to a picture of a parrot. "Bird," I said. She repeated after me and then pointed to the same picture. "Tori," she said. In these small ways we translated our worlds for one another. Sometimes Azami wrote on the wall and it looked more like stick figures dressed in a variety of different clothing than words. She asked if the other words on the walls were in my language and I shook my head and said it was Henry's language and I didn't know that either. Azami could already say many English words and learned much quicker than I did, so eventually we kept to English.

Azami and I would meet every day after I had finished my lessons with Henry and she had completed her tasks on the McCarthys' orchard. One afternoon she was late arriving. I sat on the floor attempting to read a book called *The Water-Babies*. I had found it under a board in the tree fort. The book was mildewed and the first page tore when I separated it from the next. *To Brave Bear from Stewart, your friend in God* was written on the following page. Along the borders of passages were words scribbled in the same language as the words on the walls of the tree fort. I set the book aside when I heard Azami scaling the tree's ladder. Something jingled along behind her as she climbed. When she finally got to the top she looked afraid and out of breath. She set down her sack on the floor and lifted herself up through the entrance.

"What's wrong?" I asked.

She pulled a jar of water from her sack and poured a thin stream of it into each of her hands and splashed the water on her face. Then she carefully set out other items from her sack: little pieces of wood painted red, dark hair tied in a blue ribbon, rusty nails, a mirror, a rock, an apple, and a porcelain elephant the size of my thumb. I picked up the elephant; delicate vines and leaves were painted on its torso. I thought she wanted to make another wind chime.

"Where did you get all this?" I asked.

Azami snatched the elephant back. She glared at me and made a big deal of cleaning the elephant with the edge of her shirt and what was left of the water and then set the piece back with the others. I leaned against the wall and tried to feign boredom as I watched her set up the red pieces of wood and hammer at them with the rock.

"What are you doing, Azami?" Her silence irritated me and I struggled to hide my annoyance.

She reached for my hand and motioned for me to hold two pieces of wood together against the floor so she could nail a third piece to the joint. The wood split terribly—it was old and weathered—but she managed to get the nails to hold. When she was finished, the structure resembled the frame of a tiny house with a sloping roof.

"What is it?"

"Hokora," she said finally, admiring it. "Shrine." She collected the objects and assembled them inside the little house. It reminded me of Mrs. Bell's cabinet of trinkets. "My father threw shrine away."

"Why?"

"We have book now."

"Book?"

"Bible," she said, and gestured to the picture Bible in the corner as if the flick of her hand might flip it away. She reached into her sock and pulled out a knife and began to slice the apple she had brought. She ate a slice, handed me one, and arranged the rest of the slices on the bit of mirror inside the little house.

"What's that for?"

"Offering," she said. Sometimes the priest at church spoke of offerings: coins or goats or sometimes sons, but never fruit. "Food for the kami."

Through our patchy exchange I learned kami were the *being-ness* of all things: rocks and trees and even people. Azami put her hand on my chest and said, "Kami." But kami are distinct spirits too. People who die become kami, not all of them good. The elephant had been her grandmother's and the dark hair came from her younger brother who died on the boat to Canada. She told me the shrine was a place for sacred, special things.

"You have something?" she asked, inviting me to put something into the shrine. I shook my head.

There was a thump against the side of the tree fort, and then another. Azami launched up to the window and ducked. A rock came tumbling through the window, nearly grazing Azami's head. She yelled out the window in Japanese, and I could see her sister run back through the woods towards the McCarthys' orchard.

For weeks Azami and I made wind chimes out of string, rocks, pieces of glass, beads, bones, buttons, and whatever else we could find. The chimes told us when the kami were near our fort. We hung the chimes from the ceiling and climbed up into the tree to tie them to the branches. With the slightest breeze the entire tree would jingle and ring. Each day Azami brought a fresh apple to offer the kami. The apple from the day before was always gone. The kami had steady appetites.

I was always curious about how and why people came to be in Winteridge, especially the Japanese who had begun to arrive with such regularity you might think Winteridge was the last stop of a trans-Pacific railway. When Azami's English allowed it, I asked her to tell me how she came to be here.

Azami Lin Koba, my only friend in Winteridge, besides Henry, was the eldest of the Koba children. She grew up with the guilt of being the Kobas' first disappointment—they had wanted a boy. And even after Azami's younger brother, Wu, was born, her birth was a sign of the burdens to come—three more daughters. Azami's family moved to Winteridge from Japan after Japan's war with Russia in 1905. Japan had won, but the war reparations placed on Russia were so insignificant that the Japanese families who had sacrificed their fathers, brothers, and land—and as in the Kobas' case, their fishing boats and their entire industry— went without repayment of any kind.

Azami told me that during the war in Japan, bombs thundered everywhere, and like a distant storm, it was impossible to tell how far away they were and in what direction. Azami imagined their fishing boat bobbing amongst the battleships, its yellow sail flapping in the breeze. The Kobas' boat was called *The Namazu*, named after a giant mythological catfish believed to cause earthquakes.

One day Azami and Wu were collecting clams for their mother. Azami was a terrible clam digger, easily distracted by the flotsam that washed up on the beach. She saw something glinting on the distant shore and thought it might be a coin. Azami left Wu and ran to it. Instead of a coin, Azami found a man with ruddy cheeks, fuzzy eyebrows and hair coiled so tight it might be wool. He was nearly camouflaged with the mound of seaweed he sat against. The man looked dead or asleep, except his eyes stayed trained on Azami and under his gaze she turned to stone. The glinting that had first attracted her came from a charm on a long silver chain around his neck. The man pushed himself up. One of his legs bent at a nauseating angle. His face didn't show the pain he must have felt. Azami knew he was a Russian. She knew he was the enemy. She should have run and screamed for Wu. But then the man smiled, and it seemed rude not to return the gesture. A string of drool hung from his lips like a spider's thread. The Russian soldier took the necklace from around his neck and tossed it to Azami. Then he winked and ran into the surrounding forest with surprising speed considering his injuries.

There were two charms on the necklace. One was a long, smooth square of metal with a few Russian letters and numbers engraved into it: a military tag. And the other was a ruby-red glass bead. From that day on Azami wore the necklace hidden under her clothes, flat against her chest. She said the necklace was good luck. In exchange for her silence, she understood the Russian soldier had passed his luck on to her.

Mr. Koba's family had run their fishing company for generations. It was all they knew. And so, without their boat, the Koba family was at a loss. Mr. Koba was disenchanted with Japan. When he learned of the opportunities across the ocean, in Canada, he packed up his four children and pregnant wife—another girl, certainly—and set off for Canada.

The ocean liner was cramped and hot. Each night, Azami pressed her cheek against the cool steel floor and let the grumbling guts of the ship ease her into sleep. Her baby brother, Aio, was born in the belly of that beast. Her mother had lost a lot of blood. Azami took care of the cutting and the stitching with the help of an old herbalist who laid parcels of eucalyptus against her mother's breastbone. Azami said Aio was the colour of ginger, the whites of his eyes as yellow as yolks. The Koba family celebrated the beautiful boy by opening the only bottle of sake they had brought along. Mr. Koba saw the birth of the boy as a sign he had made the right decision for his family, a fresh start.

While her mother recovered, Azami carried Aio in a shawl wrapped around her chest. The infant was sickly and slept far too much. Azami woke him every couple of hours to feed him at her mother's swollen breast, but the infant was uninterested in its milk.

Somewhere on the outskirts of Vancouver, Aio died against Azami's chest. As other families celebrated their arrival on Canadian soil and the end of the long, dreadful journey, the Kobas disembarked in the throes of mourning, their hearts in their throats and the body of Aio, shockingly small, wrapped in Azami's shawl. They were not allowed to bring the body onto the train, and so Aio was buried in the rainforest just outside the train station. Azami's mother, Lin Koba, was catatonic with grief, and Azami was left to care for her brother and sisters. From then on Mr. Koba remained stoic. His open joy had surely brought the disaster upon his family.

For a while the Kobas lived in a squalid apartment in Vancouver. Lin sold udon noodles in a broth made from what Azami was sure was not cow or chicken, for there were only dogs and cats around. Mr. Koba knew enough English to get a job mopping the docks. This was not the life he had agreed to. This was not the land of milk and honey advertised in Japan.

My father happened to be disembarking from England, and the story goes that my father had slipped while walking along the wet docks and would have fallen off the side had Mr. Koba not been there to catch his arm. My father insisted on buying Mr. Koba a drink to show his gratitude.

Mr. Koba was the only non-white in the bar. He was stared at from all angles, but my father, with his charm and his good humour, softened the crowd until every man was jolly and drunk. My father told Mr. Koba about Winteridge and the McCarthys' need of fruit pickers. A few weeks after my had father returned from that trip, Mr. Koba and his family followed him to Winteridge.

Mr. McCarthy hadn't expected a family of mostly women. My father hadn't known as much. Mr. Koba claimed his eldest daughter could pick as good as any man. Azami and Wu joined their father in the trees. Azami dressed in her brother's pants and shirtsleeves in a vague attempt to hide her femininity, while her younger sisters were put to work keeping house with Mrs. Koba.

Before I met Azami, Llewelyna and I had seen Mrs. Koba and the younger daughters scrubbing laundry at the shore of the lake while we swam. This was back when the lake monster was only a rumour and hadn't yet slipped into Llewelyna's stories, becoming far too real to ignore. The water in the bay was white with starch. Lacy puffs of soap floated to us as we swam. Llewelyna was convinced Winteridge was an island we might swim around. She had told me about Kai, a man who had trained himself to hold his breath for nine days, and we were practising swimming underwater. We waved as we swam by the Kobas. Mrs. Koba and the girls only stared and bowed slightly before returning to their work.

The Koba family was a precursor for the influx of Japanese on their way to town. My father seemed to draw a new Japanese bachelor to Winteridge with him each time he returned from the coast. Mr. Bell and Mr. Eber called my father a Jap lover. He was a man the other landowners in Winteridge wanted to hate, but couldn't. Despite his wealth and his lineage, my father could relate to anyone no matter their background. Llewelyna said he could tame any beast, charm the stripes right off a tiger's back. He said he couldn't stand to see such a civilized, sophisticated people in the grease and grime of the port and, he added, there was plenty of work for them in Winteridge. Although my father's orchard was nothing to speak of yet, he hired a few Japanese men to work in the yard. Llewelyna agreed as long as they stayed far from her garden.

6

The following summer, Llewelyna took me to the cliffs. The yellow balsamroots had blossomed as if overnight. The forest was thick with them. Llewelyna told me the wild flowers were shards of the first sun. We walked for an hour along the beach. Llewelyna walked in front. There were burrs in her hair. She wore the beaded evening slippers my father had recently purchased for her. She kept looking back and smiling at me. "Almost there," she promised.

When we finally came out of the trees, the land dropped out of sight and the lake shone in its place. Red pine needles were scattered all along the ground. Llewelyna stepped out of her slippers and had me unbutton her taffeta dress so she only wore her pale chemise, gauzy in the rising sun. She wasn't one for corsets, and she was clearly naked beneath the thin slip, the most secret parts of her body made into shadows.

"It is not known whether my body is flesh or fish," she whispered, quoting some story. Then, without looking back, she took two paces forward, and jumped. I ran to the edge of the cliff and watched her hair blaze up behind her. She disappeared in a white splash. I held my breath until she resurfaced.

"Come on, jump! It's brilliant!" she yelled up to me.

Her pale arms and legs flashed beneath the water. Her hair was flat against her head and made her almost unrecognizable. I put down our towels and slipped off my shoes. I stepped closer to the edge. When I looked down again I saw dark shadows swarm and spiral in the water beneath her.

"Look out!" I pointed at the water around her. The shadows collected into a solid shape, and a long snake-like figure breached the surface. "The addanc!" I screamed. The monster had slithered somehow from Llewelyna's story and into our world.

She kicked her legs in an attempt to lift her shoulders out of the water to see beneath her.

"Don't be a fool," she called up. She wrapped her arms around a boulder and lifted herself out of the lake.

I trembled at the top of the cliff until she hiked all the way back up. She did not slow to comfort me, but threw her dress on over her head and walked past me and into the forest. I had to run to keep up with her, clutching her forgotten slippers to my chest. We walked home in silence. The back of her dress gaped open and her wet hair dripped down her back. That was the first time I saw Llewelyna's monster, her addanc, in our own lake.

🐾

Azami took my fear of the lake and its monster as a challenge, something to defeat in me. She tugged me to the shore as if this were some kind of game. The water was so still and clear we could see the pebbles far below and fish flicker past our toes. Brown leaves from seasons past clumped along the shore and skimmed the surface beneath the birch trees. It was autumn now, and too cold to swim. Azami pulled her necklace out from the collar of her shirt and placed it over my head. I fingered the warm metal of the tag and the red glass bead. She said it would keep me safe from the lake kami. It had protected the Russian soldier from death. It had kept Azami safe on the boat from Japan.

The sun was low and bulbous on the mountains. It was the golden hour, as Henry called it, when everything is more vivid because the sun plucks the colours out into the open. A family of mallards floated past and I could see the gold flecks in their blue and green feathers. Azami took my hand. A yellow-veined leaf floated along the water at our feet and left a shadow against the bottom of the lake. Beneath the shadow, the glittery green-blue skin of the lake monster flooded past. I knew Azami could see it too because she clenched my hand so tight it pinched. She dipped her toes into the water and splashed the surface so we couldn't see the monster beneath us. Then she let go of my hand and lowered herself into the lake. Her skin was goose-pimpled; her feet treaded water in the space just above where the monster had been. She lowered herself deeper, up to her chest, and I had no choice but to follow. Our finger-tips were white, still clinging to the edge of the dock. I could feel the cool currents the monster created against the pads of my feet. A chill shot through my arches, so sharp I thought for a moment I had been bitten. Azami grinned. Then she let go and dropped below the surface. I gasped for air and followed after her.

Beneath the water her cotton shirt fluttered like fins as she swam. Her hair was as fine as ink. We swam into the darker water. Azami seemed set in a certain direction. The air in my lungs was hot and warmed my body. I realized Azami wasn't swimming away from the monster but chasing after it. The tip of its tail undulated ahead, nearly out of sight. The red bead of Azami's necklace thumped against my chest and calmed me. The deeper we swam, the larger and slower the fish around us and the cooler the water. Rainbow trout the size and girth of our calves glided past. The whiskered bottom-feeders, and carp so large they must be mammals, gave us little notice. And it was here, past the carp and into the coolest, darkest depths of the lake, that we found a sunken rowboat glittering with coins and broken china. Azami placed a chip of rose-patterned porcelain into my fist and held a triangle of blue glass in her own. Amongst the shadows on the other side of the rowboat we found the skeleton of a horse. Its teeth were clenched and furious against the sand. I went to gasp for breath and my throat burned with the choke of water. I thought I might drown but Azami's hand was tight on my wrist. Her lips puckered and her eyes went wide. We surfaced in a splash. I was surprised how close we were to the shore. I expected to come out somewhere in the middle of the lake. The greasy rocks against my soles were a relief.

"Did you see that?" I gasped. Each breath bubbled painfully out of me.

"Of course I saw."

We lay on the shore and shivered in the breeze. Our lungs pumped up and down desperately, like those of two beached fish. The golden hour had passed, and the world was ordinary again. I felt Azami turn to me. She held up her piece of blue glass and I showed her my bit of porcelain. We laughed at our tiny proof.

"What happened to that horse?" I said.

"I don't know. Drown?"

My ears filled with the horse's frantic limbs thunderous against the water. "Horses are excellent swimmers," I said.

"Kami get very hungry," Azami said. A chill crept across my legs like tiny bugs and made me itch. Azami put her hand out to collect the necklace. "Told you it's lucky."

I didn't want to give it back.

We tied our bits of glass and porcelain to chimes. A few days later, when Azami wanted to gather more of the water-softened porcelain for our wind chimes, she swam from the same spot but could never find the capsized boat and the horse skeleton again.

That winter Azami came to the tree fort with something stuffed up under her wool coat. She pulled the material up through the collar. The red silk had cherry blossoms and bumblebees embroidered onto it. Before Azami allowed me to touch it, she checked my hands and fingernails for dirt like my grandmother did before church and meals. Then she turned away from me and told me not to look. I peeked through my hands at her bare back as she slipped into the silk. Her skin where the sun hadn't touched was the colour of buttermilk. She fiddled with a tin of something but I couldn't see what she was doing. The kimono was far too long for her but she hiked it up and tied it in the back. She used a spoon to secure her hair in a bun. When she turned around her face was powdered white and her lips were dark red. She shivered.

"Here," she said and held the cube of beetroot towards me. I leaned in and let her paint my lips with the cool edge of the cut beet.

⟨⟩

In return for the stories Azami shared with me, I told her the ones I knew. I told Azami about Coyote and how he and the animal people shot arrows at the sky and waged war against the sky people. I told her how Noah called all the animals onto the ark right before the floods came. She asked how he spoke to the animals and I showed her how to call the deer and the groundhog, and when she doubted even that, I told her Llewelyna spoke to birds, spoke to spirits, to kami, using tongues.

Azami shook her head. "Not mix like that."

"What do you mean?"

"Kami or Coyote or Noah. Not all."

"Why not?"

"You can't," she said, sitting up. "My family has your God now. Father says you must decide. That's why he threw away the shrine."

"I believe in all of them," I said. I wanted to impress her with my belief.

Azami frowned at my insistence. "You can't. You must decide."

That night, as we walked home through the cool, dark forest, Azami pointed to the North Star. "There's the first kami," she said. The North Star was bigger and brighter than any of the others. "Now there are as many kami as there are creatures, but the first kami came into being alone. That, right there, is my God. See? Where is your God, Iris?"

Of course I had no answer for her.

As winter progressed, and it was too cold to visit in the tree fort, Azami and I were forced to hide away in our homes. I was restless, holed up like a rodent, and my father convinced me to accept Mrs. Bell's invitation to take piano lessons from her.

"If you don't enjoy it then there's no need to continue," he said. "But it would be rude not to go at least once." I agreed only because I wanted to see Angel, the dove.

Mrs. Bell had opened the door and inhaled suddenly, as if she hadn't been expecting me in the first place. She took me by the hand and pulled me to the parlour.

"Your hair, darling." She ran a hand through my tangled locks. She pulled me into her room, in front of her vanity, and sat me down. There were tinted bottles of perfumes, tins of powder, rouge, pins, and combs neatly arranged on the tabletop. In the reflection of the mirror I could see Mrs. Bell's bed neatly made with crisp pillows and embroidered blankets. Like most of the women in Winteridge, Mrs. Bell wore her hair in a round pompadour that nearly doubled the size of her head. She arranged my hair in the same way so that when she finished I resembled her in miniature.

I was a miserable student, not the slightest bit musical. But Mrs. Bell was patient and encouraging. After an hour or so of chords, she turned to me.

"Can I ask you something?"

I nodded, made curious by the serious adult tone of her question.

"Does your father know your mother goes off alone with that Indian?"

"Henry?"

"That *enormous* Indian." She said this as though Henry's height made the situation exceedingly worse.

"They're friends."

"Friends," she said simply, seemingly satisfied with my response, and went on to teach me scales.

It was only later, while she fetched biscuits from the kitchen to take with our tea, that I heard her say, as if to herself: "Not proper for a married woman to go off like that. Poor Noah. How shameful."

Before Mrs. Bell's comment, I wouldn't have imagined Llewelyna and Henry's relationship as anything but innocent. From then on, I became more aware of the appearance of things, no matter their truths. Mrs. Bell opened a world wherein my mother was a harlot and my father a cuckold, and I hated her for that.

One day after I watched Mr. and Mrs. Bell leave on the lake-boat, Azami and I slipped into their house through their kitchen window. It was my idea. Azami was terrified. Although she happily rebelled against her father, she was nothing but respectful of strangers.

Inside the Bells' home Azami clutched her arms around her stomach, afraid to rub against any of their expensive belongings. "Why did you bring me here?"

"I want to show you something." I took Azami to Angel's cage. She shrugged. "A bird?"

I took the silver chain out of the drawer and opened the door to the cage. I cooed to Angel as I had seen Mrs. Bell do and carefully clipped the chain to the band on the bird's foot.

"What are you doing?"

"Watch," I said. Angel launched up towards the ceiling. I looked to Azami and was satisfied by the surprise on her face. She held a hand to her mouth. Then her expression changed from shock to horror. Her eyes turned glassy.

"Please stop," she said. "That hurts her."

"It doesn't. She likes it," I said. "Mrs. Bell does this all the time." I gathered the chain to bring the bird closer.

"Birds belong in the sky," Azami said. "Let her free," she said. Her eyes turned cold. "Undo the chain."

I held the dove in my hands. Her body trembled under my palm. Her heart ticked faster than a pocket watch.

"Do it!" Azami said.

I undid the clasp from the dove's foot. Angel soared up, frantic, expecting a limit that wasn't there. She bumped against the ceiling and then soared towards us. Azami and I had to duck to avoid her flight. Then *plonk*. The dove slammed into the closed window in the sitting room and bounced onto the velvet loveseat.

Azami and I approached the bird carefully. She was on her side, yellow twiggy feet extended and twitching.

"She's just stunned," I said. But it was clear the dove was dead. Azami picked up the bird in her cupped palms and whispered into her feathers. She closed her eyes and gave the dove's head a little kiss. She carefully placed the bird back in the cage and closed the door.

As we crawled mournfully out the window of the Bells' house, we heard the dove coo. "Listen," I said. The dove cooed again. We scrambled back inside and ran to Angel's cage. The dove was perched on her pole. She eyed us sideways. I thought of the words Azami had whispered as she nuzzled the bird.

"Did you do that?" I asked.

"Do what?"

"Bring it back to life."

Azami smiled. "Of course not." She picked a white feather from the ground. "For the shrine," she said.

﷽

That spring Azami filled the tree fort with the items her parents had banned from her home and thrown away. I see now it was her re-creation of Japan, but back then I saw it only as a trove of treasure I was permitted limited access to. She found me unworthy, it seemed, to handle her precious things.

I was desperate to find something sacred, something beautiful to place in the shrine. I opened the bottom drawer of my wardrobe and pulled out one of Saint Francis's feathers and considered it. It wasn't enough. I placed the feather back. Then I found the perfect item.

The next day at the tree fort I poured my marbles from their velvet pouch into my palm for Azami to admire.

"Rocks?" she said, unimpressed.

"Marbles. Look." I held out the blue galaxy marble for her to see. "Isn't it pretty?"

Azami shrugged. Hurt by her indifference, I reached to set the marble in the shrine. Azami caught my arm and shook her head.

"You said I could bring something."

"Something sacred."

"This is sacred."

"Why? Because it's pretty?"

I looked down at Azami's objects and realized my mistake. I needed a story. "It's a marble from Germany. Handmade." Azami's disdain infuriated me. "My father gave it to me. It was his great-great-great grandfather's. Who is dead. He found it—in a northern forest."

"You lie."

"I do not." I reached again to place the marble in the shrine.

"No." Azami slapped my arm away hard. "No silly things."

I stood up and towered over her, hands on my hips. "Get out!" I said. Azami opened her mouth to say something. "I said get out!" She glanced at her shrine. I slammed my foot on the ground and the entire fort shook terribly. "Leave!"

Azami stood, her face close to mine. "You are stupid girl," she said before she disappeared through the hole in the floor. I stood over it, watching her descend. When she got to the ground she glared up at me. I snatched her porcelain elephant from the shrine and threw it down at her. It ricocheted off the lower branches. I leaned against the wall and cried into my sleeve as I listened to her rummage through the leaves and pine needles for the elephant. Then I placed my blue marble in the shrine.

The next day on my way to the tree fort, I could hear someone following me. I turned, expecting to find Azami, but it was only the silver coyote peeking at me from behind the trees. Llewelyna's she-wolf. Then something struck my back, hard. I turned to see Azami with a slingshot poised, the lake-blue marble glinting.

"It broke," she said. There was a tear in the corner of her eye. "Was my grandmother's. You understand?" Her hand that held back the elastic piece trembled. Then she let go.

I woke to the taste of iron. There were stones in my mouth. I spat them out in my palm and was horrified to see a tooth covered in blood. I felt around in my mouth with my tongue and found the gap on the bottom, near the back. The marble had struck me in the cheek. It was bruised and tender. Next to me was my pouch of glass marbles, two missing. I groped through the leaves and found the yellow marble but not the blue one.

When I got to my house, Llewelyna was reading on the front porch. My father was away, overseas. While he was gone Llewelyna often disappeared into the forest or into her books. Her constant reading gave me the sense she was never quite there, but split in two. She lived out multiple lives, one visible, the others hidden, secret. When I was very small, before I could read, I would snatch one of her books and sit next to her, gazing into it, hoping the world inside might absorb me also. We were never to interrupt Llewelyna's reading. So I wasn't surprised that as I stood there, blood seeping from the corner of my mouth, she didn't even look up to acknowledge me.

7

It rained for weeks in Winteridge and I was kept shuttered in our house with nothing but the handful of children's books Henry lent me and endless games of cribbage. One afternoon the rain fell against the roof and porch like stones and Llewelyna and Jacob and I were all sitting on the chesterfield in front of the fireplace in the sitting room, bundled with blankets. Jacob had a fever and so Llewelyna was inclined to be tender. She stroked wet locks from his forehead.

"I remember it like this," she began and closed her eyes. "Once there was a maiden, the fairest of the world, I think her name was Creirwy. She lived by the lake Tegid with her family. She was helping her mother gather herbs in the forest to make a stew that would make her ill-favoured brother who was born an idiot, and ugly beyond all means, a wise and intelligent man, for this brother was to inherit her father's throne." I expected Jacob to interrupt and protest, but he didn't. Llewelyna continued. "One day she was walking through the forest, far from her house, when she came upon a rogue magician named Gwion Bach. He had long been exiled from the town and now haunted the black mountains. The maiden hadn't realized she had wandered into his realm."

I peered through my eyelashes and watched Llewelyna and Jacob. Their eyes closed tight and their foreheads touching.

Llewelyna twisted Jacob's red curls behind his ear but they kept bouncing back.

"The rogue took hold of the maiden's wrist before she could run away. His long fingernails scratched her skin. He looked her dead in the eye and told her she would give birth to a bastard daughter. The maiden knew his words to be a threat. Whatever the rogue said always came true. This was why he was exiled. The town decided that his words were not prophecies but curses.

"The maiden was so angry at the rogue that as he turned to leave she chased after him. The maiden was a fast runner, and just as she was about to catch up to him, the rogue transformed into a hare and fled, and so the maiden became a greyhound to match his speed. When the rogue arrived at the fast-moving river he became a fish, and she an otter, and the chase continued underwater. Right as the maiden was about to snatch him up with her paw, the rogue became a songbird and launched into the sky. The maiden became a hawk and swooped after him. The rogue dropped from the sky and fell into a wheat field and transformed into a piece of grain. And so the maiden became a hen and swiftly swallowed the grain.

"Nine months later the maiden gave birth to the rogue, who had transformed into a baby girl. Although the maiden knew the baby was really the rogue, she could not kill the infant. It was too beautiful. And so the maiden put the baby in a potato sack, tied it up tight and gave the infant to the sea."

Jacob had fallen asleep. His breathing was steady and deep. Llewelyna kissed him on his damp forehead. The end of the story was so chilling I didn't want Llewelyna to know I was still awake to hear it. It seemed like something I shouldn't have heard. Although I feigned sleep, no kiss was planted on my forehead.

When the rain finally stopped a few days later, I wandered to the McCarthys' orchard to spy on Azami. She glided through the trees dressed in her brother Wu's old clothes. Her long dark hair was tucked up under a small-brimmed cap. Unlike the robotic movements of Wu and the other male pickers, Azami made picking apples look like a dance.

The first few times I spied on her I was happy to remain anonymous in the surrounding forest. Azami never seemed to look down before she jumped from the ladder. She was the only one who didn't stand at attention when Mr. McCarthy came out to give some instructions to the work crew. Azami didn't exchange a single word with the other pickers. Instead, she remained invisible in the trees.

On one of these occasions, Azami caught me spying on her. She was in a far corner of the orchard, off on her own. I thought this far from the others we might be able to talk. I waved. I thought she would be happy to see me, but she was angry I was there. She glared at me. Perhaps out of embarrassment or disappointment, I plucked some hard green apples from a bin and threw them at her, one after the other, as hard as I could.

"Stop it!" she said under her breath, no more than a whisper. She took a hand from the ladder to block an apple from hitting her head. The ladder tottered. I kept throwing the apples at her, relentless. The apples thumped to the ground and rolled along the base of the tree. She scrambled to grasp the sides of the ladder to steady it. Then there was a holler and I slipped back into the trees in time to see Mr. Koba storm towards Azami. He lifted one of the green apples and held it close to her mouth as if offering a bite.

"What is this?" he said. Azami turned her cheek to him. He said something else I couldn't hear, but I know I could have if I were nearer. Mr. Koba insisted on speaking English even when alone with his family. If Azami uttered a word in Japanese her father made her gargle boiling water and salt one hundred times.

I wondered what my father would think if he knew this ruthless side of his Japanese hero. Mr. Koba was tremendously kind to the townspeople—in fact, I knew if I were to come out from behind the tree to reveal myself to him, the stern look on his face would wash away. "Who is this pretty girl?" he said whenever I came out to the back porch to say goodnight when he and my father smoked out there together.

I kept hidden because part of me wanted to see Azami shamed.

Mr. Koba yanked Azami down the ladder and she fell to her knees in the grass. When he pulled her up to her feet, his grasp was far too tight around her arm. She kept her face downcast, away from his. He took one of the fallen apples and held it to her face again. She gave him the opposite cheek.

"What is wrong with you?" he said. Azami turned to face him. Her mouth puckered as though she sucked at something sour. I thought she might point me out and share the blame, but her eyes were cool and steady on him, defiant. If I could have escaped without being seen, I would have then. I had seen enough. Azami and Mr. Koba stayed like that for a moment, locked in one another's anger. Then Mr. Koba jolted up and dragged Azami to the house, cursing in Japanese under his breath, forgetting, for a moment, his own rules.

As I ran home, the weight of what I had done caught like a pebble at the back of my throat. I thought if only I could bring her something, a gift, she might forgive me. The next morning I went back to the orchard, armed with one of Llewelyna's cigarettes tucked behind my ear. Azami had said back in Japan she smoked all the time, but since arriving in Canada her father banned cigarettes because it looked bad—unfeminine. It must have been terribly confusing, being pushed to be both more and less of a woman at the same time.

I couldn't find Azami in any of the trees. Mr. Koba and Wu used a long saw with two handles to gnaw off some dead branches. The grating only increased my anxiety for Azami. As I walked past the McCarthys' cookhouse, I saw Mrs. Koba plucking a hen on the steps, the orange feathers scattered at her feet. The younger Koba girls were hanging up starched sheets at the side of the pick shack. One of them saw me and whispered to the others. They followed me with their eyes. I circled the orchard one more time before I went to the barn. There I found Azami stirring a barrel of milk with a paddle. She was standing on an upturned bucket, the barrel too high for her to reach otherwise. It smelled terrible—sour milk and rancid pig feed. Azami saw me out the corner of her eye and splashed me with the milk. My hand had been extended to her, the cigarette perched between my two fingers now drenched in milk. She glanced down at it for a moment before turning back to churning the milk. A grease stain ran down the skirt of my blue silk dress.

"My father bought this in England," I said. Even to me my voice was high-pitched and whiny. Still Azami did not acknowledge me. "See? You've ruined it." Although this was true—the dress was new, expensive, and surely ruined—I wasn't one to care for dresses. I twisted the cigarette between my fingers until the copper strands sprinkled the hay at my feet. Still Azami would not look up. I spat at her and ran out of the barn all the way to the tree fort. I didn't mind that I was covered in butter or that the dress was ruined. What drove me to madness was that Azami wouldn't look at me. She wore a hardened, stone face, like she had when Mr. Koba admonished her about the apples I had thrown. I knew then it wasn't so much the apples Mr. Koba had been mad about as Azami's defiance. It wrung out our rage.

In the tree fort I picked up Azami's shrine, with the carefully set orange peel and mirror, and dropped it through the hole in the floor. It crashed against the exposed roots below. For all Azami's talk of its sacredness, the shrine split so easily against the ground it hardly made a sound. I wanted to make Azami hurt, I wanted to make her feel something.

Now that it was done, the forest was dreadfully quiet. Even the birds shuttered at my actions. I knew Azami considered her shrine a holy thing, like the Eucharist or Llewelyna's tin saints she lined up on her windowsill. To see it now in so many feeble pieces made me feel like a devil. I scrambled down the ladder and checked to make sure none of the contents had been broken. And then, as if removing the shrine might make it whole again, at least in Azami's mind, I gathered the pieces in my skirt and laid them out in the bottom drawer of my wardrobe until I could decide what to do with them.

To keep myself from thinking any more of the shrine and what I had done, I left our house and ran to the river, where I knew Jacob and Ronald liked to fish. I found them sitting atop a log, fishing rods stretched out over the water. I approached from behind and was about to jump out and scare them, but something in the way they spoke to one another, as if even in these thick woods they might need to whisper, keep secret from the eaves-dropping trees, invited me to hold back and spy. I circled around them to see if I could read their lips. They were speaking too close for boys. Ronald was my age, only one year over Jacob's twelve, but his height and build made him look much older. Ronald leaned in and whispered something in Jacob's ear; his hand was on Jacob's thigh. Jacob smiled and touched Ronald's cheek. They stayed like that for a moment, locked in a gesture I had only seen between Llewelyna and my father. This tenderness between the boys startled me. A twig snapped beneath my feet and Jacob's eyes shot up to find me hiding in the trees. His hand dropped into his lap.

As I made my way back to the house, I was reminded of another moment I had witnessed between Jacob and Ronald the summer previous, when they had competed in swimming and diving competitions at the annual regatta in the city. I had never been to the event before and was impressed by all the white suits and dresses, sunhats and parasols. Sailboats studded the lake like teeth. Neither Jacob nor Ronald had done very well in the swimming competitions. Jacob was too slow and Ronald's breaststroke was awkward; he never seemed to catch his stride. After the canoe races the divers lined up on the city dock below the diving platform. It had to be twenty feet high. My father, Llewelyna, and I had found seats in the bleachers facing the platform and the lineup of nervous boys awaiting their turn to dive. Jacob and Ronald wore one-piece swimsuits with narrow straps that did little to cover their chests. The suits exposed their upper thighs and were so tight the boys' protruding groins were painfully obvious. I was shocked to see them so exposed. As if reading my discomfort, my father explained that the costumes improved their speed. Out of the water the boys looked vulnerable and skinless.

I loved the silence before each dive, as the crowd eagerly watched the diver climb the endless ladder. At the top of the diving platform Ronald straightened. Being so much taller than his peers, Ronald usually slouched. His new height and flattened hair made him look like a stranger to me. He stood there for a moment, looking stoically over the bleachers towards the mountains on the other side of the lake. He lifted onto his toes and his thigh muscles were sculpted and smooth as a horse's. He lifted his arms ahead of him, swept them down, and with that leverage made three giant bounds to the edge of the platform. Then he was airborne. He seemed to hang there, his chest pushed out, his legs straight but bent slightly back at the hips, his arms outstretched at his sides like a sparrow. Then he pulled in his knees, spun backwards, and unravelled moments before the surface of the lake. I was so taken aback by his grace I had forgotten to join the applause until Llewelyna elbowed me to do so.

Jacob's dive was a disaster. Compared to Ronald he looked bony and pale and very boyish up on the platform. On his final step he tripped and could do no better than gather his limbs together before his stomach struck the surface of the lake like a bomb. The crowd gasped. My father stood to better see. And this is when the moment occurred. Ronald stretched his arm out over the edge of the dock and easily pulled Jacob out of the water. Jacob waved off the concerns of the crowd with one hand, but his other hand remained locked with Ronald's for seconds too long as they walked away from the dive area and disappeared. They didn't return in time for Ronald to claim his blue ribbon, and so Teresa had gone up to receive it on his behalf, curtseying maniacally in her white doll's dress, tears of pride streaming down her cheeks.

Jacob knew I had seen what I had that day at the river, but he ignored me, and so I continued to spy on him and Ronald. They met in the same place every day. Sometimes they would fish, other times they would hike further into the hills and hunt snakes. They had huddled conversations I craned desperately to hear. One day, while they sat leaning against a tree, their homework abandoned at their feet, Ronald took Jacob's face and kissed him square on the mouth. My eyes burned, and I had to look away. I ran, not caring if they heard me, back through the forest to the tree fort.

Inside I found a bucket full of fish guts. All the books I had left there, precious books of Henry's—the picture Bible, a dictionary, the old red book called *The Water-Babies*, and *Peter Pan*— floated atop the guts in the bucket. They were swollen and reeked. I knew, even then, that I deserved this. I would have to tell Henry I had left the books I had borrowed from him in the tree fort during a storm.

Soon after the last time I had gone to spy on Azami in the McCarthys' orchard, the Kobas moved to their own slice of land up in the hills. The government wouldn't sign the land over to the Kobas because they were Japanese, so my father bought the land and leased it to them illegally. "It doesn't make sense," my father said. "We're strangers here too."

For decades the Kobas' orchard would be the only Japanese-run orchard in the community. Instead of relying on only one crop, the Kobas grew peaches, pears, apples, and plums and had a substantial vegetable garden. Soon the Kobas' orchard rivalled both the McCarthys' and my family's orchards.

That evening at dinner Jacob and I ignored each other. My father had recently returned from overseas. We were listening to the new record he had brought home for Llewelyna from Wales. The choir of male voices crowded the room. Llewelyna pushed her steak around her plate until my father reached across and forked it onto his.

"I purchased some pit ponies from just outside your hometown, Lew," he said.

"You went to Holyhead?" she asked, her fork poised above her empty plate, her eyes too full of white.

"No, but I was on Anglesey."

"Anglesey, the Mother of Wales, Ynys Dywyl," she said under her breath.

"What does that mean?" Jacob asked. I kicked him under the table. It was all too obvious we were meant to be invisible at this moment.

"The Dark Island," she said ominously, without taking her eyes off my father. My father was eating too eagerly, head down, as if ignorant to Llewelyna's eyes narrowed at him as though he were grazing prey. He took a long drink of milk and there was a slice of silence. Even the choir hushed. My father wiped his mouth with a napkin.

"If you want to go for a visit, Lew, just say the word."

The choir breathed back to life. Llewelyna squished a potato with her fork. "Don't be a damn fool."

"You must miss it, the old lighthouse, the woods, the olive groves."

"Stop."

"The ocean, Lew."

Llewelyna looked down at the red smear on her plate where the steak used to be.

"I'm sure your sister—"

"Noah." Llewelyna's fork slammed against her plate. Jacob and I sat stiffly in our chairs, afraid to move.

My father looked from Jacob to me. He smiled weakly and nodded for us to continue eating and pretend all was fine. I had never met Llewelyna's sister, Gwyn. All I knew of her was she was a housemaid and allergic to hazelnuts. Llewelyna told me this once when I broke out in hives after eating a piece of hazelnut pie. Because of this shared trait I always felt a vague connection to Gwyn. But Gwyn was a subject that pursed Llewelyna's lips together and made the skin on her neck flush. And with my father's brief mention of her, I watched those familiar splotches rise up Llewelyna's neck to her jawbone.

I imagined the choir voices were angels speaking tongues. The music reminded me of the hymns we mumbled at church. When the song finished the record kept spinning, and amplified the itchy silence.

"So, you've found yourself another Welsh pony to suffocate with dust," Llewelyna said.

"Lew . . ." my father warned.

"Better dan wee lads n' ladies, I suppose," she continued, dabbing the corners of her mouth with her napkin.

"That's enough." He stood from the table. "I've lost my appetite."

"I'd have worries if ya didn't." Llewelyna leaned back in her chair, arms crossed, and glared after him as he left the room. Jacob and I looked down at our plates. Lumps of gristle filled out our cheeks like a pair of chipmunks.

That night I knocked on Jacob's door.

"What do you want?"

"I need to speak to you," I whispered.

He shuffled across the room and opened the door a crack. He peered left and right before he let me in. I stood in the middle of his room. I had always imagined his room to be a mess, like mine. But it was neat and tidy, as if staged. His desk was clear, with only a pencil and a piece of blank paper upon it. A small bookshelf held a few of the books my father had brought him from London, *Treasure Island*, *The Jungle Book*, *The War of the Worlds*, and the like. They looked untouched, unread. His bed was made and there was only a crease in it where he must have been laying before I knocked.

"I said, what do you want?" He sat on the bed and looked up at me.

"I would like you to help me with something." I told Jacob about Azami and the marble and the books. I told him I wanted to return Azami's shrine to her in the bucket, burning.

"What makes you think I'll help you?"

"I saw you."

"Saw what?"

"You know."

"I don't," he said. We stared at one another for a moment. "I have some matches," he said finally.

That night we carried Azami's shrine through the woods in the stinking bucket. It took us a long time to find the Kobas' new home. The plot of land was enormous. There was a stack of fallen trees and a row of freshly planted saplings. At the edge of the land was a cabin with small glowing windows. I couldn't imagine Azami and her siblings and her newly arrived cousins all sharing such a small space.

Jacob and I set the bucket at the edge of the yard. We had siphoned gasoline from the Bells' new automobile and now we poured it all over the shrine. Jacob lit the match and dropped it in the bucket. We had to jump back from the rush of flame. The shrine sizzled and sparked. A burning piece of wood shot out from the bucket and landed in the grass. Before I could act, the flame spread, snaked through the grass towards the pile of fallen trees and brush. Over the pound of our feet and hearts, we could hear shouts and screams from the Kobas' house. I was too afraid to look back. Something nipped at my heels.

The next morning I sat at the top of the stairs and listened to my father and Llewelyna talk quietly over their morning tea.

"Imbeciles. And you were upset I gave Phillip Bell a hard time. It's his kind that'd do such a thing. He'd surely have joined those bigots rioting in Vancouver if he had the chance."

"Don't be ridiculous. Phillip would never do something so barbaric."

"Or those McCarthy boys. Perhaps Mr. McCarthy set them to it. He's probably upset the Kobas left his orchard."

"It was no mystery to Old McCarthy the Kobas would be leaving. Jon Koba has been clearing that land for the past few months."

"Whoever did it will burn for such hate."

My eyes widened. Cursed by my own mother? Hollow with shame, I returned to my bed. When Llewelyna came to wake me,

I pretended to be sick until my sickness became real. I lay in bed and retched all day into a bread bowl that Llewelyna emptied for me. I sat up only when I heard Jacob arrive home from his lessons. He ran up the stairs and stormed into my bedroom, jumped on top of me, his hands on my throat.

"I'll kill you," he said.

I thumped my fists against his back. I couldn't speak.

"I'll do it!" He tightened his grip around my neck. His face was flush with anger. I croaked. He loosened his grasp and fell backwards. His head dropped into his hands. "You promised," he said. "I should have known better than to trust you, you snake."

I coughed until I caught my breath. "What are you talking about?"

"Jesse McCarthy. You told him."

"Told him what?"

"He called me a queer." Jacob's eyes were glassy and brimmed with red. His cheek looked bruised and had a cut on it.

"I didn't tell anyone anything."

He looked at me carefully. "You didn't?"

I shook my head and fondled my neck. "Who did that to you?"

"Why would he say that, then?"

I shrugged. "Who hit you?"

"Who do you think?"

"Jesse McCarthy is an ignoramus," I said.

Jacob grinned at the word. Once he was convinced I hadn't told his secrets, he told me everyone in town was talking about the fire. It had spread to the Kobas' row of saplings. Thankfully the crackling woke them and they were able to put the fire out before it reached the house.

Jacob wriggled his nose. "It smells in here."

I knelt before the bread bowl and I retched again.

8

I sat on the wharf and watched the Jesus bugs dance along the surface of the water while Jacob swam. He had never believed me when I told him what I had seen in the water the day Llewelyna and I went to the cliffs. The wharf extended along the shore and then out towards the drop-off where the water was well over our heads. Past the wharf were a dozen or so pillars that stuck out of the water like matchsticks. A few rowboats and canoes were tied to them. On the other side of the wharf, the lakeboat was docked. Ronald and his father were unloading dry goods while a group of orchard hands waited to load crates of last season's apples. Ronald kept turning towards us, shaking his dark hair out of his face to watch us. Outside of school, Jacob had stayed away from Ronald since the incident with Jesse McCarthy, but Jacob was showing off for him now, speaking too loud and twirling and splashing obnoxiously in the water. It was late spring and the water was high. I reached out and touched the glassy surface of the lake. The clouds in the reflected sky whirled.

"Did you see that?" Jacob said, treading water. He pointed to the thick lake weed beneath him and gave a false shriek.

"Jacob . . ."

"Honest. I saw something." He laughed. "It's your monster, the addanc. Or is it Leviathan?"

"Naitaka," I said. "Henry says—"

"Henry's an Indian."

"So?" I said.

Jacob dunked beneath the surface. He swam through a school of minnows that scattered, darted in all directions at his approach. When he came to the surface he shook his head like a dog. I stood to leave.

"Where are you going?"

"I need to help Llewelyna make dinner."

"It's only three o'clock."

I shrugged.

"Stay for a bit. Wait for me."

"I have to go." I began walking up the path to the road.

"Iris!" Jacob yelled from the water. "Iris, don't."

I kept walking.

"Iris." This time my name was sputtered. "Help!"

I turned. Jacob had disappeared from the surface. I walked back down the wharf hesitantly, expecting him to launch out of the water at any moment and laugh at the terrified look on my face. The surface was calm and Jacob was nowhere in sight. Ronald and I looked at one another for a moment before he slipped off his shoes and dove into the lake.

Ronald surfaced and called to the other men on the dock. "He's drowning!" he yelled, and dipped below again. Mr. Nickel and a man who had been loading apples onto the lakeboat jumped into the water. Mr. Nickel's bowler hat floated on the surface. I was furious one of Jacob's pranks had caused such a stir. The hat would be ruined.

When they surfaced without Jacob again and again, I got chills.

"He's stuck in the lake weed," someone called, and a few other men jumped into the water. I was immobilized. I stood on the wharf and watched Mr. Nickel's hat. I wondered how long it would float there. Then I saw the shadowed figure of the lake monster. I couldn't catch my breath to say the words. A crowd had gathered on the wharf by now. I felt a hand on my back; a woman pulled me to her. She smelled of sweet bread. It was Mrs. Nickel. She held a paper bag in front of my mouth.

"Breathe into it, dear. Catch your breath." I tried to focus on the paper bag as it expanded and shrivelled with each breath. The men were still diving into the water. It had been too long. I pushed the bag away. My index finger ticked against my wrist: sixty seconds, eighty seconds, one hundred seconds. The hat sank.

"Iris." My father was beside me in his suit. "Where's your brother?"

I pointed to the water. I watched his eyes fill out as he took in the scene. The four or five men in the water yelled frantically, sputtering and gasping for air. My father handed me his top hat, took off his coat and shoes and was about to dive in when Mr. Nickel brought up my brother by the arm. Jacob's face was ashen. He was bleeding from somewhere. The water around him was rusty.

"Give him to me!" my father said. He crouched down and reached his arms towards Mr. Nickel. Out behind the men the shadows of the lake monster retreated.

"Iris, move," my father said. He laid Jacob on the wharf. He and Mr. Nickel bent over my brother's limp body. Ronald tore off his shirt and tied a sleeve above a large wound on Jacob's calf. My father knelt by Jacob's head and Mr. Nickel began pumping Jacob's chest and breathing into his mouth. Ronald sobbed openly. I realized I was crying too.

"Oh, Jesus. Jesus, help us. O Holy Father," my father said beneath his breath. They were Llewelyna's words. I had never heard my father pray. I couldn't look at Jacob's green face. His ribs would surely collapse beneath Mr. Nickel's huge hands that still pumped steadily at his chest. I heard bones crack. Finally, there was a gurgling sound. Water poured from Jacob's mouth as if he were a fountain.

"Back away, everyone. Back away," Mr. Nickel said.

My father sat Jacob up and he spat up more water. "Thank you, Lord. Thank you, Jesus Christ. Thank you, Mary." I wondered if anyone else could hear my father's mutterings. Ronald was at Jacob's feet, holding his blue toes as if he meant to kiss them. When Jacob caught his breath he looked up at me in a way I knew meant he had seen the monster too. He then looked down at his leg and the bloody rag tied around it. The crowd was quiet.

It took Jacob weeks to recover. He had several broken ribs and it was hard for him to breathe. His leg wound was slow to heal. Ronald came to our house every day, but Jacob refused to see him. He brought Jacob gifts: broth, biscuits, a book. Ronald sat with my father at the kitchen table as I served them tea. Ronald would eye me carefully, unsure of how much I knew. After Ronald left, my father would remark on what a superb young man he was, what an excellent friend. My father was convinced Ronald was keen on me. He hinted that we would make a good pair.

I was coming back from Henry's with some new books for Jacob when I saw Azami, standing in the middle of our orchard with her hands behind her back. She was looking for me from behind her cover of trees. She was dressed in her brother's pants and a loose shirt. Her hair was tucked up into a cap. I couldn't guess her intentions. A cold stone of sweat rolled down my back. Azami jumped between trees and bushes to stay hidden from the windows of the house. She approached our front porch and pulled a brown paper bag from behind her back. She was looking around for a place to put it when Llewelyna stepped outside with a cup of tea. Azami dropped the paper bag on the stairs and ran away.

Llewelyna, startled, spilled hot tea on her hands. She cursed in Welsh. I held my breath as she bent to pick up the paper bag. I imagined it would be a warning of some kind, a dead animal Azami had taken her revenge on. Llewelyna's expression was hard to read as she looked into the bag. She folded over the top edge and went back in the house.

When I got home Llewelyna was in the kitchen preparing soup for Jacob.

"Your friend was here," she said, smiling into the steam from the pot.

"Azami?"

"She was dressed like a boy. I wonder why."

I shrugged.

"She brought you something."

"She did?"

Llewelyna gestured to the windowsill, where my blue marble shone in the sunlight as if it were made of only water.

&

I entered Jacob's room one morning and sat on the bed next to him as he pretended to sleep. "You saw it, didn't you," I said. He rolled away from me. "The monster. Did you see its face?"

"I don't want to talk about it, Iris."

"Does it really have the head of a horse?"

"Get out."

Although it had seemed for a time that Jacob was getting better, his wound became infected and he and Llewelyna took the lakeboat to a hospital in the city. My father asked me again and again what had happened that day, as if the story might evolve over time into something he could better understand, pieces that might fit together more easily.

"There were these shadows in the water. Long and dark like a serpent," I said.

"Be serious, Iris. Your mother has been filling you with her stories. She must stop all that. You're getting too old." He was smoking one of Llewelyna's cigarettes at the kitchen table.

"Jacob saw it too."

"He told me he couldn't remember what happened."

"Something bit him and tangled him in the seaweed, on purpose."

"Nonsense," my father said, leaving the table for his office.

That night my father came into my bedroom and stood in the darkness with a dim lantern. Another cigarette burned at the corner of his mouth.

"You scared me," I said.

His shirt sleeves were rolled up to his elbows and his silk vest was unbuttoned. He pulled a book from behind his back, knelt down by my bed, and positioned the lantern beneath the book. There was an illustration of a long, grey, scaly creature. I ran my fingers over the drawing and traced the word *sturgeon*.

"There are a multitude of these in the lake," he said. He looked so satisfied with his discovery I couldn't tell him that this creature was merely a fish and what haunted our lake was a monster, a demon. The next morning the picture was pinned to the door of his study. The pin went right through the fish's head.

One afternoon, while my father and I were sitting on the porch reading to ward off worry, the Kobas' rugged horse carriage turned up our drive. As far as I knew, my father and Jon Koba hadn't spoken since the fire, a few months before. My father stood in greeting, and he and Jon Koba exchanged nods before setting off to walk through the orchard. Azami and her three sisters were dressed in identical red dresses with wide white collars. Their hair was pinned back into bulbous pompadours that shaded their eyes from the noon sun.

Azami's sisters embraced their Canadian names and introduced themselves as Molly, the one who had followed Azami and me around before; Dorothy; and Florence. The girls looked down at my dirty fingernails and unbrushed hair, and exchanged looks. My father would usually have encouraged me to keep better care of myself, but my brother's incident had distracted him.

"We have brought some fish and rice," Molly said, gesturing to a steaming lidded basket.

"Thank you."

The Koba sisters looked around the porch, their gazes sliding over my father's empty scotch glass, his abandoned book, his pocket watch on the armrest of his chair, ticking audibly. One of Llewelyna's tin saints, Saint Laura, the scalded one, was set on the railing of the porch. I hadn't noticed it until Florence, the youngest, considered it seriously. Azami's eyes remained fixed on mine.

"I'm sorry about your brother," Azami said. "Is he going to be okay?"

"I think so."

"He saw the lake kami?"

Dorothy rolled her eyes. Molly took hold of Azami's elbow and squeezed, her eyes narrowed in warning. Azami pulled free.

"Yes, the lake monster."

"Now that he has seen the kami, it may follow him."

"Amy, enough." Molly said.

"Amy?" I smirked.

"No," Azami said. Not turning to meet Molly's hard looks. "Did you get the marble?"

I nodded, smiling.

Florence was holding the saint now, turning it over and over in her hands.

"That's not a toy," I said. Florence looked up, froze. "Saint Laura of Cordoba was boiled alive in pitch."

Florence carefully set the saint back on the railing. Azami and I exchanged satisfied smiles.

When Jon Koba and my father returned, they were sombre. They left enough distance between them as they walked, three men could have strolled comfortably between them. My father was holding an envelope. He swatted it against his palm. Jon Koba reached across to shake my father's hand, and turned to the carriage. Azami and her sisters curtseyed and followed after him. We watched the carriage rattle down the road.

"Stubborn as mules," my father said.

I had never heard him speak unkindly of Mr. Koba. "What is it?"

"He can't own the land, not legally. And there's not a thing I can do." He opened the envelope to reveal a thick stack of bank-notes. "This is tenfold what we agreed on for the lease." My father stuffed the envelope into his shirt pocket. "That damn fire has ruined everything. He doesn't trust me."

I woke the next morning to Azami throwing meaty green wal-nuts at my window. I looked down and found her squatted low in the grass. The sky was still purple. Azami saw me and turned to walk away. She gestured for me to follow her.

We walked wordlessly to the lake. Her hand was cold in mine, the bones as fine and angular as a bird's, her grip tight. It seemed she thought I might flee or turn back if she didn't pull me along. At the shore, we hopscotched onto some boulders and perched on them, running our hands through the velvety water.

"I'm sorry," she said suddenly. "For what I did to your books. It was wrong."

Shame burned in my belly and climbed my throat. Azami poured salt from a paper bag into her hands and told me to place my hands beneath hers. She released the salt into my hands, and then I poured it back into hers. We repeated this until all the salt had slipped into the lake. Then she cupped lake water in her hands and poured that from one hand to the other and then into my hands.

"We call this *harae*," Azami said. "Purification from bad luck, disease, and—what do you call it? Guilt? Now, wash your face with that water in your hands."

Sunlight crept up the white birch trees around us and turned the far side of the lake into diamonds and the pool of water in my hands to gold. The Ebers' rooster yodelled, and this cathedral of mountains and lake valley made the sound majestic.

"I have to tell you something," I said. Azami worried over the water dripping from my cupped hands. "Azami." She glanced up at me and then back down to my hands. "The shrine is gone."

Her eyes shot up to mine. "What do you mean, gone?"

"I'm so sorry." All the water had leaked from my hands now.

"There are kami in there. My grandmother— My baby brother—"

"I know. I'm so sorry." I couldn't bear the grief in her face. "I don't know where it is," I lied. "It disappeared from the tree fort."

Azami clenched her hands into fists and slammed them against the still lake.

"Maybe someone stole it," I said.

"No, not someone," she said. I watched her nervously. She looked up at me, her pupils tiny in the glare of the rising sun. "Molly. She followed me that once. She won't leave me alone."

"Did she know you had the shrine?" I asked.

Azami nodded. "She saw me rescue it."

I felt relieved to have Azami's anger misdirected at Molly, but my guilt continued to burn despite the cleansing ritual.

"We must find it," she said.

"It could be anywhere. She probably already destroyed it."

"Molly would never do that. She knows too well the danger that comes with destroying a house of kami. Releasing them. Even my father was careful not to break the wood. Just disassemble."

A chill went up my spine. "But aren't they good kami?"

"Not if they are angry. Nothing is just one way."

We spent weeks scouring the forest for the shrine I knew could not be found.

9

When Llewelyna and Jacob finally came home, Jacob had changed in some important way. He seemed much older than me now. A darkness had crept over his features. He complained of hearing muffled voices in his right ear. My father said that was only from being underwater for too long, but Llewelyna looked at Jacob wearily. Jacob was short-tempered now and always angry. He stole matches from Llewelyna's handbag and burned things in a tin can that smouldered beneath his bed; inside it I found the charred remnants of nail clippings, hair, a square of Llewelyna's scarf, a thimble, and mouse bones.

Llewelyna spent much of her time at Henry's library. I read amongst the stacks of books while they drank coffee in Henry's kitchen with the door closed or smoked out in the graveyard. The lake monster obsessed Llewelyna. For long periods, and sometimes even at night, she would disappear. I never saw her come and I never saw her go; she would simply vanish for a few hours and then reappear. No one else seemed to notice, or cared to draw attention to her absence.

Since my father was an investor, my family was invited onboard for the launch of the *Rosamond*, the brand-new lakeboat. Jacob stayed at home. He had refused to go near the lake since the incident. My father said Llewelyna and I could stay home as well, but Llewelyna insisted she and I come along.

The *SS Rosamond* was named after the chief investor's wife, who died crossing the Atlantic. It was a sternwheeler much bigger than any of the other lakeboats. A siren was carved into the bow. The siren's breasts were bare and her stance rigid: arms to her sides, eyes painted closed. If this was supposed to be Rosamond, the investor's wife, immortalized by wood, the artist had doomed her to a particular hell: the frigid waves splashed up her scaled lower half and bare chest. The ship boasted three decks, a saloon, a dining room, and twelve private cabins that dripped with gold and enamel. The dining room was decorated like a palace. Several small round tables were set with white tablecloths and bouquets of tulips. The china teacups were gold-rimmed with roses painted on their sides. Crystal chandeliers tinkled above our heads and left us dappled in light.

Llewelyna was silent all through dinner. The woman seated beside her, the daughter of some politician who boarded in Penticton, had altogether given up on any attempt at conversation and pulled up a chair at another table. She whispered to Mrs. McCarthy and their eyes flashed at us. Llewelyna sat with her hands in her lap and stared at her uneaten fillet as if it might move, her head cocked, listening for something. I watched her nervously. Once in a while my father lifted his eyes from his plate and opened his mouth as if to speak. His black eyebrows furrowed. He silently urged Llewelyna to eat, to speak, to move. She glanced out the window nearest us. It was blue-black outside.

"I'm going to get some fresh air," she said, and pushed her chair out behind her. It screeched against the hardwood floor. The room was suddenly quiet and too bright.

"Llewelyna—" he whispered. Heads turned towards us. Llewelyna was already at the door. My father's thin lips went stiff and his moustache twitched. I watched his face flush pink right before my eyes like a kind of magic trick. "Your mother's a sea mammal," he said. "Always going up for *air*." He smiled weakly at his joke, stood, and bowed like an actor leaving the stage before walking towards the saloon.

Llewelyna refused to smoke indoors, where the trapped grey air collected in the corners and turned aged and ashy. She smoked outside because the smoke brought her prayers to the heavens.

I followed Llewelyna outside. The sky was clear and glittered with the pinpricks of stars. The wind groaned against the sides of the boat. I couldn't find her on the top or the second deck. I began looking for her in the dark water over the sides of the boat. I pictured her pale form floating spectral on the surface. I was about to scream for help when I found her on the bottom deck, at the stern, gripping the railing and staring at the moon. Her white dress and petticoats billowed and her mess of red hair whipped around her head. I stood beside her. Without looking at me she pointed to a huge mass in the middle of the lake.

"You see?" she said. "Rattlesnake Island." The waves supped against the rocky shore and the moon illuminated only the tips of trees. I imagined the island was the silhouette of a sleeping dragon. "That's where the addanc that bit your brother rests. His home."

Llewelyna reached into her handbag and pulled out something small and white. I could see feathers in the blue light. It was Angel, Mrs. Bell's pet dove. My father and I were returning from the

Nickels' store the night before when we ran into the Bells on their way to the beach to bury the dove. Although it had been months before that Azami and I had broken into the Bells' home, I couldn't help but feel vaguely responsible for Angel's death. Mr. Bell was holding a little cardboard box and Mrs. Bell was all dressed in black with a handkerchief held up to her reddened eyes and nose. Phillip was obviously pleased with the absurdity of burying the creature. He couldn't help but smile as he told my father about finding the white bird stiff at the bottom of the cage. Just the mention of Angel had brought fresh tears to Mrs. Bell's eyes. Llewelyna had appeared in the garden then. She popped out of the lilacs to join us. She held Mrs. Bell close and petted her shoulder. I had been surprised at her tenderness then. We all went down to the beach to bury the bird. In the middle of the night Llewelyna must have gone back, rummaged through the leaves for the tiny wooden cross marker, and dug up the dove. My mother the gravedigger.

"Hush," she whispered and reached out over the railing and let go of the bird. I held my breath in anticipation for the dove to flash into the dark sky, resurrected once more. But the bird dropped, lifeless, into the water. It bobbed upside down on the surface. Llewelyna watched the island carefully, as if waiting.

"I'm frightened," I whispered.

"Look," she said, nodding towards the island.

A silver ridge glided towards us along the water. It moved swift and soundless as an eel. As it got closer I realized how huge it was. Endless. The image didn't merge with the dark shadows I saw the day the creature bit Jacob. The moonlight made it luminous, made of only light and spirit.

Llewelyna clenched the railing, her knuckles white. I reached up to grab her arm and pull her back inside the dining room but she peeled my fingers away. The shimmering trail was coming closer and closer. I pushed my face into the shoulder of her dress until all I could smell were lilies and cigarettes. The boat rose up and down. There was a splash and then silence.

"Shh," Llewelyna whispered. Another splash. It bumped into the ship. Silverware and china clattered. There were screams and yells from the dining cabin. I lifted my head from her shoulder in time to see the creature rise to the surface. Its head was long and horse-like, its smooth skin iridescent.

"Leviathan," I breathed, for it was clear this wasn't merely one of Llewelyna's crude addancs. When the lake spirit opened its mouth I saw its large square teeth. In one bite it ate up Angel, Mrs. Bell's dove, then spiralled spectacularly and left the stars boiling in the mirrored sky.

"Naitaka," Llewelyna said quietly. It was the name Henry had for it. The creature sank deep beneath the water until we could no longer see it. Then, far in the distance, it appeared again, gliding back towards Rattlesnake Island. We watched until it joined the glisten of waves. I gasped as if I had been holding my breath the entire time. There were footsteps on the deck above. Llewelyna was smiling. She opened her purse and pulled out a hand mirror and puff and powdered her nose. When she was done, we joined the rest of the party in the dining room.

TWO

1912–1914

Can you draw out Leviathan with a hook?

JOB 41:1

10

Every week the *Rosamond* arrived at Winteridge with more Japanese bachelors in search of work. I would sit on the wharf and watch the men disembark with their sad, tired eyes and faraway faces. I wondered about their homes. About the people and worlds they left behind.

It had been a year since Jacob and I set fire to the Kobas' orchard but the effects carried onward; Winteridge would never be the same. Some people even decided that the burning of the Kobas' orchard was warranted. I overheard Mrs. Nickel tell a customer that the Japanese were impinging on settler land, were becoming a threat, and that perhaps the Japanese should see the fire as a warning to keep in line, to remind them of their place. The pull of nausea returned to the back of my throat like a stone I could not bear to swallow.

After the fire, all Japanese children were taken out of school. The Japanese no longer attended church or shopped at the Nickels' store. Someone had retaliated, presumably a Japanese picker, by burning a couple of apple trees in the McCarthys' orchard. The McCarthys had the largest orchard in Winteridge, and employed the majority of the Japanese bachelors. After the burning of the trees, the McCarthys fired all their Japanese pickers and from then on refused to hire Japanese. The Kobas took on the fired employees but couldn't hire all of the Japanese men who arrived in Winteridge every day. There were many desperate for work.

Azami and I met in secret. Although our relationship was encouraged by my father, who wanted nothing more than to be liked by everyone all at once, it was not approved by the community. We would practise *harae* at least once a week to cleanse ourselves of that week's disease and bad luck and, of course, guilt, but I could never be clear of it. I could never admit to lighting the fire in the Kobas' orchard, and I was sure confession was at the core of the ritual.

Azami's sister Molly did everything she could to keep Azami and me apart. In the beginning I had thought it was because Molly didn't like me, but I soon came to realize she only wanted Azami to stop with her old Shinto practices and conform to their family's new life in Canada. Sometimes she followed us to the lake and we wouldn't realize she was there until we were halfway through the *harae* ceremony and Molly would come out from behind the trees and splash us or glare at Azami so furiously that Azami was forced to stop and follow her back home through the forest.

One night, on the anniversary of her baby brother's death, I helped Azami launch a paper lantern off the wharf in Winteridge. "This will guide his spirit back to the other world," she had said as she released the lantern into the water. Ever since her family had arrived in Winteridge, Azami had woken to the cries of a phantom infant. We had watched the lantern travel for nearly an hour. It burned like a lonely star in the mirrored sky. The flame had snuffed out or sunk somewhere out in the middle of the dark lake.

It was that same night that I gave Azami back my blue marble. "I know it's just a silly thing," I said. "But I want you to have it." She rolled it between her fingers. It pulled the dregs of light from the night sky.

When our orchard finally began to produce fruit, and my father was ready to employ pickers, he went down to the docks and hired the Japanese men as they disembarked. It was his goal to undo the segregation that had begun in the community after the fire. A couple of Japanese men were adept with English, but after a patchy conversation about pruning, it was clear the newly arrived men knew little about growing or harvesting peaches. So instead of working in the orchard, my father had the men build a cabin along our property where they could sleep. Once the men were busy building, my father took a trip up the lake to Vernon to find a leader for his crew. He was gone several days before we received a telegram that his trip had been successful and he would be home that evening.

Llewelyna, Jacob, and I watched the *Rosamond* appear around the bend of land and creep towards the bay. The painted siren was already chipped away, her eyes dull and bored. My father disembarked in his suit coat and top hat and was followed by a tall man in tattered clothes and a wool flat cap. The man had a bushy, unkempt beard and thick black eyebrows. Behind him was a stout woman with blond hair and a grey bonnet, and two boys loaded down with wooden chests and canvas sacks. The younger boy looked about my age, fourteen. He was short with blond hair, red cheeks, and a solid, stout frame like his mother. The older one was thin and taller than his father and had dark wavy hair. Llewelyna ran up to my father and, despite the crowd on the dock, kissed him. He dipped her backwards to make a show of it. The dark-haired son grinned and winked at me.

My father took Llewelyna by the elbow and guided her to the newcomers. "Lew, I'd like you to meet the Wasiks. This is Taras and his wife, Mary." Mary curtseyed low, gaze towards her feet. "And these are their sons, Viktor"—my father motioned to the tall, dark-haired son, who took off his hat and nodded politely at

Llewelyna—"and Yuri." He motioned to the younger blond, who was a few paces behind, struggling to carry one of the larger wooden chests.

"Hen," the older son, Viktor, whispered to get his brother's attention. Yuri took off his hat and wiped the sweat from his forehead before bowing to my mother.

Taras had the expertise and experience my father desperately needed. "Soil's in my blood," he said. He had a strange earthy accent I later learned was Ukrainian. He and his sons had worked on many orchards in Vernon. The last orchard Taras worked on was one of the largest and most successful in the valley. My father had to bait Taras to leave his position by promising a competitive wage for him and his sons as well as a plot of our land for his own, a small corner piece near the road.

My father hadn't really thought through hiring a Ukrainian to lead a group of Japanese, and had to convince the pickers that Taras was not Russian.

The evening of their arrival, Taras and Viktor were taken by my father on a tour of the orchard. Taras's English was sparse and so Viktor was needed to translate. Yuri looked disappointed that he hadn't been invited along. Instead, he was instructed by Mary to join Jacob and me to collect walnuts for a tart while Llewelyna and Mary prepared dinner. Yuri kept glancing over his shoulder at his father and brother as we walked down towards the walnut tree. He was taller and stockier than Jacob. His blond hair and pale blue eyes made him look washed out.

"We own all the land on this side of the hill," Jacob was saying, "right down to the lake and up to the McCarthys' apple orchard." He looked up at Yuri for approval. But Yuri was staring out towards the lake. "There are three other orchards in Winteridge, but only ours grows peaches. Well, none of them have grown yet, but soon.

We did a test to see if we'd have fruit." The arrival of the Wasiks had awakened something in my brother that had been dormant for so long. It was wonderful just to see him out of the house.

"This tree is on the plot my father has given you," I said when we came to the walnut tree. "So these are technically your walnuts now."

Across the road the lake reflected the sun back up at the sky. A flock of geese flew low over the water, their wings nearly touching the surface with every beat. "It's beautiful here," Yuri said. He had a dimple on his chin.

There were yellow leaves and black-skinned walnuts in the grass. Jacob and I began collecting the nuts in a potato sack.

"Don't bother with the black ones," Yuri said. "They'll be bitter as hell. Some of those are from last season. Just pick the green ones."

"We always use the black ones, they keep just fine," Jacob said. "Those green ones are up too high in the tree."

Yuri bent down and patted his shoulders, signalling for Jacob to sit on them. I was about to tell Jacob he better not, that it might not be good for his bad leg, but the smile on his face stopped me. Yuri held on to Jacob's legs as he reached up into the branches. Sunlight illuminated the leaves, and the upper half of Jacob's body disappeared into that green glow. Yuri squinted up into the tree, his mouth open with concentration as he moved left or right to position Jacob beneath the clumps of green fruit. I noticed a circular scar on the back of Yuri's hand. Jacob threw walnuts down and I gathered them in the potato sack.

On our way back to the house we passed Taras, Viktor, and my father, walking through the orchard, ducking to dig at roots and pluck seedlings. Viktor caught me watching him and nodded my way, and Father and Taras turned to me. I looked down at my feet, my cheeks burning.

"Do you two work on the orchard?" Yuri asked.

"No," Jacob said. "We're just kids."

Yuri looked at me. "How old are you?"

"I only just turned fourteen."

"And you?"

"Thirteen," Jacob said.

"I started working when I was eight."

We were silent for a moment. I was embarrassed.

"Well, I'm off to school soon, anyway," Jacob said proudly.

"I'd like to learn to pick peaches," I said.

"Father would never let you, Irie."

"Why not?"

"Girls don't pick fruit, dummy," Jacob said

"I picked apples with a girl in Vernon," Yuri said. "She was good."

"How old was she?" Jacob asked.

"Ten. She could climb the trees without a ladder and pick the best apples in the most hard-to-reach places."

I was suddenly jealous of this girl. "I can climb trees."

"Then you would be a good picker." Yuri ran his hand through the leaves of some low-hanging branches. "It's nice here. In Vernon we lived in a shack in the middle of a muddy field. No trees. And the lake was miles away."

The three of us sat on the porch with butter knives and slit the green skins that covered the walnuts. The black mash between the skin and shell stained our fingers. Yuri showed us to slice an X on the skin to twist the peel off easily. We soaked the peeled nuts in a bucket of water and rubbed the brown shells together to clean them. When Taras and my father went back inside the house, Viktor joined us on the porch. The burn of his gaze made me suddenly aware of my body. The cotton slip under my dress itched against my breasts and tickled my stomach. "What's your name again?" he asked as he pulled a half-finished cigarette from his shirt pocket.

"Iris." I stood, my hands dangling at my sides and stained black.

"Iris," he echoed. "It's pretty." He struck a match on the railing of the porch and lit his cigarette. He closed his eyes when he inhaled, aware that all three of us had stopped what we were doing to watch him. He had high cheekbones and his cheeks hollowed when he sucked in. His thick eyelashes fluttered open. Smoke left the corner of his mouth in a wisp. "How'd these ruffians get a lady like you peeling nuts?"

"I do as I please," I said.

"I bet you do." His smile transformed his entire face and revealed two strands of surprisingly white teeth.

Llewelyna came onto the porch with a hammer. She had changed into a green silk dress with a low embroidered collar. It gathered just below her knees where a black slip was visible. Her red hair was loose over her shoulders. She seemed to avoid looking at Viktor, who stood right in her line of sight, eyes beaming at her. She turned instead to Yuri and Jacob, who sat peeling the nuts.

Yuri stood abruptly and pulled off his hat. "Mrs. Sparks, thank you for inviting us for dinner."

"My pleasure, of course." She picked up a walnut. "Splendid." She set the hammer down on the bench and pointed at the small pile of cleaned walnuts. "That there'll be plenty." Viktor followed her with his eyes. She glanced up at him before she slipped back into the house.

"She's gorgeous," Viktor said, enchanted.

"Viktor," Yuri scolded.

"You look like her," Viktor said to me.

My neck went hot. I imagined the red patches that surely crawled up my throat. "I don't."

"Maybe it's your eyes."

"My eyes are brown. Hers are green."

"Not the colour," Viktor flicked his cigarette over the railing and entered the house as if trailing after Llewelyna's scent. I stared at the closed screen door.

"Don't give him any mind," Yuri said. He raised the hammer and cracked a walnut. He handed the cracked nut to me to shell and pull the walnut meat out.

"What's that?" Jacob asked, pointing at the circular scar on Yuri's hand. Yuri shrugged, rubbed the mark with his other hand. He cracked another nut. "Looks like a burn. A cigarette?"

"It's nothin'," Yuri said.

"Look at this." Jacob pulled up his pant leg and showed Yuri the long scar where the lake monster had bitten him. "Had to get twelve stitches."

"How'd it happen?" Yuri asked.

Jacob hadn't considered his explanation. He shrugged, imitating Yuri. "It's nothing."

Yuri laughed and went back to hammering the walnuts.

Over the next couple of months the atmosphere of our quiet orchard changed dramatically. There were always Japanese men going in and out of the crowded pick shacks. They stood on ladders in the trees, walked into the forest to use the pickers' outhouse or down to the lake to fill their canisters and swim in the icy water.

Once when Azami and I were skirting the orchard scavenging for rocks and other bits to add to our chimes in the tree fort, we came across Viktor and one of the Japanese men having an argument. Viktor was trying to show the man how to use a saw, and the Japanese man was growing frustrated. He kept saying something over and over. Azami watched for a moment and then stepped in. She spoke with the man in Japanese and then turned to Viktor. "He's left-handed," she said.

"He's what?" Viktor was obviously a little annoyed at our sudden appearance. He was wearing brown suspenders and a stained undershirt.

"He can't hold it like you," Azami said.

Viktor's forehead was wet with sweat. It was a hot September. "Ah, is that it, then." Viktor released the saw and watched the Japanese man position it easily on his left side and begin to grate at the branch. Viktor mopped his forehead with a handkerchief.

"Well, Your Highness." Viktor had taken to calling me by this nickname. "Who's your little friend?" His eyes were fixed on Azami. He extended his hand to her. "Viktor Wasik," he said.

"Azami Koba," she said.

Viktor grinned. "Are you looking for a job?"

"I already work on my father's orchard," Azami said seriously.

"That's too bad. I could really use your help. Can't tell heads or tails of what these men are trying to say most of the time." Viktor looked down at the bundle of items I had gathered in a potato sack. "Where are you two off to, then?"

"Nothing," I said, before Azami could say something embarrassing about the chimes. It all seemed very childish to me now. "I mean nowhere."

"Ah, I see. Top secret." Viktor lowered his hat to Azami. I was jealous of the hungry look he gave her. "I hope to see you around more often, Azami Koba."

For the first time since I had known Azami, I watched her skin redden in embarrassment. She turned her face from me as we walked through the forest towards the tree fort.

"He's like that to everyone," I told her, my voice crueller than I intended.

"You like him," she said.

"He's too old. He could be our father." I knew this was a ridiculous thing to say. Viktor could be no older than twenty, but the gap in our ages felt like centuries.

"Hardly." She launched up the ladder to the fort.

11

The Wasiks' cottage was built between our house and the pick shacks. Mary busied herself outside with the laundry and the chickens. Llewelyna refused to hire Mary as our housemaid, even though Taras and my father had already arranged for it. My father claimed the Wasiks would likely take offence, but Llewelyna insisted she had no need for a maid, though she neglected all chores while my father was away. He spent more and more time in town or overseas now that he had Taras to look after the orchard. Dust felted the cupboards and crumbs collected in the corners. Llewelyna said she didn't want someone snooping around the house, but I suspected she was afraid Mary might witness one of her seizures if she were around enough.

Llewelyna kept out of the house that fall. Sometimes she was gone before I woke, and other times she disappeared during the day. One moment I would see her in the garden collecting seeds, or curled up on the porch with a cup of tea, and the next moment she would be gone. I was uneasy about her absences. Since her seizure in the garden years ago, I felt oddly protective of her and liked to keep my eye on her. As far as I knew, only I knew of her falling sickness. I tried to ignore the suspicions about her and Henry that Mrs. Bell had planted in my mind so long ago, but the possibility had taken root, and I couldn't shake the thought that they were sneaking away together and betraying my father.

One afternoon, I spied on Llewelyna while Jacob played check-
ers with Yuri on the porch. My father had gone to Vernon with
Taras for a few days, purchasing equipment for the orchard, and
Llewelyna had been making herself scarce. She looked both ways
before slipping out of the garden, through the orchard rows, and
into the forest behind our house. I followed her up into the hills. We
walked for a very long time. I thought we might turn back at any
moment. She didn't follow any path I recognized but would stop
every once in a while and gaze up into the trees, as if looking for
something amongst its branches. I saw then that there was a flume
of smoke in the distance and we were headed in its direction.

In a clearing, we came upon Henry tending a fire with a pitchfork. He was bare-chested and his long dark hair was untied. I
stayed back in the trees and watched Llewelyna approach him. My
skin went hot with anger. I expected to catch them in the act of
betraying my father. I expected Henry and Llewelyna to embrace
and finally fulfill Mrs. Bell's suspicions. Instead, Henry simply
nodded at Llewelyna and gestured to a bucket at the entrance of a
small domed structure behind him made of branches and covered
in canvas. Smoke billowed from its entrance. Henry faced away
from the structure and averted his gaze as Llewelyna unbuttoned
her dress from throat to belly. The heavy fabric fell from her in a
heap. Red dust rose up around her and made her naked form appear
diaphanous as she stepped out of her dress. Although I wasn't surprised to see her uncorseted, it was shocking to see she hadn't bothered with even drawers or a chemise, as though she had come to the
woods prepared to quickly undress. She pulled a mug of water from
the bucket and entered the smoke-filled dome.

I came out from behind the trees and into the open. I wanted
Henry to see me, to know that I knew what terrible people they
both were. I watched him use the pitchfork to lift a large rock from

the fire and carry it into the dome. He did not look up to see me. There was a hiss from inside. Henry emerged shortly after and placed the pitchfork by the fire, his back still towards me. Then, to my horror, he began to remove his pants, and I had to duck away again. When I looked back, Henry had gone back inside the tiny dome. I slipped through the trees, closer to the opening. I wanted to glimpse what they were doing inside. A hot current swept over my face and droplets pebbled my skin. It wasn't smoke but steam coming from the dome. One of our heavy winter bedsheets covered the entrance. I moved it aside to peer inside but it was difficult to see through the steam. Then Henry stood and poured a bucket of water over a mound of stones, and there was another hiss, louder this time, and the steam became as thick as milk.

From that day on, I continued to follow Llewelyna whenever I could. Although she and Henry were very close and spent a lot of time together, I didn't witness anything physical between them. Not even a kiss.

One day I followed Llewelyna towards the lake and she walked along the rocky shore at a pace I could barely keep up with. I slunk through the forest along the shore and watched her from a distance. A loon screamed on the other side of the lake, but otherwise the only sound was Llewelyna's footsteps on the rocks. The sun began its disappearing act behind the hills and threw back shadows like arms reaching for me. The lake was still and solid. Red and yellow leaves were plastered against its glassy surface.

A loud splash disturbed the calm. Llewelyna jumped, and I dropped back behind a birch. After a moment of silence the splashing returned. An amorphous figure silhouetted by the sun struggled in the water just off the shore. Llewelyna ran down the narrow, rocky beach towards the shape. The sun extended the reach of the creature's limbs and duplicated them in shadow. I ducked behind the bare white birches and thought of the lake demon, Naitaka. Then the shadows slipped off the figure to reveal a woman. She crawled to the shore, clutching stones; her fingertips were bleeding. Her hair draped over her shoulders like lake weed. Llewelyna ran to her, wobbled on the mossy rocks, and fell. She got back to her feet and when she reached the woman, Llewelyna lifted her up. Arm in arm they staggered up to the shore.

The woman had appeared out of nothing. I thought of the story Henry had told me about the woman who fell through a hole in the sky. She shivered. She was completely naked. The woman had dark skin, like Henry, like the Lake People I saw in the forest. She uttered something in a different language and motioned towards the water and then to the sky, as if daring it to fall down upon her. She tried to stand and collapsed to her knees and cried into her bloodied hands. Her sob echoed out across the lake and back again. Llewelyna knelt beside her and sung a Welsh lullaby I vaguely recognized. The woman was quiet for a moment, as if the song had calmed her, and then she began to cough. Her coughs were syrupy and thick. She choked as if drowning. Llewelyna looked behind her and I dropped behind a tree.

"Iris," she hissed into the forest. "I know you're there." When I poked my head out, Llewelyna was looking right at me. "Come."

I ran to her.

"Sit here. Hold her head up."

I knelt behind the woman and placed her head in my lap. Llewelyna took the woman's hands in her own and began to hum and sing in a wordless language. I watched her lips move around foreign sounds. The woman nodded to my mother and responded weakly, her words as soft as lapping water and wind against sagebrush.

"What is she saying?" I whispered.

"A child," Llewelyna said. "A girl. She has something for her." The woman looked up at me then. Her black eyes appeared bottomless.

"Me?" I asked.

The woman choked. Her voice turned to a sputter. Her eyes went wide as if I might save her. She brought a hand to my cheek and I could feel the warmth of her bloody fingers against my skin.

"Sit her up," Llewelyna said, and took my place behind her. The woman continued to cough, red-faced. There were grains of sand embedded in her cheeks. Llewelyna whispered in her ear. The woman was choking, she could no longer breathe. She sputtered as if underwater and then spat something blue onto her thighs. It squirmed and flailed. Before I could see what it was, Llewelyna scooped the blue thing up in her hand.

"Fill your hands with water," she said. I cupped my hands and dipped them into the lake and came back with the water. Llewelyna dropped the thing into my hands. It was a fish, bluer than the lake, bluer than violets, bluer than Saint Francis's jewelled feathers, bluer than blue.

Relieved of this burden, the woman lay flat on her back now, against the rocks. Her eyes glazed with the reflection of clouds. Llewelyna put her fingers against the woman's neck to check for a pulse. After a moment Llewelyna rose, face striped with tears, and performed the states of the cross on her chest. She whispered a prayer in Welsh and closed the woman's eyes with her hand. Coyotes began to yip in the hills behind us. Llewelyna lifted the hem of her soaking yellow dress and wiped the woman's blood from my face. She twisted her dress between two fists to squeeze the water out.

"Let's fetch your father," she said. I had never seen her eyes so frightened, so green and bright. I filled my hands with water for the fish before we turned back to the blue shadows of the forest.

"How did you know what she was saying?" I asked, running to keep up with her, one palm covering the handful of water that dripped onto my dress.

"What do you mean?"

"She wasn't speaking English, it was something else."

"Was it?" Llewelyna stopped. "And they spoke with other tongues as the spirit gave them utterance," she whispered.

"Was she speaking tongues?" I asked.

Llewelyna didn't respond.

We burst through the front door of our house. My father had returned that morning. He jolted up from the table where a book was splayed open in front of him. His thigh hit the tabletop and tea splashed onto his lap. He cursed. "What is it?" he said.

Jacob had descended halfway down the stairs and stared at us.

"You're soaked." My father approached. "Is that blood?"

"Come quickly," Llewelyna backed away from him towards the door.

"What's happened?" he said to me now. I stood still, stunned silent.

"A woman," Llewelyna said. "I think she might be dead. Please, will you hurry?" Llewelyna looked down at my hands. "Iris, water."

The water in my cupped hands had run dry. The fish lay lifeless against my palm. I ran into the kitchen and dropped the fish into the water basin. Jacob and my father followed Llewelyna outside. I found a jam jar in the cupboard, poured the fish into it from the basin, and screwed on the lid. I held the jar up to see if the fish was alive. It twirled its blue fins like ribbons of silk.

When I got to the beach Llewelyna was pacing the empty shore. The woman was gone. Jacob and my father watched her carefully.

"I don't understand," she said. She scanned the beach and looked out at the lake. "She was right here."

My father shook his head. "Lew, you must stop this nonsense."

"Noah, she was here." She gathered her hair in fists. "She was right here. She said her family—"

My father put his hands on her cheeks, but she avoided his eyes. "Stop this foolish talk. You're scaring the children with this lake monster nonsense."

Llewelyna moved from his hands. "Iris," she said, approaching me. "You saw her." I looked at Llewelyna blankly and then behind her at my father. He had a hand over his eyes. "Didn't you, Iris? You saw her?" She gripped my shoulder. "Tell him you saw her. And the fish. You have the fish." She squeezed hard, her thumb poked painfully into my shoulder, curled under the bone. Tears rimmed her pulsing green eyes, so bright they were difficult to look at. "She was here." She shook me. "You saw." I opened my mouth but couldn't speak, could hardly breathe.

My father came up behind her. "Enough." He clenched her wrist and wrenched her back. They glared at one another. The moment froze. He still had her wrist in his grip. Her hand was limp, dead and caught. She slipped it through his grasp and launched down the shore towards the cliffs, the whites of her bare feet flashing as she wobbled on the rocks.

"Where are you going?" my father called after her.

Once she was further away, I could speak. "It's true," I said, but it was too quiet. "It's true," I said louder this time.

My father turned his glare on me, eyes sharp and piercing. "Enough."

"I saw her."

"Your lake monster story is the reason your mother has lost herself with these fantasies." I wanted to tell him that it wasn't my story. It wasn't my monster. I had not spoken the creature into being. And I realized now that neither had Llewelyna.

"But I saw the woman. She was bleeding from her fingers. She had—"

"I said enough." I saw then it was Jacob he was concerned about. Out of the corner of my eye I noticed that Jacob was trembling; his face had lost all colour. He kept jerking his head, giving it little shakes, as if he had water in his ears. I wondered if he could hear them now, the muffled voices. It had been a year since he was this close to the lake.

The sky had turned purple. Llewelyna was a ways down the shore now, her yellow dress flapping in the wind. I shot after her. My father reached for my arm and caught my elbow, but I twisted loose and ran towards Llewelyna, who was blazing ahead like flame. She turned around once to see me running, but kept walking away. "Wait!" I yelled after her. She didn't change her pace and disappeared behind a bend of land. When I finally caught up to her I pulled at the back of her dress to stop her from moving away from me. In my grasp I accidentally clutched a handful of her hair. She whipped around and in one fluid motion slapped me across the face. I fell back against the stones and held my hand to my hot cheek. For a moment I thought she would apologize, comfort me, but her face settled back into itself, unseeing.

"Leave me alone," she said, and walked away.

I ran back through the birches and into the thick bushes, not stopping to step over the patch of poison ivy or protect my eyes from the whip of branches. The salt of my tears stung my eyes and blurred my vision. I slipped through the back door of our house just in case Jacob and my father were already home. I wrapped the fish in my shawl and placed it in a potato sack I found in the coal room. Then I went into Jacob's room and gathered his jackknife and the matches from beneath his bed.

My father and Jacob still hadn't returned from the shore. I ran to the fence that separated our yard from the Bells' and easily climbed it. The sack clanged behind me on the ground when I jumped down on the other side. I checked the jar to make sure I hadn't broken it. Through the window of the Bells' shed I could see the polished guns glowing in the cabinet. I wiggled a bit of wire in the lock on the door as I had seen Jacob do before, but it did nothing. I moved to the window and pushed; it gave slightly. I pushed again. The latch strained against my force. Something whipped through the grass towards me. The greyhound sped around the corner barking. I fell back in the grass and the dog jumped on me and licked my face.

"Edward!" Mr. Bell called from the house. "Edward, come." The dog ran out from behind the shed towards Mr. Bell. Once the dog was gone I pushed at the window one last time and it gave way. The gun cabinet inside was locked. I rummaged through some drawers and found a pistol wrapped in cloth. I slipped back out the window and put the pistol in my sack. Mr. Bell and the dog were nowhere in sight. I lifted myself back over the fence and landed awkwardly on the other side.

"Iris?" It was Yuri. He stood in the near dark with a stack of firewood in his arms. "What are doing?"

"Running away," I whispered. Yuri placed the firewood in the woodpile and came back brushing his hands on his pants. "Please don't tell anyone. And don't you dare try and stop me."

"I'm coming," he said.

"I'm not joking around, Yuri."

"I know."

"I don't have time to wait around," I said. "I'm leaving right now."

"I'm ready." He shrugged.

"Well I guess it might be nice to have someone to talk to. Just don't get in the way."

"I won't."

I could hear Jacob and my father walking up the drive. I peeked around the corner of the house. My father's hand rested in Jacob's red hair. I pushed myself up against the house and motioned for Yuri to do the same. We ran from behind the house, past the well, the outhouse, and into the forest. It was much darker among the trees. We followed the invisible path I had learned from Henry. Once we were a safe distance from the orchard, I stopped at a bush to pick saskatoons. They were hard to see in the near dark.

"What's on your legs?" Yuri asked.

I looked down; red bumps had spread along my calves. Until then I had forgotten about the poison ivy. Seeing the rash made it itch.

"It's nothing." I passed him my shawl to hold while I placed handfuls of berries into it.

"Do you even know where we're going?" Yuri asked once we returned to the path.

"It's too late tonight, but in the morning we'll make it over the hills to Oyama, where the two lakes meet."

"What's there?"

I had no idea what we would find there. I had never been to Oyama, but Henry often spoke of the place where the brown lake and the green lake kissed and he and his father had once hunted groundhog.

"You'll just have to wait and see," I said.

"This is exciting. We're like frontiersmen."

I smiled, thankful in that moment I had brought him along, although I wished desperately that things could be undone and it was Azami with me instead.

"Where will we sleep tonight?" he asked. "I can build a lean-to. I've done it before. We'll just need some thick brush and—"

I stopped beneath the tree fort and pointed up. The wind chimes Azami and I had made still hung from the branches. They jingled in the darkness. Yuri followed me up the ladder. He inspected the fort while I laid out our supplies.

"How did you find this place?" he asked.

"Henry showed it to me. I think he came here when he was a boy."

"I heard Henry killed a man."

I shrugged. "If he did, the man deserved it." I lit my reading candle with a match. It was completely dark outside now. We ate our fill of berries and then lay on our backs and stared at the stars through the hole in the roof where the tree went through. I sat up suddenly, remembering my rash, and scratched furiously at my legs.

"Stop that. You'll only make it worse." Yuri pulled me back down beside him and took my hand in his. The itch was becoming unbearable. Tears bubbled at the corners of my eyes. "You need something to take your mind off it." He was silent for a moment. "Did you bring any playing cards?" Yuri kept his fingers inter-twined with mine. I shook my head. The shadows of bats or kami flitted past our patch of sky and set the wind chimes ringing.

"Why did you run away, Iris?"

"I've always wanted to." This wasn't exactly true but rather an appetite I had taken on from the novels I read. All interesting characters wanted to run away.

"But there must be a reason."

"Why?" I watched the pine needles brush against the stars.

"It doesn't make sense. Your family is so nice," Yuri said.

"Why did *you* run away?"

Yuri rolled to his side to face me. I kept my eyes on the stars.

"My father hates me," he said.

"That's not true," I said, but I understood why Yuri might feel this way. I saw the way Taras and Viktor picked on him. I thought of the circular scar on his hand.

"He hits me," Yuri said.

"My mother slapped me today."

"Why?"

"I betrayed her."

"How?"

I turned to him. "Have you ever seen something and not known whether it was real?"

"Like a ghost?"

I had to think about it. "Yes, but more like a spirit, a being. Or maybe just something you see that no one else can."

"When I was little I saw Jesus."

"Jesus?"

"Viktor and I were in the forest gathering wood and all of a sudden this bear comes out of nowhere. A grizzly. And he's standing on his hind legs, towering over us. Viktor and I froze and just waited for the bear to attack us. But then this man came out from behind a tree. He didn't look like Jesus, not from the picture books. He was wearing a fur vest, and had long dark hair. But he was glowing. He had this ring of light around him. He stood between us and the bear. He winked at me and told the bear that we were only children, and not worth the trouble. The bear just turned and went the other way. Viktor never saw him. He says I'm crazy."

"Sounds like Coyote."

"Coyote?"

"He's an old spirit that takes the form of a coyote, but he can also take the form of a man. He likes to play tricks, but sometimes he does good things, and protects people."

"Maybe they're the same guy," Yuri said.

He meant it as a joke but I thought seriously about this.

"Have you seen him?" Yuri asked.

"Who?"

"Coyote."

"I think so. He gave me a caramel."

"A caramel?"

"And I've seen him as a coyote plenty of times. Though Llewelyna calls it a she-wolf."

"A she-wolf. Why?"

"I think it's a character from one of her old faery tales, but I'm not really sure."

"How do you know this Coyote isn't just a regular coyote?"

I turned back to the stars. "Same way you know it wasn't just an ordinary man."

We were both quiet for a while.

"So, I don't get it," Yuri said. "Your mother hit you because you saw something that wasn't real?"

"No." I could see many more stars than I had at first. The longer I stared into the dark sky the more stars there were. They multiplied. I thought about what Henry said about learning how to look. Practising how to see. "She hit me because she's angry with me," I said finally.

"Why?"

"I see more than she thinks I should. I know more than she wants me to. But I don't understand it like she does. I don't trust it."

"What do you know?"

"I don't have the dreams, the premonitions. Not yet anyways." I turned from him and closed my eyes. "But I know the lake is haunted. And I know that seeing comes easily to some and is something others need to practise."

"What do you mean, seeing?"

Just then, the yips of coyotes crowded our silence. Somehow the beasts were already right beneath the tree fort. I hadn't heard them approach. Yuri held my hand so tight I felt the beat of his pulse through his fingers.

"They're only dogs," I said. "Can't climb ladders. They won't hurt us." Amongst the cackle of the coyotes, there was a jingling. At first I thought it might be the chimes in the trees, but there was no wind. It sounded like bangles tinkling together. I peered through a gap in the floorboards and could see, amidst the darker dark of the shadowed coyotes, a glint of silver and gold. That was the first time I saw the orphan thief. She was unlike any Lake Person I had ever seen. She wore a hooded shawl made of fur. The whites of her eyes were hardly visible in the night as she lifted her eyes to meet mine. She knew exactly where to look to find me. She reached her pale palm up as if to grab me, and even though she was far below, I had to back away and break her gaze to keep myself from being pulled into her stronghold. There was a shuffle in the dirt below, a growl, and then quiet. When I looked back through the floorboards both the orphan thief and the coyotes were gone, quick as they had come.

"What was that?" Yuri asked.

The orphan thief had drained the light from the stars and left us in the ink of her absence. "Nothing," I said. "Just coyotes." I didn't know how to explain who or what I had seen. She was both implausible and the only true thing I knew, like seeing my distorted double in the underworld of the lake.

I felt the warmth of Yuri's body as he drew nearer. Eventually his chest was against my back. I stiffened. "What are you doing?" I asked.

"I'm cold," he said. "Sometimes frontiersmen would have to sleep close to survive the cold nights."

It felt good to be touched. I relaxed into his warmth.

When I woke in the morning it was still dawn. Yuri and I had fallen asleep beneath my shawl. His arm was wrapped around me and it fell with a thump as I sat up to stretch. I looked through the floorboards and saw something sparkling amongst the paw prints in the dirt below. I scrambled down the ladder and found a silver bracelet with leaves engraved on it. I recognized the bracelet; it belonged to Llewelyna. She only ever wore it to the rare dinner parties she attended in the city. I put the bracelet on, and then took it off and put it back in the dirt for the orphan thief to reclaim.

When I climbed back into the tree fort Yuri was holding the fish in the jam jar. I froze. "Don't touch that."

He set the jar down. "What kind of fish is it?"

"I don't know."

"I never seen a fish that colour."

I shrugged and put the fish back in the potato sack.

That day I showed Yuri how to call the deer. He looked at me dubiously when I brought the pine needles up to my mouth. A doe leapt out from a bush but Yuri didn't see it. "It's because you haven't learned how to see," I told him. I tried again but no deer appeared. We wandered through the forest looking for food. I had the familiar feeling of something or someone watching us. I looked for coyotes and found none. Every once in a while I saw Lake People from the corners of my vision. They carried out their parallel lives amongst the trees and paid us no mind.

Later I pointed to some mushrooms in the shade of a tree. We ate the morels in handfuls that left us even hungrier. When we found the creek we followed it uphill to where it widened and calmed and we could see glistening fish beneath the surface. Yuri sharpened a branch to make a spear while I tried to weave reeds into a net. Despite our attempts to fish, hours passed and we still had nothing to eat. We sat on a rock by the creek and washed our faces and drank.

I looked up from my cupped hands to find the amber eyes of a giant cat—a cougar, I thought. She was so close I could smell the musk of her fur. Unaware, Yuri was still jabbing at the pond with his spear. I scrambled for the gun and pulled back the hammer. A bullet shot off into the trees. The giant cat sauntered away, but she took one last look at me before disappearing into the trees. I recognized then the mottled design of her fur. I had seen a drawing of a jaguar in Henry's book on South America and had read that the jaguar was at ease both in water and on land, as well as during the day and at night, and because of these qualities, the ancient Maya had believed the jaguar could pass between worlds. When there was an eclipse, it was said that a jaguar had swallowed the sun.

The bang was so loud I couldn't hear anything for a long time. Yuri's lips were moving but I couldn't tell what he was saying. We continued watchfully along the river. It was hours later when we could hear again.

"What was it?" he asked.

"A cougar, I think." I wanted to believe it was only the shadow of leaves against the wild cat's fur.

There was rustling in the bushes near us; we stiffened. I thought it might be the cat again, but it was Henry. He towered over us.

"The whole town has been looking for you two," he said. I urged Yuri with my eyes to get rid of the gun while Henry's back was to him. Yuri had it tucked into his back pocket. He slipped the gun into the bushes behind him. Wordlessly, we followed Henry down the hills and back into town. Yuri's hand brushed against mine. I pretended not to feel it.

When we parted, Yuri smiled foolishly. "I'll see you later, Iris," he said, as if we had just spent a splendid afternoon at the beach.

The Wasiks' cottage door opened and Taras stomped out mumbling in Ukrainian. Taras took Yuri by the collar of his shirt and dragged him inside.

The door to my own house burst open while Henry and I were still on the steps of the porch. The skin beneath my father's eyes was dark. He opened his arms to me and kissed me on the head. "Thank you, Henry," he said, looking behind me. "Please tell the others she is home safe."

Llewelyna was in the tin tub. Her face brightened as I approached. Saint Francis raised his head and ruffled his feathers.

"Where have you been?" she asked.

"In the forest."

"You ran away."

"So did you," I said. She smiled, held the wet cloth towards me and leaned back into the tub. I ran the cloth down her arms. Despite the hot water, her skin remained covered in goose bumps. She stared at her toes and flexed them against the tub.

"I'm sorry."

"I'm sorry, too," I said.

"That woman, in the lake, she spoke of the addanc."

"I'm not sure it's an addanc."

"I know," Llewelyna said. "Henry says it's a spirit."

"And in the story doesn't Peredur kill the addanc? Can you kill a spirit?"

Llewelyna closed her eyes and was quiet for the moment. Then she began, in a voice that was not her own: "*A noxious creature from the rampart of Satanas—him death will not subdue.*"

I dropped the cloth. Her words frightened me. I wanted to ground her again. "What else did the woman from the lake say to you?"

Llewelyna opened her eyes. "She was in a canoe with her family. They had been forced to leave their home."

"Why?" I massaged soap into her hair as if coaxing the story out.

"Settlers chased them off their land with guns. Her husband was killed, her son was shot in the leg. They were forced to pass Rattlesnake Island, remember? The spirit's home. They didn't have time to bring an offering."

"An offering?" I poured some oil into my hands and ran my fingers through her tangled hair. It smelled of jasmine.

"A small animal, a bird or a rodent." I remembered Mrs. Bell's dove. "She said the lake became a storm and the boat flipped. Her family disappeared in the water around her. Drowned."

"How did she survive?"

"Next thing she remembered was washing up on the shore."

"I thought she said something about a girl. A gift."

Llewelyna looked at me curiously, as if she didn't know what I was talking about. "Where is the fish?" she asked. I went to my room for the jar. Llewelyna brought it up close and watched the fish's blue fins waver.

"Fantastic," she said. "Keep it someplace safe. Best not show a thing like that to anyone." I wrapped the fish in my shawl and hid the jar beneath my bed. When I returned Llewelyna had her eyes closed again. For a moment I thought she was asleep.

"I remember it like this," she said and shifted. The cloth eeled through the bathwater, wavering with the currents of her slightest movements. I understood this story was a gift, an apology. I settled against the wall by the tub and closed my eyes.

"Once there was a girl who conceived a child at an evil hour and in a dark way."

I opened my eyes and watched her, aware now that this story was no gift.

"The girl wanted to kill the unborn child—she knew it had spoiled inside of her. While pregnant she was racked with convulsions. The fetus chewed at her insides. But the girl's sister persuaded her to keep it. The sister claimed that once the child was born they could baptize it in the river, and the holy water would transform the baby for good.

"When the baby was finally born, the girl was exhausted and hollowed out. The baby was ugly and gnawed the girl's nipples when she tried to feed it. It pinched and bit and reminded the girl of the darkness from which it was conceived.

"The girl wanted to baptize the child immediately but her sister insisted that they wait for the saint to arrive from the holy city. The girl could not bear to wait a moment longer, so in the middle of the night she went to the pond to baptize the infant herself. As she held the infant under the water, she watched in wonder as the baby transformed into a hare, its hind legs kicking and paws scratching her hands, and then a pigeon, the green feathers fin-like and iridescent, then a red fox, then a kitten, and finally, a fish. The fish slipped easily from her hands and swam away towards the mouth of the river."

Llewelyna kept her eyes closed and I knew enough not to expect anything more from her. As I went back down the stairs, I could see my father and Jacob at the kitchen table drinking tea with my grandmother. I hadn't noticed her when I came inside the house before. Her boat had arrived that morning. They all turned to me as I descended the last stairs. My grandmother wore a wide hat decorated with so many feathers and flowers it must have been heavy; somehow she kept her chin up.

"Ah, the prodigal daughter," she said. "You'll ruin your reputation before you even get back to London."

I looked to my father. "London?"

"They're only children, Mother. It was nothing."

"Children? Iris is practically a woman."

I knew my grandmother's presence tamed my father's propriety. He was progressive except when it came to the future of his children. In his mind, we were only in Canada for a little adventure, experiences we would collect like shiny trinkets to bring back home to England. He didn't acknowledge our growing attachment to Winteridge.

"You smell as terrible as that Indian," my grandmother said to me, recoiling.

I looked down at my dirty dress. "Once Llewelyna is finished in the bath I will bathe."

"How is she?" my father asked.

"She's fine."

"Fine?" my grandmother said. "That woman is not fine. This house is in complete disarray, an utter shamble. Fowl roaming the halls. This is no way to greet company. If you ask me, she has become quite the sluggard." My grandmother picked up her teacup and gazed at my father over its rim. "Noah, what a shame. If you had only waited a few more months. Annabel Linus, she's still available, you know. No children. She would make a fine wife."

"Mother, please," my father said, sounding exhausted.

I was so thirsty. I took a teacup from the tray on the table and poured myself some tea. Jacob chewed a biscuit from the tin my grandmother had brought along from London and grinned at me.

"A woman should not read so much. Planting ideas in her daughter's fertile imagination," my grandmother went on. "Just watch. Under that woman's negligence Iris will surely become a scoundrel."

"Stop," my father attempted.

"And attending that barn of a country school along with any tramp and vulgar brewer's daughter, it's no wonder."

"Well at least you and Lew might agree on something."

"Oh, and what's that?"

But just then there was a knock at the door. It was Yuri.

"Excuse me, sir," he said to my father. "You must come quick. It's Henry. A mob is headed to his shop."

"Whatever for?"

"What in the world kind of place is this where just anyone storms into your private home! Don't you hire—"

"Mother, hush!" It was rare for my father to raise his voice.

"Mr. Bell says Henry stole his gun." Yuri's eyes caught mine for a flash.

"Where did he get an idea like that?" My father followed Yuri onto the porch, hatless. I stepped out after them.

"My father saw him snooping around the Bells' shack, sir." Yuri and my father went from walking to running. I followed them to Henry's home. A mob of men stood around a pile of books; each carried one of Mr. Bell's rifles. Viktor and Taras held Henry's arms, though he didn't appear to be resisting, and another man was yelling threats. Mr. Bell dangled a match over a pile of books.

"What in God's name is going on here?" my father said as we burst through the bushes.

A few spoke at once, claiming what Yuri had already told us, that Henry had stolen Mr. Bell's pistol. Taras and Viktor were silent.

"Put your bloody guns down," my father demanded, and the men complied. He turned to Henry. "Did you take Phillip's pistol?"

"No, sir," Henry said, straight-faced.

"Henry is an honest man. He does not lie. He does not steal. Let go of him already." Taras and Viktor released Henry. "You should all be ashamed."

Mr. Bell approached my father. "Taras here says he saw him steal it, Noah. I won't rest until we search the house."

My father glanced down at the pile of books. "It looks as though you already have."

"We weren't able to get into the back room."

"Henry, I know you have nothing to hide. Will you allow Phillip to respectfully search your home for his goddamned gun if he promises not to touch one more goddamned thing while he's at it?"

Henry nodded. He would not look at anyone but my father.

"There you have it," my father said. He walked up close to Mr. Bell. "But if you don't put everything back exactly as you found it, I swear to God . . ."

I stepped away from the crowd and went back into the forest to look for the pistol. I would slip it back into Mr. Bell's shack while everyone was gone. When I finally got to the place on the river where Yuri had hidden the pistol, I searched in the bushes, beneath rocks, and behind trees, but I couldn't find it anywhere. I thought the orphan thief might have found it and this terrified me. After what felt like hours of futile searching, I ran back through the forest to Henry's shop. Everyone was gone except for Yuri, who was carrying a precariously tall stack of books back into the library. He looked at me, expectant.

"I couldn't find it."

"I threw it into the bushes."

"I looked everywhere. Nothing."

"Do you think Henry saw me throw it?" Yuri said, ignoring me.

"I don't think so."

"Maybe he went back for it."

"Why would he do that?"

Yuri shrugged.

"Where is everyone?" I asked.

"Your father and Henry have gone for a walk, to cool off."

"We have to find that gun," I whispered.

"If it's gone, it's gone. There's nothing we can do," he said, and handed me a stack of books. "Let's just get Henry's books back in order. That's all we can do now."

I watched Yuri's face carefully. His eyes wouldn't meet mine.

12

The Japanese no longer lined the back wall of the church as they had before the fire in the Kobas' orchard the year before. They attended their own church now, built near the lake. In their stead, the Wasiks and some of the other poorer, white picker families sat at the back of the church. When I looked back at the Wasiks, Yuri glanced down as if he had already been looking my way. There was a bruise on his cheek. Viktor slouched beside him, his eyes opening and closing drowsily. On the other side of Yuri, Mary wore a grey veil over her face. Beside her, Taras was rigid and upright. Since the incident at Henry's, he and my father had hardly spoken all week.

Someone poked my shoulder. I turned to find Mrs. Bell. She gave a playful little wave with her gloved hand. Mr. Bell nodded at my father, and my father, never one to perpetuate drama, smiled back.

The priest motioned for us all to stand and sing the hymn. The congregation rose with a shuffle. Llewelyna remained sitting. She was unusually pale, amphibian. She knit and unknit her fingers. The congregation stole glances at her. My father pretended not to notice, while my grandmother threw Llewelyna glaring looks she didn't acknowledge.

"Are you feeling okay?" I whispered in her ear. Llewelyna closed her eyes and smiled. She mumbled something in Welsh.

"For shame!" my grandmother hissed at us for talking. Llewelyna's eyelids lifted heavily and she smiled dumbly up at my grandmother, who shook her head, furious.

I stood for the hymn and stared at Jesus pinned to the cross. He looked as gruesome as ever, his mouth distorted in a terrible grimace of death. A bead of blood had collected on the tip of his big toe. It dripped off and stained the white mantel below. I mouthed the words to the hymn. Jacob's new, erratic voice quivered above the rest:

"Cast thy bread upon the water,

"Christ will watch the rolling wave,

"As it ripples slowly onward, to the soul he seeks to save."

When the hymn was over we all sat back down in the pews. Llewelyna's eyes opened and closed slowly. Her lips twitched with language too quiet to hear. Father John asked us to bow our heads in prayer but I kept watching Llewelyna. My grandmother stared at her also, until she saw me looking and glared for me to close my eyes, and I did.

Llewelyna's leg began to vibrate against mine. By the time I knew what was happening she had slipped off the pew to the ground. I dove down beside her. Her head jolted back and forth between my hands. There was noise all around us as people stood, and then shuffled to get a better view. Llewelyna's hair was already plastered against her forehead with sweat. My father was too large to fit between the pews at her feet and so remained seated. "No, no, no," I could hear him saying, but wasn't sure who he was directing those words to. Father John, eyes closed, continued with his prayer, his voice projected towards the ceiling. No one was praying with him now.

Llewelyna's eyes were closed and her mouth long and tense. Her hands were in fists at her sides. She had told me once, after that first time in the garden, that during her tremblings she often saw the end of the world as Saint Francis described it to her: fire, earthquakes, exploding stars. It was important I didn't tell anyone about these visions, it would only scare them, she said. The trembling in the garden felt surreal, otherworldly, as though I had witnessed her exit the physical world for another. But now, surrounded by people, her trembling was made corporeal: just a body ravaged by convulsions, made electric. I thought I might throw up, faint, or die right there beside her. The trembling seemed to last hours. I couldn't help but look around at all the faces. People held white-gloved hands and handkerchiefs against their mouths as if there were a contagion in the air. At the back of the church Mary fell to her knees and uttered a prayer of her own. Viktor's and Taras's eyes were to the floor in shame, but Yuri's met mine.

A voice hissed, *devil*. It made my skin bristle. I looked up at my grandmother but her mouth was sealed with a frown. I was glad Llewelyna couldn't hear those words spat out like a curse upon her: *devil, devil*. I was nauseous at the thought of my beautiful mother thrashing on the floor beneath the pews, with common, unspectacular people bending over her and whispering. I realized then that Father John had taken on the hissed word and was praying the devil out of Llewelyna.

When Llewelyna finally opened her eyes she smiled at me. The whites had turned dark red and emitted gasps from onlookers. She took in the scene around her slowly, then closed her eyes and fell asleep. Despite my grandmother's quibbling—*Mightn't we leave her be? Mightn't there be harm in moving her? Mightn't we call the doctor?*—my father slipped his hands beneath Llewelyna and picked her up. Her head hung limp over his arm; her white neck curled back impossibly, the bulge of her throat visible through the skin, her hair loose, almost touching the ground. I picked up her yellow lace veil and pinched the fabric so hard it left imprints on my fingertips.

There was a crowd outside the church and I stood alone, lost in it. My father got inside our carriage with Llewelyna still in his arms. My grandmother and Jacob got in behind them, and the horses tugged the carriage towards the road.

"Are you all right?" Yuri was beside me. I turned as if to walk away from him, but I knew he would follow me into the forest.

We ducked under fallen trees and stomped through low bushes.

"Were you afraid, Iris?" Yuri asked. He ran up ahead and stood in front of me. "Iris?" His eyes were big as two bluebird's eggs. I couldn't speak. I didn't want to release the bubble rising up my throat. "Are you all right?"

I shook my head and pinched my lips together. The hot tears were ready at the insides of my eyes. I couldn't stop shaking my head. Yuri pulled my shoulders into him and petted the nape of my neck softly as mothers are supposed to. My knees gave out and we sank to the forest floor, my face planted into Yuri's shoulder. The bubble in my throat burst.

Llewelyna's fall in the church confirmed my grandmother's suspicions about her: *She has always been a little "off," hasn't she?* She called the trembling a fit. Dr. Cross was called from the city to see to her, and he gave my father a bottle of white pills Llewelyna refused to take. She stayed in bed for days.

I wasn't quite sure how she had done it, but Llewelyna had hidden her illness from everyone but me. Although my father was often away, I thought he must have suspected something, but he didn't seem to know about her tremblings. Perhaps he was naive to it or maybe Llewelyna had a kind of control over the falls. Later she told me she usually knew when one was coming. It began with the smell of lemons, sharp at the back of her throat. She would have a dizzy spell and need to sit down, and then everything would go black and all of a sudden she would be in a thick forest, following Saint Francis to the lake. She knew when she dove into the water that she was convulsing, that her visions of the end of the world would begin. She said that day in the church, the dizzy spell had come upon her too quickly. Before she realized what was happening it was already too late.

My grandmother had called upon a proper priest from the city, dressed in white robes and with a heavy gold cross around his neck that thumped against the kitchen table when he reached for the sugar to sweeten his tea. The priest arrived on the *Rosamond* early one morning. While he was in Llewelyna's room, I strained to hear his murmurings from my bedroom. His voice surged in a kind of chant.

"Why worry yourself?" my grandmother was saying to my father as I descended the staircase. "There is no harm in it." She sat alert at the kitchen table with the handle of her teacup pinched between index finger and thumb. My father was slumped over, head in his hands.

"You've brought an exorcist into my home."

"Simple prayer. No harm in simple prayer."

"The entire neighbourhood watched the man disembark. Do you understand what you've done?"

"It's a matter of spirit. And spirit must be fought with spirit." My grandmother lifted her face to me. "Good morning, darling." She smiled and gestured to the teapot. "Tea?"

My father got up from the table without looking at me and went outside.

This wouldn't be the last time I would feel as though I were interrupting something when I walked into the room. For weeks after Llewelyna's fall in the church, I often found my grandmother

and father sitting close, leaning towards one another like schem-
ing thieves who couldn't quite agree on a plan. During one of
these heated whisperings in the sitting room, I hid around the
corner where I could just barely hear the conversation.

". . . in Hertfordshire," my grandmother was saying. "A lovely
building, and new. Designed by Rowland Plumbe. It doesn't even
look like a hospital. An estate, really. A palace. The grounds are
stunning. Gardens. Plenty of fresh air."

"I'm telling you she won't cross the Atlantic again. She won't
leave. I've tried."

"Perhaps she hasn't a choice?"

"Are you suggesting I kidnap my wife?"

"Of course not, Noah. But something must be done. You
cannot continue in this manner."

Then one evening my father entered the spare room where
Llewelyna now slept since her seizure in the church, and announced
he would be accompanying my grandmother and Jacob back to
London. My grandmother stood at the doorway, her arms crossed.
I remained in the hallway, a safe distance from the scene but close
enough to see my father and the lump Llewelyna made in the bed.
She didn't say anything, just let my father keep talking. His words
were practised and precise but his chin quivered ever so slightly
as he spoke.

"Surely you can see that it is best for Jacob to get acquainted
with London. Mother has arranged for him to receive instruction,
a tutor who will prepare him for the rigour of boarding school."
He looked to my grandmother as if for encouragement. My father
did not go on to say why it was necessary he go along with them,
but my grandmother's firm nod dispelled all uncertainties.

Llewelyna sat up then and reached for a glass of water on her
bedside. My father regarded her squarely and awaited her response.

She propped herself up on a pillow. She was pale, her eyes still bloodshot, as pink as her robe. She held the glass of water to her chest and turned towards the window. I wanted so desperately for her to demand he stay, or go hysterical, cry, curse him, jump from the window, anything at all. I could tell by the way he watched her, the muscle of his jaw pulsing, that he wanted that too. But she didn't appear to be interested, or even listening, at least not to him.

The day they left on the *Rosamond* I refused to walk them to the lakeboat. My grandmother and Jacob were already at the bottom of the drive. Viktor and Yuri carried their trunks for them. My father had stalled at the threshold of our house and waited until everyone was a distance away. He bent down and pulled me in close.

"I just can't bear it," he said into my neck, his voice muffled by my hair. He was crying. "You understand, don't you? To see her like this again, I can't. I just need some time." He peeled away. His eyes were red and puffy, his cheeks wet. He kissed me on the head and wiped his face on his sleeve before he left. That word *again* rang in my ears.

❧

Mary was hired to care for Llewelyna, who no longer had the strength to refuse her services. I couldn't tell whether this last seizure had been so much more intense than the ones before or if it was grief that weakened her. My grandmother had told me to expect the priest every Monday morning after his initial visit, but he never came back. Instead, Henry came to visit every week with a paper bag of what must have been tobacco for Llewelyna. During his visits the house would fill with the smell of sweet smoke. I walked up the stairs once to find Mary standing at Llewelyna's door—it was slightly ajar—and peeking in through the crack. When she saw me watching her she straightened and shuffled past me and down the stairs. I took over her spot at the door. Through the crack I could see Henry holding a jar of smouldering leaves and herbs. Smoke rose from it in ribbons. He positioned the jar under Llewelyna's face. She closed her eyes and waved the smoke against her face as if it were water. Henry put the jar by Llewelyna's bedside, where it continued to fill the room with its creamy smoke.

Taras despised Henry's visits. He'd glare pointedly at Henry whenever he walked up our drive. Mary told me that Henry shouldn't take it personally. Taras didn't trust Indians; thought them sneaky devils. Some bandit Indians had run off with four of the horses from the orchard Taras had worked on in Vernon. He had chased them into the hills until nightfall, shooting at their shadows until they dissolved into darkness. Taras still claimed Henry had Mr. Bell's gun hidden away somewhere, and that we all underestimated what a man of his size and breed was capable of. I told Mary that Henry was my family's closest friend, and if she and Taras thought anything had changed now that my father was gone, I would be happy to send my father a letter and ask him as much. That seemed to silence her for a time.

Against Mary's wishes, I helped her with the washing and the chicken coop. I liked to be awake in the blue light of dawn with the rest of the work hands. Every morning I rubbed the fuzz of sleep from my eyes, threw on my father's coat, and slipped through the orchard to the coop. The rooster yodelled at my arrival, as if in warning. Hens clucked at my feet, awaiting the handfuls of seed I offered. I had to nudge the sitting hens off their eggs. Before I set the eggs in my basket, I liked to hold those warm globes in my palms and marvel at the possibility, the vulnerability, pulsing inside.

After my chores I would slink through the orchard and spy on the pickers. They balanced on the ladders like industrious acrobats.

The absence of Noah and Jacob allowed Llewelyna to slip deeper into her own world. She read voraciously. When she wasn't reading, she slept, only to rest her tired eyes, she said. A blood vessel in one of her eyes never healed from the seizure, and that eye remained bright red, flooded, the emerald iris still absurdly lucent.

Some nights I woke to Llewelyna stumbling around in the room above, or mumbling in her sleep. One night I went up the stairs to her bedroom and cracked open the door. I could hardly make out her inky shape in the darkness. She was rummaging through boxes in her closet.

"Mum?" I asked. The forbidden name fell from my lips like a stone, like a small hope I had sucked dry. I had once imagined the word might unlock an intimacy, a tenderness she still had for me.

She startled at my voice, the forbidden word. "Neb?" she asked the darkness.

"What are you doing?"

"Ba ba bach," she said so tenderly I hardly recognized her voice. "Babi bach gwael."

I took a step into the room. "Are you looking for something?"

"That photograph of you," she said and continued to rummage. "It's here somewhere, it is."

I approached her. "What photograph? The one at the waterfront?" One summer we had our portraits taken at the photographer's booth in the city during the regatta.

"The only one I have, *cariad*." When we were very small Llewelyna sometimes called Jacob *cariad*, a Welsh term of endearment, but she had never used this pet name for me. She stopped rummaging for a moment. Despite the darkness I could feel her eyes on me. "You forgive me, don't you?" she asked.

My eyes adjusted to the darkness of the room enough that I could light a candle. Even in the fluttering light her face sank, darkened, as if she had expected someone else.

"Ah, yes. It's you, of course," she said. "Back to bed you go, Iris."

᧙

My father's letters to me were sparse, and often summed up in the front cover of some book he sent along. Inside *The Seven Wonders of the Ancient World*, he simply wrote: "And the eighth is you!" The illustration of Nebuchadnezzar's wife brushing her hair in the hanging gardens of Babylon reminded me of Llewelyna. At first, I was so angry at my father I hadn't even bothered to write to him, but as Llewelyna became more ill, I wrote him false little notes about the weather, or the orchard, so he might think everything was okay. I didn't want him to know about Llewelyna's decline; I was afraid he would never return to us.

He hadn't sent Llewelyna anything until now. I passed her the book. It was wrapped in butcher's paper. "It's from Father," I said, although this was already painfully clear to her. She traced the postage stamp briefly before she tore the paper open. The book was dark olive green. Llewelyna looked at the cover with both wonder and confusion.

"What is it?" I asked.

She opened the cover and flipped through the first few pages. "How did he . . . ?" She closed the book and looked at the back of it for too long, for even I could see it was blank. "I don't understand," she said. "Who is this Lady Charlotte Guest?" She fanned through the pages again.

"Is that the author?"

"These are old Welsh stories. But she writes in English. And the title—*Mabinogion*. It isn't even a word."

I remembered the branches of the Mabinogi that she had often referred to before, and thought again of our maple. "Is it like the Mabinogi tree?" I asked.

"You foolish girl. Mabinogi means story. It isn't a tree."

I reddened at my mistake. "Did he write something in it?" I asked.

She turned to the first pages of the book. They were blank. "Why would he do that?" She gave me a hard look then, and for a moment I thought she might throw the book right at me. Instead, she placed it gently on my lap. The green book had a chimera on the cover: a red dragon with a lion's head.

"Can you read it to me?" she asked. "My eyes are so tired today."

The first story was called "Pwyll Prince of Dyved." I recognized the name; he was married to Princess Rhiannon, the heroine of some of the faery tales Llewelyna told Jacob and me when we were children. But this particular story wasn't one I had ever heard. Llewelyna had her eyes closed, and as I read she interrupted every now and then with a groan or a bitter laugh. "Ah, Charlotte, it's all wrong. The story just doesn't work in English," she kept saying. "This Guest woman is a complete fool." And yet she insisted I continue reading.

In the story, Rhiannon bears Prince Pwyll an heir, but the infant disappears one night while six of Rhiannon's handmaidens are meant to be watching him. Instead of admitting his disappearance, the handmaidens kill a litter of puppies and spread their blood on Rhiannon's face and leave their bones beside her bed. When Rhiannon wakes, the handmaidens claim that despite their attempts to restrain her, Rhiannon ate her infant son in her sleep. The nobles want Prince Pwyll to put his wife away for such a crime, but he begs their mercy. Instead, Rhiannon's penance is to sit on a horse-block in the town square and tell the story of how she ate her own son, over and over again to passersby.

Meanwhile, her lost son is discovered and raised by a good family. As the boy grows, his adoptive father recognizes the child's unmistakable resemblance to Pwyll and decides to present the boy to the prince. Overjoyed with the discovery of his lost son and his wife's proved innocence, Prince Pwyll shows the boy to Rhiannon at the horse-block.

At this point in the story, Llewelyna sat up and stared at me as I read: ""I declare to Heaven," said Rhiannon, "that if this be true, there indeed is an end to my trouble."" I flipped the page. ""Lady," said Pendaran—""

"Stop," Llewelyna said. "Give me that." She reached for the book. Her eyes scanned the page. She threw the book to the floor. "Complete and utter rubbish."

"What's wrong?"

"That's not at all how the story ends." She leaned back into her pillows and her stare was so direct I had to look away. "Rhiannon doesn't accept the child. When they bring her her son, she denies him and only repeats the story of eating her baby. She recalls the snap of tendons and the taste of iron in the infant's blood. Then the next day she attacks another child, and is hanged by the neck for her crime."

This story wasn't particularly darker than some of the other stories Llewelyna had told me about mothers and their infants, or ferocious black knights or monsters or dragons, or the one about the deathless boy caught in a fish weir. But there was something unbearable about the way she watched me so directly as she spoke. It made the story feel like a kind of warning to me personally.

13

Winteridge had made a few decisions about my family. Llewelyna was mad, a witch or devil, and my father had abandoned us because of his shame. When I walked into the Nickels' store for supplies, everyone turned quiet as if I had interrupted them, and then they watched me sympathetically. Mrs. Nickel puckered her lips when she spoke to me, as if I were a toddler. I started asking Mary to do the shopping for me instead.

Llewelyna continued to sleep in the spare room on the top floor. She needed the still air, the white sheets, the blank. The only colour in the room was the fire of Llewelyna's hair and Saint Francis's plume at her feet. Although she threw the *Mabinogion* aside that first time, she spent the cold days and nights with it in her lap, the gold nib of her pen scratching away at the pages as if there was something just beneath the surface she might unearth. She never asked me to read from it again. Instead she kept the book and its stories to herself and faded into that faraway world. Llewelyna's other books collected dust beside her bed. She even turned Henry away a few times, saying she had work to do. He visited less and less often, to Mary's and Taras's satisfaction.

Once, while she was asleep, I picked the *Mabinogion* up off the bed beside her. It felt much too heavy for its size. Llewelyna groaned in her sleep and then quieted. I opened the book—I wanted to know what she was writing inside. Her scrawl was more neat and delicate than I could have imagined. She was scribbling over the text in Welsh. I thought she must be translating the stories back into their original language, fixing the flaws in the tales she found along the way.

Llewelyna turned in her sleep and I placed the book back down on the bed where I had found it. She reached for it immediately and opened her eyes.

"Do you need anything?" I asked. Just then Mary entered the room and began to sweep beneath the bed.

"Water." Llewelyna's empty glass was rimmed with lip prints.

"I'll see to that," Mary said.

"It's okay, I—"

"Don't worry yourself." Mary took the glass from me. She went all the way down to the kitchen to fill the glass even though there was a water basin full of water right in Llewelyna's room.

Every once in a while Llewelyna asked to see the fish. I would pull it out from its hiding place and climb into bed beside her. We would marvel at the blue fish's luminescent scales. They shone like young flame even in the dim evening. One night, Llewelyna held the fish up towards the starlight coming through her window and told me that fish were the wisest of all creatures because they were the very first to be created, water being made before land. She quoted Genesis: "And the earth was without form, and void; and darkness was upon the face of the deep. And the spirit of God moved upon the face of the waters." She went on to say that some fish, this one for example, had lived since the beginning of time. And if you were to eat one of these ancient fish, its wisdom would be born inside of you. I took the fish from her then, and was careful to hide it in a new place each week.

❧

Even as the long, dark nights of winter approached, Azami could rarely get time away from working on her family's orchard, and we hardly ever saw one another. We no longer performed the *harae* together. Since the seizure in the church, I didn't like to leave Llewelyna's side for too long. I missed Azami's friendship, but whenever I saw her, my guilt about the fire and her shrine blossomed into an unbearable ache. Not only that, ever since I destroyed the shrine I had a creeping feeling that something was watching me, stalking me. Sometimes I could feel its breath on the back of my neck. I thought that admitting to Azami what I had done might make it go away.

We met one afternoon on the shore by the boulders. Azami's face went very stiff when I told her I had destroyed the shrine. Of course I couldn't tell her about the fire. That was something I could never admit to anyone. Azami's face shifted from fury to urgency. The sun had moved out from behind the shade of trees and she had to peer through it at me.

"Where?" she said. She was gripping my wrists now. Shaking them. "Where is the shrine?"

"I'm sorry. It's gone."

"I must know where it was destroyed. And how."

I panicked. "In the lake. I threw it in the lake."

"Show me where."

I told Azami I had thrown the shrine off the side of the cliff, where Llewelyna had jumped off so very long ago. I thought this would dissuade her, but it didn't. She tugged my arm towards the cliffs as if it were my leash. She was walking so fast. Her grip on me was brutal. I wasn't dressed warmly enough for how cold it was and my skin prickled beneath her touch. I had the strange sensation that my legs were not connected to my hips. I lost command of them and stumbled after her. Then my vision became blurry. I couldn't tell near from far. My mouth filled with the sting of lemon. I fell.

In that in-between world I saw the jaguar again, the rosettes on her coat as clear as coins. I ran my fingers through her silken fur. It smelled of pine needles.

When I returned, Azami had my head in her lap. Her breath blossomed in a white plume. Her eyes were wide and fearful.

"What happened?" I asked. The sweat on my forehead was already beginning to cool and I began to shiver.

Azami explained how my body had gone stiff, my eyes open but vacant. She tried to show me with her own arms the velocity of my trembling, but said she couldn't imitate it, it was too fast. As I listened to her, I couldn't keep my eyes off the jaguar. It had followed me from my seizure dream and now wandered through the surrounding forest behind Azami.

"What is it?" she asked. She clutched my chin in her hands to steady my gaze, but my eyes still followed the cat.

"A jaguar," I said.

Azami jumped, turned around. I could tell by her reaction she couldn't see it. "A kami?"

"I don't know. I've seen it before. You don't see it?"

"They decide who sees them," Azami said. Then: "It makes sense."

"It does?"

She shaded her eyes from the setting sun and looked out towards the lake. "You destroyed the shrine. It makes sense she would stalk you." We had arrived at the cliff, and from the top we could see all the way to where the lake met the purple mountains to the south.

The jaguar stayed by my side for a few days before she wandered back into the woods, but I could still feel her amber eyes on me, tracking my every move.

I decided to build Azami a new shrine. I thought rebuilding it might satisfy the kami and make the jaguar leave me alone. With little explanation, Henry agreed to help me, and we built the little stick house in a matter of hours.

"Aren't you a little old for doll houses?" he said as he held one side down and I hammered away.

"It's not a toy. It's a shrine for Azami. I broke her other one."

"Her *other* one. You people are funny. You think all you need to do is build a house and God will already live inside."

I walked to the Kobas' orchard with the carefully built shrine in a wagon, covered with a potato sack. The forest floor was firm, but it hadn't yet snowed. Azami was digging for potatoes with Molly. Molly was the first to spot me in the woods. She stood to stare as if her gaze itself could propel me away. I gestured for Azami to come to me and lifted the potato sack to give Azami a glance at the shrine. I had painted it red, just like the other one. Henry had carved ornate designs on the wood, birds, bears, and coyotes. It was a much more beautiful shrine than the one Azami had before. But she looked unimpressed. I could tell her anger had hardened against me. Only my seizure had protected me from its full force before.

"A shrine isn't like your cross," she said. "It isn't some symbol you can make of sticks. A shrine is a space apart from the ordinary world. Not about the thing itself but what it made inside."

She walked back to Molly, who squatted down again to dig when Azami returned to her side. I left the shrine in the grass and walked away. My confession had broken something, and I wished that I had never admitted the truth. My sins could not be undone. From then on Azami and I did our best to avoid one another, and it was easy to do in the winter. Our bustling summer town grew cold and stiff during those dark months. We each isolated ourselves in

our homes and only went outside in the meagre daylight hours to
work or go about our errands.

My father wrote that Jacob was thriving at boarding school in
London. I offered him no news in exchange, and the less I
responded, the more seldom his letters and books came.

✿

The following summer, Viktor and Yuri swam carelessly through
the waters I feared. I would sit on the wharf and count their laps,
timing them with my father's old pocket watch. Between swims
they lifted themselves up onto the dock and panted next to me.
Water slipped down Viktor's chest. The skin there was smooth
and firm as a seal's. I wondered how it might feel to the touch.
How it might taste. In the water Yuri's blond hair became trans-
lucent; his eyebrows and eyelashes disappeared completely. His
body was in no way formed like his brother's. Despite the long
hours he worked, Yuri's stomach remained pudgy. His large pink
nipples were visible through his wet undershirt.

"How long?" Yuri asked, pushing his hair off his face and rubbing the water out of his eyes with his middle fingers

"You each did fifteen laps. Eighteen minutes for you, Yuri,
twenty and a half for Viktor."

"That's worse than yesterday!" Viktor said. "I don't believe you."

"I never miscount."

"Never?"

"Never."

Viktor crawled on top of me. "Never?" He shook his hair and
body like a dog, spraying water all over me. I covered my face and
squirmed beneath him, laughing.

"Viktor, get off her," Yuri said.

Viktor ignored him. He dropped his chest onto mine. The wet cloth of his shorts soaked my dress. I went still, removed my hands from my face and looked up at him. Viktor's face changed. I didn't push him away like he expected. Yuri pulled at Viktor's shoulder until he got off me, awkwardly. He left me soaked and still catching my breath.

"Why don't you ever swim with us, Your Highness?" Viktor asked. The nickname had stuck and I hated it. His eyes wandered over my body and I knew he was imagining me naked. I crossed my arms to hide my unimpressive breasts.

"I don't like to swim."

"You don't know how, do you?" Viktor teased.

"Of course I know how to swim."

"Well, what are you afraid of?"

"Leave her alone," Yuri said.

Viktor wrapped his arms around me. "What if I just picked you up and threw you in." He stood so I was dangling from his arms. I looked down into the water below. My stomach rose to my throat.

"I said leave her alone." Yuri ripped at Viktor's arms, red-faced.

"Damnit, hen." Viktor put me back down so he could inspect his arm. "You scratched me, you little woman. I was only fooling around." Viktor gathered his clothes and stomped down the wharf, back towards the orchard, their midday swim finished.

Later that evening, I couldn't find Viktor as I walked along the edge of the orchard while the pickers were just finishing the workday, putting away ladders and carting the last few bins into the storehouse. In the dead of summer, the men worked early mornings and late evenings and spent the unbearably hot middle hours of the day at the lake. Pink blossoms filled the trees and the entire world smelled of their nectar. It would be an hour until Mary called me in for dinner and so I hiked up into the forest and climbed the ladder to the tree fort.

For the most part, my days were taken up with tending to Llewelyna and helping Mary around the house, and so I hadn't been up to the fort for a while. When I pulled myself up through the hole in the floor I found myself staring into the wide eyes of a beautiful woman, a grown face I vaguely recognized. She was lying beneath a sheet, her shoulders bare. Sweat glistened her forehead.

"Azami?" I asked. She patted her hand on top of the sheet where another shape moved. The blanket was pushed back and Viktor's dishevelled dark head emerged.

"Your Highness?" he said with a crooked smile. He pulled the sheet up to his chest and lay next to Azami. Long black eyelashes rimmed her dark eyes. Her face had grown dimensions, cheekbones, a delicate chin. It had only been months since I had seen her, and yet she looked so much older than me. The peaks of her breasts rose up from beneath the sheet. I was humiliated by my shapeless child's frock, much too short for me now, but I refused to wear the suffocating gowns my grandmother sent. Azami reached for her clothes and pulled them on beneath the sheets.

"Could you pass me my trousers, Iris?" Viktor said.

I found his brown work pants and threw them to him. He scrambled around beneath the sheets as he put them on. Azami twirled her long black hair around and around. She knotted it somehow on top of her head, stood, and slipped a flat cap over her hair. She was wearing a button-up shirt and trousers. A button was missing from the shirt. I found it on the floor and passed it to her. Wordlessly, she squeezed past me and down the ladder. I heard her jump to the ground.

Viktor was sitting against the wall watching me, his chest still irresistibly bare and glistening. He patted the floor next to him and I sat. His rough fingertips tickled my arm. "You'll keep this between you and me—what you saw. Azami and me." He looked directly into my eyes as he traced figure eights on my skin. "You can't tell anyone. Not your brother, not Yuri. Not anyone. I can trust you, can't I?"

I nodded.

"I knew I could." He ruffled my hair as though I were a child. I wriggled away from him. "Hey, don't be like that," he said. I gave him a final glare before stomping down the ladder and running home.

The vision of Azami and Viktor opened me up to the world of flesh and bodies and sex. That night I lay in bed and imagined Viktor on top of me, his body pressed up to mine, his lips hard against my neck, my shoulder, my breasts.

Some days Viktor and Yuri would pick up huge rocks, hold them against their chests, and wobble along the mossy rocks into the water. I'd watch their backs slip below the surface and timed how long they could stay underwater, walking along the lake bottom. Reminded of Jacob, I was always anxious for them to rise. Just when I would be about to scream for help, one of them would burst through the surface. It would usually be Yuri, who was a better swimmer than Viktor but couldn't hold his breath as long. After they dried off, Viktor would light a cigarette, pass it to Yuri and me, and we'd watch the sun go down.

"I want to work on the orchard," I said one day.

Viktor scoffed. "A woman? Father would never allow it."

I turned to Yuri. "You told me once about the girl you knew that could pick better than some of the men." I didn't want to bring up Azami. I didn't want her name to enter our triangle. Yuri coughed smoke and passed the cigarette across me and back to Viktor.

"Cleo Winston!" Viktor said, taking the cigarette. "You were in love with that little half-breed, weren't you, hen?" he teased.

"She was my friend," Yuri said.

"She wasn't that good a picker."

"What about Azami?" Yuri said. "Wouldn't you agree she's quite efficient?" Yuri's face was serious, challenging.

The moment of tension between them exposed a glimpse of the sibling rivalry I could never understand. Viktor broke the moment with a hearty laugh the joke didn't warrant and that enraged Yuri further.

"And with my father and Jacob gone, and the trees full," I went on, "I'm sure you could use some help."

Viktor took a final puff and flicked the cigarette into the lake. He placed a hand on my head and ruffled my hair. "You'd like that, would you, Your Highness? Working on the orchard with the lowly peasant men?"

"I'd earn a wage, of course," I said.

Viktor smiled. "And who would teach you to pick fruit? It's no easy thing you just wake up doing. It takes exceptional talent." Viktor rubbed his fingernails against his chest, playing the dandy.

"It's not that hard," Yuri said.

"You could teach me, couldn't you?" I asked Viktor.

"I've no time to teach little girls how to pick peaches."

"I'm fifteen," I said. My irritation was unwarranted, he was only kidding, but I was fed up with him treating me like a child. "And I learn quickly. I've been watching the men, I know how to do it."

"I could teach you, Iris," Yuri said.

"All right," I agreed, looking at Viktor but speaking to Yuri.

For a week Yuri and I met in a hidden corner of the orchard during his lunch break. He showed me the best way to pluck peaches, by slightly twisting my wrist, not so hard that the delicate skin peeled or wrinkled but enough that the stem broke from the branch and didn't separate from the core. It was messy work. The peaches were sticky with nectar and bugs. The pick sack was heavy and made my back throb and shoulders burn, but it felt wonderful to be outside in the fresh air, up in the trees with the birds. Once I was fast enough, and Yuri inspected the peaches I had picked and found no badly damaged ones, I performed my act for Taras.

Taras laughed when he first saw me put the pick sack over my shoulders and climb the ladder. I quickly filled my sack. After he inspected the peaches in my batch, he shrugged and gave me a job. "What harm?" he said.

Despite my attempts to engage the Japanese pickers, they avoided me. Most could not speak English anyway, but they also knew that to speak to a white woman, and the daughter of the landowner besides, was unacceptable. It wasn't anything anyone had to say. I tried to tell myself their unease had nothing to do with the fire.

That summer the trees were heavy with peaches. I would wake in the mornings to the groaning branches. Taras hired more and more pickers to keep up with the work. There was a constant flurry of new faces. Men slept on floors in the workhouse or in hammocks hung between the pine trees bordering the orchard.

I kept the money I earned in a coffee tin under my bed, next to the blue fish. I had no idea what I would use the money for, but I felt better having it. If I wanted, if I needed to, I could jump onto the *Rosamond* and disappear. I thought of Llewelyna's faery money that she claimed would turn to fungus if Jacob and I didn't go spend it quickly at the store, and sometimes I checked the tin just to make sure my coins were still there. Each time I put my wages away, I would take out the blue fish and remember the words of the woman who crawled out of the lake: *A gift. A girl.* I didn't understand what this gift might mean, and why she had brought it to me, but I hoped one day I would understand. I dropped a dead fly into the jar, a ribbon of lettuce, a bread crumb; the fish didn't seem to eat anything and eventually I had to transfer it into a fresh jar of water.

At the end of a hot summer workday I was in the top of one of the taller trees, my pick sack nearly full, the straps rubbing my shoulders raw, and I was about to head down the ladder when I saw one last peach, reddened by the sun, just out of reach. My mouth watered for it. As I stretched my arm out for the peach I had an intense feeling of déjà vu. The green filtered light, the tickle of sweat down my arms, and the men laughing while they carried a bin of peaches—it was all eerily familiar, as though I had already lived through this precise moment. Then my vision became splotched, full of burning holes, like the jaguar's fur. I realized the peach I reached for was much too far away. A metallic taste filled my mouth, like the smell of lightning, then lemon. The world began to shake. A branch whipped my face. I was in the air. Then darkness.

I was on the rocks at the bottom of the cliff face. The jaguar was swimming through the lake towards me. I pulled my knees to my chest. Before me, the lake was swollen, swarming with blue fish. I scooped one from the water and dropped it down my throat.

A cold splash on my face made me open my eyes. Viktor, Yuri, and Taras looked down at me. Taras held an empty bucket, his face recoiled in disgust. My pick sack dangled from Viktor's hand. Peaches were scattered everywhere. One was sticky beneath my back; the pit pricked my skin. Some Japanese pickers kept a polite distance and craned their necks from where they stood amongst the trees. Yuri had me propped up on his knees. His face was upside down and his hands cradled my head.

"Are you okay?" he asked.

I moved my fingers, my toes. "I think so."

He tried to pick me up.

"Let me," Viktor said as he put down my pick sack. "I won't have you dropping her." He took me from Yuri's arms. I let myself lean in against Viktor's chest and breathed in the smell of his skin, peach nectar and tobacco and salt. I thought of my father when he carried Llewelyna out of the church. I had never loved my father more than at that moment.

When I woke hours later I was in my bed. I had been stripped down to my drawers. Yuri sat on the edge of the bed, staring at his feet. He tapped his work boots against the floor. There was someone else in the room but I was too tired to turn my head to see who it was. I shifted, and Yuri looked at me.

"You're awake," he said. "How do you feel?"

"Tired." It was hard to speak, exhausting to move my jaw.

"Mother is preparing you a bath."

I tried to sit up but my torso was iron. I fell back into the pillow. "Who else is here?"

Yuri looked left and right as if he may have missed someone. "It's just me."

I tried to sit up again, not believing him. "There's someone else," I said.

"Relax, Iris. Rest." His face was terribly serious. "There's no one else." He kept his eyes trained on me as if I might disappear.

"What's wrong?" I asked.

"Do you remember what happened?"

"I fell."

"You don't remember anything else?"

I thought for a moment and remembered the dream I had before I woke up in the orchard, the jaguar and the fish, but this couldn't be what Yuri meant.

"When I found you on the ground you were shaking terribly. Thrashing."

I stared up at the ceiling. There was a yellow stain in the plaster. "Thrashing," I echoed. The room spun around me. I rolled away from Yuri and there was the jaguar, her enormous head resting serenely atop the bed covers.

"I'll give you some privacy," Yuri said, and shuffled out of the room.

The jaguar yawned. Her teeth were as long as cigarettes.

🐾

I woke the next morning to hushed laughter and the clatter of tin plates. The jaguar purred steadily on the bed next to me. I moved to the window, careful not to wake her. The sun wasn't up yet but the sky was violet from its hidden glow. Blue mist collected in the peach trees and undulated as if underwater. A lantern was on the picnic table in the orchard. Faces moved in and out of the dim light. A steaming pot was passed around. The workers took turns sitting at the table to eat while others warmed themselves by the cook fire or bathed in the dark by the well. Some men, their backs to the orchard, relieved themselves into the surrounding forest, whistling into the darkness to scare off bears.

Yuri must have been down at the lake still. He said that swimming in the dark was like disappearing. I never asked him why he would want to disappear because I understood that thrill. But for me the lake wasn't where things disappeared but where they came alive.

I had spent much of my childhood invisible. If I was bothering Llewelyna she would simply close her eyes and make me disappear in the darkness of her mind. I knew then to walk away and leave her be. As a girl I would slink around the house on tiptoe and watch her from behind furniture and around corners while she went on not seeing me. The spell would break unexpectedly—*little minx, you are*—her hand reaching for me, her eyes finally meeting mine.

Yuri walked out of the dark lake more real than when he stepped into it. I watched and waited for him to return to camp wet and shivering. When I finally saw him with a quilt over his shoulders, I let the disembodied babble of the workers and the purr of the jaguar lull me back to sleep.

Later, it was silence that woke me. Outside the sun swelled against the hills across the lake. The mist had burned off the trees. The men were no longer at the table. There was nothing left of their meal, no plates or scraps. The scene had been wiped clean as if it were a dream. The orchard looked empty, but on the far side of the property, the trees rustled.

I pulled the blankets up to my chin. The hush of the house emphasized the silence. The screen door moaned on its hinge. A breeze yawned through cracks in the walls. I could even hear the clock in the kitchen ticking. I was sore and exhausted. Each joint was stiff and swollen and my body ached from the fall. I touched the bump on the back of my head and winced. In that quiet, the rustle of her blankets in the room above mine and the creak of the floor as Llewelyna shifted her body were thunderous. My eyes snapped open. I jolted out of bed. For a moment I had seen a cross-section of the house, our rooms stacked atop one another and our bedrooms identical, our positions in bed the same, her with her peacock and me with my jaguar. I imagined books piling up around my headboard as my hair grew wild and red around my face.

In the mirror my eyes were bloodshot and there was a long streak of crusted blood all the way from the corner of my eye to my chin. Red and blue bruises mottled my arms. The jaguar paced behind me. I poured out some water from the basin and splashed it on my face. I undressed and checked the cut on my back, where the pit of the peach had pricked me. The jaguar's hot tongue lapped at the blood. I recoiled.

"Get away," I stomped. She didn't even blink. I tried clapping and snapping to scare the jaguar away but she did little more than glance up and lick a paw. I found Jacob's matches and held one out towards the jaguar. The small flame flickered in her eyes before she turned from it and sauntered down the stairs and out of the house.

I found my brother's trousers, peeled a peach skin from the pant leg, and slipped on my boots. The orchard was busy with birds and thick with the sweet-sour smell of ripe and rotting fruit. I reached up, plucked a peach from a branch, and let its nectar revive me. On the far side of the orchard I found the familiar hustle of workers and disappeared into its rhythms.

Yuri was helping a picker bring down a tree that had gone to rot. As soon as I set my eyes on him he looked around, sensing it. Once he and the worker had set the tree down, he came towards me.

"Iris," he whispered, glancing behind as if followed. "You can't be here."

I looked down at him from the second rung of the ladder. "Why not?"

"You fell."

"I won't use the ladder, then." I took a step down.

He shook his head. "Please, before my father sees you."

It was too late. Taras was coming towards us, ruddy-faced. The cigarette out the side of his mouth was stiff and angled upwards. "Nee, nee, nee," he said as he approached. Yuri took a step back and looked down at his feet. "All right now, little lady, back to the house."

"Taras, really, I'm fine—"

"Not asking." He began to turn away from me.

"You're not one to give orders," I said.

Taras swung back around. The workers near us watched from the trees. Taras took a few steps forward until our feet were nearly touching.

"Listen here. Your father left me in charge. Your time playing is over. You understand?" I thought of Azami and stared back at him defiantly. I had never heard him speak so much English at once. "You understand?" His spit speckled my cheek.

"I'll walk her back to the house," Yuri said, nudging his father away.

Taras swatted Yuri's hand and walked away.

"You shouldn't have done that." Yuri kicked a rotten peach as we walked through the shade of the trees. I was too upset to speak the whole way back. "He didn't mean to scare you. It's just his way." I started up the porch steps. "Iris," he began. He opened and closed his mouth like a fish. I turned from him and went into the house. The screen door slammed behind me.

The silence of the house made it enormous. A slight breeze fell against my shoulder and bristled my skin. Our peculiar house was a world with its own weather patterns, its own atmosphere. Outside it was summer; in the kitchen it was the dead of winter. I walked up to Llewelyna's room. It became warmer with every level of the house I passed. The top floor was hot and airless. The lace curtains cut the sunlight into shapes that shrunk and stretched against her blanket. Llewelyna's eyes were closed and she lay on her back. Saint Francis was in his usual spot at the foot of the bed. He lazily raised his small head at me and unravelled his feathers.

"Llewelyna?" I said. Her eyelids fluttered open. "Do you need something? Tea? Toast?"

"Your eyes. They're red."

I looked away. "Do you need anything?"

"Bring me the fish." After some hesitation, I brought the fish out from behind my bookshelf and handed it to her. It radiated a blue glow against her white sheets.

"I need water," she said. Her glass by the bed was full.

"You have plenty there beside—"

"Not to drink," she whispered mischievously, although there was no one to overhear. Mary was outside doing the washing.

"I don't understand."

"I want to go for a swim." The corners of her mouth turned up. She set the fish on her bedside table, atop the *Mabinogion*.

"I'm not sure that's a good idea."

"Help me up, you." She tossed the blanket off her body and pushed herself up with one arm. Her white nightgown blended with her skin. She had never been a voluptuous woman, but now she was angular and emptied out. Muscles that were once long and lean had dissolved. I couldn't look at her without a sickening pull at the back of my throat. To see her as a body—a body that was wrinkling, melting away—made me nauseous and depressed. It inverted my universe, like discovering God was dead. She had always seemed so magical to me, so unreal. I gave her my arm and tried not to look at her. She ran her hand over my skin. Her palm was dry and cold.

"You're so brown."

"I've been working. Helping in the orchard."

"I know," she said. "Don't forget the fish." I collected the jar in my dress pocket. When I pulled her up her legs buckled beneath her and she collapsed back into the bed. She looked out the window towards the lake and then tried again.

"No use," she said and fell back. She pulled the sheet up to her chin and closed her eyes. I knew this meant I was to leave. She had made me invisible again.

I walked down to the wharf. It was early afternoon and already so hot even the breeze was warm. I dangled my bare feet in the water. The cold was sharp and full and cooled my entire body. The water in the well was never cold enough in the summer, and Llewelyna's room was stifling. It was no wonder she craved the lake. Sitting on the wharf staring at my feet beneath the surface, I had an idea. I moved our tin bathtub into the sitting room, and then filled the well buckets with lake water and carried them back to the house. I repeated this until the tin tub was full.

I sat Llewellyn up again in her bed. "I've a surprise for you," I said. She looked at me wide-eyed and wrapped her arms around my neck, putting her weight on me as we walked down the stairs to the tin tub in the sitting room. It was terrifying how light she was.

"I bathed yesterday," she said, referring to the sponge and pail Mary had brought up to her.

"This is not a bath. It's a swim."

She dipped her finger in the tub, tasted it. "Lake water," she grinned.

I closed the curtains in the sitting room and helped Llewelyna lift her nightgown over her head. I tried to avert my gaze but her body was so shocking to me I couldn't look away. Her rib-cage and sternum nearly poked through her thin amphibian skin. Her breasts had shrunk and they sagged as she bent to take hold of the tub's edge. Her stomach was a hollow. She nearly lost her balance.

"Help me," she said. I held her as she lifted her legs into the tub. Water splashed the floor as she sank down with a long exhale. She slipped her head beneath the surface; her hair licked the sides of the tub like flames. When she brought her head out of the water, her cheeks were pink and her freckles dark. She inhaled and lay back, her hair draped over the edge of the tub, dripping to the floor.

"Thank you," she said, before closing her eyes to make me disappear again.

I went into the kitchen, restless and unsure of where to go. Above the stove a horsefly was caught between the yellow curtain and the windowpane. I reached for the window latch but stopped when I heard Llewelyna speaking.

"A full set of teeth," she said. I stepped towards the sitting room and stood still in the doorway. I wasn't sure whether she was talking to me or to herself. "I wouldn't let you feed. Gave you goat's milk instead. The most ridiculous-looking baby. Covered in dark hair too. Even in my belly I knew you would be ugly." Llewelyna's eyes remained closed as she spoke. "It was Gwyn's idea to baptize you. She thought that might get the evil out. I just couldn't let go."

Until the mention of Gwyn's name, I had thought this might be one of Llewelyna's stories. "Gwyn?"

Llewelyna's eyes snapped open. She took in the room as if she had been asleep.

I hadn't meant to interrupt her, but I was shocked. As far as I knew, I had never met Llewelyna's twin, not even as a baby. Jacob and I were born in Canada. "Are you okay?" I asked.

She muttered something in Welsh.

"When did I meet Gwyn?"

"You didn't." She raised her foot out of the water and rotated her ankle in big, slow circles; water dripped from her foot and speckled the floor.

"But you just said—"

She turned away from me and towards the light beaming against the curtains. I knew she wanted me to leave. I was breaking another one of her rules. But I couldn't.

"Who, then?" I asked.

"You'll never understand what a mother will do, what sacrifices she'll make." She put her foot back into the water. Her emerald eyes opened and absorbed all the light in the room and directed it at me, through me. "I pray to God you never become a mother. You couldn't bear it." I looked away and hardened myself against her. I could never understand where her cruelty towards me came from. She kept her eyes trained on me. "Did you bite your tongue?" she asked.

"What?"

"When you fell from the tree. Did you bite it? I often bite my tongue when I have a *fit*." The word brimmed with bitterness. "You saw it too, didn't you?"

"Saw what?"

"The end. All those bombs. All that fire. Death, death, death. Your father and brother are never coming back to us."

"Don't be ridiculous." I left the house. I wanted to be far away from her.

"You're just like me, Iris," she said. Her voice was clear, even from outside.

14

I walked down the road, past the cannery, and through the forest to Henry's library. Although I had often briefly spoken with Henry when he visited with Llewelyna, Mary watching us disapprovingly, he rarely came to our house now, and we no longer met like we used to. The business with Taras and Mr. Bell's gun changed something between us, or perhaps it was simply my guilt that kept me from him. The silver coyote watched me from behind a tree as I entered the library. All the books, neat upon their shelves, calmed me and gave me a sense of order. Some spines glistened with gold or silver and others had thick, dark letters. There was a ladder against one wall and a few footstools and chairs in the corners. The wood floors creaked with each step. I turned the corner to the next room and found Ronald Nickel at one of the shelves, holding a book. We spotted each other at the same moment, and both turned to avoid one another's glance, like two negatively charged magnets. Then, as if changing his mind, Ronald turned back to me and nodded. His shoulders had grown full and round and his face had thinned out. I hadn't spoken to him since the summer Jacob was bitten by the lake monster. After a while he had given up on visiting my brother.

I nodded at the book he was holding. "What do you have there?"

"*A Study in Scarlet.* Have you read it?"

"Llewelyna read it to Jacob and me when we were little." The mention of Jacob spread a flush up Ronald's neck. He looked away and fiddled with his earlobe. "It's good." I smiled in an attempt to comfort him.

Henry was sitting at his desk at the back of the library and looking over the ledger. I sat down across from him.

"Has she begun reading again?" he asked.

"Nothing but the *Mabinogion*. I didn't come for books, though."

Ronald approached the desk holding *Sherlock Holmes*. "Some tobacco from the city." He placed a paper bag on the table.

Henry pinched the orange coils between his fingers and smelled them. "Wonderful," he said, and wrote something in the ledger.

I looked at the globe on Henry's desk. As a little girl I would close my eyes and spin the globe. I would hold one finger gently against the surface and wherever my finger pointed when the globe stopped spinning would be where I would one day run away to: Lima, New Caledonia, Bavaria, Saxony, Kirin, Dongola. When I shared these names with Henry he would tell me what he knew of them, if anything, and reminded me the map was old and some of the places no longer existed.

"Hope to see you soon, Iris," Ronald said as he left the library.

"I think he likes you." Henry tucked the tobacco away. A book on his table was open to the title page. In the top corner was a familiar name, handwritten.

"Stewart Brewster," I said. "I've always wanted to ask. Who was he?"

"A friend." Henry looked down at the open book and ran his thumb over the name. "A priest, actually."

"A white man?" I went on with my questions carefully. Henry was closed about his past. These moments of openness were rare.

"He wanted to learn our language."

"Did he teach you English?"

"He taught me to read. Most of the other villages had already taken to his teachings about God. But we were nomadic. He had a hard time finding us."

"I thought your people lived here, in Winteridge."

"This was our winter village. Otherwise we travelled all around the lake and deep into the hills. We rarely stayed in one place for long. Stewart stumbled upon our village one winter. From then on he came every year. He brought me books, and so I taught him what I could."

"And that's why your books have his name in them?"

"That's right. For a time I worked for him at the mission ranch in town, caring for the cattle, harvesting wheat, tobacco." Henry stretched out his arm, palm up. "He gave me this so I would know when to pray." I had seen the brown leather strap before. He wore the wristwatch backwards so its face was at his wrist. The hands of the clock did not move.

"It needs a wind."

"I don't wear it to tell the time."

"You wear it to remember to pray?"

"I wear it to remember."

"Did you kill him? Stewart Brewster?"

Henry was taken aback. "Are you here to examine me, Iris Sparks?"

"I mean, I'm sure he deserved it if you did . . ."

"Would you like to search my house? Am I under arrest?" Henry leaned back into his chair and crossed his arms.

"No, of course not. I'm sorry." I looked down. Shame soured my stomach. I couldn't be certain how much Henry knew about the pistol. Surely he heard it fire, two years ago, when he found Yuri and me in the woods.

"What about the grave in the backyard?" I asked hesitantly.

"So you've been snooping around."

"I've walked past the graveyard a hundred times." I had thought at first there were only four or five graves, each marked by deliberately placed stones and some larger rocks with names written in that same backwards language as the words in the tree fort, but once I learned to recognize the pattern of the stones, I realized the graves were everywhere, countless. They took up an enormous portion of the forest behind Henry's library.

"He died just like everyone else."

"From smallpox?"

"I had taken him fishing one summer. He wanted to know our route. Then he became very ill. My people were settled here for the night, and so I brought him here for help." Henry looked at me warily. "I've told you many of my people's stories, Iris. Perhaps I've told you too much." He tapped the face of the watch against the table. "There are some things you don't get to know. You must remember these stories don't belong to you."

My cheeks burned. I was reminded of when I was a little girl and Henry told me the name of his people in his own language and laughed when I tried to repeat it. "Language limits understanding," he had said then. But he hadn't tried to teach me how to say the word properly.

Henry seemed to be reading my thoughts. I wanted to turn his gaze away. In the centre of his desk was a tin statuette of Saint Francis with a bird on his shoulder and a book under his arm. It was only about two inches tall. I recognized the saint from Llewelyna's collection she kept on her windowsill. I picked it up and considered the saint's sad face.

"She gave that to me. To protect me," Henry said. "I must admit I'd prefer Saint George the dragon slayer."

I smiled, relieved that his tone had lightened. "That's Jacob's favourite." I put the statuette back down. "What do you need protection from?"

"She said I would know when the time came."

I rolled my eyes. "She's gone completely mad."

Henry smiled. "Why do you say that?"

"You know that she thinks our peacock is a saint. Speaks to him. Prays to him. Says he tells her things."

"Who are we to say it isn't true."

"Henry—it isn't true."

"How many people must experience something for that experience to be valid?"

"But it cannot be true."

"It is true to her." Henry began to pack his pipe with tobacco. "And don't her premonitions, the things she sees or says the bird tells her, often come to pass?"

"I don't really know. She doesn't tell me much about them. What about the fits?"

Henry lit the pipe and took two puffs. "I once knew a man who had the same kind of tremblings as your mother. He said he could see things."

"What kinds of things?"

"The unseen. The invisible. The worlds within worlds. When his tremblings came more and more often, like your mother, he became too tired to leave his tent. It was at this time that he became the most wise. He was only half in the world, you see, and half someplace else. Soon he was more in this other place than where his body was. One day, we entered his tent and found him gone. Disappeared."

"You think Llewelyna will disappear?"

"She says the *Mabinogion* keeps her here."

"Have you seen what she's been doing? She's writing over the words in Welsh."

"She's revising. She knows the stories as oral tales, accumulating, growing, and losing layers like a wet stone rolling through sand. It is hard for her to see those stories written down like that, trapped on the page. If you write a story down, then you can preserve it. Keep it. Own it. If you don't write it down, then it is forever free."

"And you think that is keeping her here?"

"Seems to. Maybe she will stop when she gets the story right."

"But I thought the point was that it will never be right if it is written down."

Henry shrugged.

"Has she told you about the world's end?"

He nodded.

"And you believe her?"

He looked back at the ledger and wrote something. "Nothing ends. Only shifts. Takes on a new shape. That new shape can resemble an ending."

"And the baby with teeth. Has she told you about that?"

Henry looked up from the ledger he was scribbling in and seemed almost disappointed that I knew about it. "She's mentioned her."

"Her? Do you know who she is?"

"Sometimes profound guilt or grief can bear skin, grow teeth, take physical shape. I think that is who Neb is."

"That's her name?"

He shrugged again, realizing he'd revealed more than intended, and went back to writing in the ledger. "I believe I've heard her call it that."

"Henry, do you think my father knew about the fits? I mean, before the one in the church?"

"Why do you ask?"

I told him what my father said the day he and Jacob left.

"I know she had her first seizure when she was pregnant."

"Pregnant with me?"

Henry just smiled sadly and went back to writing in the ledger. I pulled the jar with the fish out of my coat pocket and set it on the table to get his attention again. Henry picked the jar up and brought it close to his face. The fish's blue silken fins flowed over its small body.

"Where did you find this?" he asked.

"I've had it for a year or so now." I leaned in close. "Can I tell you something? You have to keep it a secret." As I told Henry the story of the woman who crawled out of the lake, his eyes stayed on the fish. I didn't tell him about what I heard the woman say about the fish being a gift for me, a girl. It seemed unlikely, and I felt silly and presumptuous.

"I saw her," he said.

"You did? We went back to the place where she was and she had vanished. My father—"

"I carried her body into the lake. I told your mother this long ago."

I was speechless.

"The woman was naked on the shore. I didn't want anyone to find her like that. I recognized her. She belonged in the lake. Not buried in the ground."

"How did you know her?"

"She was from my village," he said. "I thought she had died years ago. It was said she had drowned. When I first saw her there I thought she was a ghost." He set the jar down. I kept quiet with the vague hope he would go on.

"Perhaps the fish is her spirit," he said finally.

"Llewelyna thinks the fish is ancient and if one were to eat the fish she would absorb its wisdom."

"Yes, she's told me that story."

"Story?"

"I think it's in the *Mabinogion*." Henry bent forward to peer at the fish through the jar. "And this is not a natural animal. It doesn't eat, does it?"

"No. But the lake monster eats and it isn't a natural animal."

"Naitaka doesn't need to eat."

"What about the birds and squirrels people give it for safe passage?" I said.

"Does God eat his sacrifices?"

"Is Naitaka a god?"

"Many believe Naitaka was once a man who murdered an elder in cold blood."

"I know that story."

He ignored me. "And so the gods cursed him by turning him into a lake serpent."

"So it's a beast, then, not a demon."

"Others believe Naitaka is the spirit of the lake, as old as time."

"What do you think?"

"Aren't we all a little of both? Beast and spirit?"

"Is Naitaka good or evil?"

"Are you good or evil?"

"I'm good."

"According to who?"

"Me, I guess."

Henry grinned. "We're all the heroes of our own stories."

"What about the people who don't see the lake monster?"

"Just because you don't see something doesn't mean it isn't there. But you know that already."

I thought of the deer Henry had taught me to see, the Lake People in the trees, the holy spirit, Azami's kami. "That man we saw in the forest that time, he's Coyote, isn't he?"

"Coyote?"

"The man with the caramels."

"Who? Oh, Frank!" Henry laughed so hard he had to cough to catch his breath. "I'll have to tell him you said that. He'll like that."

I walked back home along the shore of the lake. Some Japanese women were washing laundry at their usual spot in the small bay. The water there was very clean and the pebbles were the perfect size for grinding out dirt. I looked for Azami amongst the group. Soap bubbles foamed the shore. The women smiled as I passed. Azami turned her back to me as she hung a pair of trousers on a drying rack made of branches.

Further down, three of the McCarthy boys stood at the end of the wharf with crates of apples stacked behind them. They were waiting for the lakeboat to arrive. When they heard me walking along the shore, they began to push and shove. Jesse wrestled both of his younger brothers into the lake. Out of the corner of my eye I saw him turn back to see if I was watching.

A ways past the wharf, I walked through some bushes to a rocky beach. It was a secluded spot, forested thickly from behind and surrounded on one side by raspberry bushes and on the other by a curtain of willow branches. The sun's reflection on the lake made it look as though it were glowing from its depths. I took off my picking trousers and placed them on the shore beside the blue fish in its jar. I was still dressed in the long shift I had tucked into my trousers. I found a large rock and clenched it against my chest. It tore at the silk of the shift. The midday stillness had turned the lake to stone and when I took my first step into the water I was almost surprised to see my foot sink beneath the firm surface. I wanted to walk along the bottom of the lake like Yuri and Viktor. I wanted to cleanse myself of disease, bad luck, and guilt. The mossy rocks made it difficult to balance. I let the weight of the rock in my arms anchor each step. The water felt thick and smelled of iron. I was in halfway up my calves. Despite everything Henry had said, I thought if I could only enter the lake, if I could face what terrified me, I would no longer be afraid—a kind of conquest, like Azami had tried to teach me. I didn't want to be like my mother, seeing things that were not there, allowing some invisible realm to take over.

A heron flew above me and its shadow washed over my face. I watched it soar over the lake and shrink into oblivion. Then the familiar taste of lemon filled my mouth, the lake was full of dark holes. I looked down. My feet were in murky water. Something slithered down the insides of my legs, like in my mother's story of the girl and the monster. I dropped the rock. It landed hard on my feet and rolled off. I turned back towards the shore and slipped on the mossy rocks. I knew I had to crawl out but I was too exhausted to fight. I collapsed on the shore and let the waves come over me.

I was walking through a hallway, following the jaguar. There were many doors along the way. Each door was closed to me except one, open just enough for a slice of light to escape.

When I returned to the shore, I was trembling in ankle-deep water. The jaguar had followed me out again. I was growing used to her, this old kami. Although I had no reason to, I had decided she was the spirit of Azami's grandmother, and this nearly comforted me. She licked at my thigh. There was blood all the way down it. I rubbed the blood with a finger and held it up to the sun before washing it away with handfuls of water. In the distance, I saw the crest of the lake monster. I closed my eyes and told myself it was only a wave. It was only the way the sunlight hit the surface of the lake. I would not invent out of shadows.

I limped through the strip of forest and up the driveway to the house. I passed the Wasiks' cabin, where Mary sat outside mending Taras's jacket. "Iris?" she called. I didn't answer. Mary came rushing at me. "Iris, what's happened?" She stood in front of me. "You're bleeding." She dropped down to inspect my swollen foot. Hot blood trickled down my thighs. She lifted my shift above my knees and hurried me up to the house.

I sat on my bed with a wad of rags stuffed into my drawers. I was fifteen years old, and this wasn't the first time I had menstruated, although Mary may have mistaken my astonishment as ignorance. I let her take care of me as though I were a child. I was exhausted and in shock. My hands were shaking. My own experience was muddied by Llewelyna's story about the girl in the pond that birthed the monster.

Mary returned with a basin of warm water. "First you fall from the tree and now this? You need to be more careful, love." Mary clucked as she cleaned the cuts on my feet and knees. When she was done she sat on the bed beside me.

"Is everything all right?" she asked. I looked up at her. I had never noticed how smooth her skin was. She was younger than Llewelyna. "I know it's been hard, with your mother ill and your father and brother away."

I straightened. I had forgotten Llewelyna in the tub.

"She's fine. Don't worry. Yuri heard her hollering and came in to find her stark naked in the sitting room."

I bent my head in shame. "I'm sorry."

"Was it your idea to give her an ice bath?"

"She wanted a swim."

Mary pushed my hair from my face. "Hush." She laid me back into bed. "It's all right. Everything is going to be all right." She placed her palm on my forehead before backing out of my room.

It was dark when I walked through the orchard that night, the peaches aglow like crescent moons. I had forgotten the blue fish on the shore. I crossed the road to the lake and searched the beach. The jar was easy to find. The fish emitted a dim blue light. I sat on the beach with the fish in my hands and watched the *Rosamond* pass by, all lit up and heavy with goods. The water around the boat was stringy with light. Waves lapped against the shore. Once the boat was gone, darkness settled back into the water.

Then there was a splash. I could see movement in the lake further down, coming towards me in a steady pattern. I hid the fish in the folds of my nightgown and stood, ready to run. As the shape got closer I could see it was a man, swimming. His strong arms broke the surface in silvery breaststrokes. I sat back down. I thought the swimmer would pass and I could watch unnoticed, but he stopped in front of me. He shook the water out of his hair and walked carefully on the moss-covered stones and out of the water. It was Yuri, his blond hair incandescent. When he finally saw me sitting on the shore he froze.

"Iris?"

I stood, embarrassed. "I just came to get some fresh air." I was horrified at how much I sounded like Llewelyna. Yuri was bare-chested and dripping wet. He went a little way down the beach, dried off with a towel, and returned wearing his shirt.

"I thought you swam in the mornings," I said.

"I didn't have time this morning."

We sat down and stared off into the water.

"Aren't you afraid?" I asked.

"Afraid? Of what?"

"The dark water. The things in the dark water."

"You mean the monster your mother sees?"

"I see it too."

"My mother says we see only what we want to."

"I don't want to see it but I do."

"Maybe you can teach yourself to un-see," he said.

"Maybe."

It was completely dark now. The moonlit sky reflected on the glassy surface of the lake, making it seem as though we were out in that abyss and not on the cold rocky shore. Somewhere a fish jumped and splashed back into the darkness.

"You know in the ocean there are *real* beasts, sharks and octopus and eels with razor sharp teeth," Yuri said. "These beasts could hurt you, but they usually don't. My mother says she swam in the ocean every day as a girl. She was never harmed by anything other than a piece of broken glass in the sand." He picked up a rock and skipped it along the void before us. "And this is just a lake. Nothing but big fish in there." He passed me a flat, smooth rock and put his arm over mine to show me how to skip it. His skin was shockingly warm and soft. The rock skipped once or twice into oblivion. "Do you want to try?" he asked.

"Try what?"

"Swimming in the dark. It might help."

"I could never."

"There's nothing in there to be afraid of, I promise."

I saw Llewelyna's thin arms and her rib bones sticking out of her chest like the salamanders Jacob and I used to chase in the forest. I thought of her mystery and her devouring sickness. I remembered how I would sneak into her room as a child and spray on her perfume, slip on her shoes, run my sticky hands over her clothes. I would study her gestures until I could copy them perfectly. And now, our likeness terrified me.

"I haven't swum in years," I said.

"You wouldn't have to go in far. Not at first."

I wiggled my toes in my boots. My feet were still swollen and bruised from when I dropped the rock on them. "I'm not ready," I said.

"Well, when you are, let me know. I'll show you it's safe."

We were quiet for a moment. Crickets stirred and gave the lake back its invisible dimensions.

"I think I should be the one, not anyone else," he said.

I knew he meant Viktor. I could feel his gaze against my cheek. I turned to him. All I could see were the whites of his eyes, his crown of hair.

"Sure," I said. I reached for the fish and pulled it out of the folds of my nightdress. It didn't seem to glow as brightly as it did before, but I could easily see its form in the water. "Do you remember this?"

Yuri took hold of the jar and marvelled at the blue fish. "You've had it all this time?"

"Llewelyna says it's an ancient fish. Deathless. She says if you were to eat it you would absorb its wisdom."

"That's madness," Yuri said.

"I know," I said, and tucked the fish back away. "She told me to be careful who I showed it to."

Yuri smiled and looked back out towards the water. There was a rustle behind us.

I stiffened. "Did you hear that?"

"Hear what?"

"Something in the bushes."

"Could be a million things."

"What are you two lovebirds up to?" The amber tip of Viktor's cigarette floated like a comet through the night sky. He sauntered out of the darkness and into the moonlight. He sat down next to me. "Have you recovered from your fall, Your Highness?"

"I'm fine," I said. A carriage rumbled up in the hills somewhere.

"You fell at least ten feet. And then you had that fit, like your mother in church last summer."

"Viktor, stop," Yuri said.

"Has that happened to you before?"

"Viktor, leave her be."

"That's the first time," I lied.

"Father says it's the sign of the devil."

"He doesn't, Iris. Don't listen to him."

"Says we should bring back that priest. The exorcist."

"Piss off, Viktor."

It was difficult to read Viktor's face in the darkness but I knew it wasn't as cold as his voice sounded.

"Calm down, hen. I'm not saying I believe the madman."

On our way back to the house, Viktor turned around and faced me right before we were about to emerge from the forest and onto the dirt road. Without realizing we had stopped, Yuri continued on without us. "I've been meaning to ask you." His hands were warm on my bare arms. He was so close I could smell the tobacco in his breath. My stomach rose to my throat. "Azami and I want to meet again next week in that tree fort." My hate for Azami bubbled like vinegar. "I'm supposed to buy a few things for my father from the Nickels' store." He took my hand, squeezed it. "Would you do me a favour?" His dark eyes shone. "Would you go to the store and purchase them for me?"

"Where are you two?" Yuri called from across the road.

Viktor pulled me into him. "Will you do it?" he whispered into my neck.

I nodded. "Sure."

"You're a doll."

"Iris?" Yuri yelled, his voice nearly tremulous. "Are you okay? I can't see you. Where—"

"We're coming, little hen, we're coming," Viktor called to him.

✿

I was meant to hide the items behind a peach tree in the exact middle of the third row of trees. In a paper bag, I carried a tin of nails, some antiseptic cream, a bottle of thick red syrup, and a roll of twelve ginger lozenges. I set the items in the long grass beneath the tree.

"What are you doing?"

I spun around. Yuri was up in the lower branches of the peach tree beside me. I hadn't noticed the ladder. I stood with my back to the loot. "Nothing."

Yuri made his way down. "What did you put in the grass?"

"Mind your own business."

Yuri attempted to lean around me to see what I had hidden but I moved my body to block him.

"If it's nothing, let me see." He reached into the paper bag and pulled out the bottle of syrup. He inspected it. "This is Father's medicine. Did Viktor put you up to this?"

"I offered. He was busy."

Yuri found the other items and gathered them in his arms. "I don't understand why you're helping him. He doesn't even—"

"It's just a favour. I don't mind."

"Viktor's not your friend, Iris. He's using you."

"That's not true."

"Where is he right now? Why couldn't he get these things himself?"

"He's busy."

"Busy with what?"

I shrugged. Yuri turned towards his house.

"Yuri, please. Just leave it. This has nothing to do with you."

"Nothing to do with me?"

"Please." Bit by bit I could see him relenting. "Put the things back."

Yuri placed the items back under the tree. "Don't say I never warned you."

"Don't tell anyone. You must promise."

"Fine. But not for his sake." Yuri walked through the peach rows towards his house, kicking the long grass.

15

The next winter Llewelyna's condition worsened. Soon she hardly ever got out of bed and rarely ate the scant meals Mary prepared. Some days she only spoke in Welsh. Other days her body twitched uncontrollably. It wasn't like during a seizure. This twitching was isolated to only certain body parts: her hands would tremble as if from cold, or her head would jerk back and forth, *no, no, no*. Her arms and legs were covered with red splotches, and the rash spread daily. A patch of what appeared to be pimples sprouted on her hip and spread up her back. The bumps pussed horribly and became infected.

After a particularly cold night, I thought I had lost Llewelyna. When I entered her room in the morning, her blankets were on the floor. Her skin was blue and her teeth chattered. She told me she was hot; her forehead was wet but her skin was ice cold. Mary and I boiled water in all the pots we could find and forced Llewelyna kicking and screaming into the bath.

The pickers continued to work despite the cold. They wrapped their hands in cloth and their breath rose into the bare trees like spirits. To keep the men busy, Taras had them build a fence around the property and clear out rotten fruit and dead branches.

The frost had come upon us so quickly that year, my mother's flower garden froze mid-bloom. The purple asters were stiff as spurs and the sunflowers glittered with ice. The marigolds flaked off in gold coins. Mary's vegetable garden also froze. We chipped the carrots out of the solid earth and let the late tomatoes sit in a bowl of water before we sliced or canned them.

One morning I found a dead cat on our porch. Its mouth was open and its claws stretched out as if it were about to pounce. Then three horses died at the Ebers' ranch. The ground was solid and so they had to wait until spring to bury the beasts. I wondered how Henry's people survived the cold back when Winteridge was their winter village.

For the very first time, the lake froze over. Months went by without any news from Jacob or my father because the lakeboats that brought our letters and our food, and delivered our goods, could no longer run. We were left to live off our scarce pantries. After a while, men were hired by the lakeboat company to break up the ice using saws and axes. Taras, Yuri, Viktor, and the other pickers joined the crew. It was dangerous work and several men fell through the ice. One died. Yuri said he could hear the hollow thud of the man punching and kicking the ice from below.

When the lakeboats could finally run again, Taras received a letter my father had sent months prior. It said to lay off the workers for the winter. Most of the Japanese bachelors, using the money they had made that season, went back to Japan to find wives they would bring back with them in the spring. Other men found work on ranches in the valley. Only the Wasiks stayed on our orchard, but soon even Viktor and Yuri left for Vernon to work as ranch hands. Taras tinkered with various projects around the property and Mary tended to Llewelyna full-time. I busied myself with canning the cellared peaches. Mary taught me how and I enjoyed the work. Steam warmed the kitchen. We survived off those peach preserves. I traded them with neighbours for potatoes, rice, or salted pork and beef.

Later that winter I received word that Jacob and my father were coming home in the spring. Inside the envelope was a sealed letter for Llewelyna. She often received mail from my father now. Usually she put the letter in her lap and waited until I left the room. I assumed she read them after I left. This time she opened the drawer by her bed and slipped the envelope in atop a pile of other unopened envelopes.

"You're not going to read it?"

"Bring me some water, would you?" she said, twirling one of Saint Francis's feathers between her fingers. The bird seemed to be losing more feathers than usual. His chest feathers were patchy; he had become worn and ravaged alongside Llewelyna.

"Have you read any of them?" I asked.

She smiled. "Please?"

I poured some water from the basin into her glass and handed it to her. "You were wrong. They're coming home," I said.

She took a drink and grimaced. "What is this? It's bitter."

I went to the basin and poured myself a glass. "It tastes fine."

She put the glass on her bedside table. "Have Mary get me some water."

"Did you hear me?"

"Her water is sweet. I'm not sure but—"

"Llewelyna. They're coming home."

"Who?"

"Father and Jacob. They'll be here in the spring."

Her mouth twitched in a smile she tried to hide.

"They're coming for my debut," I said.

"Debut?"

"I'll be sixteen in July."

She looked at me as if for the first time. "So you are."

A month or so later, I was waxing the floor in Llewelyna's room and took a sip from her water glass. I wouldn't usually have done such a thing, but the basin in her room was empty and my throat was parched. I spat the water back into her glass. It *did* taste sweet. That night I watched Mary in the kitchen from the darkness of the sitting room. She was preparing to bring up the small bowl of soup Llewelyna would sip and probably vomit up later if she managed to get any of it down in the first place. Mary looked over her shoulder before reaching up into the top cupboard for the yellow biscuit tin that had once held Saint Francis. As far as I knew, the tin contained only the seeds Llewelyna harvested from her garden. I watched Mary withdraw a glass bottle from the tin. I recognized the white pills the doctor had prescribed that first visit, so long ago now. Mary dropped a pill in Llewelyna's glass of water before she put everything back in its place.

She brought the medicine water to Llewelyna three times a day. I didn't confront her; instead, I switched each glass Mary brought with a glass of sugar water. Over the next few weeks Llewelyna improved. Her terrible rash cleared and she began to eat.

꿏

That spring, despite Llewelyna's curses and premonitions, my father and Jacob returned to Winteridge on the *Rosamond*. It was dawn and the air was still crisp with the memory of winter. The lakeboat came around the bend and a thick tongue of fog lolled out behind it. There was pink in the staunch siren's cheeks. Her eyes were closed in sleep. I stood on the wharf shivering in my father's old wool coat. Yuri and Viktor had accompanied me to the wharf to carry my father's and Jacob's luggage. They had arrived from Vernon only the week before. The hard winter work had thinned them out. Yuri had lost his childish softness. He was solid and strapping. Viktor's muscles were more sinewy; his limbs seemed longer. He looked taller.

The passengers disembarked in the fog and seemed to appear out of nothing. Jacob walked down the wharf with his shoulders back; the limp in his step was almost indistinguishable. He was fifteen and taller than my father now. He wore round wire-rimmed spectacles. His red hair no longer looked feminine and awkward like a wig. He had grown into it, learned a way to comb it down and tame it to make it his rather than something Llewelyna had thrust upon him. He still looked a lot like her but in a way that wasn't so imposed. I breathed into my hands to warm them. I wondered if I had changed. It had been nearly two years since I had seen my father and brother.

My father's waxed moustache was stiff and his cheeks pink from the cold. When he embraced me I smelled the tea tree oil he rubbed behind his ears. "Where's your mother?" he asked.

"At home," I said. Although Llewelyna had improved since I had begun switching out the water glasses, she still kept to her bed most days.

"Oh?" His face changed. I realized he might not know a thing about her decline. Judging by the stack of unopened envelopes next to Llewelyna's bed, she hadn't written to him in a while.

"Hello, Iris," Jacob said and bowed slightly. His formal demeanour stunned me and made me aware of my hollow cheeks and unclean hair. I pulled Llewelyna's scarf up higher on my neck.

"She won't believe how you've grown," I said. But Jacob had already looked on past me to Yuri. They exchanged glances, as if to measure one another up. Before Jacob went off to school, Yuri was one of the only people he could stand to be around. Some evenings they sat in silence for hours on the back porch and played chess or cribbage.

"Hi, Jacob," Yuri said.

"Yuri. Viktor. Nice to see you both." The porters dropped the luggage off near us. Jacob looked down at his trunk and then up at Yuri. He straightened, stepped past the trunk, and walked down the wharf. Yuri watched him go before he reached down to lift the trunk.

On our walk back to the house my father kept an arm around me. He pulled me close and kissed my head. I wanted to prepare him for Llewelyna but didn't know how. "We've missed you," was all I could muster.

The house was cool and quiet when we arrived. Mary and I had cleaned it top to bottom. We had sparked fresh fires in the sitting room and Jacob's room, and in the master bedroom where I imagined my father would sleep alone. The heat and dusting hadn't shaken the chill.

My father took a breath and went up to see Llewelyna.

"Would you like some tea?" I asked Jacob.

"Don't we employ Mary to do that sort of thing?" Jacob's voice was deep and low like my father's and had acquired a lilt, a piece of England he carried with him.

"She helps me with Llewelyna, but she isn't a maid. This isn't London." In fact Mary helped me around the house much more than she ought to and much more than I cared to admit. She washed our clothes, bought our groceries, and often cooked and cleaned. I had asked her to stay home the day Jacob and my father arrived.

"I'll have mine with lemon," Jacob said.

"Lemon? We don't have any lemon."

"Cream is fine, then."

I brought the tea to the table and sat down across from this stiff new stranger. Jacob fidgeted with his handkerchief and cuflinks—gestures I didn't recognize. The glare from the window on the lens of his new spectacles made it impossible to tell where he was looking.

"What's the matter with Mother?"

"Llewelyna," I corrected him.

"It's perverse to call our own mother by her Christian name," he said, and I could hear our grandmother's shrill voice echo inside him.

"She hasn't been herself since you left."

"I don't understand. The doctor said she just needed a little rest."

"And she's been resting."

Jacob shook his head and poured cream into his tea.

"How is school?" I asked.

"I enjoy it."

"Have you made many friends?"

"A slew. In fact, I'm rather impatient to return." He sipped his tea.

We sat in silence until Father came down the stairs. He looked sullen and worn. I poured him a cup of tea.

"Was she awake?" I asked.

"She woke for a moment." He sat down with us and I passed him the teacup and saucer.

"It's quite early still," I said. It was the blueberry of dawn. Birds had only just begun to sing in the peach trees.

"How long has she been like this?" my father asked.

I opened my mouth to speak but Jacob spoke for me. "Since we left, can you imagine?" I looked down into my tea.

"But it's been nearly two years," my father said. "Why didn't you tell me?"

The rare letters I sent my father were brief and vague; anything more would have been unfaithful to Llewelyna. I was still her confidante. And to betray her illness would be to betray my own. Her recovery was central to my own health. I hoped desperately she could beat whatever had come upon her. In fact, I half expected that with the arrival of my brother and father, she would be sitting at the table with a spread of breakfast awaiting us as she had done in the past, allowing only me to see her at her worst.

"There are good days," I said, raising my head to look at him. This was true. Some days Mary, Llewelyna, and I sat at the kitchen table and played bridge while Saint Francis pecked at crumbs on the floor. Before, when she could still walk, Yuri and I supported her between us and took her for walks through the orchard or to the lake. Once, in spring, I carried a kitchen chair into the garden so Llewelyna could tell me how to plant the geranium seeds I had purchased at the Nickels' store. I even got her to paint a couple of times. But most days she stayed in bed with the *Mabinogion*, mumbling to Saint Francis in Welsh, or slept. "She's getting better," I said.

"And the doctor, what does he say about it?"

"She won't see a doctor."

"Won't see a doctor," my father resounded, leaning back in his chair. "She could be dying and she wouldn't see a doctor. You call Dr. Cross without telling her. Don't give her the choice."

"Mary has been helping me care for her. We bathe her, feed her, what else can we do?"

He started at that, as if remembering something. "Where is Mary? I need to speak to her."

"I told her to stay home today. I thought we'd appreciate some privacy."

"I am disappointed in you two. You've neglected her. She's shrivelling away up there."

"Neglected her?" I stood as I said this. "I didn't run from her. I didn't—"

"Iris," my father said, lowering his voice so I would also. "I apologize." He waved me to sit back down. "You're right. I'll call Dr. Cross. I'll deal with this. Please, sit down." I did. "I'm home now. She isn't your burden." I didn't like the way he spoke of her as a chore, a weight. "I really must find Mary." My father left the house and stomped through the grass to the Wasiks' cottage.

"Jacob?" asked a raspy voice from the top of the stairs. I scrambled to my feet and walked Llewelyna down the last flight. She had rouged her cheeks, spun her hair up with her ivory pin, and put on her blue silk dress. It sagged at her chest and revealed her bony sternum. "This can't be my boy Jacob." She brought her hand to his cheek. Jacob stood at attention, stiff and speechless as if afraid of being slapped. She moved his spectacles up and down his nose, and then jiggled them. "How sharp you look. How smart." I found a certain satisfaction in seeing Jacob struck dumb by her presence. She fell on him with her full weight and hugged him. He nearly toppled over.

When my father came back inside, Llewelyna was wearing Jacob's spectacles and attempting to read out loud from the newspaper. We laughed at the ridiculous things she pretended it said. I caught my father looking at her in that old way.

Mary and I were mystified by Llewelyna's recovery, but I had seen her do this in the past. When I was little we would live in shambles while my father was away, cocooned until the night before he was due to arrive. Then Llewelyna would burst out in familiar magnificence. She would clean, cook, launder, and be dressed like a duchess by the time his lakeboat docked.

Things returned to normal for a few weeks. I continued to switch out Llewelyna's water glasses whenever I could. My father was the one slipping the pills in now, and he was much more secretive about it than Mary. Jacob obsessed over his schoolwork and bent over his books in my father's airless study. Although the summer was still young and the lake ice cold, Yuri and Viktor had been swimming all spring. I invited Jacob down to the beach with us, but he refused.

After I timed Yuri's and Viktor's laps, we sat on the wharf and passed around a customary cigarette. "Are you going to the festival tonight?" Viktor asked. Every year the McCarthys threw a solstice celebration on their orchard. There were often games during the day for the children, and a bonfire, music, and dancing for the adults at night. I hadn't gone for years, having long outgrown the children's games but been too young for the night festivities.

"If I can convince Jacob to come," I said.

"He's a real stick in the sand these days, isn't he?" Viktor said.

"He hasn't said more than two words to me since he's been home," Yuri said.

"A lover's quarrel?" Viktor teased. "I hear he's quite the kisser."

"What's that?" I said.

"Shut up, Viktor."

"Calm down, hen. Everyone knows he—"

"Viktor."

"He what?" I asked.

"Oh, nothing."

Later that night Viktor and Yuri arrived on our porch. "Evening, Mr. Sparks," Viktor said. He looked sharp in a freshly starched collared shirt. His black hair was oiled to one side. Yuri smiled at me. His hair was slicked back in the same way. He was a pale reflection of Viktor. "We're here to escort Iris to the festival, if she would still like to join us, that is. And Jacob, of course, if he likes." Jacob heard the conversation from the sitting room and lowered his book.

"Sounds like a wonderful idea," my father said. "You are due for a little fun, Jacob. Get your head out of that book. What do you say?"

"I'd really rather stay put."

"No, no. Come now, put that nonsense down," my father said.

"Fine," he said, and I was surprised to see Jacob close his book. "But I won't take part in any of those ridiculous pagan games."

"Bobbing for apples is hardly pagan," my father said.

"It's too late in the day for any of that," Viktor said.

"I'm not dancing either."

My father gave Viktor a wink. "You're only afraid you might enjoy yourself."

Viktor gave me his arm and held me back to let Jacob and Yuri walk ahead of us. He pulled a flask from his pocket and took a drink before he offered it to me.

Lanterns in the trees guided us towards a bonfire at the centre of the McCarthys' orchard. My belly was warm from the whisky and my head floated, making the lit-up orchard dreamy and surreal. Viktor and I ducked beneath boughs and hopped over logs, giggling like children. He plucked an apple and handed it to me. I took a bite. The flesh was young and sour but I swallowed anyways. There were some people at the festival I had never seen. While most were work hands from the surrounding orchards, some were strangers from other villages on the lake. I scanned the crowd for Azami, but couldn't find her or any of the Japanese pickers from the Kobas' orchard.

"Is Azami coming?" I whispered to Viktor.

"She's done with me," he said.

"Really—I mean, don't say that."

"It's true. Her father wants her to marry her second cousin. He's here from Japan."

"And she said yes?"

"Not yet. But their families are ten steps ahead." Viktor took another swig from the flask. Some musicians took up instruments near the fire. One of them was Ronald Nickel. He nearly dropped his fiddle when he saw Jacob enter the glow of the fire. Jacob kept his head down and didn't acknowledge him. Ronald caught me looking at him and smiled, placed the fiddle back under his chin, and joined in with the song. Some of the white pickers from our orchard sat at a table playing cards and drinking. One called out to Viktor and he went to join them.

I sat with Jacob and Yuri on a log by the fire. The music was so loud there was no silence to fill. Some couples began to dance in the clearing. A girl I recognized from church sat alone on the other side of the fire. She had long curly blond hair and a warm-looking face. I elbowed Jacob. "Go ask her to dance."

"I said no dancing."

"Yuri." I reached across Jacob and poked Yuri's shoulder. "Ask that pretty girl to dance."

"I don't like dancing either."

"Go on, please."

Yuri stood nervously and patted down his pants and shirt. He walked around the fire and sat by the girl. He said something that made her laugh. Jacob and I watched the two of them dance. Viktor came out of the crowd and offered me his hand. I took it and he launched me up and pulled me into him. We danced too fast to the music. Every time we spun Viktor lifted me off my feet. He fed me more whisky and everything became fluid and loose. I stared at

Viktor's face while the rest of the world spun around it. I couldn't
stop laughing. We danced until we were dizzy and stumbling. The
colours from the fire made everyone look yellow. It was only when
we slowed down that I realized we were the only ones still dancing:
the centre of attention. Yuri tapped me on the shoulder.

"Trying to cut in, hen?" Viktor said. "Don't worry, I'm not
going to steal your girl." Yuri rolled his eyes. Viktor offered him
the flask and he pushed it away.

"We're going to leave now, Iris," Yuri said. "Let me walk
you home."

"But we've only begun!" Viktor said, his eyes wide and bright.
His hand fell down my waist to my hip and he pulled me away
from Yuri. Yuri grabbed my hand.

"Viktor, let her go." Yuri glared at Viktor with a ferocity I
didn't think his gentle face could muster.

"All right, all right, hen. Let's go, Your Highness." Viktor didn't
take his hand from my hip, forcing Yuri to let go of my hand.

"Where's Jacob?" I asked. Then I saw him, talking with Ronald
near the flickering fire. I hadn't seen my brother smile so openly
since he had been home. He saw that we were leaving, left Ronald
with a brief embrace, and followed us.

On our way home Jacob and Yuri walked steadily ahead while
Viktor and I sang into the trees, arm in arm and stumbling. He was
trying to teach me an old Ukrainian song, and my attempts made
us both hysterical. Right before we got to the edge of the orchard,
Viktor pulled me down into the long grass between the trees. I fell
on top of him. Yuri and Jacob didn't notice our absence and kept
on walking. Viktor brought his finger to his lips for me to be silent.
I covered my mouth with a hand to keep from laughing out. Then
Viktor's eyes become serious. He ran his knuckles along my cheek
and down my neck. His other hand lowered further and further

down my back. He craned his neck and pulled me into him hard. We kissed.

"Iris? Viktor?" Yuri called. He and Jacob had backtracked through the orchard. Viktor stood and helped me up.

Yuri looked at me as though I had struck him. "What are you doing?" he asked.

"We fell," Viktor said, grinning. He let go of my hand.

The next morning my family sat at the kitchen table eating breakfast. I looked out the window for Viktor. Sunlight came through the trees in patches. The disembodied arms and heads of the pickers popped out through the tops of trees on the far side of the orchard.

"You seem in high spirits, Iris," Llewelyna said, peering at me from across the table. I realized then I was smiling. I looked down at my eggs to hide my hot face. She grinned. "You have the look of Blodeuwedd about you."

"Blodeuwedd?" I asked.

"Flower face. I never told you the story of Blodeuwedd?"

I shook my head.

She put down her fork and folded her hands together. "Lleu Llaw Gyffes was cursed to never marry a human wife, and so he had magicians make him a wife from broom, oak, and meadowsweet blossom. They named her Blodeuwedd and she was the fairest and most beautiful maiden anyone had ever laid eyes on. Very soon after she was created, she fell in love with another man, and this love made her even more beautiful than before. When her husband found out about her new romance, he had the magicians change her into the form of an owl, for the owl is hated by all other birds. And that's why, in Welsh, Blodeuwedd is the ancient name for owl."

My father was smiling at her. He was about to say something when there was a knock at the door. It was Ronald Nickel.

"Pardon me, sir," Ronald said, taking off his flat cap. He

passed my father an envelope. "Says it's urgent so I thought I better bring it by." He looked past my father and smiled at Jacob.

"Thank you, Ronald. I appreciate it." My father closed the door and brought the envelope to the table to open it. We watched silently as he read. His expression was difficult to discern.

"What is it, Noah?" Llewelyna asked. He didn't respond. "Who is it from?"

"My mother," he said finally.

"What does it say?" asked Jacob.

"My father has died."

My grandfather had always been too busy to visit us. My father had apparently taken me to England to meet him when I was hardly two years old, but I didn't remember a thing. My father always insisted I had memories I did not: "He walked you around the pond of the estate. You pointed at the ducks. You loved to play with his walking cane." He was incredulous at my inability to recall such moments. "He took you to the fair, you must remember the fair. There was a giraffe." I imagined my grandfather as a stocky man with a large grey beard. There was a painting of him in my father's study. I later discovered this was a painting not of my grandfather but of King Edward VII.

The added weight to the event of my estranged grandfather's death was one that only Llewelyna understood at first. Her head dropped to her hands. A strand of red hair dipped into her egg yolk. My father picked the letter back up, more to hide his face from her than to reread it.

"She wants me to return, to help with the funeral. She's asked me to manage the Rhondda mine."

"But what about your brother? Isn't he—"

"John already has a lot on his plate. He has been managing the London mine on his own for years now."

"You've only just arrived. Surely she—"

"My father has died, Llew." He reached for her hand but it slipped beneath the table. "You could go home to Wales, visit your sister." Llewelyna stood and went upstairs. My father followed her.

"Did you love him?" I asked Jacob once they were safely upstairs.

Jacob jolted. "Love who?" he said, defensive.

"Our grandfather."

He looked down and chipped at an undercooked potato with his fork. "I hardly knew him." He jerked his head in that strange way I had seen him do before.

"But when you visited Grandmother, wasn't he there?"

"He didn't like me," Jacob whispered.

"Father seems to love him."

"Father respects him, that's all." He scraped his last bits of egg and potato onto his fork.

That evening, Jacob, Yuri, and I played cribbage on the front porch and secretly smoked a package of old cigarettes I had found in Llewelyna's wardrobe. She and my father were at the McCarthys' for the night. I looked for Viktor over Jacob's and Yuri's heads and found him drinking with some of the other pickers. There was no work done on the Sabbath. Viktor's eyes met mine and he winked at me. My stomach was full of flapping birds. We had made plans to meet down by the lake that night after dark.

Jacob kept saying, "It's your turn, flower face," and asked, obnoxious as ever, why I wore such a stupid smile.

We weren't expecting the McCarthys' carriage to pull into our drive. Their house was only a couple of miles away and Llewelyna had preferred to walk. We scrambled to stub out our cigarettes and toss them into the bushes. I hid the package in the folds of my dress. My father helped Llewelyna down from the carriage. Her neck was limp and she couldn't carry her own weight. She looked like a drunkard. Yuri and I ran to them. Yuri put one of Llewelyna's arms over his shoulder and helped my father bring her to the house.

"She's had a terrible fit," my father said between gritted teeth, his eyes stern and shining with a holy kind of anger.

Later that week Dr. Cross arrived from the city to examine Llewelyna. I could hear her sobbing even while I was downstairs with Mary preparing dinner.

"I feel so terrible," Mary rambled nervously as she shelled peas. "I don't understand. She was doing so well. The medicine, it must not—"

"She's not taking medicine," I confided.

"Well, I've gone and said it now. Your father didn't want you or Llewelyna to know."

"No, you don't understand. I've switched it."

"What do you mean?"

I explained how I had been switching the medicine for sugar water and how much better she became after I started doing so.

Mary froze. "Oh love, what have you done?"

I didn't see Llewelyna until my birthday dinner the next day. It was a warm evening so we ate on the front porch. My father carried Llewelyna out of the house wrapped in blankets and sat her up in a chair. Her eyes were wide and blank. She gazed around like a tamed bird.

I had tried to persuade my father not to make a fuss for my birthday, but he wouldn't hear it. He said he had intended to throw a much larger party for my debut, an event usually celebrated in a ballroom with hundreds of young men to look me up and down as if I were a new suit they'd like to try on. He had meant to decorate the orchard and invite the Nickels and the McCarthys, *and* the Kobas, he added purposefully, but with Llewelyna's condition the way it was, it was best to keep the festivities intimate. I convinced him to invite the Wasiks. All but Taras, who said he was much too busy with the orchard, joined my family for dinner that evening.

After we ate Mary's vanilla cake I opened the presents gathered at one side of the table like an offering. Yuri gave me a hummingbird carved out of wood. It was delicate and hung on a long string so I could tie it to the ceiling of my room. He had expertly painted the bird blue and green and given it golden eyes. Viktor gave me some chocolates that had already melted to the bottom of the paper bag. My father handed me a parcel from my grandmother. Inside, wrapped in tissue paper, was a pale green dress. Father made me stand and hold it to my chest. Lace was sewn all along the hem and bust. It had short sleeves and a high collar.

"For your London debut. The real one," my father said.

"My what?"

"Your grandmother has paid for you to return with Jacob to London, so she can throw you a proper debut."

"I won't," I said simply. Llewelyna had a slight smile on her face. "I don't know anyone there."

"That's the point. To meet people."

"I don't want to meet people. There are people here I already know."

Mary stared down at her lap and Yuri and Viktor looked off into the orchard, obviously uncomfortable with our arguing.

"I mean a husband, Iris." My father whispered, as if doing so would prevent the present company from overhearing. "A husband suitable to your stature."

"I won't go to England."

"We'll talk about that later. Let's not ruin the party." My father smiled to the guests. I folded the dress and put it back in the box.

"Here, Iris." Jacob handed me a parcel wrapped in brown paper and tied with a yellow ribbon. Inside was a rectangular black box with nickel fittings and leather coverings.

"What is it?" I asked.

"A camera, silly," Jacob said.

"But it's so small."

"It's the newest of its kind, a Kodak Brownie."

My father took the camera from me and turned it to show me a place at the bottom where it had been engraved. He handed it back so I could read it for myself. *Beauty is in the eye*, it said, followed by an ellipsis, as if this line was easily completed. Although I knew the saying "Beauty is in the eye of the beholder," I was confused with my mother's own sense while painting—*without your eyes you're nothing but a husk.*

"Thank you," I said finally.

The next day I went to take a picture of a robin perched in the walnut tree. By the time I held the camera down to my chest, focused, and opened and closed the shutter, the bird was gone. Later I walked down through the birch forest to photograph the glittering lake. Just as I opened the shutter there was a splash. The lake monster's green back crested. I closed the shutter too slowly. From what Jacob had told me about using the camera, I knew the image would be blurry and indeterminate. I aimed the camera again and waited. The lake monster surfaced, its long neck stretched out of the water and its horse-shaped head turned to look at me. I took the photograph.

Later we were in the sitting room drinking tea. Llewelyna sat on the faded yellow chesterfield in a gown much too large for her now. She held a glass of water at her chest in both hands. I couldn't stop watching her. She looked sedated and sad. Banished from the house by my father, Saint Francis paced along the porch outside, forever Llewelyna's sentinel. His feet rasped against the wood. He pecked at the window.

"Have you taken any photographs yet?" my father asked, to break the charged silence.

"A few."

"In London," Jacob said, "you could walk across the street and have the film developed in a couple of days. Out here it'll take months." Jacob had taken up the habit of pointing out the downfalls of living in Winteridge in comparison to London. Although tiresome, I found his efforts endearing. He seemed to want me to come back with him.

"I have proof now," I said to him.

"Proof?"

"I took a photograph."

"A photograph of what?"

I was hesitant to pronounce the name of the creature we hadn't mentioned in so long. It had become unspeakable. "Naitaka," I whispered, carefully watching Llewelyna. She didn't even flinch.

"Of what?" my father said.

"The addanc," I said to get Llewelyna's attention. She still didn't acknowledge the name.

"She's talking about that bloody lake monster," Jacob said. "You're unbelievable, Iris. You really are."

"It wasn't on purpose. I was photographing the lake and when I—"

"Stop." Jacob looked at me with such urgency it conjured me speechless. He angled his head and fidgeted with his ear.

"Aren't you much too old for that sort of thing," my father said in a voice he reserved for precisely this brand of foolishness.

"I cannot wait to leave this dreadful place," Jacob said. "We should have never returned." He stood and walked to the window. My father and I watched him uneasily.

"But what about Jacob's leg? That wound proved . . ."

My father wiped some invisible crumbs from his lap. "Iris, his leg was injured by something in the water. It could have been a cut anchor, a splintered piece of wood. It could have been anything."

"But I saw it. Jacob, you saw—"

"I don't know what I saw," Jacob said, still facing the window.

"You did. I know you did. Just try to remember."

"We were children."

"You've been in this house too long. This town too long. Your mother's stories have gotten to you."

"Don't speak of her as if she's not here," I said. We turned to Llewelyna, who sat oblivious as a fish at her end of the chester-field. "What have you done to her?"

"The doctor said there would be side effects. She might be out of sorts for a little while."

"Out of sorts? She's tranquilized." I watched her carefully. "Llewelyna?" She didn't respond. "Llewelyna?"

She looked up. "Could you pass the sugar?" she asked Jacob.

Later I caught my father crushing up the pills and putting them in her water glass. "It's inhumane," I said, standing behind him. He froze. "What you're doing. It's not right. Sneaking it into her water like that."

"You know it's the only way she'll take the bromide."

"Hiding it from her, and from me. I know you had Mary doing it for you before."

He turned to me. "She told you?"

"She didn't have to." I told my father what I had done. I tried to explain to him the extent of her illness before—the rash, the tremors, the nausea and vomiting—and how much better she was after being off the medicine. "The seizures are minor compared to what the bromide did to her."

He looked down into the glass as he stirred in the powder. "You're a doctor now, are you?"

I watched him ascend the stairs as I stood, furious, in the kitchen. Then, after a little while, I ran up and burst into Llewelyna's bedroom. "He's poisoning you," I said.

Llewelyna started, water spilling from the glass and onto her lap.

"Iris, get out," my father said. But he didn't interrupt me as I went on to tell Llewelyna everything.

"My dear, it's for your own good," my father said when I was done. He sat on the edge of her bed. Llewelyna's face had dropped. She turned away from him. He brushed her hair out of her face with his hand. "Lew, sweetheart?"

She slapped his hand away. "Do you think I'm a child, Noah? An animal?"

"The doctor—"

"Get out," she said. "Both of you."

The next morning while Jacob and I sat at the table eating breakfast, we could hear Llewelyna and my father arguing in her room two floors above. My father calmly urged her to come with him to London and go to some kind of specialized hospital for epileptics. Llewelyna kept telling him she wasn't epileptic. That it wasn't some kind of illness. The falls were a gift. She saw things, she said. Prophecies. And to take them away would cost her her soul, would surely kill her. My father was livid. I could tell because his voice became quieter and quieter, until we could no longer hear him. He was never one to shout when truly upset. If made angry enough, he quit speaking entirely.

"Will you come back with us?" Jacob asked me, when we could no longer eavesdrop.

"No," I said.

"You'll never leave here if you don't find a husband."

"Who says I wish to leave?"

"Don't you?"

"No."

"Who will you marry?"

I shrugged. Outside, Viktor unloaded peach boxes from the horse cart. I could see the shape of his muscles through his thin shirt.

"Iris, you can't marry a work hand," he said. I ignored him and spread some peach jelly on my bread. "And you won't inherit the orchard either."

I looked up. "I'm the eldest."

"You're a woman."

"But you don't even want it."

"I'll sell it. It may be worth something someday. You need to look out for yourself. I don't want to have to take care of you. Cousin Peter, he's a bit older, but he is the heir to—"

I let my fork drop to my plate with a clang. "I'm not going to England, Jacob, and that's final."

Jacob shrugged. "Viktor's a flirt."

"What?"

"I saw you at the festival, falling all over him like a hussy. Everyone watching. You need to be more careful. You'll cause a scandal."

I scraped my chair back and left Jacob with the dishes on the table.

The next week, while Jacob and my father packed their trunks and prepared to leave, Llewelyna stayed in her room. My father had asked feebly if I would come along, but Llewelyna had worn him down and he didn't push the issue once I refused him again. He knew I had to stay with her.

As Yuri and Viktor loaded the trunks onto the *Rosamond*, I hugged my father and Jacob goodbye. The wooden siren had wide-open eyes painted atop her lids. She appeared foreboding and afraid. It was late afternoon and there were a number of people on the wharf, waiting to board or load and unload goods. Above the hustle and bustle there came a shrill call from the forest behind. Everyone turned to look. To our collective horror, tripping over roots and rocks and dressed in only her pink robe, Llewelyna thrashed through the bushes towards us. With every step, her bare white legs flashed out the slip in her robe. None of us wanted to watch and many of those on the wharf looked away, as if there was something more interesting out in the distance, at the centre of the lake.

"Noah, please," she sobbed, finally performing the hysterics I had wanted from her before. She could hardly speak. There were scratches all over her arms and a tear in her robe. Her bare feet were dirty. Jacob took a few steps away as if being a little more distant allowed him the perspective to watch his family with the judgment of an outsider. When Llewelyna reached my father she fell to her knees and whispered, but it was useless in that quiet. Everyone could hear.

"I told you I . . ." She had to catch her breath. "And our son. I saw it. Before my very eyes, I swear to you. It's the end of everything."

Jacob bowed his head and took off his hat as if he had just realized he was in a church or graveyard. My father squatted down to her level. There were tears at the insides of his eyes. He took Llewelyna's head in his hands. "I believe you," he said. "I do. I believe that you have seen these things. But you understand I must go." They stared at one another for a long moment, as if the rest of the gaping world had fallen away. Tears streamed down

Llewelyna's face. "I must," he said again. He kissed her and stood, wiping his face with his handkerchief. He placed his hand on Jacob's head, ruffled his red hair as he would when Jacob was a boy, and they walked towards the *Rosamond*.

I helped Llewelyna up. Even heavy with despair, she weighed nothing at all.

16

A few weeks after my father and Jacob left for England, Yuri invited me to take a walk with him to the lake. We sat on a grey quilt on the shore, close to where Llewelyna and I had left the woman who had crawled out of the lake. Apples covered the beach. A crate had tipped over the edge of a lakeboat the day before and the current had carried the apples gently to the shore. They were still fresh and hardly bruised. Yuri polished us a few and gathered them in the tails of his shirt. We ate them, the juice dripping down our chins.

"Look there," Yuri whispered. He pointed down the shore behind me. Two whitetail deer bowed to lap up the lake, a fawn and doe. The speckles on the fawn's back glowed in the long shadows of the trees. Its spindly legs nearly buckled beneath it. At Yuri's voice, the deer spun towards us: ears wide and long and glowing pink in the light of the setting sun. We stayed still until the deer turned, cautiously, back towards the lake and drank. Yuri raised a hand to my back. His callused fingers snagged the lace of my collar. I pretended not to feel a thing.

When the sky went black we lay down on the blanket and gazed up at the stars. I kept looking around to see if Viktor was going to leap out of the bushes to scare us as he usually did. I touched my lips at the memory of his body pressed against mine as we danced. We had made several attempts to meet in secret, but something

always interrupted our plans. Before my birthday we had planned
to meet at the cliffs, and I had arrived at the agreed-upon time and
waited there for hours. When I realized he wasn't going to come,
the thrill of our meeting cooled and was quickly replaced by my
terror of the invisible world around me. I felt my way back home
through the blue darkness with only the burning heads of balsamroots to guide me. I had expected Viktor to come find me and apologize with some excuse, as he usually did, but weeks had gone by
without my hearing from him. Like a fool, I thought that agreeing
to meet Yuri might make Viktor jealous.

"I wonder what would have happened," Yuri said, "if Henry
hadn't found us that time we ran away together."

I laughed. "We'd have been that jaguar's lunch."

"Jaguar?"

"Cougar, I mean."

From the corner of my vision I could see Yuri watching me
carefully. "Maybe we would have made it to Oyama. Maybe we'd
still be there now."

"Look," I said. A star flashed across the sky, and then another.

"Iris?" he whispered, his eyes still on me.

"What?" I kept looking at the sky. "You're missing it. Look,
another."

Yuri swallowed audibly. "I think, I love you." I turned to him.
"I think I've always loved you," he said. His bottom lip trembled.

"Yuri, I—"

"Please don't say anything. It would only embarrass me. I just
want you to know. So that whatever decision you may make . . ."

"Decision?"

"Well, I know now you're looking for a . . . I just couldn't forgive myself if I didn't—"

"Yuri—"

"Please," he said, halting me. "I know I don't deserve you. I don't have much money, but I work hard and I would take care of you." He pushed himself up on his elbows. He looked out towards the water. "I just want you to know that." A muscle at his jaw pulsed. I didn't know what to say. We watched the sky spark in silence. "No matter what, I would never leave you like that."

His words struck a tender chord I didn't know I had. I bolted upright. In truth, to see Llewelyna abandoned by my father in such a distressed state had terrified me. I thought seeing her desperation might make him stay. And yet I was defensive of my father, and resentful of any judgment Yuri might have to offer.

"You don't understand a thing," I said. I picked up a rock from the shore beside me and whipped it at the lake.

"It's true, I don't."

"You're a fool."

"You're right. I didn't mean anything by it. I'm sorry."

His docility irritated me. I stood and slipped on my shoes. "You know what else you are right about, Yuri Wasik?" My cheeks burned, tears beaded the insides of my eyes. "You *do not* deserve me. You don't now and you never will."

"Iris . . ." He reached for my arm but I slapped his hand away. I turned from the lake and ran into the shadows of the forest. I was sure Yuri would chase after me. I heard coyotes yip, far away at first and then closer. Once I was a ways from the shore, there were footsteps, but they came from the direction I was going rather than where I had left Yuri. The white eyes of the orphan thief blinked at me. Her black hair and dark skin made her difficult to see, but her jewellery caught the scant starlight. She reached her hand out towards me, bangles ringing, as if I might place a coin in her palm. I realized then we were surrounded by yellow-eyed coyotes. I could feel the breath of one against my ankle. I looked down and the coyote licked my leg. When I looked up again the orphan thief was gone. As if this were their signal, the coyotes leapt into motion and disappeared into the forest, their yips growing fainter and fainter.

After that, I saw the orphan thief more often around our orchard. I asked Henry about her once. "Many have been killed or chased from their land," he said. "Families are separated. Children are forced into white people schools. She's probably a runaway."

⌀

Llewelyna's neglected garden was thick with blindweed and poppies. Some days she walked through it, a shawl over her shoulders, Saint Francis trailing behind her. Other days she had me bring out a chair from the kitchen so she could smoke and read. Mary returned to help with the housework. She moved about the house like a shadow. Although Llewelyna told her she didn't blame her for what she did, slipping the crushed pills into her water, it was clear that Mary's conscience was still uneasy.

Although we hadn't spoken for weeks, I continued to watch for Viktor in the orchard. The waiting only made my desire for him more desperate. I imagined that I could feel his eyes on me, taking in the shape of my legs through my cotton dress or my bust pushing up at the collar where I had undone a button or two. It took everything I had to keep myself from chasing after him. One day I saw him headed towards the house while the rest of the pickers were working at the far end of the orchard. I walked along the path to the well with the hope he would follow me there. I thrilled when I heard his footsteps quicken in my direction.

"Iris," he whispered. I turned. He gave his crooked grin. "I've been meaning to talk to you in private." I gestured for him to follow me. As I bent down to the pump my skin tingled with the anticipation of his touch. "I need to ask you a favour," he said behind me. My back stiffened. I turned and let the water pour into the bucket. He looked boyish, bursting with excitement.

"Azami and I have been seeing each other again." His smile was bold and naive. "Could you tell Mother you've sent me to Vernon for some errand? We're going to meet tonight after work." Water slipped into my shoes. "You've overflowed your bucket," Viktor said, grinning. I halted the pump and glanced at my reflection in the clear water. A ghost. I turned back to him. "You'll do it?" he asked.

"Of course."

Viktor kissed me on the cheek before he ran back into the orchard.

From then on, he and Azami met regularly once again. I couldn't bear to see them slip away together. Azami would wait for Viktor at the edge of the forest, and when she saw him coming towards her through the orchard her face opened up in a joy so pure and transparent I wanted to shatter it.

Yuri and I avoided one another. He knew too much and I couldn't stand the way he looked at me, his eyes needy and sad. I kept to the house and helped Mary take care of Llewelyna.

There had already been talk around Winteridge about the assassination of an archduke in a faraway place. I had no idea what this event could have to do with us. Then it was whispered that the Russian army was mobilizing, and Germany had declared war on France and Belgium. And then, a month later, we were at war, too.

Peach-picking came to a halt. The men sat around and spouted their opinions and argued in a flurry of languages, while Yuri read out the newspaper . . . *Germany sweeps through neutral Belgium* . . . *Flanders under fire.* Viktor translated into Ukrainian for Taras, and a picker relayed the news in Japanese. Yuri and I still wouldn't look at one another directly, though the excitement in Europe eased our personal discomfort.

A recruitment office appeared one day on the wharf next to the packinghouse. The officers who manned it stayed at the Pearl Hotel. These men wore stiff peak caps and olive uniforms with tight collars and gold buttons up the front. When they weren't manning the office they smoked on the patio of the Pearl and drank well into the night.

Taras and some men from our orchard went to the office to enlist. The Japanese workers were denied and told this wasn't their war. Similarly, Taras was led out of the office. He screamed in his furious accent: "*East* Galicia. *East*, damn you. Ukrainian, you idiots." Yuri and Viktor relayed Taras's spectacle to me while they smoked on my porch.

"But how will we enlist if we can't state our names?" Yuri asked.

"We won't use our names," Viktor said. "We don't need them."

"Whose name will we use?"

"Wilson. Mother's maiden name. It's a good English-sounding name."

"Surely they'll know," I said.

"They have nothing to check against. There hasn't been a census in Winteridge for a few years, and since then there have been so many new settlers, and all the Japs. There's no clear record."

"Take Mother's name? That's absurd. Father won't like that."

"Well, hen, do you have a better idea? If we are any kind of men, we need to be there, whatever it takes."

Yuri sucked hard at his cigarette.

"If they don't want you fighting, then why enlist?" I asked. I couldn't imagine the orchard without them.

"They think we're the enemy," Viktor said. "Part of Galicia is under Austro-Hungarian rule. They don't realize the east sides with Russia if it sides at all. But the Japs aren't fond of Russia, of course. It's all very complicated. Father has always told the pickers he was from Hungary. And now Hungary is the enemy."

"I thought he was Ukrainian," I said.

"He is. But you see, the Ukraine doesn't exist. It's a people split in two. Besides all that, little hen and I are Canadian." He elbowed Yuri. "And so we must fight. It's our duty."

"Then why lie about your name?" I asked.

"The Wasik name will have been blacklisted now," Yuri said and stubbed his cigarette onto the porch with his thumb.

"I just wonder why you should go in the first place."

"Well you see, Your Highness, like I said, it's the only thing for a man to do." Viktor flexed his muscles in mock pose. "Any man who doesn't fight for his country is a pansy." His words were directed at Yuri. Yuri gazed out towards the orchard. The branches drooped, heavy with ripened peaches. I wondered if I should mention that our harvest was beginning to fall from the trees and if the men didn't get back to work everything would go to waste, but it didn't seem like the right moment.

"It's a mistake for them to deny the Japs," Viktor went on. "They've just as much right to prove their citizenship as anyone else. It doesn't settle well."

"Who will care for the orchard?" Yuri said, echoing my concern.

Viktor took Yuri's head in his hands in a gesture that was embarrassingly intimate, as if he might kiss his brother square on the lips. Yuri's cheeks reddened and I had the urge to look away.

"Listen to me, hen. You want to grow old in these trees? You want to turn out just like Father? This is all life has for us, you understand? This is our chance to escape. We'll get to see places we never would otherwise." He released Yuri's face and spread his arms above his head like the perfect picture of Atlas. I imagined him shouldering the globe from Henry's library. "We'll see Europe, Asia, maybe even Father's Ukraine."

There was a bang from inside my house. Saint Francis shrieked. I left Viktor and Yuri on the porch and ran upstairs. The sound had come from my parents' room, the room Llewelyna refused to sleep in. Saint Francis squawked and flapped his wings on the bed. Llewelyna was frantic, her face pink and eyes narrow and sharp. She didn't seem to notice me enter behind her. She took her jewellery box, full of gifts my father had brought her from his travels overseas, and emptied it out the window.

"What are you doing?"

"I told you, Iris." She opened a compartment in the jewellery box that hadn't opened on its own, scooped a strand of pearls from it, and tossed it through the window. "They won't be back. It's the end as we know it." Once she had emptied the jewellery box with the spinning girl inside of it, she dropped it out the window. "All this, every single thing, is meaningless. Nothingness."

"I don't understand," I said.

Llewelyna gestured to a crumpled letter on the bed. I recognized my father's large, emphatic writing. The letter was brief. Its few lines announced my father and Jacob were joining the British armed forces and would be sent to France any day. It was dated two weeks prior.

Llewelyna opened the drawers of her vanity and spilled out more of her fine things, all gifts from my father: shawls, dinner gloves, silk nylons. I looked out the window at her belongings scattered in the lilac bushes below. "He thought his absence could be replaced with this . . . this trash," she said. Viktor, Yuri, and a few other pickers stood around the pile and looked up, curious. Llewelyna tossed an emerald green dress out the window. It snagged on the side of the house and hung there.

"They'll be back," I said to her.

Llewelyna raised a hand to her tangled hair as if something ached there. She closed her eyes. "Everyone thinks this war will pass in a couple of months. Your father treats it as a vacation. 'It'll be good for Jacob to see some of the world,' he says. 'Gain experience.' It's idiotic. This *world* they imagine is unreachable. Idealized. A place they'll never set foot on. It doesn't exist." She opened the closet and reached up to the highest shelf. She pulled down a wooden box and took the lid off. Inside were photographs and letters. She went to throw them out the window, but I caught her wrist. Her arm vibrated against my strength. She looked up at me.

"Stop," I said.

Later that day I went to collect her things from the bushes, but they were gone. I looked for the thief amongst the pickers, but there was no one around for me to glare at. The green dress still hung snagged on the side of the house, too high for me to bring down. It hung there for years. I often mistook the dress for someone scaling our house, Rapunzel stuck mid-escape. Eventually the sun and rain dulled the emerald fabric beige, and birds and other rodents tore it to shreds and furnished their homes with strips of it.

Taras was proud when Yuri and Viktor were both accepted into the Canadian army. He walked around town as big-chested as a robin. His voice boomed with the news of it. Although Mary was British, she begged her sons not to go. It wasn't until Yuri and Viktor were sent their letters of appointment that Taras realized his sons had changed their last name to Wilson. Yuri carried a plum-purple bruise on his jaw that hadn't disappeared even when he boarded the boat to leave. He said he fell from a tree but I knew different.

Despite Henry's visits having stopped completely, one day he arrived at our house to see Llewelyna. Taras threw him threatening looks as he passed the Wasiks' cottage and Mary disapproved so fervently that she had to leave the house when Henry entered. Henry and I nodded our hellos before he went to Llewelyna's room. They spoke quietly for hours. At one point Llewelyna gave a sharp little whimper and began to cry. From my room I could hear the bed creak as Henry lay down beside my mother. With that, I too had to leave the house, though I could no longer blame them for their unfaithfulness. I knew they had loved each other for a long time. My father had betrayed Llewelyna, twice now, abandoned her completely. Henry, on the other hand, had seen Llewelyna through everything. He understood parts of her that my father couldn't bear to know.

The approaching reality of war had everyone acting desperately. We each searched for something solid, if only for a moment, to hold on to.

ɾɛ

I was running on the road. I had no destination, I just wanted to get away. When I passed the Pearl there was a group of men in olive suits gathered on the porch drinking beer.

"Iris!" one of the men called. It was Yuri. He stumbled down the steps and met me on the road. I realized the group wasn't made up of strange men but of local boys disguised in uniforms. Ronald, the McCarthys, the Ebers, and of course Viktor, who whistled and hooted licentiously.

"Ah, yes. Now is your chance, hen!"

Yuri could see I had been crying. He took me by the elbow and led me to the lakeshore, beneath the cover of trees. "What is it?" he asked, and his sincere concern was so welcome, so refreshing after everything, that I reached for the back of his neck. Kissing him in that moment felt like the only thing in the world left to do, but I couldn't bring myself to do it. I ran my fingers through the short hair at the nape of his neck, shaved close to the skin and smooth as velvet.

"I am so afraid," I said. "I am so afraid of being left alone with her." I could see the disappointment on his face. He took my hands in his. His palms were warm. His breath was sweet with brandy.

"It will be a short time. We'll end this war and be back in no time. And when I return . . . I don't know. Maybe we can be together."

I could still hear the men in the Pearl laughing and singing foolish songs. I was angry how casually everyone was treating this war. I didn't see the apocalyptic images Llewelyna did, but her response to the visions frightened me. And here Yuri, my tender friend, was to enter this world of Llewelyna's imagination, brimming with explosions and fire and blood.

"Llewelyna says it's sure death. The end of the world as we know it. She's dreamt my father's death a hundred times."

"I know, you told me that." He brought a hand to my cheek and wiped a tear away with his thumb. "Those are just dreams, Iris. I'll come back. I promise."

❦

The *Rosamond* was docked at the wharf. Someone had repainted the siren. She was garish with her pale skin, pinched cheeks, and blue eyelids. Her areolas were the size of peaches, or perhaps they were meant to be clamshells set upon her breasts. Her lips turned up in a wolfish grin. The *Rosamond* had already been around to many of the nearby towns and villages along the lake. It sat low in the water, crowded with uniformed men who shouted and cheered at the crowd gathered in the bay. Taras hadn't come down to the shore to see his sons off.

"Have you seen Viktor?" Mary asked me.

"He forgot something at the house," Yuri said. He had a cloth bag over his shoulder and seemed much older in his starched uniform and cap and with his hair shaved behind the ears. I spotted Henry in the crowd. He too was dressed in one of the olive suits, his hair shaved like Yuri's. I left the Wasiks and ran to him.

"What are you doing here? It's Britain that's at war."

"I've as much of a right as anyone to fight," Henry said, a little defensively. Then his face softened and he leaned down to my level. "There is only so much knowledge to gain from reading books." He smiled. "But in truth, I need to get away from these ghosts for a while."

From the corner of my vision, I saw the Lake Person with the blistered face dart between the trees not far from us. "Is she here? Your half-sister?"

Henry nodded.

I remembered how she had approached us in the forest so long ago. She had looked as though she had wanted to hurt Henry then. Now she seemed worried, flitting between the trees, desperate to stay near him.

"Please be careful," I told Henry.

He pulled Llewelyna's Saint Francis statuette from his pocket. "I have my lucky charm." He tucked it away.

"Iris!" Yuri waved to me from the other side of the crowd. "We'll board soon."

I kissed Henry on the silver scar down his cheek. "Thank you," I said.

"What for?"

"For loving my despicable mother." I smiled.

Henry's face went stoic. He gave a little nod and looked away.

I hurried to join Yuri and Mary. Mary dabbed her eyes with a handkerchief as she said goodbye to Yuri. He turned from her and approached me. He stood close. Too close. Then he was on his knees. The crowd in the bay hushed. Even the birds went quiet and the fish went still in the water.

"Iris Sparks," Yuri began in a whisper I could hardly hear over the pounding in my ears. I could feel the hot red splotches inching up my neck. "Will you give me something to come back for? Will you marry me?" I looked around. Henry smiled at me from across the crowd, nodding, as if I had already given my answer. One of the McCarthy boys snickered but was quickly silenced by his mother.

"Yuri, I . . ." He was trembling. In his eyes I could see a reflection of the clouds, the fringe of pine trees. I thought of Yuri swimming through the dark water. I thought of us as children, asleep in the tree fort, his arms wrapped around me. I looked behind Yuri and saw Viktor emerge from the forest in his olive suit, his mouth agape at the scene. Azami approached from the trees further down the shore. Something greedy boiled in my gut. People started to whisper. The men on the *Rosamond* cheered, finally realizing the situation. Yuri was about to stand back up, my silence too long.

"Yes," I said, finally, catching Viktor's eye. "I will." Yuri nearly fell as he stood. He pulled me in and kissed me square on the lips. "But only if you come home, you understand?" I said. The already exuberant crowd laughed and cheered around us.

Yuri took my face in his hands. "Thank you," he whispered. It was an odd thing to say. He pushed something into the palm of my hand.

Viktor patted Yuri hard on the back, then pulled me close, kissed me on the cheek. I could see the chain of Azami's lucky necklace at his neck. "Goodbye, Your Highness," he whispered in my ear.

Yuri and Viktor joined the lineup of identical men boarding the *Rosamond*. Yuri kept turning around, waving to me, his face bursting. Mary wrapped an arm around my waist.

"It's no mystery," she said. "Our Yuri has loved you for so long."

I opened my fist and found a ring carved from purple lilac wood and sanded smooth. There was an imprint in my palm from holding it too tight. I fit the ring on my thumb; it was far too big for any of my fingers.

"Wait!" I called as I ran towards the lineup of men. I found Yuri and planted another kiss on his lips. My eyes found Viktor's. He stood just behind Yuri. And in that moment I thought I had finally made Viktor want me back.

The crowd in the bay cheered again as the *Rosamond* set off. I couldn't tell Yuri or Viktor from the other men on the boat. They all looked the same, waving and shouting their final indecipherable offerings to the crowd. When the lakeboat turned past the last curve of land, a silence fell upon Winteridge, one that wouldn't lift for four years. All our young men gone in a single stroke. The war was a darkness our men disappeared into. Those few who did eventually return to Winteridge never recovered from the dark.

THREE

1914–1919

The world is full of abandoned meanings.

DON DELILLO

17

Soon our men's letters arrived as if to replace them. Those of us left behind in Winteridge lived half our lives through their words. Jacob wrote to Llewelyna, and though she didn't share his letters with me, I could hear her open the envelopes when I left the room. The letters I received from Yuri relayed only common, mundane events like the weather and the details of this or that supper. Yuri was a poor writer, having never gone to school, and I suspected Viktor had transcribed his words. Yuri called me his beloved. The word already felt worn and tired and plucked from some song he might have heard. He and Viktor were about to leave the dusty training base in Valcartier where they slept in tents. They would be part of the first Canadian Division and would leave Quebec for Europe in a few days.

One day I received an especially thick letter from Yuri. Inside, along with his letter, was a sealed envelope with *Azami* written on it in Viktor's handwriting. Yuri's letter instructed me to deliver Viktor's sealed envelope to Azami. I held Viktor's letter to the sunlight but couldn't see through the cream paper. I slipped my fingertip beneath the seal. I could tell Azami it was the censors. Although Yuri's dull letters were rarely altered, I heard some of the women received letters that were blacked out with ink. I made a little rip and stopped, visited once again by the guilt of the shrine and the fire. I put the envelope down.

The next day I untied one of the cart horses and rode to the edge of town and then through the forest to the Kobas' property on the other side of the hill. I tied the horse up to a pine tree and slipped along the edge of the orchard. I hadn't been there since I had delivered the new shrine to Azami. The apple trees were lush with fruit and there were many pickers up in the branches. Although the peach season was now over and the majority of our unpicked harvest had gone to rot, the apple season didn't end until November. Even after, there was plenty of sorting and packing to be done. I recognized some of the Japanese pickers who had worked on our orchard. Those who had been denied service in the war had promptly left our orchard and joined the Japanese workforce at the Kobas', leaving only Taras to tend to our peaches. Viktor was right: preventing the Japanese from joining up didn't settle well. Our community was more divided than it had ever been before.

Azami was up in one of the apple trees. I whistled to her from the bushes. She scanned the forest and when she saw me came down the ladder and walked casually between the trees, then ducked into the woods. Viktor must have told her to expect me, his little gofer. When I passed her the letter she slipped it into her overalls.

"Thank you," she said. She had a small cut beside her eye. Someone called to her. She handed me a brown envelope and kissed me on the cheek. Her smile revealed an open trust I did not deserve.

I dropped Azami's letter, unread, into the river on the way home. I followed the brown envelope along the bank until it got clogged amongst some roots and sank.

℆

Our rotten harvest continued to fester beneath the trees well into the fall. Taras didn't bother to clean it up. He had taken to whisky and had grown negligent of his responsibilities. Insects and mice made their homes in the fruit. The fetid smell was inescapable even inside our house. I was relieved when the mess was covered by snow that hardened into sheets of ice that cracked underfoot. Mary worked tirelessly all day nursing Llewelyna and returned to her own cottage at night to nurse Taras, who drank himself into a sickness.

I opened our front door one morning to find Azami holding a basket of shining red apples, like a character in a faery tale, a Japanese Snow White. The branches of the peach trees behind her were ornamented with icicles.

"Merry Christmas." She put the apples down between us. A Japanese man held another basket of apples behind her. She gestured to him. "This is my cousin Kenta."

"Hello, Kenta. Merry Christmas."

He bowed slightly.

"He doesn't speak English," she said, and came a little closer. "Any word?" she whispered. Her eyebrows arched with a desperation I couldn't help but enjoy. It was strange to see worry on a face that was usually so numb.

I shook my head.

"You'll let me know?"

"Of course," I said.

In a few weeks a letter for Azami from Viktor *did* arrive, and then another, and another. I cherished the power of keeping the letters from Azami and used the incessant snowfall to excuse my inaction. When I finally decided to ride to the Kobas' orchard to deliver the letters to Azami, there was a foot of fresh snow on the ground. I wore several wool sweaters, and an overcoat, and wrapped a scarf around my neck so my own breath could warm my face. I tied the horse to a tree just outside the Kobas' orchard and walked carefully in the snow along the perimeter. The apple trees were as bare as bones and covered in snow. There were no workers. My boots were not high enough and my feet were already wet and cold. I knew I couldn't approach the house, and I was about to turn back when I heard a voice. I followed the sound down a hill to the far side of the property. I didn't know the Kobas' land extended this far north. What I found below fascinated me. From above it looked like an enormous crystal sparkling among all that fresh snow in the winter sun. I walked carefully down the steep hillside, nearly forgetting what I had come here for. As I got nearer, I could see the building was very low; the glass roof came no higher than my shoulder. The walls were made of wood, and panes of glass angled up to form a peaked roof. I would have to crouch or crawl to get around inside. I had never seen a greenhouse before.

I leaned over to see what was inside and found Azami and Kenta rocking together amongst the greenery of spinach and onions and garlic shoots. They were naked and it was a wonder to see bare skin and lush vegetables on such a white, cold day. The window-panes were slightly steamed. Kenta was on top of her, and Azami's legs were around his waist. Her hair spilled out beneath her like syrup. She arched her back in pleasure, her eyes pinched closed. I felt for Viktor's letters in my pocket and hiked back up the ridge to my horse.

When I got home I ran my finger over Azami's name scrawled on the envelope in Viktor's writing. I peeled back the flap and slipped his letter out.

What a fool I was to complain of our training in Salisbury. We're in France but we could be in any Hell. It's been

three days of rain. These trenches are full of blood water.
Yesterday a man died in my arms. He had two children
and a wife back home in Winnipeg. As blood spilled from
a hole in his chest, and bombs exploded in the near distance, I told him about our house in the sky. The beaded
chimes ringing in the morning breeze and the sun falling
on your face like melted butter. I dream of it, you know.
I dream of your warm nakedness pressed up to me and
then I wake to this nightmare. I regret everything. I am a
selfish coward. I would do anything to return to you now.
I would lose a limb to be next to you. The man closed his
eyes and eased into death. Once his spirit was gone his
body became so heavy another man had to help lift him
off me. When I come home I will take you away. Never
mind what our fathers might think. Life is much too
short. Я тебе кохаю. I love you.

I set the letter down. Then picked it up and read it again,
slowly. Yuri never wrote of love or death. His self-censorship irritated me. He only asked about Winteridge and told me about
different men in his battalion and the food he did and did not get
to eat. After I read Viktor's letter for a third time, I set it on fire
in the stove. Then I read the other letters.

Only time separates the land of the living and the land of
the dead. And here, in Hell, time has disappeared. I pinch
myself to make sure I am still alive, still awake, but it's so
cold this no longer proves useful. Only the thought of you
warms me. I relive that night you told me about Coyote,
the trickster, and we made love until the church bells rang
in the valley. Do you remember? Yesterday I thought I saw

you in the trench. I followed you until you changed back
into a yellow tarpaulin whipping in the wind. Я тебе
кохаю

Why don't you write? I need your words. Today I killed a
boy. Pimples freckled his forehead like stars. He wore a
silver cross under his uniform. I was close enough to smell
the fresh piss in his pants. I was close enough to hear his
last words. The words were in German, but I know he
called for his mother in that final breath—mutti, mutti,
mutti. He stuck his bayonet in my chest but I did not feel
a thing. No matter where I go, his blood cries out to me
from the ground. I am forever half of whoever I was
before. Pray for my soul. I have lost it somewhere in the
bloody mud.

I burned these letters up too.

⟊

One night, a few weeks later, I woke to a pounding on the door.
I had to pull the door open hard against the wind. Spindly branches
from the orchard whipped across the porch. Azami stood there,
bundled in her scrubby picking clothes, a lock of hair swept across
her face and into her mouth.
    "Iris. You must tell me what to do."
    "What is it?"
    "Is he dead?" Azami bit her lip, her eyes full of water. "He's
dead, isn't he?"
    "Come in for a moment."

Once we were at the table in the low light of the lantern she went on:

"Kenta has proposed," she said.

"And what did you say?"

"That I needed a day to think about it. It hurt him. I could see that." Azami looked down at her hands, callused and marked with cuts. "He's a good man. I don't know what to do."

"You should do what you feel is right," I said.

"It's not that simple." Her eyes rose to meet mine, the black pupils aflame from the lamplight. "I'm pregnant."

I looked to her stomach but it was impossible to see beneath all her clothes. I thought of her and Kenta in the greenhouse and my cheeks grew hot.

"I told Viktor in that first letter. But he never responded. I am afraid he is angry."

"Is it Viktor's?"

She tilted her head, askance. "Of course." Her face went hard again, cold.

"Does Kenta know you are pregnant?"

She turned away to face the darkness. "He believes it is his own. But if Viktor's alive and if he—"

"Does your father know?" I asked, remembering his anger towards her that one time in the orchard when we were just girls. Azami shook her head. The tears ready at the corners of her eyes streamed down her cheeks. She wiped at them with a sleeve.

"You must act quickly," I said simply.

"If we marry, Kenta will inherit my father's orchard. He's a good, honourable man," she said. "I might not get another offer like this. If I say no, and Viktor abandons me . . ." I handed her a handkerchief. Azami's face lifted to the dim pulsing light as she blotted the tears beneath her eyes.

"Do you love him?" I asked.

"Who?"

"Kenta."

"I think I could," she said.

I smiled, as treacherous as Judas, and promised never to tell anyone what I knew.

Azami's marriage to Kenta was announced in the newspaper the next month. I should have written to Yuri of it, but I knew this would mean Viktor's letters would stop. And so, instead, I picked up my father's good pen and paper, and I wrote a letter to Viktor. I attempted to copy Azami's hand, small block letters like from a child's copybook. I wanted to give Viktor the intimacy he craved. But it came out foolish. I couldn't capture my emotions in the words. I attempted three times before I gave up.

&

Every month I took the money our household received for Yuri's and Viktor's service to the Wasiks' cottage. Taras scornfully accepted it and then drank it away. Some nights I woke to him hollering Ukrainian at the darkness.

One morning I watched from the kitchen as a young soldier holding a clipboard walked up our drive. I wiped my sticky hands on my apron and waited for his dreadful knock on the door.

"Mrs. . . ."

"Miss Sparks."

"May I speak to the lady of the house, please?"

"She's unwell," I said.

"I need to speak to . . ." He looked down at his clipboard. "Mrs. Lew-Wall— Mrs. Sparks. It's important."

I led the man to Llewelyna's room. She smiled and waved him in as if he were a long-lost friend she had been expecting all this time. Saint Francis nestled deeper into the duvet. On her bedside table the blue fish spun in its jar next to the *Mabinogion*. I wondered if Mary had found the fish in my room and taken it to her. Llewelyna's nightgown scooped low at her chest. The officer was obviously unsettled by her appearance. He took off his cap. His black hair was plastered to his head like a helmet. I remained in the doorway.

"Mrs. Sparks, my condolences that you are unwell." He spoke to her but faced the peacock at the end of the bed, his eyebrows high on his forehead in wonder. "I'm looking for a man named Taras Wasik."

"Taras Wasik," she repeated. "Never heard of him." Mary had left our house to give Taras his medicine. She could be back at any moment. "What has this man done?" Llewelyna asked.

"He's an enemy of the Allies, ma'am. Aliens of enemy nationality must register with authorities, as stated in the War Measures Act."

"Oh dear."

"You're not familiar with the man?"

"Certainly not. I assure you we will report him if ever we come across him. You have my word."

"That would be much appreciated." The officer nodded and then, after an awkward silence, left the room. I walked him to the front door.

"Mind if I check that cottage there?" The Wasik house was dark.

"It's really not necessary," I said. "Been vacant for months."

"There are some clothes drying on the line. Is someone living there?"

"Those are my clothes." In truth they *were* my clothes. Mary had washed them for me.

"You dry them way down there?"

"They get the most breeze closer to the lake."

"And over there, some firewood, and it looks like a pair of old shoes."

"Sir, many of our workers enlisted and left our orchard in a hurry. The men didn't have time to clean up or organize their things. Even our harvest spoiled beneath the trees. As my mother said, we promise to let you know if we see anyone or know of any enemies. She gave her word. Please do not offend her by questioning it."

He nodded and put his cap back on. "My apologies."

As he left our land I saw Mary's moon face lighten a window in the Wasiks' cottage, but the officer was looking in the opposite direction.

The next day there were bruises on Mary's cheek and up her arms. Her lip was split.

"What's happened to you?" I asked.

She pulled the collar of her dress up around her neck. "Really, it's none of your concern," she said, and poured water from the kettle into a teapot.

"You don't need to put up with him. You can stay in our house if you—"

"I won't leave my husband. I would never."

"You're British. They're not looking for you."

"What are you talking about?"

"An officer came snooping around here yesterday, looking for Taras."

"What do they want with Taras?"

"He said he's an enemy to the Allies."

"Nonsense," she said and turned from me to take the tea tray to Llewelyna.

"Did you bring Llewelyna the blue fish yesterday?" I asked as she was about to ascend the stairs.

"She asked for it. It calms her."

"Please do not go through my things."

Mary bowed her head and climbed the stairs without another word.

I didn't dare try to take the fish from Llewelyna, but I checked on her regularly. She often clutched the jar against her chest as she read, or gazed into the blue light and watched the fish spin.

Along with various letters from Jacob, Viktor, and Yuri, every few months Llewelyna and I received a blank postcard: Montreal, Morocco, Spain, France, England. These postcards were the only things that made Llewelyna smile. When I showed her the first one, with the trams and crowded streets of Montreal, she laughed. "The rascal," she said. "Out to prove it is a vacation." We both knew the postcards were from Henry.

18

That spring the *Rosamond*, the very same lakeboat that carried all our men away into Llewelyna's apocalyptic nightmare, returned to deliver one single officer, carrying one single letter. We women, who were left behind, shut ourselves in our homes and observed the uniformed man from behind curtains as he walked dutifully along the road. We all knew a hand-delivered envelope was a very bad sign. There had already been one delivered to the Ebers. The exhalation of each household he passed was almost audible as he neared our drive. I stood at my bedroom window and waited for him. I knew he was headed to our home. It was still early morning, the sky a pale pink. I had woken from a night seizure and my tongue was raw and my limbs tired. The jaguar purred, sprawled on the floor next to my bed. It was hard to breathe. I felt as though I had feathers stuffed down deep in my chest. The officer walked up our drive. Mary peered through the curtains of her window and closed them as he passed the Wasiks' cottage. The man disappeared from my view. I heard the hollow knock at our door.

I stepped over the jaguar and started down the stairs. I could hear her pad down behind me. I held the railing tight to keep my balance. The house spun, pulled me into some central, empty space. The jaguar stopped at the bottom of the stairs. She was timid of Llewelyna.

In the kitchen, the floor shifted and slanted beneath my feet. I
ran my fingers along the walls, the cupboards, and nearly nudged a
teacup off the counter. Every step felt heavier and harder than the
last. The knock at the door resounded inside me like a heartbeat. I
entered the dining room. Llewelyna was at the table. She had somehow made it down all of those stairs on her own. She was visible
to the officer who watched her curiously through the window by
the door and continued knocking. It wasn't until I stood in front
of her that I saw the paring knife on the table before her.

"It's your father," she said simply. "I saw it." She stared into
the grain of the table. Her fingers felt for the handle of the knife.

"Llewelyna . . ." I began, easing my way towards her. She
stood, took hold of the knife. "Llewelyna, please." She walked
into the kitchen and began slicing a carrot on the cutting board.
I exhaled, and let the man in.

"Miss?" he said, his chin vibrating. He was young, only a few
years older than me. "I regret—"

"Out!" my mother yelled from the kitchen behind me.

"I regret—"

"Get out!" She turned to us. "I said, out!" She held the carrot
like a knife and took a threatening step towards the door. The
young officer dropped the letter. She threw the carrot and it flew
out the door and bounced off the porch. The officer ran down our
drive and walked briskly towards the dock, where he embarked
for the next town to perform his role in the nightmares of other
mothers, sisters, and daughters.

Llewelyna returned to the cutting board and chopped steadily.
There was a pile of carrots on the counter beside her. Mary had
brought out the bundle from the cellar the day before. I picked up
the envelope and read the dead words, then I threw the letter into
the stove, as if fire might make the words untrue.

The thump of the knife on the cutting board echoed through the house. Hours seemed to pass while I lay on my bed upstairs staring at the corner where the rosebud-patterned paper peeled from the wall. The jaguar and I watched a bud loosen, unravel, and fall open into a brassy blossom. Its petals fell from the wall and dried immediately along the baseboards. I swept the petals up in a tight fist and squeezed, and when I opened my hand there was only a layer of fine dust. I blew the specks into nothingness.

When I went back downstairs Llewelyna was looking out the window behind the sink. The knife was still in her hand. Carrot moons covered the floor at her feet. She turned, smiled at me. "An owl," she said. "Old Blodeuwedd, the poor girl."

❧

While Llewelyna slept her sadness away, I watched the bare branches of the peach trees swell with yellow buds that unravelled into green and then pink flowers, thinner and more delicate than silk. When the wind blew the petals away, the leaves of the trees became thick and lush and the green stone fruit could hardly be seen until the sun transformed them into its own blushing, velvet-skinned children. That summer I did not pluck a single peach although they grew enormous, ballooned, their clefts deep-set, and ripened to the exact colour of sunset. The swollen, heavy fruit pulled the branches to the ground until they dropped, finally, into the long grass like dead stars. The leaves turned yellow and then orange and then one morning they were gone. The long, cold winter better resembled our grief.

Although we kept it dim and cool inside our house, we could not keep spring from returning. Once more the peach trees were speckled with pink blossoms and grew lush. I could not bear to watch another season pass by, the ripe fruit left to fall and rot in the grass. Instead I let the orchard consume my days. I wore an old pair of my father's trousers and raked up all the old, rotten fruit left from last season. I trimmed and pruned the trees just as I had seen Taras and Viktor do one hundred times. By the end of the summer the peaches were swollen and made the branches sag. I could only manage to pick one tree a day. The peaches grew far too quickly; I couldn't keep up on my own, so one day I went door to door collecting workers—women who had been locked up in their houses all season living off rationed scraps—and offered them jobs on our orchard. I would pay them at first with what money I could scavenge and the small pile I had collected in the coffee tin beneath my bed when I worked for Taras.

The blue sky reflected in the window on the door to Grace Bell's house. I could hear King Edward VII whining in the backyard. Mrs. Bell appeared at the window of the door and an arrow of geese crossed between us on the glass. She opened the door slowly, as if careful to not disturb someone sleeping inside. She had a pair of knitting needles and a whorl of grey wool in one hand.

"Mrs. Bell, it's good to see you."

King Edward barked furiously now. She gave a thin smile and yelled at the dog to be quiet. "How are you?" she said. Her face was worn and colourless except for the violet skin beneath her eyes.

"I'm well."

"I'm so sorry about your father, I meant to come by, but I just . . ."

"It was a kind thought. And you, do you have news from Mr. Bell?"

She brightened slightly and exhaled as if she had been holding her breath. "I received a letter yesterday." She felt for her apron pocket. "Phillip was about to be sent to the front. The letter is a month old. I have a bad feeling."

"I'm sure he's all right." I smiled in a way I hoped was reassuring.

"Just trying to keep my hands busy." She held up the wool. "Do my bit and all, though I'm a miserable knitter. Feel sorry for the lad that ends up with these socks."

I admired her knitting, full of gaps and cinched too tight in places. "Every bit helps, they say. But I'm here today to see if you'd like a job."

"A job?"

"On our orchard. You see, the harvest is just wasting away again. But with some help we could pick enough fruit to send off to Vernon and Kelowna. We could even make preserves to ship over to our men."

Mrs. Bell was looking past my head towards the lake. "They've come back."

"Excuse me?" I turned to see what she was looking at.

"The geese. They've returned as if nothing has changed."

The geese descended to the shore behind the trees and rustled amongst the rocks, honking joyously. I turned back to Mrs. Bell. Her eyes shifted, saw me again.

"I plan to start tomorrow," I said. "I'll give a wage. Not much at first, but once we begin selling . . ." Mrs. Bell was already closing the door. "Wear trousers if you decide to come," I said.

She opened the door a crack and peered out. "Wear what?"

"You'll need to wear trousers to climb the ladders. Mr. Bell must have left some around," I said. Mrs. Bell closed the door.

I got up early the next morning to get the extra picking ladders from the shed and clear the bins of leaves and the spiders and rodents that had made their winter homes in the corners. The first of the women to arrive was Juliet Pearl. Juliet was tall and broad-shouldered with long curly brown hair she wore on the top of her head in a tight bun. Since the war, business at the Pearl Hotel had slowed. Mr. Pearl had to let go of the cook and the maid they had employed during the summers. The recruiting officers had kept Juliet busy cooking and cleaning for a time, but once they departed the Pearl was forced to close.

I knew Seamus Pearl had been ill in the past. Juliet and I had attended the country school together for a short time when we were small, before Llewelyna pulled me out entirely and sent me off with Henry. Juliet had arrived at school with her hair braided neatly down her back. And I had wondered how Mr. Pearl executed such a perfect braid with his callused, arthritic fingers. Then Juliet's hair came loose when she took off her overcoat, and from the desk behind, I watched her raise her arms above her head and blindly twist her fingers through her hair. When Juliet was eight, her father had a stroke and she was forced to leave school to care for him and help him with the Pearl.

As a little girl Juliet had been quiet. And as a woman she was still quiet, but in a way that made you realize she knew something you didn't. Her mother had died when Juliet was only an infant. Llewelyna once told me that while pregnant with Jacob, she and Juliet's mother had compared their growing bellies. Juliet's mother had a complicated birth and had to be taken to the Vernon hospital. A few months later Mr. Pearl returned with only the little girl swaddled in his arms. Despite his advanced age, he raised Juliet on his own and stubbornly refused help from the eager women in Winteridge.

Llewelyna said the death of Juliet's mother had disturbed her terribly. She held the outcomes of their births in each fist, weighing them like stones. "It could have been me," she had said, again and again, with almost a sense of yearning.

The day before, when I had stopped by the Pearl to collect workers, Juliet had been feeding her father soup straight from the pot. Despite the warm summer day, he was dressed in a wool sweater and had a blanket draped over his legs. I watched Juliet through the windows in the living room as she put the pot down on the side table and wiped her hands on her apron before coming to the door. Seamus Pearl had always been an old man to me, but these days he looked ancient.

"We've nothing to trade," she said as she opened the door and glanced at my jar of peaches.

I handed it to her. "A gift," I said.

"What for?" She took it tenuously.

"I need help on the orchard. I'll pay. If you'd like to join us, we begin tomorrow. Sunrise."

Juliet had thrust her chin up then and I knew I could expect her on the orchard the next day.

Joan and Ida Eber followed Juliet Pearl up the drive at a distance. Juliet must have heard their footfalls, but chose to ignore them and did not wait up. Ida Eber walked with the same limp she had as a little girl. She was born with one leg three inches shorter than the other, and often wore a shoe with a wedge of wood nailed to the sole. The runt, they called her. Now she had a rose-coloured stain all up her neck. Joan later claimed it was a birthmark, but I couldn't remember seeing it on Ida's neck before. It was puckered like the burn I got as a little girl when a drop of hot oil landed on my arm. Her sister Joan was tall and haughty. She wore a constant scowl, a hardened look I understood must have come with living with the seven Eber brothers, crude boys that couldn't be trusted to fill a bucket with water.

When I had ridden up the Ebers' drive the day before, their vast land had felt desolate with the sons off at war. The eldest

Eber boy had been eaten up by the war already. Mr. Eber was tending a burning mound of waste. The smell was putrid. I could feel him staring at me but knew not to make eye contact.

I came across what remained of one of the Ebers' hounds. It had been torn apart by hungry coyotes and left to rot. Ida and Joan were on the front porch pinching the ends off wooded beans and scrubbing nubby old potatoes. A little grubby boy was seated at their feet, dressed in only a long shirt. There were rumours about this boy, for Mrs. Eber was far too old to have birthed such a young child. She had to have been nearing fifty when she gave birth to Ida, her last. The little boy opened and closed the wings of a dead bird, a house finch. I noticed then he had mismatched eyes, one blue and one brown, like Ida. Joan and Ida hardly lifted their gazes to acknowledge me. Like their father, it seemed the sisters despised my presence. I was an outsider and unwelcome on their land. A trespasser.

I hadn't thought they were interested in my proposition and was surprised to see them walk up our drive the next day. I hadn't expected Mrs. Bell to show up either. She looked incredibly small and bird-boned in Mr. Bell's overalls. Her thin hair was in two narrow braids tucked behind her ears, so unlike the pompadour she had worn before. The girlish hairstyle made her look old and thin.

After we toured the orchard I offered the women the black tea and sourdough I had Mary prepare for us. Teresa and Daphne Nickel joined us a little later in the day. The Nickels' store had slowed, and there weren't enough customers to warrant Teresa and Daphne working the storefront. I had always found Teresa an ignorant, melodramatic sort. She talked endlessly about Ronald, her twin brother. If I didn't like Ronald so much myself, I might have revealed his and Jacob's secret romance to Teresa just to silence her.

On that first day, I taught the women how to safely operate the ladders, how to wear the pick sacks, and the best way to pluck the ripened fruit without bruising its tender skin, just as Yuri had once taught me. Mary watched us from the windows of our house where she cared for Llewelyna, or sometimes from the wash tub outside where she scrubbed at our clothes.

Every morning we sat at the pickers' table as the sun turned the edges of the trees gold and read the latest news from the front. Teresa bought the newspaper from the lakeboat captain, who brought copies from the city and charged tenfold for them. We would also share with one another our most recent letters. We kept these letters in breast pockets and waistbands, as if their contact to our skin might bring our men closer to us.

Though I couldn't share Viktor's illicit, stolen words with the women, I often read them Yuri's humdrum letters. His way of evading any emotion or detail about the war became a kind of game. The women laughed as they counted the number of times Yuri mentioned food, the absence of food, or the weather. When Yuri began writing me overwrought love poems, it was only natural that I read them out to the women, too.

"'Your cheeks soft as peaches, your lips like rosebuds.'" I said the words indulgently while Teresa wrapped her arms around herself and turned from us so it looked as though she were kissing someone. "'Your hair like crow feathers, and your eyes like fire.'" I was being remade by these elements in Yuri's imagination, like Blodeuwedd, built from broom, oak, and meadowsweet. And with every new iteration, I disappeared a little.

Teresa claimed she had the ability to see and feel the war through Ronald. "I felt it in my bones. I saw it all in my mind's eye," she said one day. I busied myself with setting the dirtied teacups on the tray so no one would see my eyes rolling. "Like your mother, Iris. Like how she saw your father's death before it even happened. I can see things too."

I let the stack of saucers clang to the tray. "How do you know about that?"

"Ah, now you should know you can't keep a secret in a town like this."

"Did your mother tell you that?"

"My lips are sealed." Teresa made a motion as if to button her lips. I knew she was just a fraud looking for attention, a girl so ordinary she had to invent and lie to make herself feel important, and still her ignorance irritated me. She didn't understand that foresight was a burden that wore you down and could make you lose yourself.

One evening that summer, I fell asleep on our back porch after a long, hot day of picking and woke to the sound of someone running through the orchard. There was the jingle of silver. Once my eyes adjusted to the dark I could make out countless shadows moving amongst the trees. For a moment I saw the shapes of coyotes. I thought I heard one howl. Then the moon came out from behind a cloud and the shadows dissolved. It was only the trees remaking themselves in the dark.

Since my fall by the lake, my seizures came only while I was asleep. I would know one had occurred by a few telltale signs the next day: bloodshot eyes, stiff arms and legs, and a sore, bleeding tongue. Even more than the physical markings, I knew I had had a seizure by the dream I always woke from. Like the forest Llewelyna walked through during a seizure, I was often in a long, unfamiliar hallway trailing after the jaguar. Then, once I returned from the dream, I would find the jaguar had followed me out. Sometimes she would stay for a few hours; other times she would stay for days. Even once the jaguar disappeared, I still felt as though I was being watched, even in the most private of moments.

Llewelyna's seizures were frequent and getting worse: longer and more intense. She often complained of pests in the house, mice scurrying across her bedspread, a squirrel climbing along the curtain rod, sometimes invisible fruit flies clouded her vision and she would wave a hand in front of her face to clear them. She couldn't understand why Mary and I couldn't keep the house free of the creatures. Admittedly, the house was difficult to keep clean at that time. A mysterious layer of coarse animal hair coated the chesterfield, and dirt crusted the floor. I found nibbled bits of food in Llewelyna's wardrobe and along the stairs. She once claimed to have a coyote beneath her bed, and later said she had found a fawn asleep in the tin bathtub that morning. Of course Mary and I thought these were only hallucinations, but then I came across a muddy paw print on the wood floor. After days of her complaining about a robin trapped in her closet, the bird finally materialized, and Mary and I madly raced about and finally caught the bird with a lampshade and a newspaper.

It was around this time that Mrs. Bell's greyhound was attacked. She arrived home from picking one day to find King Edward VII torn to shreds. It was a terrible mess. We helped her bury the dog in the forest. Mrs. Nickel had claimed she had seen a cougar stalking the perimeter of their yard a few days before, but I couldn't help but wonder if it was my jaguar that killed her greyhound.

After an especially brutal seizure, Llewelyna slept for an entire week. When she finally woke, Mary fetched me from the orchard and said, "She's asking for you."

The door to her room whined as I pushed it open. She was propped upright and her eyes were closed. Saint Francis sat at her chest and pecked at crumbs in her hair. He squawked when I brushed him away. Llewelyna opened her eyes. She stared at me blankly.

"Mary said you asked for me," I said.

Her eyes narrowed. She shook her head. "No. I asked for my daughter. Not *you*."

When I told Mary what Llewelyna had said, she suggested putting her back on the bromide. At last, I complied.

19

Most of the women got along quite well and our days were filled with chatter. Since the death of King Edward VII, Mrs. Bell claimed to have seen a little Indian girl climb a maple tree in her backyard. She crawled along the limbs to get in and out of the Bells' yard. Mrs. Bell threatened to call the mounted police. She said things had gone missing from her house, jewellery, a few figurines from her cabinet, and her collection of butterflies. I grinned at the obvious work of the orphan thief.

Mrs. Bell and Teresa spoke so much and with such velocity that I often had to escape the sounds of their voices to cool the gears in my ears. Juliet was the only other one who also seemed irritated by the racket and, after a brief exchange of looks, we would escape, saying we had to chop firewood, or collect the rubbish and branches beneath the trees at the far side of the orchard, or help Mary prepare lunch.

Juliet's silence always urged me to speak. I revealed things to her I had never told another soul. One day we shared a pair of Llewelyna's leather gloves my father had once bought her, and carried a long, poky branch between us, and I found myself telling her about Yuri's proposal, and my growing distaste for him. I had to stop before I told her about Viktor's letters. Juliet didn't comment on what I had said. Instead she offered a piece of her own story in return. In this way we quickly became friends.

Mary left platters of bread and cheese on the porch for us to snack on while we worked in the trees. She looked at me with sullen eyes that shifted every time I tried to make eye contact. I asked her several times to join us for lunch at least, but she claimed there was simply too much work to be done in the house, and someone had to care for Llewelyna. Finally she admitted:

"Taras hates it. He thinks you women are stealing his men's jobs."

"But his men aren't here."

She shrugged. "He won't have it."

Taras's health had declined significantly. I only saw him when he stomped past the orchard on his way to the outhouse, cursing us women beneath his breath like a madman. The women would freeze on the ladders or hide in the trees whenever he passed, afraid to move. Once he had returned safely back inside his house we would snicker and mock his awkward gait, or inhale dramatically as if we had been holding our breath to keep from breathing in his stench.

Some nights I woke to Taras and Mary fighting. Taras's voice boomed in the stillness while Mary's words, if she said anything at all, remained inaudible. Often when they argued I heard things fall to the ground. Pots and pans slammed against the walls, glass shattered. They didn't own many things, and I thought they must only have a couple of dishes left. During these episodes, I would sit at the window and watch the dim windows of the Wasiks' house, seeing nothing but the dance of shadows, afraid and unsure what to do.

One night I was jolted from sleep by a gunshot. I walked through the halls of our house, running my fingers along the walls to remind my body of its dimensions until my eyes got used to the dark. Once I was outside, the sky was clear and cloudless. Stars twinkled innocently. The Wasiks' house was dark and the orchard was so quiet that I thought I must have imagined the shot. The only sound was the beating of my heart in my throat and the chirp of crickets in the bushes by the lake. Just as I was about to return to the house, a shadow sped out from behind the workhouse and disappeared into the orchard. I pushed my body up against the side of the workhouse and slid along the building. Right when I was at the corner, Taras lurched out of the darkness and raised a pistol at me. I closed my eyes as the shot rang out. It echoed into the hills. I opened my eyes to see if I was dead or alive. Taras wasn't looking at me. His gun was aimed into the orchard.

"Coyote," he said, and cursed in Ukrainian as he walked past me. I remained stiff against the house and caught my breath. My thighs were sticky with urine.

"Did you hit him?"

"Dunno."

Despite my fear, I followed Taras through the forest. I worried over Llewelyna's silver coyote, her she-wolf. Had he hit her? Moonlight bounced off the gunmetal as he swung the pistol at his side with each step. It was then that I recognized Mr. Bell's gun from all those years before. Under the trees the darkness was thick, more pronounced. For a moment I lost sight of Taras. I froze and listened. I heard the crunch of leaves and followed the noise. Taras was bent down at the bough of a tree. He ran his finger along a dark splotch. Blood. I backed away slowly and ran to the house.

The next morning, I went back to where Taras and I had trailed after the coyote. I couldn't see any blood or other evidence of what had occurred in the night. Later, while the women went down to the lake for their afternoon swim, I saw the orphan thief slip out the window of Mrs. Bell's kitchen holding a few of her treasured sugar spoons. She was wearing a necklace strung with Mrs. Bell's butterfly

collection, the kaleidoscopic wings more brilliant than any gem-
stone. I ran after her. She didn't turn around, but she slowed every
now and then, as though she had intended that I follow her.

The orphan thief was leading me to Henry's tree fort. I hadn't
been inside since I had interrupted Viktor and Azami's lovemaking three years before. As we got closer to the fort, the surrounding trees became more and more ornamented with the orphan
thief's scavenged things—rings were glued with sap to bark, silverware hung from threads, pearl necklaces draped from branches.
Llewelyna's gold scarf was wrapped around a trunk, and her ruby
earring punctured a broad leaf.

A sound was coming from up in the tree fort. I slowly climbed
the ladder and carefully peeked above the floor, but the orphan
thief was not inside. I found Llewelyna's jewelery box against a
wall. It was left open and the dancing girl turned around and
around to mechanical music. There were new chimes hanging from
the ceiling. The strings were invisible, and so the charms and trinkets seemed to float mid-air. The deer statuette from Mrs. Bell's
china cabinet clinked gently against her emerald brooch and silverware. In a corner I found Mrs. Bell's little house figurines lined up
amongst some moss, bark, and stones. I realized the display resembled Winteridge in miniature: the schoolhouse, the Nickels' shop,
the homes, Henry's library, the orchards, it was all there—a little
map of the town. I carefully thumbed a house painted green, meant
to resemble my own home. The peach trees were made of green
snips of cedar and rolled bits of marigold petals.

In the opposite corner of the tree fort was a square of buck-
skin mottled with holes, a stone bowl full of ash, and a long brown
feather. The collection reminded me of Azami's shrine, her precious, meaning-filled items. I knew the orphan thief was trying
to show me something, but I didn't understand why she collected

these stolen items. What did Mrs. Bell's trinkets and Llewelyna's jewellery mean to the orphan thief? What use did she have for them besides decoration? And why the miniature town? I wondered if the very act of stealing was the point the orphan thief was trying to make. Had I taken something from her? I considered this, and although it was beginning to come clear, I wasn't ready to acknowledge my part in her suffering, my own bit of thievery.

The next morning, when Mary didn't arrive to nurse Llewelyna, I went to check in at the Wasiks', thinking she might be ill. She answered her door with a blackened eye she attempted to hide by bowing her head obviously. She walked with a limp. I tried to persuade her to gather her things immediately and come stay in the house. Mary refused and gestured for me to keep my voice down.

"You have no business prying," she said. Her voice was so stern I hardly recognized it. She closed the door on me.

While the women worked in the trees and Mary stayed home and nursed Taras, I kept to the house and took care of Llewelyna. I was outside at the well filling a bucket for her bath when the officer who had come looking for Taras before appeared again on our porch. I approached him from behind as he knocked at our door. Water from my bucket sloshed onto the porch. He turned, clearly startled.

"Iris Sparks, is that right?" he said kindly, his hat in his hands. He was holding the clipboard again. I invited him inside and we sat at the kitchen table.

"You have quite the operation here," he said. "I've never seen so many hardworking women in trousers." He laughed.

"They pick as well as the men, I assure you. We sell every week at markets in the city, and in the fall we hope to send preserves overseas to the soldiers." I leaned forward, tired of his small talk. "What are you here for, if I might ask?"

"We're still looking for this"—he glanced down at the clip-board—"Taras Wasik character. One of your neighbours says he worked for your father. Is that true? Strange your mother didn't mention it."

I stared at the crystal vase in the centre of the table where I had placed some of the purple asters and marigolds that still thrived in Llewelyna's wild garden. I hadn't changed the water for a few days. A beetle struggled to crawl up the glass and out of the water, his little legs spinning.

"What will you do with this man once you find him?" I asked.

"He'll be held safely, just until the war is over."

The fact that Taras had had Mr. Bell's gun all this time terri-fied me. That night, the moment before I had closed my eyes, Taras had aimed the gun right at me. He had lied about Henry snooping around Mr. Bell's shack and stood by as the mob ran-sacked Henry's bookstore. He had wanted Henry destroyed. And how did he get the gun, anyway? Taras couldn't be trusted and I could no longer bear him spending his sons' money on alcohol. He scared the women and took his misery out on Mary. I looked up at the soldier. One of his eyes turned outward, as if he were look-ing at two things at once. I wondered if this was why he couldn't join the forces overseas. I leaned in.

"He's in the workhouse. That cottage down there."

"Taras Wasik?"

I nodded.

"Were you hiding him?"

"He forced me to," I said. "He said if I didn't protect him he would kill me."

The officer nodded gravely.

I watched from the kitchen window as the officer burst through the Wasiks' door. I imagined Mary's fear. I hoped, finally freed from him, she would forgive me and come stay in the house with us, maybe even join the women in the orchard. Some female company would be good for her. The officer pulled Taras out and bound his arms behind his back. Even in his weakness, Taras struggled against the soldier. Then, to my horror, Mary followed Taras out of the cabin. She searched the windows of our house for my face, her lips clenched tight. I ran onto the porch.

"Mary, what are you doing? Don't go."

Taras cursed me in Ukrainian.

"She has no choice, miss. She's his wife. She must come with me also."

"But she's British."

"Doesn't matter. She's his wife. An accomplice. We've no idea what side she's on. It's a risk we can't take."

Mary offered her wrists to the officer, but he hadn't come prepared with restraints for two. I should have realized, even if she had been given a choice, Mary would have followed Taras anyway.

I ran down our drive babbling to the officer that Mary was innocent, British! And had no part in whatever Taras was involved in. Mary shot me a look in an attempt to silence me. Everyone had come out of their homes now to watch us parade down the road towards the wharf.

"Go home, Iris," Mary said. "You're making a scene."

I fell to my knees in the middle of the road. I had never felt so helpless. Taras fought against his restraints, shoulders straining, and the officer struggled to keep hold of him. Mary limped obediently behind them. Tears burned my eyes. People on the road bowed their heads and pretended not to watch Mary and Taras pass. Another man in uniform joined the officer and tied Mary's wrists behind her back with rope and pulled her roughly by the shoulder. She tripped and fell headfirst, her arms unable to break her fall. When she stood, her nose was bleeding. Blood dripped down her chin.

I knew it was Mrs. Bell who had told the officer about Taras, although she didn't admit to it when I told the women what happened. Even still, it wasn't Mrs. Bell's fault Mary was taken. It was mine.

I searched the Wasiks' house for Mr. Bell's pistol, but I couldn't find the damn thing anywhere.

ﯼ

That autumn it was sad to see the women return to their homes. Only Mrs. Bell and Juliet stayed on to help me jar peaches and make preserves. Mrs. Bell talked on and on about London and her teenage years. She told us the dull story of how she and Phillip met, and the silly things he had done to win her over. Although her talking had annoyed me at first, it soon became a comfort, a kind of hum. The sound of her voice made the house feel full and warm.

That winter Juliet loaned me romance novels. Henry's library never held such books. We exchanged them wordlessly, smiles creeping up our cheeks. I filled the narratives out with the bodies of Viktor and me and used these scenes to inspire my own words. Soon I was writing letters back to Viktor. I didn't sign my name. I didn't sign any name. And so I decided this wasn't exactly a betrayal. In truth, Viktor moved around so much it was impossible to know if any of the letters ever reached him.

20

Only Juliet and the Eber sisters returned to the orchard the following spring to work. We couldn't keep up with all the picking, and most of the peaches went to waste again that summer. The first men returned to Winteridge late in the fall of 1917, and everyone in town went down to the wharf, hoping to see their son, brother, or husband. Although the crowd consisted of many of the same people who had once gathered to send our men off three years earlier, we had become thin and pale, worn, weak and disenchanted. We had heard of the battle in France—our men had finally taken Vimy Ridge—but it was difficult to celebrate success so far away when all we were faced with was absence. By this time we had learned that any triumph came with a death toll; we were still waiting to find out who.

Further down the shore I saw Azami and her husband, Kenta. I had heard from Teresa, who kept up on Winteridge gossip, that Azami's brother, Wu, was the only Japanese man in Winteridge accepted into the Canadian forces. He had been so determined to fight that when he was barred from enlisting, he travelled to Alberta because he heard they were accepting Japanese volunteers. From there he was swiftly sent off to Europe with a Canadian battalion.

A toddler was crouched at her feet picking up stones and turning them over in his tiny hands as if searching for a message written on one in particular. I knew Azami had named this son Juro, after her father. A name her father had tried to leave behind in Japan. Azami held a swaddled baby in her arms also, another boy, only a few weeks old. I wondered if he had a name yet and what it might be.

When the *Rosamond* first came around the bend, the crowd in the bay cheered it along, and then, as the boat approached and the weakened condition of the soldiers was made clear, we all grew quiet. Only a cough or two punctured the silence. There were few men returning, and they were wounded at that. These were not the warriors we expected, but men who could no longer fight, could hardly stand. The painted face of the siren on the ship's bow was smeared. She looked like a whore after a long, terrible night.

Although I hadn't received word from Viktor, Yuri, or Jacob for months, and had no reason to believe they were returning that day, I looked desperately for Jacob's red curls, Yuri's blond hair, and of course Viktor. But the men all wore hats and bent awkwardly over crutches or slouched in wheelchairs. I didn't recognize any of them. A couple of girls squealed as they ran up to a young man with a pale face and pushed the bewildered soul down the wharf in a wheelchair.

Azami was staring at something, her eyes wide and unmoving. Her brother had not arrived and so her family had turned towards the shore, but she remained, looking out at the boat. I followed her eyes and found Viktor on the upper deck. He had a dark beard and was unrecognizable except for his eyes, which gaped back at Azami. His mouth was open in shock. The baby in Azami's arms began to cry but still she didn't move. The ramp was being lifted; the *Rosamond* was about to set off. Azami's husband came up beside her, tapped her shoulder. Finally Kenta looked up to where Azami was looking, saw Viktor, and more forcefully tugged at her shoulder. She gave in.

"Viktor!" I ran down the wharf. The man securing the ramp to the boat stalled and looked up at me. "There's someone still on the boat. Wait."

"Are you sure, miss?"

"Yes, my . . . my friend. I see him. He must be confused. Viktor!" I called out to him. He didn't look at me. I pointed Viktor out and he was led off the boat, helped by a man with a mangled hand. Viktor looked at me dully, a bottle tucked in his pocket. I had imagined him so thoroughly in my mind that it seemed strange he should still possess a body at all.

"Well hello, Your Highness," he said in mock earnest. I was passed Viktor's cloth sack; the very same one Mary had packed for both him and Yuri when they left. It had bulged with supplies then; now it was limp and light and might not have contained anything at all. I took Viktor by the arm. He used a crutch to walk. The bottom half of his right leg, from the knee down, was gone. He leaned on me heavily as we walked home, arm in arm, and despite the tragedy of it all, I couldn't help but smile at the thought that this body, however worn and disfigured, was mine to care for. Viktor needed *me* now.

"I wonder why my mother didn't come to the bay," Viktor said quietly as we hobbled together down the road. I hadn't thought through what I would tell him about Taras and Mary and so I pretended not to hear him. When we got to the driveway I tried to steer Viktor towards my house. He stopped outside the Wasiks' cabin, already searching the windows for Mary.

"Come inside the house, I'll make some soup," I said.

"I should go home right away, my mother will want—"

"They're not home."

"Ah. Have they gone to town, then?"

"No, Viktor. They've been taken."

"Taken?" He stumbled, his crutch dropped. He grabbed my arm and I struggled to stand under his weight.

"I did everything I could," I said. I thought I would vomit from guilt.

Viktor shook me. "What are you talking about?"

"Some officers took them to a camp in Vernon."

"What? Why? A work camp?"

"I don't know. They said it's just until the war's over."

"This goddamned war will never end."

"I'm so sorry, Viktor." His hands were cinched tight around my arms and the pain felt good, earned.

"But why did they take them?"

"Because they're considered enemies, like you once said."

"Enemies?"

"Hungarians."

"My mother's British, for God sakes, and their sons are fighting for the Allies against the Huns. Their sons . . . I have to find them. Help me with the crutch." I positioned the crutch back under his arm. He took his cloth bag from me and wobbled towards his parents' cabin.

The next day, I went to take Viktor some breakfast, and he was gone.

ಕ

It was while Viktor was away, looking for his parents, that I received another letter. This one was not delivered by a young soldier but came instead with the regular post. I had to read the name over and over: *Jacob Sparks*. They were balanced by the next words, *missing in action. Passchendaele.* At first I didn't know how to understand this message. Missing? Then I closed my eyes and I saw it. I saw Jacob fall. I didn't want to tell Llewelyna of this news. I could hear her upstairs, singing softly. She must not have forseen this particular tragedy. I wanted to go upstairs and join the world that still existed for her, a world in which Jacob was alive and well and the words from his last letter still trickled through her mind. When I had taken up her breakfast that morning she had been in a good mood, alert and upright and writing in the *Mabinogion*. Her hands were always blackened with ink now. The work seemed to keep her seizures at bay along with small doses of the bromide.

I went upstairs and found Llewelyna in the tin bathtub. It took me a moment to realize the fish was gone from the jar beside the tub.

"What have you done?"

Llewelyna smiled eerily. "Was wasting away in there." She shrugged. "What's the harm?" She lifted her chin and sniffed as if tracking a smell in the air.

"You swallowed my fish?"

"*Your* fish?" She spoke as if her tongue was swollen.

"The woman said it was for me."

"For you!"

"Yes, she said it was for a girl."

"And you think that girl is you? Ha!"

"Did you eat it?"

She smiled darkly.

"I hate you."

That's when the trembling began. Her head jerked back against the tub. Her neck was strung with tendons, her jaw clenched, and her teeth locked. Her eyes went wide, the pupils slowly eclipsing the green irises. Her arms were stiff against her sides and her hands made fists. The thrashing created a wake and bathwater splashed the floor. I cradled her head in my hands to keep it from slipping underwater. Sweat pebbled her temples and pink drool trickled from the corner of her mouth and onto my hands. The whites of her eyes flooded red as the blood vessels burst. The seizure lasted forever. When the trembling slowed, her body remained stiff. I could feel the moment she was finally released. Her mouth went slack, and her bloodshot eyes finally blinked.

"Water," she said.

I returned from the kitchen with a pinch of bromide dissolved in water. She was sitting up now, amused by something near her feet.

"Look," she said. The blue fish was darting through the bathwater, dipping and swirling past her limbs. She giggled when it grazed her skin. "It won't have me," she said, a little sad. "Rejected me. Just like it did the woman who walked out of the lake."

"But she died."

"Yes, and now it needs a new body. Wisdom like that needs a home."

We watched the blue fish flash through the water.

"Why didn't you tell me Henry found the woman? That he put her in the lake?"

"Well, you didn't seem much interested. Apparently you never even saw her in the first place." She cupped her hand and caught the fish against her leg. I refilled the jar and she placed the fish back in it.

"Maybe I should just put the fish back in the lake," I said.

Llewelyna shot forward and grabbed the wrist of my hand holding the jar. She clutched the jar with her other hand, but I wouldn't let it go.

"Don't you dare. Don't even think of it." Her fingers pressed against the veins of my wrist and my hand swelled with trapped blood. "You don't even know what this is, you fool." She squeezed my wrist even harder. My hand went numb. "Let go," she said.

"You can't swallow it."

"It doesn't want me anyway."

I let go of the jar. Llewelyna lifted it close to her face and smiled at the blue fish. I passed her the lid and she screwed it back on. "I had a dream," she said. "A vision."

I swallowed hard. I thought she might know about Jacob now. Llewelyna lifted her eyes to mine before she closed them. I knelt beside the tub but I did not close my eyes. I didn't trust her.

"I remember it like this," she said, and I was confused because this was how she began her old stories, not her visions. She hummed. "Ba ba bach. Babi bach," she sang in Welsh. "The baby was so small. She had white fuzz on her skin, like a peach. Not quite ripe. Hardly two days old." Llewelyna wore a smile that unsettled me. "When the mother carried her to the water, the infant spoke, for she was wise and had lived many lives before this one. 'Where did you come from?' the mother asked the infant. 'My original country is the region of the summer stars,' the baby responded. 'It is not known whether my body is flesh or fish.' The mother asked, 'What should I call you?' And the infant said, 'You shall call me Neb. For I am no one.' And with that the mother placed the infant in the water until she was no more. And then the mother—"

"This is you," I interrupted. "This is a story about you. All of these horrible stories are about you."

Llewelyna's eyes shot open. "Are they?"

"You drowned your baby." I stood and looked down at her. Her body was grotesque, sinewed and starved, all bone and joint. Her skin was faintly green. She kept her eyes on me. I wanted to take the fish from her but her knuckles were white around the jar and she had the look of a snake about to strike.

"You did," I said, "didn't you."

Llewelyna threw her head back and laughed heartily. I slammed the door.

"One day you will understand," I heard her say.

I busied myself with housework on the main floor until dark. I didn't want to see her. I didn't want to hear her confess her evils. I didn't want to understand her. Around midnight I heard her step out of the tub and walk around. I heard her fall. I might have gone up then to see if she was okay, but I didn't. A few minutes later I heard something break. And still I refused to go upstairs. I remained for hours on the ground floor standing at the bottom of the stairs. It was far too quiet. It is possible I knew. It is possible I wanted it to happen.

I can only recall a few vivid details: her arm, palm up, veins exposed, resting on the edge of the tin tub. The broken jar. A bloody shard. The blue fish frantic in the rusty bathwater, darting around her limbs. I used my hand to scoop up the fish. My fingers grazed her cold, lifeless skin. I don't remember running to the Nickels' store with bare feet. I don't remember watching Mr. McCarthy and Mr. Nickel carry the tin tub down the stairs and out of the house. I don't remember the water spilling on the kitchen floor or slipping in that puddle and bruising my elbow. I can't connect her death to any of that. It was much too unreal to be true. What I do know for certain is that Llewelyna knew about Jacob the whole time.

I am still haunted by a recurring dream of Llewelyna's death. In this dream she is standing at the shore of the lake in the blue light of stars. The moon is enormous. She is in the white dress she wore that first night on the *Rosamond*. The lake is calm. She clutches a large rock to her chest. As she walks into the lake her dress floats up around her knees, her hips, her stomach. The monster raises its head from the lake. I can't see it in the dark but I know it is there. The lake becomes turbulent and takes Llewelyna with it.

In part because of this vision, but also because I knew my mother and her wishes, I refused to have Llewelyna's body buried. Instead, I had it sent off in the lakeboat to the city. It returned in a parcel of ash. Giving her to the water was the only kindness I could bear to offer Llewelyna. Mr. McCarthy paddled Juliet Pearl and me out into the middle of the lake in his rowboat. Juliet held my hand tight and sang a beautiful song about angels and white-robed martyrs and it all sounded like sacrilege coming from her heavily lipsticked mouth. Old Mr. McCarthy kept his face turned from us, as if only looking directly at my grief would make him privy to it. He looked towards the horizon as I poured my mother's body into the icy blue water.

Llewelyna would have been satisfied to know that the night she died, she entered into myth. Everyone in Winteridge had his or her own version of her death. Juliet said that the night she died, her father had seen Llewelyna walking towards the lake, the peacock trailing behind her. He had asked her what she was doing out in the cold at that hour, and she had said she was going for a swim. The similarity between Mr. Pearl's vision and my own recurring dream of Llewelyna's death made me shiver. Later Mrs. McCarthy told me she saw Llewelyna wandering through the wooded hills the night she died. A fisherman from another village reported a woman on the cliffs, standing over the edge and looking down at the water below, her dress blowing in the wind. He called to her but she didn't respond. There were rumours about Saint Francis too. He disappeared the same night Llewelyna died. Kenji, a picker on the Kobas' orchard, saw Saint Francis, the flightless bird, soaring above the apple trees. Mr. Nickel saw the bird stalking the shore of the lake, squawking mournfully.

I placed the blue fish in a new jar of water and set it by the window to take in the light.

I found Llewelyna's *Mabinogion* hidden beneath her bed. I ran my fingers over the dragon on the cover and considered throwing it into the stove unread, both out of respect for Llewelyna's wish that I not intrude on her work, and because I wasn't sure I was ready for what I might find inside. I knew her words, her secrets, would appear as nothing to me. I knew she wrote in Welsh. And still, the fact that she kept this book secret from me made me imagine I might make some sense of it. Llewelyna had bent over this book for years, scribbling furiously. She saved whatever energy she could muster for this one final task. I understood that she was not only translating the text back into Welsh but, like Henry had said, she was attempting to rewrite the stories, revise and fix them until they better resembled the stories her grandmother had told her as a young girl, the stories Llewelyna had told and retold Jacob and me. But I realized too that these written stories and Llewelyna's grandmother's stories and Llewelyna's own stories could never be the same. They were bent by memory and experience, twisted to fit whatever meaning the story-teller might require at that moment. And because I thought there was something inside I might inherit, something I might bend and flex and mould into my very own, I opened the *Mabinogion*.

There was nothing left of the original text. Llewelyna had written over the words, crossed out her own writing, and rewritten something else in its place so that in the end, all that remained inside the book were indecipherable puddles of black ink. I almost laughed when I saw it. What kind of sense did I expect from madness? Then I realized I didn't need these stories. I already had them.

I walked to the edge of the wharf and dropped the *Mabinogion* into the water. The book floated for a moment, the red dragon burning like an ember, before it sank into the bottomless lake.

21

Viktor returned early one winter morning. He had been away for months looking for Mary and Taras. It was still dark outside when I opened the door to him. He shivered in his thin coat. His shoulders were dusted with snow. I sat him on the yellow chesterfield and warmed us both some broth. He looked into the flames of the fire and said nothing. His broth remained untouched on the side table. He looked as though he hadn't eaten in a very long time.

"Viktor," I said. I put my wrist to his forehead. "You're not well."

"You're in black," he said. "Has someone died?"

"Everyone has died."

"Yuri, is he . . . ?"

"I received a letter from him yesterday. He's been offered some award."

"Is it Jacob?"

I nodded and tried to keep the familiar bubble from slipping up my throat. As I told Viktor about Jacob and Llewelyna, my words turned to sobs. I could hardly breathe. Viktor clutched my head against his chest until I calmed down. His heart thumped against my cheek. Then my sadness was replaced by doom. Had Viktor found out what I had done? That I had betrayed Taras? I sat back up.

"Did you find your parents?"

"It's terrible." He wouldn't look at me. He stirred his soup as if it were something he could read from.

He knows, I thought.

"I've never seen my mother so worn. I only recognized her by her old bonnet."

"So you found them?" I managed.

"We spoke through a wire fence, the kind we keep the chickens in. They're at a work camp. The prisoners carry boulders in wheelbarrows, work day and night, hard, hard labour. It's inhumane." He began to break down, his words gurgling out. "I had no choice. My mother's hands were cracked, her nails torn and bleeding. And my father . . ."

I pushed Viktor's oily hair back, away from his face. He wiped his tears with his sleeve.

I was relieved. It was clear he didn't know. "What is it? What's happened to Taras?"

"He's dead."

"Dead? How?"

"I brought him the pistol, hidden in a loaf of bread. I thought he could use it to get out."

"Oh, Viktor . . ."

"They saw the gun. Shot him dead."

Viktor slept in Jacob's old room. We spent those first weeks taking turns being the invalid, reminding one another to eat, to sleep, to bathe. One unusually warm winter evening, Viktor brought up the whisky from his father's liquor cabinet and a stringed instrument. We sat on the porch wrapped in blankets and watched a pair of loons nibble at the long grass in the orchard. Their white-speckled backs glimmered.

"This was my grandfather's." Viktor strummed a few notes. He played it like a guitar, but it sounded more like a harp.

"Did he teach you to play?" I asked.

"No, my father taught me. I didn't know my grandfather. He died before I was born. He was a kobzar."

"What is that?" I asked.

Viktor continued to play softly as he spoke. The strings of the instrument appeared made of light. "A kobzar is a travelling bard. This here is called a kobza, but kobzars play banduras and liras too. In the Ukraine these bards organized themselves into brother-hoods and guilds. My grandfather was blind and it was common for kobzars to be blind. I'm not sure why." Viktor smiled as he spoke. It was good to see his sadness break for once. I urged him on. "He sang well. He was nearly famous for a time, played in concert halls in Kiev until the Russians put a stop to it. The brotherhood nearly dissolved, forced underground. The Russians banned the use of the Ukrainian language. The Tsar's wife was fond of my grand-father's songs, and so he had them translated into Russian, but my grandfather refused to sing them. My grandfather's songs were symbolic, political, about the Ukrainian state, independence. To translate those songs into Russian was treasonous. But my grand-father continued to sing his Ukrainian songs in the streets, for anyone who would listen, until he was arrested."

"Just for singing?"

"His language was illegal. The Ukrainian culture was a speck in the eye of Russian sovereignty. Even my father's name, Taras, after a great Ukrainian poet, was a kind of rebellion. When he was finally released my grandfather was weak and poor—and blind, remember. He died a few years later. But before that time, and in secret, he taught my father to play this kobza."

"And Taras taught you?"

"Yes, in secret, just like his grandfather did. He said that is the only way to play the kobza. And someday I am to pass the skill on to my children." Viktor stopped playing to take a drink of whisky.

"But why in secret? Taras could speak Ukrainian freely here."

Viktor looked at me cruelly. "Don't be daft. His language got him sent to that prison camp."

"Why did your father want to fight with the Russians if he hated them so much?"

Viktor returned to the instrument and strummed. "The other side is Austria-Hungary and he hated them just as much as he hated the Russians. He wanted to fight for the Ukraine. For Galicia. But since those countries don't exist on maps, he wanted to fight for Canada. All he really wanted was a place to call his home, his country." He closed his eyes and continued playing the instrument.

"Viktor," I interrupted, "I stole that gun."

"What are you talking about?"

"The pistol you gave Taras. I stole it from Mr. Bell when I was just a girl."

He jolted upright. "That was you?"

"Don't play coy. You were the one who found it in the woods."

"You let Henry take the blame for the gun."

"I didn't know what to do."

"All those books were destroyed . . ."

"It was terrible."

"I had never seen that gun before," Viktor said. "I found it in the liquor cabinet." Something startled the pair of loons and they launched into the painted sky, their wide wings beating.

"If you didn't find Mr. Bell's gun, then who did?"

The question hung in the air between us, but we both knew it could only be Yuri.

ɾℇ

I hadn't received a postcard from Henry for a while. At first I had thought the worst, then wondered if he somehow knew about Llewelyna's death. When a letter came from Wales for her, I recognized Henry's handwriting. What was he doing in Wales? I fingered the postage stamp. The red dragon's outline was so severe the ink had ridges I could run my finger along. There was no return address. I convinced myself there might be a clue inside as to where Henry was and how I could contact him about Llewelyna's death, and that was enough to give me reason to open the letter.

A photograph slipped from the envelope. At first I thought it was a picture of Llewelyna and me. The girl was pale with thin dark hair and the woman beside her was surely my mother, but something was off about it all. The two were sitting in the sand, wearing breezy spring dresses. The ocean stretched out behind them. The girl was about ten or eleven years old. She held a clutch of marigolds to her chest. Her eyes appeared closed because she was looking down at the flowers. I flipped the photograph around: *Gwyn a Nia, Ebrill 1905.* I wondered if this girl was my Aunt Gwyn's daughter, my cousin. I ripped out Henry's letter and read it voraciously.

From the fragments of poor Henry's rambling, broken thoughts, I learned that Llewelyna had asked him to travel to Holyhead to visit her sister. There, he learned from Gwyn that Llewelyna's daughter had not died as an infant as Llewelyna had told him, and as I had gathered through her stories. The truth was, Llewelyna had simply vanished without a word when the child was only days old. She had refused to name the infant, referring to her only as *Neb*, Welsh for no one, and so Gwyn had named the girl Nia and raised her as her own. And although Nia did not die as an infant, Nia did die. At twelve she caught pneumonia and passed in her sleep. Nia's father was never known, but Gwyn had assumed it was a violent pairing; Llewelyna was fifteen years old when Nia was born.

Henry's letter was full of questions. He couldn't understand why she would make up something so horrifically, monstrously false. To me it was clear. The stories Llewelyna told about killing her baby were not confessions, as Henry and I had both assumed, but revisions. These terrible retellings were easier for her to face than the truth: she had abandoned her daughter, her firstborn. Instead, she revised the events so she could attempt to make sense of what she had done, even if it meant turning herself into a monster. I thought then of Llewelyna's version of the Rhiannon story, where Rhiannon has told the tale of eating her own son so many times that despite its fabrication it becomes true to her. Like Rhiannon, Llewelyna became trapped in a story of her own making.

If Llewelyna had sent Henry to Wales, she wanted him to know the truth. I wondered if she had ever meant for me to learn about this sibling. I wished I could see into my sister's eyes, which were forever looking down at those marigolds. But she would never see me, nor I her. And so, what of this new sibling I had gained in a photograph and lost in the space of a paragraph?

I had Viktor to care for now and I didn't have any room for this loss. I slipped the photograph and Henry's letter into the oven with the rest of the words I would rather have scalded from the earth.

❧

Viktor and I continued to hear good news from Yuri. Thankfully he had given up on his poetry. I responded to Yuri's letters with a new kind of enthusiasm, as if I already had something to hide from him and cover up. Yuri was championed by his regiment and was to achieve an award for service. Viktor scoffed.

"You don't want to know the atrocities a man must commit to get an award like that," he said. I didn't have to remind Viktor that it was he who convinced Yuri to join up in the first place, for Viktor's guilt was apparent in everything he did. The weight caused him to hunch over. He resembled a man twice his age. His hair greyed at the temples. Viktor wouldn't let me write to Yuri about their parents. He said it was best to wait until Yuri returned home.

Most evenings that spring, Viktor drank at the Pearl Hotel, which had become much more popular since the wounded soldiers had returned to Winteridge. Juliet worked tirelessly pouring ale and liquor for the soldiers. Viktor would leave the house angry and stumble back hours later whistling eerily cheery tunes.

One night I woke to the familiar tick-tock of him climbing the steps with his crutch. He stopped outside my bedroom. My stomach tightened and my entire body grew hot. He pushed the door open just a crack, then stepped in. As he approached, I was shocked to find my exhilaration was not unlike fear. I pretended to sleep as he slid into bed next to me. He ran his fingers up and down my arm; my skin tingled. He breathed in my hair, kissed the back of my neck. His beard tickled my skin. I forced myself not to move, afraid I might break whatever moment we were suspended in. Then he got out of my bed, picked up his crutch, and limped to the door.

"Viktor?" I whispered. I still faced away from him.

"I thought you were asleep."

"I was."

"I'm sorry. I'm a fool."

"It's okay."

"I've been drinking. My bed is cold. I just . . ."

"Come back."

"No. I should go."

"Come back," I said again. He didn't move towards the bed, but he didn't turn to leave either. I rolled over to face him. His body was silhouetted by the moonlight coming in from the window. "My bed is cold too."

Viktor hopped forward. "But, Iris . . ."

I lifted the blanket. "Just lie here with me until morning." We faced one another in the darkness. I could smell sour alcohol on his breath. "We'll pretend we're frontiersmen and we have to keep each other warm to survive." I was thankful the little joke was enough to make Viktor laugh, though my easy betrayal of Yuri scared me. I thought of the two of us as children, curled together in the tree fort like puppies.

"Give me your hands," I said. I held his hands in mine and blew warmth into them. We lay there for a while and listened to one another breathe. Azami's necklace slipped from Viktor's shirt. The silver tag caught a sliver of light.

"Did you see Azami?" I asked.

"Azami? When?"

I could make out the whites of his eyes, the gleam of teeth when he spoke.

"When the boat landed, she was there. Did you see her?"

"Of course I did."

"Is that why you stayed on the boat?"

"There were many reasons."

"Do you wish I hadn't made you get off? Do you wish you were somewhere else?"

"Do you?" He ran his fingers down my cheek. "Do you wish you were someplace else?"

"No." I smiled.

"I am glad Azami found happiness," he said, though his tone was flat. "Two children."

"Yes," I said. It made me sad to think that Viktor might live his entire life not knowing he was a father.

"It's so cold. My feet are—my foot is like a stone," he said.

"Come closer," I said.

Viktor wrapped his arms around me.

"You know I can still feel it sometimes, my missing foot. Isn't that ridiculous?"

"I don't think so."

"I'll never run. I'll never work on the orchard again. I'm forever half a man."

I thought of Viktor's letter and what he had said about killing the German soldier. The boy. I knew this was the real reason he felt like half the person he was. "You're not half. You'll be okay." There was a silence that was broken by his stalled breathing, then a kind of whimper. "You're not half." I pulled him close. His face was wet with tears. "You're not half," I kept repeating until we both fell asleep.

In the morning I woke to an empty bed. Viktor was asleep in Jacob's room. For a moment I had to wonder if it had all been a dream. Then that night Viktor came to my room again. This nighttime routine of ours continued for a few months. After leaving the Pearl, Viktor would slip into my bed and return to Jacob's room before morning. Some nights we talked until we fell asleep, and Viktor would tell me about his childhood in Vernon, about his mother and father. We never spoke of Yuri. Some nights, instead of speaking, we communicated only in the smallest of movements. Viktor's hand would slip between my knees until it was warm. My foot would push up against his calf. My fingers would find the crescent scar beneath his shirt where the bayonet had once punctured him. We wouldn't speak about these evenings in the light of day. It was a kind of rule. I thought of the Maya, who believed the night and day were separate worlds and the jaguar was the only one that might traverse from one to the other. I hadn't seen my own jaguar for a while, and I wondered if having Viktor with me at night kept her away.

When I ran into Juliet at the Nickels' store, the young girl in me was tempted to tell her all about Viktor and me, but I knew what I was doing looked terrible and cruel, and I wasn't ready to face the truth of it and what it meant, never mind her opinion. Although Viktor and I didn't speak of the changes that came over us at night, he looked at me differently now. His eyes settled on me as if in deliberation, as if each part of my body presented a mystery he might solve.

Sometimes Viktor called out in his sleep: *mutti, mutti, mutti*. He thrashed back and forth, his skin slick with sweat. I would shake him awake from the night terror, and he would jolt up terrified and tell me of dead horses as far as the eye could see—fields of dead horses, killed by poison gas. And tunnels underground, men crawling like worms, and German boys screaming for their mothers. And then Viktor would weep.

22

One evening late that spring, Viktor and I sat drinking whisky on the secluded beach curtained by willows. It was dark and the water was calm. We passed the bottle back and forth until our minds became heavy and our bodies light. A flock of geese appeared out of nothing in the sky. We looked up to see their white bellies moon past. They honked above our heads and faded into the distance.

"I wonder where they're coming from," Viktor said.

"Mexico, maybe. Or even South America," I said.

"I'd like to go there someday," Viktor said.

"You would?"

"South America is as far as you can get from the war." Viktor pulled a cigarette from his pocket. "I'd like to think there are countries in the south that don't even know of this *Great* War. For them it doesn't even exist."

I looked out towards the lake and thought of what Yuri had once told me about the beasts in the sea. The beasts that could eat you, but usually didn't. "What was Europe like? Did you swim in the ocean?"

"We were such fools." Viktor lit a match and held it to his cigarette. He breathed in until the tip glowed. "We thought we'd see the world. What I saw of Europe were muddy trenches scattered with the body parts of young men."

I remembered Jacob as a boy. His curly red hair and his tiny fishbone chest the day he was bitten by the lake monster. Then I imagined this little boy in a bed of poppies and I had to fight down the tears.

Viktor took off his shoe and sock and extended his foot into the water. "The ocean, though. Now that's a sight. The picture of eternity. Nothing but water."

"I can't imagine."

The dark lake glittered with stars. Molasses waves lapped the shore. I pulled my knees to my chest. "I'm sorry," I said. The words soured my mouth.

"For what?"

"About what happened. About your father."

"You should have seen his face the day he found out we got in using Mother's maiden name. I've never been so ashamed. I thought he'd be proud of me, thought he'd know it was just a means to an end, is all. He died still hating me, I'm sure. He was ashamed of me. We took away that last thing he had to pass down, his bloody name."

We sat quietly for a while. Viktor took a long pull on the whisky. Coyotes yipped in the hills behind us.

"Do you still refuse to swim, Iris?"

"I've tried."

"There's nothing in there. Nothing but fish. There's no demon, no monster. What did your mother used to call it?"

"An addanc. Henry called it Naitaka. Azami called it a kami."

"Azami believed in it?"

I nodded.

Viktor passed the cigarette to me. "There are so many real-life monsters. You can't even imagine. You don't want to imagine. There's no need to go making them up. The world has enough, believe me, the world has plenty of monsters. If we're not careful, we become them."

"But I've seen the monster, the lake spirit, whatever it is. I've seen it countless times. I saw it bite Jacob."

"Jacob was bit?"

"Before you moved here."

"Did Jacob see it?"

"He saw. I know he did."

"But did he say so?"

"He denies it. Or he did."

"Are you the only one who actually saw the lake monster?"

Although I knew Azami saw the lake monster at least once, I didn't like to say her name. "Henry saw it. And Llewelyna, of course." I passed him back his cigarette.

"Iris."

"What?"

"Llewelyna was very sick. Delusional. Remember on the wharf? That day your father and Jacob left?"

"Even before she was ill she saw it."

"You were always protecting her, even when she didn't deserve it, even when she treated you so terribly."

"She was my mother."

"I understand that." He stubbed out the cigarette. "But now you must face your fears. You need to swim. Don't inherit your mother's monsters or they'll destroy you too." He splashed his foot in the water. "At least you *can* swim." His trousers were pinned up around the end of his one knee.

"You'll swim again."

"Not with one leg."

I slipped off my mother's nylons and rested my feet on the surface of the water. "I'll only swim if you come with me," I said.

"I don't know, I—"

"If you don't swim, then I won't either."

Viktor took a long drink from the bottle. "Temptress," he called me, and began to unbutton his shirt. He placed it behind him in a gnarl. I looked down at Azami's necklace around his neck. The Russian tag caught the dregs of moonlight. Remembering how it had once protected me quelled my fear of the lake.

Viktor caught me looking at the necklace and picked it up off his chest. "Azami gave this to me." He lifted it over his head and fingered the letters on the tag and the red bead. "She said it was lucky." He kicked up the phantom leg that began at his knee. "A lot of good it did me." Then, to my horror, he threw the necklace overhead. It splashed into the darkness. "Now, let's go for a swim," he said.

"Viktor—"

But he was already pushing himself up off the rocks with one arm and reaching for his crutch. I stood to help him. He unbuttoned his trousers and leaned on me as I slipped them down his hips and legs. It was the first time I had seen the nub of his knee. The skin was folded over itself in a pucker.

"Isn't it dreadful?"

"No, it's not." I put my hand on the knotted skin there. It was warm. I ran my fingers over the fresh scars. Viktor looked down at me, his mouth open slightly. "Does it hurt?" I asked.

"Sometimes."

"When I touch it?"

"No. That feels nice." He took off his undershirt. The crescent scar on his chest glowed in the dim light. He was only in his underpants now. "Are you going to swim in that?" he asked. I looked down at my dress.

"I don't have a bathing suit."

He smiled. "Do you need one? It's so dark. No one will see."

Feeling brave, I lifted my dress over my head and slipped it off. My skin burned from the whisky and the exhilaration of being seen so bare. I tried to calm myself by folding my dress neatly on the rocks. I stood before Viktor in only my bloomers and Llewelyna's old corset.

The corset was a foolish, bulky thing that pushed my stomach in and my hips backwards. Llewelyna had told me it was a wedding gift from my grandmother and had surely been meant as an affront. Llewelyna had tossed it to the floor then. "These old-fashioned things enslave us, Iris." The corset was made of golden silk and yellow lace, with pink ribbons up the back. I had picked it up, unable to allow such a beautiful object to go to waste, and tucked it into my wardrobe. I had begun wearing the corset only recently. I liked what it did to my shape and how solid it made me feel.

Viktor grinned at my appearance. I offered him my hand and pulled him up off the log. "Should I fetch your crutch?" I asked.

"I can lean on you, can't I?" He wrapped his arm around my shoulders and together we stumbled along the mossy rocks into the biting lake.

"It's freezing," I said.

"It's not that bad."

When the water was knee high I slipped and we both splashed in.

"Are you all right?" I worried over his wounded leg. Viktor just laughed as he attempted to push himself up. I had to help him by the elbow. We continued into the dark water until it came up to our shoulders.

"Funny—in the lake it feels like I have two legs again."

"Maybe you do," I said. "Maybe it's grown back like a lizard's tail."

A flock of geese swooped down to the lake, landing not far from us. "We've got company," Viktor said. Out in the distance, near the geese, I saw the water ripple.

"Let's go back now," I said.

"It's fine. Just geese."

"No. There's something coming towards us."

"There's nothing. It's just a wave."

"Viktor, I'm afraid. I want to go back." I turned towards the shore, but I couldn't leave him there.

"Hush." He pulled me close. Cool currents tangled between my legs. I imagined the lake monster approaching us. "Close your eyes," he said, and I did. His breath was warm against my neck. "Just listen to my voice. Nothing can hurt you." The currents slowed. All I could feel were Viktor's warm hands on my back and his beard prickling my skin. Despite the cold, I felt so warm. "Not anything. I won't let it." His lips moved down my neck to my shoulder. "I promise." He moved my bloomers down my hips. He kissed me on my cheek, my mouth, my neck. With one foot I slipped my bloomers down the rest of the way and I stepped out of them. He hoisted me up and I wrapped my legs around him. In the water he balanced easily on his one leg. It surprised me how natural it all felt, his skin against mine. He kissed my collarbone as his hands worked at the knot at the back of the corset. I kept my eyes closed, afraid if I opened them I'd break the magic of darkness. I didn't try to help him with the knot. I just let myself be kissed, awestruck, speechless, and blind. I ran my hands up his back. I wanted to map the flex of each muscle, the pull of every tendon and bend of each joint.

The geese took flight and startled us. I opened my eyes at the sound of their splashing and the beat of their flapping wings. We both paused to watch the moons of their bellies float past again.

Then, over Viktor's shoulder, I saw the ripple, closer now, a string of light along the water. The corset unfolded from me like an extra set of ribs and left my breasts abandoned to the icy water. My nipples tingled. Goose bumps budded up my arms and neck. Viktor's hands were on my back, in my hair. He pulled my gaze back to him.

"Close your eyes," he said, his mouth warm on my nipples. But I didn't want to close my eyes. I slipped Yuri's wooden ring off my thumb and let it sink. I could only see the parts of Viktor the moon illuminated, disembodied. An earlobe. An eyebrow. A jawbone. I could no longer distinguish between Viktor's skin against mine and the water. In the lake we were weightless, we were invisible, we were somewhere else, we were nowhere at all. I closed my eyes when he fit himself into me and for a moment, we were only water.

Viktor and I filled our nights with drinking and lovemaking and stories of the dead. I felt as though I was living out one of Juliet's romance novels. My body bloomed under his heated gaze. One evening he traced his finger along my collarbone to my sternum. "This would be a nice place to sleep," he said.

"Where?"

"Right here. This little hammock." He made circles in the curve of bone with his finger. "This looks like home. Yes, I could live right here forever."

Each day he found a new part of me to admire, the curve of an ankle, a calf, the soft skin of my sole, my wrist, my thighs. Viktor's sense of wonder made me look down at my body like a stranger. I watched my reflection in the windows to see what I would do next.

The town was desolate and quiet. It felt wrong to feel so good. They were surely talking about us, but my family was never without scandal, and Winteridge was all whispers anyway. No one escaped the gossip. Each of us was followed by a trail of stories.

Viktor said it was rumoured that Jesse McCarthy hadn't said a word since returning from war. Some believed he was struck dumb. I often saw him stalk through the forest surrounding our orchard. Mrs. Bell whispered to me through the fence that it was said Juliet served the young soldiers more than beer at the Pearl Hotel, and I couldn't help but wonder if Viktor had taken such liberties with her. The only time I could see Juliet was if I helped her with some task or other. We were scrubbing tablecloths when, as if in response to Mrs. Bell's words, Juliet joked that Mr. Bell had contracted syphilis while at war, and Mrs. Bell was forced to nurse him, spreading salves on his genitals like a mother. Although she hadn't seen Ronald for herself, she said that the men at the Pearl joked that the war had melted half of Ronald Nickel's face and made him into a masturbating recluse.

One day I walked to Henry's cabin to return the books Llewelyna had last borrowed. Even when Henry was gone it didn't feel right to keep his books for so long. I knew how much he valued order. When I came to the cabin, I saw someone jamming something through the window, trying to force his way in. He didn't hear me as I approached.

"Ronald?" I asked. He flinched like a coyote. When he saw me he turned the burnt side of his face away. "Is that you?" I asked. He didn't respond.

"It's not how it looks. I just wanted to borrow a book. I've read everything my father owns a dozen times."

"I can get you in," I said.

His gaze softened and he turned his ruined face towards me. The skin at his cheek was creased like the shell of a walnut. His eye socket on that side was empty. I caught myself staring. "I'm sorry," I said, and took a step back. He looked down and away to hide that side of his face from me again. He rubbed his shoe in the pine needles.

"So you know how to get in?"

"I'll show you where Henry keeps the extra key." I walked into the graveyard hidden by the willow and dusted off the rock with *Stewart Brewster* written on it. I lifted the rock and showed Ronald the skeleton key.

"You can't tell anyone. It's just for you. And you have to fill out the ledger. Write down the book you return and the one you borrow so everything is in order when Henry comes back."

"*If* he comes back. You can't be sure of anything these days."

I opened the door to the library. Ronald looked around while I put some books on the shelves and filled out the ledger.

"Have you read this?" he asked, and held a book towards me. It was *Dr. Jekyll and Mr. Hyde.*

"It's a little dark."

"I don't mind dark."

"Balance it with this." I passed him Nesbit's *Five Children and It.* "It's a children's book but it's fantastic."

Ronald browsed the pages. "What's that?" He pointed to an illustration of a creature with a monkey's body and insect antenna.

"The Psammead. The children find it in a sandpit. It grants them wishes."

Ronald smiled.

I looked for a book for myself. I rarely read in those days. Ronald handed me a large novel with a thick blue spine. On the cover it read *Moby-Dick* in gold letters. "Jacob liked this one," he said, his face turned towards the window.

I tucked the book under my arm. "Thanks."

"He told me about the voices," Ronald said.

"What voices?"

"Ever since the accident in the lake, he heard voices, mutterings in his one ear."

I remembered Jacob shaking his head as if to clear them. "When did he tell you that?"

"That last time he was here."

"I'm glad he had you to talk to."

"Do you think he's alive, Iris?"

A woodpecker began to tap against the ceiling of the house.

"No," I said simply. "I'm sorry, Ronald, but I know Jacob is dead."

Ronald turned to me. The side of his face that was still his own went slack. His eye watered. "The only reason I joined up was to find him. Protect him."

"There was nothing you could have done."

"I couldn't find him. I tried, Iris, I swear to God, I tried."

"It's okay."

"I loved him," he said.

I approached Ronald carefully. "I know," I said, and he let himself be embraced.

23

That summer Viktor and I often returned to the lake and swam naked in its depths, always at night so no one could see us. Viktor didn't cure me of my visions, although I told him he did. I still saw Naitaka's scales in the moonlight, but I was no longer afraid. After we swam we would return to the house and lie, still wet, in the small bed upstairs. I read to Viktor from *Moby-Dick* until he fell asleep. Yuri's letters continued to arrive but I was too ashamed to read them now. I kept them, unopened, beneath my bed. We hardly noticed autumn's arrival.

Every week Viktor took the *Rosamond* to Vernon to speak to his mother through the chicken-wire fence. Each time he left I worried Mary would finally tell him of my treachery. Viktor would return in low spirits, muttering about Mary's shrunken body, the yellowed whites of her eyes. Then he'd disappear for a few days into the Pearl or the forest. One night after he returned, I found him sitting on my bed. Open envelopes and Yuri's unread letters in a pile on his lap. His eyes were glossy and red.

"We must stop this at once," he said.

"Stop what?"

"He loves you." Viktor held one of Yuri's letters towards me.

"But I love *you*."

"No, Iris. You don't."

"I do."

"I'm nothing. I'm worthless. I'll never work. I'll never be anything."

I knelt between his legs. "It doesn't matter to me. I'll take care of you. I like taking care of you. We take care of each other."

Viktor leaned away from me. "He'll be home in a few weeks. He's been discharged. We'll burn these, say they never came." He began to gather up the letters.

"Stop," I said. He ignored me. "Stop." I grabbed at the letters.

"Iris, this is over."

"But we're in love." The word was thick in my mouth and already sounding foolish.

Viktor looked down at me coldly. "No, Iris, we're not."

"We are."

"I don't love you," he said, reaching for his crutch. He stood, and the letters fell from his lap and scattered on the floor. "Read them and then get rid of them." He went past me and down the stairs, his crutch thumping. I heard him nearly stumble once. The door slammed.

That November, the newspapers declared the war was over, and everyone in Winteridge besides Viktor and me was in good spirits. The rest of our soldiers were to arrive home soon. Yuri was to receive the Victoria Cross for his bravery in the battle of Passchendaele, and the name of that faraway place never failed to evoke hollowness in me for Jacob. The war photograph next to the article in the newspaper revealed a new version of Yuri, a young blond man I barely recognized, with stiff, square shoulders and flat cheeks. *Captain George Wilson of Winteridge* appeared below the photograph. While some believed the soldier's hometown was an error, for there was no George Wilson in Winteridge, others whispered about Taras being taken prisoner and knew that this was his quiet boy, Yuri.

In the midst of all the excitement, Ted Carson, captain of the *Rosamond*, sighted the lake monster. He had been transporting fruit when a long, green ridge crested, perpendicular to the other waves. Despite the clear sky, the water spiralled and caused the lakeboat to wobble terribly. The lake became so turbulent that Ted Carson and the carter had to grab on to beams and railings to keep themselves upright. Boxes of fruit turned over and apples, pears, and peaches rolled through the cabins. Then, just as quick as it had begun, the lake became as calm as before. There was no evidence in the sky of the storm they had suffered. The carter hadn't seen the creature himself but supported Ted Carson's every word, as did Viktor and the group of men he was drinking with on the cliffs. One of these men was Ronald Nickel. Ronald saw the monster's horse head rise up out of the water. He and Viktor arranged a mob to go hunt the lake monster. Most of these men were the war's wounded and injured. They gathered in the Pearl and sang drunken songs that echoed through Winteridge:

I'm looking for the Ogo-pogo, the funny little Ogo-pogo.
His mother was an earwig, his father was a whale.

Ogopogo was the name they gave the demon to tame it. For each of these broken men the monster meant something else. Something they might defeat. An enemy they might finally kill.

I was in the kitchen steaming jars for preserves when Viktor stumbled onto my porch. We hadn't spoken for weeks. "I'll kill it," he said. "I'll do it for you." He was drunk and leaned against the doorframe to steady himself. "We have them all on our side. Everyone believes you now."

"You can't kill a spirit."

"It's a beast," Viktor said.

"And would you hang a mouse for thievery?" This was something Llewelyna had said once, and the words were bitter in my mouth.

Viktor stepped off the porch and began to walk away. "It's my Moby Dick," he called to the sky and laughed. I had no time to tell him what happened in the end of the novel, that if he wanted to play the one-legged Ahab then he should finish the book and see how the captain fared.

The next morning the men went out on the *Rosamond* to hunt the lake monster, which, like Moby Dick, was only ever a vessel they poured their individual evils into. There was a crowd on the shore to see them off. I stayed back in the trees. The men howled their Ogopogo song, armed with spears and axes. It was an odd group. Some were missing arms and legs, others eyes and ears. Each and every one was disfigured in some way by the war. Viktor looked for me in the crowd on the shore but I did not want to be seen.

A large net and several hooks were rigged onto the once elegant *Rosamond*. I remembered the tinkling china and the chandeliers the night Llewelyna offered the lake monster the dove. The siren on the bow was of indeterminate shape now. She could be a woman, a man, a fish, a seal. Only the divots of her eyes were recognizable.

For seven days the men travelled up and down the lake hunting Naitaka, the lake monster, half spirit, half beast. They returned rank with booze and fish. Again a crowd gathered on the wharf as the men carried a long, grey carcass between them. They laid the stinking thing on the shore. The ageless monster that haunted our lake was startlingly small, at about six feet long. It had smooth skin with prehistoric-looking parallel spines up its back and long whiskers on either side of its snout. Its wide blank eyes were those of a fish. I recognized this creature from the picture my father had pinned up in his study after Jacob was bitten: a sturgeon.

Women covered their mouths at the smell of the dead fish and children kicked and poked at it. There was a slice in the side of the creature where blue and pink insides spilled out. This sturgeon might have been seventy-five years old. The only way the men could have caught this deep-water swimmer was if it had risen to the surface to spawn. Henry had once told me that sturgeons are an ancient species that can live for over one hundred years. They feed on the bottom of the lake, and since the bottom of our lake did not exist, I believed that sturgeon, like the lake monster, could pass from our world to another. The damming of rivers endangered the sacred places sturgeons came to spawn in. Henry said that since so many developments had sprouted up along the rivers and the shore of the lake, the sturgeon rarely surfaced to spawn and their numbers were dwindling.

Viktor stood behind the ancient fish and smiled, awaiting my approval. When, after a while, I didn't respond, he stepped forward and stabbed his crutch into the blue tubes that hung from the carcass. The guts popped and squirted. The crowd laughed and the children squealed with delight. I took a step forward and slapped Viktor across the face. Thrown off balance, he fell. He landed on his back, atop his crutch, and held his cheek.

"You should be ashamed," I said between my teeth. I didn't recognize the rage that filled me as my own.

⟡

Yuri came home on a clear day in early December. The sturgeon was still rotting on the shore. Ants and maggots had made their homes between its bones. Every now and then a breeze caught the stench and carried it to where we gathered on the wharf. Viktor kept back behind the crowd.

The moment the *Rosamond* turned the last bend of land, Yuri's eyes found me on the wharf. He was one of the first soldiers off the boat. His face, although a little thinner, had maintained its boyishness, but his body had changed dramatically. He stood straight with broad shoulders and thick arms. He was taller than Viktor now, who slumped over his crutch and pulled his shoulders forward as if to protect a hollow chest.

Yuri pulled me into him. "Iris," he whispered. "Oh God, Iris, I've been waiting so long for this moment." He pushed back to look at my face. I tried to return his excitement but my eyes fell from his; they were too bright.

The three of us walked together to the house. Yuri held my hand and Viktor hobbled beside us.

"Did you get my letters?" Yuri asked.

I caught Viktor's eyes. "None for a while," I said. "I was worried. I thought something had happened."

"I wrote to you as often as I could, I promise."

"I believe you, Yuri." I smiled up at him and hated myself for it.

"Call me George," Yuri said.

"George?" I asked.

"Everyone calls me George now. George Wilson."

Viktor did not delay in telling Yuri about Taras's death and Mary still held prisoner. Within the hour, Yuri had set off on the next boat for Vernon. Viktor had tried to go along with him, but Yuri forced him to stay, declaring that Viktor's one leg would only slow him down. Viktor tipped back his bottle and shrugged as if he didn't care either way.

It was while Yuri was gone that I told Viktor I was pregnant.

I had known for a month or so, but with Viktor's denial of me, and then my anger at him, it had never seemed like the right time. Now, with Yuri back, reality came hurtling forward.

Viktor paced awkwardly around the Wasiks' tiny kitchen. "What have we done, oh God, oh God," he kept saying. I sat at the table and fiddled with the frayed embroidery on the tablecloth. The house smelled like vinegar. "You must marry. You'll marry immediately," Viktor said, not looking at me. "As soon as Mother gets back."

"Marry who?"

"Yuri."

"Don't you mean George?" Viktor ignored me. "I won't," I said simply.

"When he gets back you'll tell him you're ready. You'll marry as soon as possible. We need some cheer around here, anyways."

"I said no. I won't marry him. I hardly know who he is anymore."

Finally Viktor raised his face to mine. "You must. I can't be a father. Look at me." He spread out his arms so I could admire his narrow chest and scruffy clothes. His beard was patchy around his cheeks. I wanted to tell him right then, "You already are a father." But my deceit and my loyalty to Azami were one and the same and impossible to expose.

"I've told you already, Viktor. I love you and only you."

Viktor stood in the middle of his kitchen, arms still extended from each side as if about to take flight. "Me?"

"Yes." I stood up now.

"You're sure?"

"I'm sure." I took a few tentative steps towards him.

"But Yuri's my brother. It's all wrong."

"We'll run away. We'll leave tomorrow. Catch the first lakeboat. I have money saved." I stood in front of him now. Viktor dropped his crutch and fell to his knee. He looked up at me and ran his hands up the backs of my legs. There were tears at the insides of his eyes. He pressed an ear to my stomach.

"It's a girl," I said. "I'm sure of it."

"I'll be a father," he said.

"Yes."

"I'll teach her to play the kobza. I'll teach her the old songs." He lifted his ear from my stomach and looked up at me. I massaged the back of his head. His hair was waxy and in need of washing.

As we waited for the water to boil, Viktor and I made love on the floor of the kitchen, fearless of onlookers despite the wide, gaping windows. We filled the tin tub and took turns washing each other's hair, as we had in the beginning. We made plans to leave for the coast, a place so foreign to me it could have been Rome, or Egypt, or the Never Never Land. Viktor had a well-connected friend in Vancouver he had met in the war. After a while we sat facing each other in the tub and watched shadows puddle the kitchen floor.

"It's funny how things turn out." My words were brimming with secret meaning. I wanted desperately to give Viktor a child he could claim as his own. I reached out my hand. I wanted to touch Viktor's face but I couldn't quite reach. I slid closer and wrapped my legs around his waist. "I never expected to be as content as I am right now." Viktor smiled in a sad, far-off way. My fingers fell from his face and settled on the white scar on his chest, where the German boy's bayonet had pierced him. He squirmed under my touch and looked away.

"What's wrong?" I asked.

"Nothing. It's just, I don't deserve to be happy."

"Why not?"

"I've done terrible things."

"It was war. It was—"

"You couldn't understand."

"He haunts you, doesn't he?"

"What did you say?" he asked.

But I had already said too much. My entire body went rigid. I couldn't speak. With all the stories Viktor told me, he had never said a thing about the young German soldier he killed. He had shared that only with Azami. It was a secret I had stolen.

"Think of who, Iris?" he repeated. If I had responded faster I might have made something up, but it was all too clear. Viktor understood. He used the side of the tub to lift himself out and hobbled through the dark kitchen, bracing himself on chairs and counters until he found his crutch.

"You read Azami's letters." It wasn't a question. He stood naked in the kitchen, painted silver by a pillar of moonlight.

"Not at first," I said. There was no use hiding now. The water in the tub had turned cold. I hadn't noticed until the heat of his body left mine. I told Viktor what happened with the letters, that only after I saw Azami had found someone else did I stop delivering his letters to her. Of course I still could never tell Viktor that Juro was his son. That betrayal was too immense and would only cause more difficulties for Azami.

Viktor dressed in silence. I shivered and gathered my knees to my chest. I couldn't read the expression on his face. All was darkness. He was standing at the counter, looking out the window above the sink. The moon was snagged in a net of stars. All was silent. What I had really wanted was an exchange of horrors. A balance of some kind. I had hoped Viktor, with all the wrongs he claimed, might forgive me in exchange for bearing witness to one of his own demons. I wanted a safe place to be honest and true, a love bigger than evil.

I thought Viktor might need some time on his own, to process what I had told him. As I stepped out of the tub to embrace him before I left, Viktor swept his arm along the counter and dishes crashed to the ground.

"Viktor, I—"

"Get dressed and leave."

I put on my dress and slipped on my shoes.

"You'll marry Yuri. You'll marry him as soon as he returns."

"But, Viktor . . ."

"He'll never know about this. The child will be his."

"I can't. I don't love him, and the timing . . ."

He began to gather his things.

"Where are you going?"

He stopped. "You don't deserve love, Iris Sparks."

I choked from the shock of his voice, transformed by hate.

"I'm leaving town. You'll marry Yuri and soon be expecting your first child. Do you understand?" His face was deformed by shadow. "You're selfish, Iris. You destroy everything you touch."

"Viktor . . ."

"You'll marry Yuri this weekend. And if you aren't married by the time I get back—I'll kill you, I swear to God." He spat at the floor near my feet. "I pity Yuri."

The next day, when I saw Mary walk up the hill to our house, my breath escaped me. I stood at the window with a hand on my throat. Mary's body was impossibly frail. Yuri had an arm around her shoulders, supporting her. Despite the distance, Mary found me in the window. I backed away from it slowly.

I couldn't think of an excuse for why Viktor might have left before seeing his mother, so I told Yuri and Mary I didn't know where he went, that he had simply disappeared one night. Yuri admitted to his mother that he noticed Viktor had grown rather fond of whisky. He guessed Viktor had gone away because he was ashamed and didn't want Mary to see him in such a state. He assured her he would be back.

I prepared one of the skinny hens the coyotes left behind for dinner that evening. Mary and I exchanged cool glances across the table. She met my eyes and held them until I had to look away.

"So when's the wedding?" she said in a voice that flaked at the edges. I could tell by the way she looked at me that she suspected Viktor and me. Perhaps he had mentioned our relationship to her.

"There's no rush." Yuri smiled. "Time is one thing we have now."

I set my fork down. "How about this weekend?" I said. My hands twisted together in my lap.

Yuri choked on his food, coughed, and covered his mouth with his napkin. "This weekend?" he said when he caught his breath.

"Why not?"

"Shouldn't we wait until Viktor returns? And don't you want a fancy dress, a party, flowers, what about all that?"

"I don't care for any of it. I'm impatient." I smiled in a way I hoped looked eager and sincere. Mary gave me a nod of approval while Yuri smiled down at his food.

"All right, then." He shrugged. "Whatever my bride desires." He leaned forward and planted a kiss on my cheek.

Mary and I cleaned up after dinner and I was relieved she filled the silence with a story about how she had met Taras. Her family had just recently moved to Canada from England and her father was a shopkeeper in Alberta. Taras was working on a nearby potato field. He came to the store every day to buy cigarettes. She said he brought Mary poems he wrote for her in Ukrainian. She couldn't read them, of course. Taras couldn't speak a word of

English. But they fell in love without the aid of language. I thought of Yuri's poems to me then, and felt sorry for making a show of his vulnerability.

When Mary's father found out about her romance with Taras, he disowned her. The lovers fled to Vernon, where Taras got his first job on an orchard. Although Taras had often gone on to my father about being born to the soil, Mary told me he came not from a line of labourers but of musicians.

I turned my face from her and tried not to think of the night Viktor played me the kobza. I took a plate from the soapy water and held it out for Mary to dry. Instead of the plate, Mary took hold of my shoulders and looked at me directly. "You may think you are in love with him. But what begins as love can become a nightmare."

"What are you saying?"

"Yuri is the better choice. You will learn to love him."

Mary's directness took me by surprise. She walked out of the kitchen and left me standing there, the plate still dripping in my hands. I stared blankly at the now empty space she had occupied.

As Viktor demanded, Yuri and I were married that weekend.

The last time I had been to the church was when Llewelyna convulsed on the floor between the pews. Now, sunlight came through the stained glass in slates that painted us all blue, red, and yellow. Mr. and Mrs. Bell and Juliet Pearl and her father were the only ones to respond to our last-minute invitations. They sat on opposite sides of the aisle. Mrs. Bell did not want to be associated with Juliet, now that Juliet had become so mixed up in scandal. Of course Mrs. Bell didn't know the stories whispered about her own shameful husband visiting the upstairs room of the Pearl in the middle of the night.

I carried a bouquet of snowberries and wore Llewelyna's old wedding dress. Mary pinned an opal brooch to the collar to cover a rust-coloured stain. Old Father John's voice echoed in the small, empty church and lent it the dimensions of a cathedral. Yuri was handsome in his olive uniform. His bluebird eyes had darkened, their pupils huge. As Father John read out the verses, I lifted my head to count Jesus' wounds and found the cross bare and painted eggshell white. Jesus' body had been stripped from the cross. I wondered where he was buried and when he might rise again.

That night Yuri and I made love on a quilt spread on the floor of one of the empty rooms on the third floor of the house. So many of the rooms had become closed off. The doors to Jacob's and my parents' rooms remained closed. The door to the spare room where Llewelyna had faded year after year was locked, one of Saint Francis's feathers still on the bed, the window open in case he decided to return. And the room I had as a child, where Viktor had explored parts of my body I didn't know I had, was surely off limits now.

As I undid the buttons at my throat, Yuri told me he had saved himself for me. Even in Paris, where the beautiful young girls threw themselves at the soldiers in the pubs they went to on their nights off, Yuri said he would return to his room early, make himself a pot of tea, and write a letter to me. I had been glad he was behind me as he spoke, because my eyes surely revealed my shame, and my face went as red as the devil's.

As we made love, I could tell Yuri had lied about being a virgin. He pulled my hair and clutched the back of my neck hard enough to leave bruises. And, despite myself, he knew how to please a woman with his hands. As I listened to him snore, I remembered Azami and Kenta in the greenhouse and understood, for the first time, why Azami had given herself so easily to him. I had never thought of her actions as strategy before. I was only then struck by the parallel nature of our misfortunes, or if it could even be called misfortune when I was so great a part of orchestrating the fate of Azami and Viktor's relationship.

I stared up at the ceiling and let tears bud at the insides of my eyes. I had ruined the lives of the ones I loved. How could I go on to live in the shadow of such evil? I brought a hand to my stomach and felt for that orb of life beating inside of me. I couldn't help but imagine the fetus as the form I once saw emerge from a chicken egg. The chick was eyeless and sinewed, born a few days too soon. I had carried the cracked egg to one of the hens, with the hope she might take to it, keep it warm, and it might survive. When I went to check on the chick the next day, it was shredded, eaten up by hungry relatives. With that memory, I had to jump up, reach for the chamber pot beneath the bed, and retch, careful not to wake Yuri.

I was desperate to get away from Winteridge before Viktor returned. I thought if I could just leave everything for a little while, Yuri and I could be happy. He was as good a man as any. It turned out that during the war, Yuri and Viktor had met a Scot named Jeremy, whose grandfather owned a shipping company that ran between Seattle and South America. All through the war the shipping company took tourists and passengers to a casino off the coast of Chile. Yuri said before Viktor got hurt, the three of them would often talk about this luxury liner that existed in a world so far away from the blood and mud. Jeremy promised that if they made it out of the war, he would make sure Yuri got to take his fiancée on a cruise to South America. Jeremy never survived the war, but Yuri still had his father's address. He was the one to write to the family and alert them of their son's death.

And just like that, Yuri took the lakeboat to the city one day and returned with two tickets for the *Jezebel*. We were set to leave the following weekend. The brochure Yuri showed me had a jagged mountain range with *Tracey Brothers Shipping: North to South Shore* across it in bold font. On the opposite page was a drawing of a three-storey casino with a red roof. Ocean waves splashed against the shore.

"What do you say, wife? Care for a little trip?"

I was flooded with such gratitude that I took Yuri and kissed him, and for the first time my actions were not forced.

24

From the window in our room on the *Jezebel*, we watched the busy Seattle port fade into the distance. The view was soon replaced with the sandy beaches of California. Then for days we were too far from land to see anything but water. I went out onto the deck with all the wind and water and eternity around me, and thought of Viktor. I wondered where he was at that very moment. I tried to imagine good things.

In our room, red panels of silk draped down around the bed from the ceiling, and a claw-foot bathtub was in the middle of the room. When we asked to have the tub filled one night, an endless train of maids carried buckets of water all the way up the stairs from the kitchen. We watched from the bed as the dark-skinned girls, Chilean natives, poured the water into the tub, their faces turned away to avoid the rush of steam. The water smelled faintly of salt.

I had hidden the little blue fish in my suitcase. Since Llewelyna's death I was more protective of it than ever. I kept the jar wrapped in a cloth and didn't dare remove it when Yuri was around.

There was a games room next to the dining room meant to prepare us for the Palacio, the renowned casino of the Americas. In the games room, the maids carried trays of sweating cocktails and martinis. Yuri and I were sitting at the blackjack table when

I was overcome once again with nausea. I had been plagued with it the day before and blamed my illness on seasickness. I excused myself from the table and went to the ladies' restroom. A woman with straw-yellow hair twisted up in a tight chignon eyed me curiously as I leaned over the marble counter to steady myself. She smelled strongly of lilac. She reached into her purse for her powder compact and suggested I borrow it for my shiny forehead. I shook my head. I wanted her to leave me alone. The room was spinning and the new dress Yuri had bought me was too tight. The woman was saying something about sea legs when I vomited into the sink. All that mint julep and lamb heaved out of me. The woman held my hair away from my neck and rubbed at my back. Her palms were cool and her voice was soft and calm. When I was done, the woman poured me a glass of water from the pitcher and poured the rest of the water down the drain to rinse the vomit.

"Thank you," I said finally.

"Don't mention it." She was fixing her own hair now. A few strands had come loose and she pinned them back as she watched me in the mirror. I began to fix my own in the reflection next to hers.

"Here," she said, and turned me towards her. She brushed some powder on my forehead and painted my lips the same dark red as her own. The woman wore a blue dress with floral bead-work up the sides and long earrings that nearly touched her shoulders. She looked like someone who belonged to the city.

"It's my first time on the ocean," I said.

She held her handkerchief between my lips for me to blot them. "Seasick, are you, then?" she said, unconvinced. I nodded. "Whatever you say." She gave me a sympathetic smile as she put her compact and lipstick back in her purse.

"What do you mean?"

"I don't mean to pry. It's none of my business."

"I don't understand."

"You're pregnant, no?"

"Why would you say that?"

"How far along?" she asked as she stroked her hair into place again.

"A couple months, perhaps."

"You're starting to show, dear."

I turned sideways and looked at my profile. "Hardly."

"That man with you the father?"

"Of course," I said.

"Fine. Only ask because he was giving me eyes yesterday. Then he tried to convince me to join him on the top deck."

"Don't flatter yourself."

"You tell him you're pregnant yet? I wonder why." Before I could answer, she swung wide the door and left.

Even after retching, I still didn't feel much better. As I walked back to the blackjack table it seemed I was traversing stormy waters. The floor rocked. I spotted the woman seated with a man at least twice her age. She watched me carefully.

Yuri had the ear of one of the waitresses cupped in his hand and whispered to her. The waitress saw me coming. She stiffened, placed his martini on the table, and turned to leave. Yuri took hold of her wrist and tried to pull her back down towards him, but she slipped away.

"Did I interrupt something?"

"These silly girls go mad for uniforms," Yuri said as I pulled my own chair out to take a seat. I was still reeling. I tried to grab hold of the table for balance but it slipped from my grasp.

"What a nuisance," I said and stumbled to the ground.

I woke a few hours later in a cold sweat and with a terrible pain in my stomach. Someone had dressed me in my thin nightgown. There was a faint knock on the door. I thought it might be Yuri, but in walked one of the maids. She was young, no older than twelve or thirteen, but already gorgeous. I can see her face now as clearly as that first day. Her skin was dark against the white of her apron. Her wide cheekbones gave her a noble appearance. She set a cool, wet cloth on my forehead. The presence of this girl's exquisite beauty made me feel better. She said something to me in Spanish I didn't understand and slipped something into the pocket of my nightgown.

When Yuri opened the door the light he let in burst into painful shards. My vision went kaleidoscopic. "Something isn't right," I told him.

"You've a fever." He tore off my blankets.

"Yuri," I said.

"George," he corrected. I could hear him bustling around the room. The very young maid from before stood at the door, waiting for direction. Her presence gave me strength. I thought as long as she remained, nothing terrible could happen.

"I'm pregnant."

Yuri's face brightened. "Well, that's wonderful—"

"Yuri." I didn't have to say anything else. The maid left and a darkness swept over us. The pain in my stomach returned and made it hard to breathe. Soon a doctor appeared and I was lifted onto a gurney and rolled out.

What seemed like days later, but could have only been hours, I woke in a white room. There were several other small white beds around me. I stared at the back of a man in a long white jacket. My vision was blurry. Sweat dripped into my eyes. He turned to me.

"You're awake," he said. His eyes were purple and he wore a paper mask over his mouth and nose. He put his hand on my forehead. "It's important we try to keep your temperature down, for the baby." A woman moaned in the bed next to mine, her blond hair honeyed against her forehead. Brown splotches covered her cheeks. "The child is okay, might still survive."

"What's happened?" I asked. On the other side of me was a dark-haired man I recognized as the carter who had brought our luggage up to our room. His skin had turned a faint blue. He sat up to cough and foamy blood slipped down his chin.

"It's a bacterial infection, I believe," the doctor said. "Spreads very quickly, though. You were one of the first to become ill, but there have been fifteen other cases since." He dipped a white cloth in a bucket of ice water and held it against my forehead. "You need to stay relaxed, to rest."

Through the window opposite I could see orange rays of morning against the rocky bluffs. For some reason it was important for me to know where we were and how far we had travelled.

"Ensenada, Mexico," he said. "We aren't in the harbour, so don't fret. The last thing we need is to be contaminated by that filthy place. We're just anchored offshore." The doctor turned to help the carter, and I fell back into oblivion.

When I woke hours or days later, the carter was no longer beside me. One of the Chilean maids who had helped fill the tub in our room had taken his place. The blonde was still in the bed next to mine. Her skin was a dark blue. Her breathing laboured, as if she were drowning. We were all underwater. There were green aquamarine currents in the air. I thought of the woman who had emerged from our lake in Winteridge. I yearned to have the blue fish with me now.

I remember it like this: Saint Francis was perched on the edge of my bed and eyed me suspiciously. My legs were propped up and spread. The doctor's hands were covered in blood. He called for the beautiful young maid who had helped me before and handed her what looked like the insides of a fish. She wasn't prepared for the bundle and stared down at the fetus in her palms. Even covered in blood, I could make out what might be a tiny fist. The maid saw me watching and scurried away with the mess that was to be my daughter. I wanted to ask her if I could hold her, just for a moment, but the maid was already gone. I tasted lemon and knew I was about to be overcome with trembling.

In my vision I was swimming after Llewelyna, who was a sturgeon now. I had rocks in my pockets. Silver minnows sparkled past like flecks of glass. She led me towards the ruins of a capsized ship, the *Rosamond*. Peaches rose like bubbles from a spilled crate aboard the lakeboat and floated up to the surface like countless suns. The siren on the bow was Jesus. Ribbons of blood streamed from his wrists and ankles. The ghosts of the drowned were thick in the water around us.

I swam to the capsized lakeboat, and once I was inside, it became the *Jezebel*. I was no longer underwater. The hallway was dark and quiet. The jaguar's spots shone like coins. Her swishing tail guided me down the hall lined with closed doors. There was a weight in my pocket. I had forgotten about the item the young maid had placed there. I reached inside and found a warm, purple egg, a thin crack running down it. I knew my daughter was inside. If I could only cradle her in my palms, keep her safe and warm, she might return to me.

Then, as if born in that oceanic silence, a girl screamed. Her cry was muffled. Something forced into her mouth. The jaguar led me around a dark corner and disappeared into shadows. I walked up to the door the girl's screams came from. It was number twelve, the room Yuri and I were staying in. I heard the scream again. A child's voice. Spanish words. Words that begged. It was the young maid who had disposed of my unripe child. I could hear Yuri now too, struggling against her. I eased the door open a crack and I saw them. He had her pinned against the wall, his fist full of her dark hair. He kept banging her head back against the wall each time he rammed himself into her. She saw me over his shoulder and cried out to me in Spanish. She was just a girl. I eased the door closed.

A matronly maid, short and round-faced, appeared at the end of the hallway holding a candle set on a plate. She was about to walk away from me with her beacon of light. I called to her, still cupping the purple egg in my hands. I had something to protect. I didn't want to be alone in all that darkness. "I'm lost," I said to the maid. She nodded and guided me down the hall and back to the white room where I faded into the rhythm of laboured, drowning breath.

When I woke the next day, my hands still clutched the egg. The doctor asked to see what I held. For hours I refused to even look for myself. I had to keep it warm. When I finally opened my palms for the doctor, I found not an egg but a small purple potato. The doctor was not surprised.

"Did the Mapuche girl give this to you?" he asked. I nodded. "It's a superstition," he said. "An old wives' tale to fend off illness."

Even then, I would not let the doctor take the potato from me. It was a cruel exchange for a daughter but it was all I had of her. I begged for death to find me. It claimed many in the beds around me. One by one, their faces turned indigo and blood poured from their mouths, noses, and ears. Then they drowned in their own fluids.

With very little ceremony, seven bodies were lowered into the ocean off the coast of Ensenada, and mine was not one of them.

I was haunted by Llewelyna's many stories of drowned infants and wondered whether I had misunderstood them. If her stories weren't confessions, perhaps they weren't revisions either, but premonitions. Maybe Llewelyna's stories weren't about the past, but the future. Maybe the stories weren't about Llewelyna

at all, but about me. I considered the possibility that she had
been trying to shield me, to warn me about the central tragedy
of my own life—the death of a daughter.

I was thankful I never saw that beautiful young Mapuche maid
who had given me the purple potato and disposed of my ill-born
child. I know she kissed my daughter before she dropped her into
the ocean to be swallowed by fish. I know it was when she had
gone to tell Yuri of the death that he realized everything and had
punished her for my colossal betrayal of him. And still, I hoped
not seeing her might mean it was all a dream. I never asked Yuri
about what happened that night. In return, we never spoke of the
origins of the daughter who died inside me. But after that trip,
Yuri no longer insisted people call him George. He changed it
back to Yuri, but he couldn't fool me. I knew who he really was
now. I knew the kind of man he had become.

The day the captain deemed the ship safe to travel and pulled
up the anchor to go north, I saw the jaguar scouring the bluffs of
Ensenada, so near to the city I thought someone was sure to shoot
her before nightfall.

When we arrived in Seattle our ship was quarantined for
twelve days. They used pulleys to bring us water and food. Many
of the more affluent guests found our quarantine humiliating. It
would be weeks until we discovered that the Spanish flu had been
widespread, catastrophic, and many years until we learned nearly
one-third of the entire world population had been infected. Back
then some believed the Germans had committed a kind of bio-
logical warfare against us. Of course the central powers couldn't
have planned it better if they had: successful soldiers returned
home only to spread disease amongst their own dearly beloved.

25

The curious thing about fire is its silence. On the Kobas' orchard, before Jacob and I had turned to run, I had watched the flames slither through the grass towards the Kobas' home. Bats scooped the darkness above our heads, and the beat of their wings was louder than those deadly flames. I imagined the fire that flooded Winteridge years later in this way: silent as night and bright as day.

In Vancouver we learned from a merchant waiting for the train that Winteridge had been burned to the ground. Spanish flu had swept over the town with such force that few families were untouched by death or tragedy. In fear the plague would spread to other communities, the town was set aflame. Of course we went to Winteridge anyway, not willing to trust the words of a stranger. I tried to persuade the lakeboat captain, a young man with missing fingers, to stop in Winteridge, but he refused.

Yuri shivered when we turned the last curve of land. I reached over to hold his hand. The other passengers held handkerchiefs to their mouths as if the tragedy might still catch. Our bay was a gaping mouth. Even the wharf had burned. The fire had levelled most of the buildings we could see from the lake, the blackened mounds of their foundations like the rotten roots of teeth. Somehow the birch trees in the bay were untouched by fire. They seemed to float above the destruction as white and solid as pillars.

Upon seeing the remains of his family's cabin, Yuri went very quiet. He dropped my hand. All of the blood slipped from his cheeks. He squatted low on the deck of the lakeboat and pressed his palms to his eyes. The guttural sounds that escaped him were new, unfamiliar to me. I bent down and touched his back, but he flinched away.

"Leave me," he said.

I gladly did. It was hard to see him like that, ragged with grief, but after what I knew he had done on the *Jezebel* to that maid, that child, I was unwilling to feel sorry for him. We had already begun to harden ourselves against one another. As the years went by I wanted to know less and less about Yuri's life outside of our home. Our marriage was sown with a lie that could only sprout more seeds of the same.

I walked away from Yuri to the far side of the boat's deck. An older man in a tweed suit leaned against the railing and smoked a pipe.

"Used to be a settlement there, you know," he said.

"I lived there," I said, irritated.

"No, no. Before that. An Indian settlement." The man looked weary. The smoke from his pipe smelled of vanilla. "A town built upon a burial ground. Bodies upon bodies." I thought of Henry then and wondered where he was now, what he would think of the burning of Winteridge. I worried about his books.

Mary was in the hospital. She had been infected by the great flu. Her body was too weak and worn by tragedy to come through the other end of illness. Yuri had her buried in Vernon, next to the remains of Taras.

Azami's brother Wu never returned from the war, and so the Koba family, secluded in their orchard up in the hills, remained untouched by both the epidemic and the fire. The isolation of the Japanese in Winteridge protected them in the end.

Many of the McCarthys and Ebers died, but the sizes of those families meant they could afford tragedy. They restarted somewhere else in the valley. I heard that Joan and Ida Eber and their youngest, that little boy, caught a lakeboat out of town during the first couple of nights of the epidemic, when things were so hectic their family would not notice their absence. Years later, I learned that Ronald and Juliet moved to the prairies together. As far as we knew, Viktor never returned to Winteridge. They found his body days before the fire occurred. It had washed up on the shore in Peachland. The newspaper described his limbs as "nibbled." One leg was missing from the knee down. There was a hint in the article that the lake monster might be responsible, but it was only in jest. We knew the corpse was Viktor's by the crescent-moon scar observed on his chest.

Yuri was gifted a plot of land in Kelowna for his participation in the war. And once we had moved in, I buried my potato daughter in the grave of the garden.

FOUR

1941–1942

. . . for they are all beasts of burden, in a sense,
made to carry some portion of our thoughts.

HENRY DAVID THOREAU [ON ANIMALS]

26

Somehow I drag the buck's body down the steps and across the yard to the side of the snow-covered garden. I hope it will be easier to dig a shallow grave there, in the soil. The winter is still young and I have dug a couple of feet when Juro, Azami's eldest son, who goes by Joe now, arrives at my house in the Kobas' fruit truck. He marvels at the dead deer, the path of blood. Snowflakes dust the deer's hide and gather in its eyelashes, its eyes still wide. Joe takes the shovel from me.

"Where did this come from?" he asks with a grin pinching the corners of his mouth. I know he sees me as some eccentric middle-aged woman. I imagine he might collect these instances and laugh about them later with his friends, or maybe with Azami. I am surprised that the thought of it doesn't bother me.

"The forest, I suspect," I say, and get a laugh from him. "I found it this morning. On my doorstep."

"Ah, I see. Have you made friends with a cougar?"

"A cougar, no."

"We might take it to the butcher and have sausage made from it."

"Can't eat an offering," I say, a little too quiet for Joe to hear.

Joe has been at my house every day since he brought me home from the hospital. He helps me out around the house, repaired the fence, fixed a stubborn door jamb, and replaced a few windows. At first I thought his visits were at Azami's urging, that she felt sorry for me, lonely, sick woman that I am, but now I believe his visits must be against her instruction. A few days ago, Japan bombed Pearl Harbor and the news of this distant event has turned our valley sour. Someone broke the windows of the Kobas' grocery store and the Kobas were forced to close for the winter. They had opened their shop in Kelowna shortly after the first war, and I had gone there regularly, in hopes that I might come across Azami and we might confront one another for once, but she was never there.

I often tell Joe he should stay home and care for his mother, but he refuses. I have to bite my tongue around him, for I am becoming reckless with words. I wonder if he suspects Kenta isn't his real father and hangs about my house because he somehow knows I might tell him the truth. In fact, I almost told him once, but when I opened my mouth, one of Llewelyna's old faery tales came rolling out instead.

Joe sometimes meets up with his red-haired lover, Mirabelle, in my backyard. He says it's the only safe place for them to visit. I told him to invite Mirabelle over for tea sometime, but he prefers secrecy. They usually slip into Yuri's old woodshop together. He says Azami will not hear of their relationship. She insists he be with only Japanese girls. Better yet, she wants him to return to Japan and find a bride—maybe even settle down in her old village.

I can understand Azami's stubbornness. She is only trying to protect him. I was a mother for only a handful of seconds to only a handful of organs and a few wrinkles of tenuous blue skin—a soul already departed to the world of eternal sleep or maybe never fully awake in the first place—but a daughter nonetheless. And despite my inexperience I have learned something about being a mother. A child is an opportunity to do things differently, to undo the

mistakes of the past. But a child is also a resilient echo. And sometimes a child must be permitted this echo. Sometimes old mistakes,
mimicked by a child, can lead to something beautiful.

"Best saw these off," Joe says, gesturing to the antlers. He has
nearly completed the grave.

"I suppose you're right." I doubt I can bear the grind of the
saw. "I'll get some lunch ready." I head for the house.

I warm the last two slices of the meatloaf Azami sent along
with Joe on the stove. Snow has begun to fall again. It collects in
the cedars and the bare branches of the two pear trees in the
backyard. When the meatloaf is ready, I call Joe in to join me. He
breathes into his red hands.

"Any word from Kenji or Emiko?" I ask. Joe's brother and
sister live on the coast. Since the bombing in Pearl Harbor, he
hasn't heard from them.

"Japanese are being shipped from the coast to mountain
towns. I imagine they are on board one of those trains."

"I'm so sorry."

"I just feel so helpless."

I serve Joe a piece of meatloaf and pour hot gravy on it. "You
should stay home with your mother. I'm sure she could use your
company."

He ignores me, bored with this topic.

"I'll be fine on my own," I say.

"Who will bury your dead?" he asks in jest. "And what if you
fall again?"

As if in response, my hand rises to the stitches and miserable
green bruise on my chin. "I'm okay, really. Much better."

"Have you had one since?"

"No," I lie. He doesn't want to use the word *seizure* and I am
thankful for this small kindness.

27

A month ago bone cancer took Yuri to his grave. A week after his death I was in the Kobas' grocery store holding a vine of tomatoes and the smell of lemon struck me out of nowhere. I hadn't had a seizure since aboard the *Jezebel*. I thought that, along with my child, the illness had left me for good.

When I gained consciousness, Joe had his palms on each side of my face to keep my head from banging against the fruit bins. I had wet myself. Some customers stared at me in fear or disgust. Others tried to be helpful, and offered their purses as pillows, or brought me a glass of water when Joe sat me up. Some casually walked around me as if I weren't there. They stepped over my spilled groceries: a split watermelon, cucumbers, and rolling oranges. I had hit my chin and was bleeding on the tile. Joe Koba's eyes were the only kind pair I could find. They were Viktor's eyes.

"It's over," Joe said. He dabbed my chin with the edge of his apron.

I glanced towards my feet and saw the jaguar, licking her paws.

Joe drove me to the hospital in the Kobas' fruit truck. I made Joe promise not to tell the doctor about my seizure. I had slipped, that was all. As she had before, the jaguar stalked me for a while after the incident. She lay on the floor beside my hospital bed and purred me to sleep. She didn't bother to move when the nurses tended to me. They casually stepped over her.

Once my chin was stitched up, Joe drove me home. I slumped in the passenger seat and drifted in and out of sleep. A vaguely familiar porcelain elephant hung from the rear-view mirror. I could see where it had cracked and been glued back together. The elephant swayed from side to side as we turned corners.

Joe walked me up the stairs of my house as if I were a much older woman. "Do you want me to come in? Help you get settled?" he asked.

"Don't worry yourself," I said.

"You'll be all right?" He held the door open. It was clear he really didn't want to leave me.

"Of course." I winked. "I've made it this far."

That night I found a peacock feather on my pillow. It was only a small azure chest feather, but that feather was the first of many I later found. I searched the house for the source, but Saint Francis was nowhere.

That next morning I woke to hammering in the backyard. I looked out from behind the curtain and saw Joe fixing a break in the fence with some fresh wood. It had snowed overnight and the heat of his effort steamed from his shoulders. I went downstairs and found the refrigerator full of fresh produce and a meatloaf. I boiled water for tea and took Yuri's tin cup out to Joe. Despite the cold, sweat beaded his eyebrows.

"How long have you been here?" I asked.

"Couple hours. Mom sent along some food."

"I saw that."

"She said you two are old friends."

"She did?" I couldn't keep myself from smiling at the thought. I felt the urge to tell Joe about Viktor, and the letters I had destroyed, and how it was me who came between Viktor's and Azami's union. But I couldn't.

The last time I had seen Azami was during a lantern procession in the city a few years before. I had been surprised the Japanese community had decided to contribute to the parade at all. I hadn't thought they cared for British royals. It was spring 1937, and the parade was a celebration of the coronation of King George VI and Queen Elizabeth. There were cars covered in flowers, cows with the British flag painted on their sides, and beauty pageant contestants with crowns made of cherry blossoms and lilacs. The sunshine had fooled me and I had worn only a thin sleeveless dress. The swooping breeze from the mountains was still crisp. Yuri offered me his coat but I was already angry at him for some triviality. I refused his offer and hugged my elbows tighter.

I easily picked out Azami from the crowd gathered on the opposite side of the street. She clutched a pink shawl over her head and shoulders as if it might disguise her. She looked the same, dark eyes and prominent cheekbones. She kept wetting her lips and they shone red. Kenta stood next to her wearing an old Vancouver Maroons baseball cap and his easy smile. Arthritis and hard work had turned his hands to claws.

Azami's face appeared neutral, uninterested in the parade before her. Her excitement was only revealed when she craned her neck and rose up on tiptoes to see past the crowd. The sound of flutes and drums approached from around a corner. I couldn't see past a float decorated with a grinning papier-mâché Ogopogo to find the source of the music. Azami had a better vantage point. She smiled at what she saw. A troupe of children from the Japanese school danced out from behind the Ogopogo. The girls looked like butterflies swinging in their colourful kimonos. Azami's eyes followed one of the girls in a red kimono, Emiko, her daughter.

I recognized the kimono from my childhood. Unlike the other straight-faced, serious children, Emiko grinned wide for the crowd, or maybe for only her mother. Azami brought her hands up to her mouth and although she tried to hide it, her face broke with joy. The crowd clapped for the children as they dispersed to find their parents in the crowd. Azami put her arm around Emiko's shoulders so they both faced the parade. She clutched Emiko against her, lips tight with pride. I tried to catch Azami's gaze, but she would not meet my eyes.

The sun had ducked behind the hills and left us in shadow. From behind the scrambling children came a crowd of Japanese teenagers. They each held a square paper lantern. These teenagers were dressed in their street clothes, trousers and sweaters, dresses for the girls. Joe was taller than the rest. His face was solemn in the warm light of his lantern. He stared down intently at the glow, as if the light there was something alive and precious.

We followed them slowly towards the shore of the lake. Not one lantern went out despite the breeze. The teenagers walked into the water up to their knees. As they released the lanterns into the lake, everyone cheered, or everyone but the Japanese who had gathered. They remained solemn as saints. I looked to Azami and she wiped a tear from her cheek. I had been confused by the gesture of the floating lanterns on what was a celebratory occasion. Azami had taught me the lanterns were meant to guide the dead.

28

Yuri and I had lived simply and, for the most part, separately. I started a bookstore in Henry's honour called Brewster's Books. Sometimes I saw Mrs. Bell downtown in the shops. We neglected to recognize one another, preferring to let our joint histories rest.

Yuri spent his days in his workshop. He made tables, beds, and chairs out of pine and maple and sold them at a shop downtown. Sometimes he whittled me butterflies, birds, and woodland animals that reminded me of Winteridge. These little gifts, left for me like secrets, made our life together bearable. They reminded me of the boy Yuri had once been, before the war. And sometimes, even those memories of him were enough.

The lake monster Henry called Naitaka disappeared from local memory the day Viktor and his mob gutted the fish on the shore of the lake. The demon was replaced by the Ogopogo, a mockery of the original. The Ogopogo has snail-like antennae, forest-green flesh, and cartoon eyes. Children still sing songs about the Ogopogo and dress up as the comic creature at parades and festivals.

Although the town still chooses to ignore it, the spirit of the lake continues to haunt its depths. Naitaka does not require our belief, nor our food. It does not need our stories, nor our forgiveness. It took me years to understand this, and though I would never claim to have a kind of innate wisdom of this place, for I will forever be a stranger to the land, a thief, I believe the lake monster is not one thing but multitudes. It is a memory, a premonition, a haunted history, and a cursed future. It is a culmination of all our sins and all our wonder.

I travelled once on the old *Rosamond* to purchase a collection of encyclopedias advertised in an estate sale in Penticton. I stood on the deck and watched Rattlesnake Island approach. The waves rose and fell against the rocky beach as if the island were floating past the lakeboat instead of the other way around. A canoe was anchored near the shore. A couple of native women were bent over the hull of the canoe. When the lakeboat neared them, the women looked up briefly to return the stare of our gawking white faces. I had a dead mouse in my handbag for a sacrifice. I held it by the tail and dropped it in the lake. One of the women in the canoe saw what I had done. She looked at me quizzically and then laughed at my meagre sacrifice. Long after the *Rosamond* passed, one of the women reached her arm over the side of the canoe and dropped a long strip of bloody flesh into the water to ensure our safe passage past Naitaka's home. No one else on board knew how these women had kept us safe.

Every few years someone disappears in the lake. And every decade someone reports a long, dark crest rising up out of the water. But these are never more than ghost stories. Some people have even tried to photograph the lake monster, but even the clearest image does not convince most. I never did develop the photograph I took. My belief does not require proof.

There are sightings of Llewelyna too. She takes the form of a mermaid or water nymph. Cliff jumpers often report seeing a woman sitting on the rocks below or swimming in the water beneath the cliffs. They only see her once they've jumped and are

in mid-air. When they come up out of the water, she is gone.
They call her the lady of the lake. They've named a beauty pageant after her.

For years I have kept the little blue fish in a jam jar wrapped
in a bit of velvet and tucked in a locked cabinet in the attic. Like
any good robber with a treasure she doesn't understand, I can
hardly bear to set my eyes on the extravagant creature. And yet
the fish serves as a token, a reminder of the things I have experi-
enced. It's all I have of Winteridge. I am not tempted to eat the
fish. I know the wisdom it offers is not for me. I'd like to think I
am its caretaker, but in truth I have held on for too long and have
grown attached to the little thing. Like any secret, like any sin,
the fish has become a part of me.

*

This morning I open the back door of my house and find a raccoon,
an orange house cat, and two magpies splayed on the stairs, dead.
The jaguar is nowhere to be seen. What am I meant to understand
by her presence now, this ancient kami I angered so long ago?

When Joe doesn't arrive I have a bad feeling and call the Kobas'
house, but no one answers. I step over the dead animals and take
a taxi to the Kobas' store. Most of the windows have been smashed
and someone has painted *Leave Japs* in crude letters across the
front. There is nothing inside but fruits and vegetables shrivelled
in their dark bins.

From there I take the taxi out of town and up the hill along
a dirt road to the Kobas' house. I stand for a moment and take in
their land. There are endless rows of fruit trees dusted with snow.
A greenhouse leans against the house. Inside the greenhouse are

peas, beans, and even a few miraculous strawberries. The windows of the house are dark. The front door has been broken in. I wander through the abandoned rooms; photographs of Azami's children line the walls. A half-finished bowl of porridge is still on the kitchen table. A cup of coffee has spilled over. In what I imagine is Azami and Kenta's bedroom, I am astonished to find the red shrine I built for Azami so long ago. It is filled with the old items and a little china plate of sliced orange, still untouched. I pick up the dove feather and spin it between my fingers. Then I see my own old blue marble set upon a nest of yellow silk and it brings tears to my eyes.

At the police station a Mountie comes to help me at the front desk. His belt is cinched tight and a gold button is missing from his red jacket, so I can see his white undershirt. When I ask about the Kobas, he tells me they have been taken to an internment camp in the mountains. "It's for their own safety," he says. The Mountie refuses to tell me where exactly. When I ask about the broken door he claims there was an altercation when they came to collect the Kobas. After further questioning, the Mountie says that officials intercepted letters sent to the Kobas from Vancouver, written in Japanese.

"Of course," I say. "They have family there, children."

"Did you know fishermen on the coast have been communicating with flashlights to Jap submarines?"

"That sounds a little far-fetched."

"Ma'am, we found explosives in the Kobas' cellar."

"Stumping powder, surely, for clearing land."

Fed up with me now, the Mountie puffs his cheeks and slowly releases his breath. It smells of eggs.

"What harm could they possibly cause, anyway?" I ask.

The officer leans in close, as if the secretary rat-a-tatting on the typewriter at the far side of the room might care to overhear. "We've got word the Japs are planning an attack on our irrigation system. Do you have any idea what kind of damage that would cause?"

"But it doesn't make any sense. The Kobas depend on that system more than most. Why would they bomb their own home?"

The Mountie crosses his arms, finally satisfied with my line of questioning. "This is not their home," he says. We exchange steady looks and I am pleased that he is the first to look away. I can tell, beneath everything, he too is pained by it all. This war has stirred up so much hate. "Listen," he says. "We'll be sure to fix the door for them. Just holding on to the property for now."

I know this is a lie. There are already rumours about Japanese homes and ships and belongings being auctioned off for the bottom dollar on the coast, and so I counter his lie with one of my own:

"The Kobas' land, I believe, is still in my father's name." I recall what Llewelyna said about us never belonging to the land, and that our claim to it is forever false. Even still, I am quite confident that my father was never able to legally sell the land to the Kobas. The Mountie leaves the front desk to check some paperwork and returns apologizing for the intrusion on my property. He promises the damage will be corrected immediately and the place will be protected from vandals.

When I return home there are more dead animals on the back steps. I don't bother digging graves for them. I bury the dead in snow. My door was left wide open, and inside the house I have the sense that someone has entered. I am not alone.

29

The jaguar has stalked the yard for months now. I share with her whatever I can spare from the pantry to keep her from killing the animals: canned peaches, tuna fish, pickles. I leave the food in a saucer on the back porch.

Every day I find more animals have infiltrated my house. It started with spiders and flies. A silk web bloomed against the window and I marvelled at the lacework. The red-bellied spider perched at the centre, attuned to the strum of her instrument. I aired out the house one morning while I had a bath, and emerged to find a couple of chickadees and a wren nibbling at some crackers I had left on the counter. A grey cat licked at an empty can of condensed milk next to the teapot. Soon sparrow nests appeared in the eaves of the house, and now the cries of their hungry young are everywhere.

Coyotes howl in the yard and scamper through the house. Sometimes I walk into a room and find paw prints on the wood floor. Mice have made nests in the backs of all the drawers. At first I attempted to keep the pests out. I chased after birds and rodents. I destroyed spiderwebs with a broom and stomped at coyotes, only to have the animals overtake the house again.

And if these creatures are not kami or ghosts, perhaps they are manifestations of my own mind. What if I have created these animals somehow? Then I recall Llewelyna in her final days and I realize it doesn't matter. I am losing time.

Outside, the white snow piles upon itself, collapses, and then finally begins to melt. In the garden, the potatoes blossom. Day by day their purple star-flowers flood the yard.

By spring the house is so crowded with animals, it is difficult to move. Ghosts swarm. The howl of coyotes and the hoot of owls and the buzz of insects are a new kind of silence. I feel myself fading, slowly disappearing into the chaos. The taste of lemon is ever present at the back of my throat. Over the past few days the jaguar's food has gone untouched, and I know she has returned to Winteridge.

Llewelyna said once: we're all just beasts with our animal hearts aglow. I know this to be true. We are beasts, crude and cruel, but *aglow*, nonetheless, aflame with something so brilliant it cannot be seen. It cannot be known or ever understood.

I glance out the window to find Saint Francis pecking at the potato flowers. I rush out onto the porch to scare him away. Although he is an aged, wild bird now, he has lost none of his splendour. He launches up into the sky, his blue tail of many eyes streaming behind like the all-seeing face of God. I know now it is time to go home.

I buy a ticket to Vernon and persuade the lakeboat captain to let me off at Winteridge. I recognize the captain with the missing fingers from when he was a young man and I first saw Winteridge burned to the ground, and I think he might recognize me also. I have dressed in my best coat and in its pocket I carry my fish.

Once the white birch of the bay come into view, I pay the captain to bring me to shore in a rowboat. The other passengers look on from the anchored lakeboat in disbelief. The captain says he will return at four o'clock to collect me. I explain that I have made other arrangements and will not need a ride back.

The trees are thick in Winteridge. No one lives here anymore. At least not to the city's knowledge. It is a ghost town, but it has always been a ghost town. As the lakeboat pulls away, I see the Lake People in the trees, congregated in tight circles, weaving, picking, and collecting in peace. My shoes are soft-soled and I make very little sound on the rocks. The Lake People have grown brave in their solitude. They do not even turn to watch me.

Henry told me once that each story is a continuum of where another left off, and I believe this is true, but I also think that the stories we tell are not chronological but overlapping, interacting with and forever altering one another. I believe the Lake People are simultaneously the ghosts of the past and the future, spectres from a parallel world that could have been, that could be, that still is.

I am pleased to see the forest has taken back the town. The dining room of the Pearl Hotel is exposed to the road. The four walls have collapsed around a pile of charred wood, which I imagine was once the dining table. All that remains is a cut-glass bowl atop the rubble. It collects milky water.

The fire dissolved our house and the Wasiks' cabin and left nothing but grey foundations. I look for some item, some piece to collect, and find nothing. A family of mice has made their home in the debris.

I walk through our peach orchard, now a field studded with charred stumps. I imagine the flame spreading quickly from branch to branch, peaches bursting. Henry claimed fire and smoke were sacred entities, used to purify, to cure, and to communicate with the spirit world. I thought of Winteridge turned to smoke, refined by fire. New ghosts mingle with those that existed here long ago. This land is anything but empty. It is brimming, fuller than ever before. The fire only burned down walls. Now, it seems, the land has gone back to the way it was before settlers arrived here.

A single tree remains on our orchard. As I approach it, I picture an impossible lone peach dangling low from one of its branches. I crave the sweet flesh of that tender heart. The grass is long, and as I step through it I hear the jaguar behind me. There is the rattle of a snake. I imagine the little Satan sifting through the grass, hoping to sink its teeth into my heel. But the rattle multiplies; it is only crickets. The tree is lush. Its greedy roots have stolen life from the other withered trees around it. I realize it is not a peach tree at all, but the maple tree where Llewelyna would spread out her blanket and lie with Jacob and me, telling stories. There is a slight breeze, and frog-wings spin from the maple's branches. This makes me think of Jacob and my heart breaks for him anew, just a boy who died so long ago.

I walk up into the surrounding forest. New growth and fireweed are thick where the forest must have burned brightest. I pick some of the purple flowers and set them in my hair. The deeper I go, the cooler and greener and fuller the forest becomes. It begins to rain. I cannot feel the drops yet but I can hear their music in the trees. Coyotes yip in the hills. How strange to hear them this early in the day. As I near the tree fort I find the jewelled trail of the orphan thief, the little magpie. Her pines have grown even more dazzling, their branches heavy with the items she stole from homes. Some items were taken after the fire: Llewelyna's singed slippers and a charred pearl necklace. Now the orphan thief's collected treasures are all that remain of Winteridge. They are a hanging gallery. A museum. I think of her miniature Winteridge made of Mrs. Bell's figurines safe inside the tree fort, untouched by fire, the only version of the town that remains.

I understand now that all this time, the orphan thief has been trying to show what's been taken from her, to demonstrate the extent of her loss. But this loss can never be met, can never be filled with gold and emerald and silk. And so her collection can only grow. There is no end.

From a distance, the tree fort appears the same. There are what look like stores of food all around the trunk of the tree: a box of potatoes, a bundle of asparagus. The orphan thief tends a small cook fire with her bare hands. She remains unchanged, ageless, though her hair has turned silver. She stands as I approach. The tips of her fingers are blackened. We are not alone. From behind the tree, a boy aims a slingshot with a jagged rock at me. His face is firm. The orphan thief whistles and with that signal seven other children reveal themselves from the trees or lean out of the windows of the tree fort above. They have dirty faces and shining, keen eyes. Their hair has been cropped short, close to the scalp. These children are not ghosts but runaways. In front of them I feel as though I am nothing but a spectre from a terrible dream they have only just woken from.

Coyotes come out of the bushes and curl their lips back at me. I put my hands up in surrender and point to my pocket. When I pull out the fish, burning blue, the orphan thief's eyes spark.

"This belongs to you," I say and walk right up to her. "I'm sorry I have kept it for so long. It was never meant for me. I realize that now." I place the fish at her feet and turn to leave. I hear her unscrew the lid and swallow the fish.

Once I have left the clearing I am struck on the back of the head by something. Some of the children giggle. I look down and find a large pine cone. The orphan thief smiles before she recedes back into the forest. Azami's necklace with the Russian military tag and the red bead are tangled around the pine cone's scales.

30

At the shore, Saint Francis pecks at a dead fish. Rain pocks the still lake. Coyotes yip in the distance and the jaguar is behind me, licking her teeth. The sun has dipped into the mountains and in this crowded world I am alone. Out in the distance the lake spirals, turns white, and I know it is Naitaka. I let my heavy, rain-soaked coat fall from my shoulders. Beneath it I wear only an old nightgown. It collects in a pool of pink silk at my feet. I step out of my shoes. The stones are cold and hard against my heels. I put Azami's necklace over my head, clutch the pulsing red bead in my fist, and step into the cool waters of our bottomless lake.

ACKNOWLEDGEMENTS

This is a work of fiction; however, the Okanagan landscape I have attempted to portray is a real and very meaningful place to me and to many others. Although I have lived in the Okanagan all of my life and am constantly moved and inspired by the lake and the land, I recognize that as a descendant of settlers, I am a guest of the Syilx/Okanagan people to whom this land belongs, and to whom I am grateful.

Our Animal Hearts has been my companion through university, marriage, motherhood, and into my nine-to-five adulthood. While some passages were written only months ago, other sections were put to paper when I was only nineteen. Since I have been plucking away at this story for ten years or so, it feels a little strange to release it, no longer able to tinker and revise. Like Llewelyna's copy of the *Mabinogion*, this novel would be puddles of ink if handwritten.

There are far too many people and books and influences to acknowledge—regardless, I will try to name some. First of all, I want to extend my gratitude to Zoe Maslow, my brilliant editor at Doubleday Canada, who so eloquently intuited what I was trying to accomplish in this novel and provided pivotal feedback that encouraged and challenged me, and to Martha Webb, my wise, patient, and steadfast agent, who was the first to take a chance on me and this book. I am also grateful to Jennifer Griffiths for her stunning artwork, to Shaun Oakey for his keen eye, and to the entire team at Doubleday Canada—thank you for championing my debut.

I have many people at the University of Victoria and the University of British Columbia in the Okanagan to thank, such as Lee Henderson, Adam Lewis Schroeder, and Anne Fleming, who read very early versions of this novel and pushed me forward, and especially Michael V. Smith, who has been a mentor and friend, and guided me through challenging terrain. I am grateful to my accommodating colleagues in the AIC, to Allison Hargreaves for her conversation, and to members of my MFA writing workshops, thesis committee, and the creative writing faculty at UBC Okanagan.

My friends and family have been ridiculously supportive during this long venture, particularly my mom, Linda Christie. Her wisdom and bizarre insight during our many long, meandering talks about this book have often buoyed me. One of the central inspirations for *Our Animal Hearts* is my Welsh-Canadian grandma, Aerona Wilson, née Griffiths (1921–2010). Despite our closeness she remains a mystery to me, and this fact will forever spur my imagination.

This novel is for my daughter, Wren, whom I love ferociously, and for my husband, Brad, who has never lost heart. Without you, nothing.